SILENT BLUE TEARS

Voice of the Victims

by

Detective Ron Bateman (ret.)

Ron Bateman
Ronwood655@verizon.net
Website: http://www.ronbatemanbooks.com

Silent Blue Tears, Voice of the Victims © 2018

The characters and events in this book are fictious. Any similarity to real persons, living or dead, is coincidental and not intended by the author.

Copyright © 2018 by Ronald Bateman

All rights reserved. The scanning, uploading, and distribution of this book without permission is a theft of the author's intellectual property. If you would like permission to use material from the book (other than review purposes) please contact ronwood655@verizon.net. Thank you for your support of the author's rights.

This book is published by SBT Entertainment LLC and found at ronbatemanbooks.com. The publisher is not responsible for websites or their content that are not owned by the publisher.

ISBN 979-8502216616

Cover designs by Zoe Neely

Printed in the United States of America

Dedicated to my brothers in the Unit,

thanks for the memories.

Shithead

Ruthless

Robin was a lady who no one from the unit ever had the good fortune to meet alive. In fact, the first time anyone laid eyes on her was when Detective Michaels saw her lying face down on the cold tile where she worked, partially submerged in a thick pool of her own blood. Unlike most homicides, this one occurred in the morning when normal people are either off to work, or just waking up. Just shy of 8:00 a.m. Michaels heard his call number over the police radio.

"*Christ, why are they calling me this early?*" He took a quick sip of coffee and grabbed his portable radio.

"Detective 132 to dispatch, go ahead."

The news from the other end wasn't what he expected or hoped for, in fact, just the opposite.

"Respond to Clarke's Saloon, located at 1400 Ritchie Highway in Severna Park and meet Detective 130 for a homicide," the female dispatcher recited without emotion.

Michaels knew Detective 130 was his Sergeant Tommy Suit's radio call number. "Fuck" he blurted out, knowing most likely he would be tied up for the next few days. Still holding the radio, he acknowledged with a "10-4" in the same monotone voice.

Clarke's was in a small line of businesses located off the main drag that ran through the section of a well to do portion of the county, known as Severna Park. Next to Clarke's was a small liquor store, and on the other side was a large grocery store that kept the parking lot full of cars and people most of the day and night. Behind the stores were the rear entrances to the businesses used by employees and vendors throughout the day.

It was a local hangout, with its regular customers and a new jukebox equipped with a variety of country and good old rock and roll tunes. The inside was simple, equipped with a bar suited for 10, and six dark, scarred up, wood stained tables with matching stools. It wasn't the classiest place, but a nice hole in the wall, nonetheless. The doorman was a fella named Steve, who knew Michaels was a cop and always let him in without paying a cover charge.

Detective Ronald Michaels was no stranger to criminals, big cases, or court. Having just completed a 4-year assignment as an undercover narcotics detective, he knew his way around the criminal justice system, and earned a reputation as a meticulous cop who settled for nothing but success. Standing an even six-foot tall, he was the newest member of the 5-man elite Homicide Unit. Michaels dressed like a contemporary detective, sporting quality suits, nice ties and shirts so heavily starched they could stand on their own. Like most, he was divorced after 6 years, but was blessed with a precious 5-year-old daughter, Nicole, who he adored deeply, but saw rarely. Most people referred to him as Ronnie, but not long after joining the unit, he was branded with the nickname of Young Shithead by Sergeant Suit. Everyone in the unit had their own unique nicknames. Some were created from things that happened from years past, while others were based on appearances or appendages.

Michaels wasn't too far from Clarke's when he got the call. He parked behind the emergency medical vehicles who were packing up to leave. He grabbed his reporter style notebook, which everyone in the unit carried. Before getting out of the car he took a last sip of coffee and jotted down his arrival time on the scene.

With notebook in hand, he grabbed his suit coat and climbed from his car. He walked toward the front door when he noticed his father, Ray, inside the bar taking pictures. Ray had worked in the department's Evidence Collection Unit as a technician for the past year. It was a job he had taken after retiring from the Maryland State Police at the rank of Lieutenant. Evidence Technicians are responsible for photographing crime scenes, gathering and submitting evidence for analysis, lifting fingerprints, and anything else necessary to solve a case. Having been on a police force for over 25 years, Ray knew his role. This was the first case he and his son had together. This was the first time in Michaels' life he got to tell his dad what to do. Here was his hero, someone who had forgotten more about police work than his son would ever know, being told what to do at a crime scene by his youngest, and that was okay with Ray.

Approaching the front door of Clarke's Saloon, Michaels could see a young rookie uniformed police officer posted outside the door allowing only authorized people in.

"Good morning Detective Michaels," he said respectfully.

"Good morning. Are you keeping the Crime Scene Log?" Michaels replied.

"Yes sir," he said as he held out his clipboard for review.

"Not now but be sure I get that from you when we clear the scene please."

"You got it detective. I'll make it happen."

"Have you been inside?"

"Yes sir. I was the first to arrive, of course, after the employee who called it in."

"Tell me what you saw."

The officer was very excited and nervous to be talking with a homicide detective. "Well sir, the bookkeeper, Mary Bell, discovered the body and called 911. Ms. Bell said she came in through the front door, which was locked, and when she called for her co-worker, Robin Collins, she didn't answer. She went to the back room where the safe and storage room is, and that's when she saw Robin lying on the floor. She said there was blood everywhere and immediately she called 911. Sir, I went in and observed a deceased white female and as she said, blood was everywhere. There is no doubt she's dead. The guy standing right over there is the Coors Light distributor who talked to the victim earlier this morning," he said motioning his eyes toward the liquor store. "And the bookkeeper who called 911 is sitting in my car," he said talking fast, barely taking a breath.

"Wow, good job officer, keep up the good work. I'm going over to talk with the Coors Light fella and see what he has to say."

Michaels approached the man standing next to the Saloon. He seemed both eager and anxious to talk to the detective.

"Good morning, I'm Detective Michaels from the Homicide Unit. Thanks for sticking around, I'll get you out of here as soon as possible." Michaels shook the gentleman's hand which he noticed was weak and flimsy like a wet noodle.

"Oh, that's no problem. I'll stick around as long as you need me. I already called our warehouse and told them I'd be delayed on my deliveries. Whatever I can do, Robin was always so sweet to me. I really respect law enforcement officers. So, whatever I can do to help, I'm at your service. I can't believe it. Is she really dead? Who would do such a thing?"

"I don't know sir, hopefully we will get to the bottom of this."

For once, Michaels was surprised he didn't have a witness who refused to cooperate or was in a big hurry to leave. "Great, Mr. Cooke. That's good to hear."

"Uh, how did you know my name"? he asked with a puzzled look on his face.

Michaels smiled and pointed to the name embroidered on his company shirt. Mr. Cooke looked down. "Oh, oh that's right. So, are you taking me to the station?" he asked in an excited voice.

"Not right yet Al. First, can you tell me what happened this morning?"

"Well, I arrived at my normal time, which was 7:30 a.m. I deliver to Clarke's every Monday and Friday. When I pulled up to the back door, I beeped twice like I always do so Robin would know it was me."

Al was talking so fast, Michaels had to stop him a few times, so he could catch up with his notes.

"I always brought Robin a black coffee and a blueberry donut. She loved that."

"What happened after you pulled up and beeped your horn?"

"Normally, Robin would unlock and open the back door, but today the door was already open, and I walked in, which I thought was odd because she always kept it locked, especially when she was counting money. Something seemed weird today and this time she wasn't alone."

"Was she usually alone in the mornings?"

"Yes, at least on Mondays and Fridays as far as I know. I think another girl comes in later to help her out. But this morning, I saw the back door partially open and there was a heavyset black guy, about 20 years old standing in the back room talking to her. He was leaning against the beer cases stacked in the room next to her desk."

"Do you know who this guy is?"

"I don't know his name, but he's the bar-back who worked the evening shift. I've seen him before when I would stop in sometimes for a beer. I really didn't think anything was wrong because he worked there, but I've never seen him here in the morning. Do you think he did it?"

"We don't know yet Mr. Cooke."

"Should I have done something? I mean, I know they don't open until 3 p.m., but he seemed ok. I handed Robin her coffee and donut and got a big hug and a thanks. I loaded up my hand truck and brought in 16 cases and stacked them against the wall. While I was doing this, that guy walked to the front of the bar and Robin stayed in the back talking, drinking her coffee and eating her donut with me."

"Did anything appear to be bothering her?"

"No, not that I could tell. When I finished, I left and continued with my route. I came back when I drove by and saw the all the police cars and ambulances out front. Oh my God and she just had a baby girl a few months ago. Oh my. Does her husband know?"

"Not as of yet, so please if you know him, do not make contact with him."

"Oh no, I don't know Mr. Collins. Boy, I know she sure did love him and their new baby."

Michaels retrieved Al's information and told him he would be in touch later if he had more questions. Al was a good man, who genuinely wanted to help and was very upset that something had happened to his friend.

"Now go ahead with your day, I'll be in touch and thank you," Michaels said as he shook his hand.

Michaels made his way toward the front door of Clarke's Saloon, when he noticed his partner, Detective Dave Hart getting slowly out of his car. Referred to as Dredge by most, Dave had been Michaels' partner since he joined the unit three months ago. No strangers to one another, he had been Michaels' Field Training Officer in patrol for a few weeks when Michaels first graduated from the Academy 7 years ago. Dredge looked like an old fashion television homicide detective. At forty-two, his hair was rapidly thinning, eyes were shaded by dark circles and always a pen and a pack of Merits in his shirt pocket. He was an excellent detective who taught Michaels a great deal about his new line of work. He was a quiet man, that is, until he downed a few cocktails, then it wouldn't be odd for him to tell you just how he felt about the topic at hand, while he chained smoked one cigarette after the other. When he did speak, it was normally something you should listen to.

Dredge and Michaels were an excellent mix, each complementing the other with their own unique talents. Dredge had a slow deliberate pace, while to the contrary, Michaels couldn't get anything done fast enough. The younger detective had more energy than the energizer bunny, just like a caged dog who never wanted to stop working. Dredge was a master of note taking and report writing, while Michaels could stay organized in a category 4 hurricane, coupled with the knack to talk to anyone.

Dredge's nickname was tagged on him by a former partner. As legend had it, his dick was so big it could be used as a dredging device, like those used to make shipping canals deeper. Michaels didn't know the authenticity of the rumor, until one time while using the urinal next to Dredge, he did give it a quick peek. Jokingly, he used to tell everyone his dick was so big, if you put glasses on it, you could haunt a house. Everyone knew Dave as Dredge, even the Chief of Police, but not everyone knew what it stood for, except for a handful of cops and of course, his wife.

"Dredge, you bag of shit. What are ya doing?"

"Tommy told me to come over and see what you need."

"Thanks, my brother. I'm told I have a white female dead in the backroom of this bar. She apparently is an early morning employee and was found by another employee. I have no idea as to how or why, but I do know she was alive when the Coors Light delivery guy was here. He said it was odd that a young black guy who works the evening shift was here talking to the victim."

"Why is that odd?"

"He said he's never seen him here in the morning, that's all."

"Umm mmm. What do you need me to do?"

"Can you interview the employee who found her? Her name is Mary Bell. See what she can tell you about who was here. Find out what his deal is. She is sitting in the patrol car parked in front of the bar. She can leave when you're done."

With that, Dredge turned and walked toward the patrol car parked nearby.

Michaels walked over to the rookie standing proudly near the front door. "Ok, it's time for me to go in, so put me in your log please."

"Yes sir, done. Will that other fella be coming in as well?"

"Oh Dredge?"

"Who sir?"

"I'm sorry, uh yes that's Detective Hart, as soon as he gets finished with the witness in your car, he'll be coming in."

"Yes sir."

"Shithead. Good morning. How the hell are you?" Tommy shouted in his normal chipper voice. "Your victim is in the back room along with your dad," he said pointing to the *Employees Only* door next to the bar. "Here are some rubber gloves your father brought in. He's back there taking some preliminary photographs, waiting for Jeff Cover."

"Jeffery is coming? Great."

At forty-four years old, Tommy was a former respected homicide detective and polygraph examiner. One thing everyone knew, he was proud and guarded of his unit. The administration allowed him to hand-pick each person. He demanded each member be relentless in their work ethic and fit into his cohesive team, with no exceptions.

Michaels snapped on the protective gloves, writing frantically in his notebook as he started toward the crime scene. The door had been propped open by a five-gallon bucket of floor cleaner which blood had pooled around.

"And I've already talked to Doc Johnson and he's on his way," Tommy yelled out.

"Good, thanks."

After scratching out a few final notes about the front part of the bar, he stepped around the trail of blood and got close to where the victim laid. It was a sad sight, one that would be forever etched in his mind. The room where this brutal crime occurred doubled as an office space and storage for liquor and other supplies needed to keep a bar running. Saying the area was cramped would be an understatement. With a table mounted to the wall as a desk, and several shelves and boxes stacked on the floor, there wasn't much space available, but still enough to kill someone. In the back of the room was the rear entrance, accessible only to employees and vendors. After a quick observation of the back door, he could see it was partially open, with a heavy metal padlock dangling in the unlocked position from the hasp.

Michaels couldn't see his victim's face. She was face down on her knees, with her back slightly humped up on the hard tile floor, soaking in her own blood. The office chair was directly behind her, lying on its side, pressed up against her back. Michaels surmised that she must have been sitting in the chair when the attack occurred.

Next to her body was a section of Formica tabletop, approximately 2 feet in length by 10 inches wide, two 2 inches thick and weighing nearly 3 pounds. Noticeably missing from it was a portion of a splintered corner. It was a leaf made for a narrow table like the one mounted to the wall and was obviously the weapon of choice left behind by the killer. Michaels could see it had blood smeared on it, along with a thick wad of dried blood and light brown hair embedded in one of its ends.

"This was obviously the convenient weapon used by this asshole," Michaels said to Ray who stood beside him snapping off pictures.

"Yeah that's pretty heavy and capable of doing some real damage to a skull, and boy did it," Ray said while he kept the camera close to his face.

Blood was everywhere. There were spatters speckled across the wall in front of her desk, on many of the papers where the victim had been working, and a large pool of thick coagulating blood covered the floor around her body, some still oozing from her skull. It was difficult to make out the color of her shirt from the blood that had drained from her. From the spots on the wall, Michaels could tell his victim had been struck with great force causing the blood to travel a good distance. This was no accident; it was premeditated homicide without a fight.

Michaels was quickly filling up page after page with detailed notes, taught to him by no other than his partner, Dredge. Unlike Tommy and Dredge, Michaels' handwriting was sloppy, and his mini drawings were crude, but suited him just fine. He stared at the back of her mutilated head and wondered for a moment what her face looked like.

Ray strategically moved around the room, photographing the disarray caused from the thoughtless and vicious violence.

What was her expression going to be like when we turned her over? Michaels thought to himself. Ask any cop about turning over a dead body and they'll tell you it burns an indelible picture in their mind.

"Hey boys, what's going on?"

Michaels and Ray turned to see the Evidence Collection Supervisor, Jeff Cover, standing in the doorway leading to the scene, wearing a full paper jump suit and rubber gloves.

"Well look who came out to play. We got the full-blown varsity team now," Michaels said.

"I figured since Ray was working alone, I'd come give him a hand."

"Thanks Jeffrey," Michaels said.

"Thank you, Jeff. Did you bring any more of those paper gowns? This is a mess," Ray asked.

"Yes sir, they're in my case at the front of the bar."

Jeff and Ray took photographs and measurements of the outer bar area and the final resting place of the victim. For hours they meticulously dusted and lifted fingerprints from the rear door, walls, the desktop and some of the beer and liquor cases. They carefully packaged bloody papers and money strewn about the floor and table. Several of the bills lay soaking in the blood, while others were on the desk. With his trained eye, Jeff pointed out that one of the smaller denominations contained a partial bloody fingerprint. This was promising.

While in the backroom, Michaels could hear Tommy call for him. "Detective Michaels."

Michaels figured someone of importance must be with Tommy by the way he called his name. "Coming sir." He quickly finished his notes and walked to the front of the bar. Tommy stood talking to two well-dressed men in their 40's with worried looks on their faces.

"Detective Michaels, this is Mr. Alan Levy and Mr. Ed Powell. They are the owners of this establishment."

"Nice to meet you gentlemen."

Michaels shook their hands and Mr. Levy got right to the point. "We were told a woman was found murdered here. Is it Robin or Mary?"

Michaels was very eager to talk with the owners, but not quite ready to reveal the victim's identity. "Well, I was hoping you could help me with that and maybe shed some light on who may have done this. First, which employees were supposed to be here this morning?"

"We have one girl, Robin Collins, who comes in at 7:00 a.m. and Mary Bell who comes in at 8:00 a.m.," Mr. Powell said.

"If I can see her, I can tell you who it is," Mr. Levy stated.

Knowing he would never allow either of them any further than where they were standing, Michaels ignored his question and asked him to describe each of the ladies. As he began, Michaels heard the all too familiar sound of Ray summoning him to the backroom. "Excuse me gentlemen. I'll be right back," Michaels said hearing a sense of urgency in his father's voice.

"We found this purse covered by papers under the table, it belongs to the victim. Her driver's license was inside. Her name is Robin Collins."

Shithead, I think we've done all we can until the on-call Medical Examiner gets here and we can move the body. Once that happens, then she'll be ready to be taken to the morgue. Who is coming anyway?" Jeff asked.

"Well that would be me."

Michaels looked up while flipping through some pictures in the victim's wallet. There stood Dr. William Johnson, waving a Polaroid snapshot he had taken of Michaels. "Yo Doc, what's up?" Michaels greeted him.

Dr. Johnson, or Doc as he was referred to, was one of the on-call Medical Examiners. At 59 years of age, Doc was a general practitioner with his own successful practice in Annapolis. The short, balding Doc would frequently respond to scenes sporting his round spectacles, preppy attire and his ancient Polaroid One Step camera. He was extremely educated and very knowledgeable when it came to interpreting causes of death and other signs on a body. He, along with one other doctor, would serve as the on-call representative for the ME's office in Baltimore, for which they would be compensated.

"Do you know who did this? This looks bad," Doc replied.

"A fucking asshole is all I can tell you right now. I don't know much yet; except she was alive this morning."

Doc bent over Robin and pulled her left arm from under her body. "She's married, does she have any kids?" he asked inspecting her corpse.

"Yeah, a little girl, a month or two old. Ain't that fucked up?"

Ray came over and handed his son a new pair of disposable gloves and shoe booties to put on while Doc was cranking off photos of the head wounds.

"Dad can you please get a few of those with your camera, I would like to take them with me?"

"Sure, Ronnie. I can do that."

"He really hit her hard. Come look at this," Doc said to Michaels.

Careful not to slip, Ray and his son tiptoed through the blood to get next to Doc, who had pushed some of Robin's hair to the side, exposing one of the wounds.

"Shit," Michaels said in shock noticing the frayed corner of the tabletop stuck in her skull. "Get a picture of that Dad."

"I don't know why whoever did this had to hit her twice. She would have never survived either one these hits alone," Doc said.

As Ray took pictures of Robin, the doctor continued with his examination. Most of her hair was matted down with dried pasty blood. A closer look revealed two very large holes on the back and side of her cranium. They were big holes, three inches wide, that split her skull wide open, exposing parts of her brain.

"Alright guys, if everybody has got their pictures and measurements, let's turn her over," Doc said.

"Let's slide her toward us first and move her away from some of this blood," Doc suggested.

Michaels grabbed Robin's right calf while Doc took ahold of her left ankle. The men had a difficult time turning her over in the tight space with the slippery blood on the floor, but eventually they managed. You could have heard a pin drop when she came to rest on her back. No one said a word for what seemed like minutes. Everyone stared at her eyes, each half open. Doc pulled a small pen light from his shirt pocket and shined it into her eyes. Michaels and Jeff remained squatting and couldn't stop looking at her glazed over green eyes. They were cold, dull and lifeless.

"Dead people never seem to look at you. They look right through you like you're not even there," Michaels said.

Doc leaned over close to Michaels and quietly whispered, "Give me a call if you lock someone up for this, would you?"

"No problem."

A short time later, Doc stripped off his gloves and his paper shoe coverings and threw them in a pile of trash separate from the evidence. "Nice seeing you all again. I gotta run. Is Dredge here?"

"Yes sir. He was out front interviewing the girl who found the victim. He should be about done," Michaels said.

"Ok, I'll say goodbye to him on my way out. Good luck boys."

"See ya Doc, don't forget that high tech camera of yours," Michaels said jokingly.

"What's wrong with my camera, Young Shithead? Why are you always on me about that?"

"Well let's see. You're a successful doctor, got your own practice, making big bucks and you have an early 1970's version of a one-step Polaroid. Now you tell me?"

Doc left the room laughing and shaking his head while Jeff and Ray followed behind.

Michaels pulled his notebook and scribbled some notes about the piece of table remaining in one of the wounds. The scene was almost complete and a strange quiet came over the room. He and the deceased were the only two remaining, but he had the feeling he wasn't alone. It was a sensation hard to describe. He looked down at Robin and felt an enormous sense of sorrow for her, her husband and child, neither of whom he had ever met, and neither knew she was dead. He walked over and knelt beside the distorted body of Robin Collins. He looked over to be sure no one was coming in or watching him. "Don't worry Robin, I'll get him," he whispered knowing her spirit was near. He wondered why this poor girl had to be struck repeatedly so many times. He couldn't imagine what she could have done to deserve this. He couldn't help but think how this lady must have kissed her husband and baby goodbye while they were sleeping, so she could go to work to help her family. And all for what? So that some cold-hearted son of a bitch could snuff out her life to rob the business of a few bucks, leaving her baby girl without her mother and her husband without the woman he loved? He hated this motherfucker and didn't even know who the person was.

A brief time later, the Medical Examiner's Office van arrived, along with two workers. In the tight space they had, Michaels and the crew managed to get Robin into the dreaded zipper coffin, a long, one size fits most, thin grey plastic bag.

"What a sad way to go. One day you are a respected, loved, cherished, valued person, and the next minute you're zipped up in a cheap piece of plastic and laid in the back of a cold metal van like an old tire being taken to the dump. It just doesn't seem right," Michaels said aloud with a cold chill racing through his body.

By now Dredge had finished with Ms. Bell and was standing outside the bar talking with Tommy, Mr. Powell and Mr. Levy.

"Mr. Levy and Mr. Powell, I see you met my partner, Detective Dave Hart," Michaels said as he approached.

"Yes, and we've provided him a full list of our employees, their work schedules and their addresses. If there is anything else you need, let either of us know," Mr. Levy stated.

Now that the body was gone from the scene, Jeff and Ray continued with a few final tasks.

"What else do you need Young Shithead?" Tommy asked.

"If I could get someone to canvas the nearby businesses, that would help."

"I'll take care of that for ya," Dredge offered.

"Thanks. Then I'm off to find the husband and do this death notification. God, I hate doing these."

"Do you want someone to go with you?" Tommy asked.

"No, I got it, but thanks."

He sat in his car and looked through his map book to see where the Collins' lived. It was only two minutes away. Normally before he did a death notification, he would drive long enough to gather his thoughts and prepare himself. Not this time. As he began the drive, like always, he imagined how her husband was going to take the news and before he knew it, he was at their residence.

There was a new minivan parked in the driveway of the modest style rancher. He raised his head and looked at the ceiling of his car and let out a deep sigh. Michaels dreaded the long walk to the front door on a notification and even more so once the door opened. He knew he was about to change the lives of so many people and his news would bring the ultimate in sadness raining down on them. Being the bearer of such news was the worst he could ever imagine. Since working in the unit, there were times he felt sorry for himself for having to perform such a task, but soon erased his self-pity. After all, he thought, it was far easier to deliver such horrible life-changing words, than to hear them.

He knocked on the door and was greeted by a man holding a newborn in his arms. The man didn't even know that he was a widow and a single father.

"Mr. Collins?" He was startled Michaels knew his name and his eyes opened wide.

"Yes, I'm James Collins. Who are you?" the man demanded.

He showed his badge and credentials. "Sorry to bother you sir, I'm Detective Michaels with the Anne Arundel County Police Department. Can I come in and talk to you?"

Mr. Collins moved to the side. "Is everything ok?" He knew something was wrong. He could sense it.

"Is there some place we can sit down?"

"Yeah sure come into the living room. He clutched onto his infant daughter, sound asleep in his arms. Michaels could see the peaceful look on the baby's face, who was far too young to realize her mother had been taken from her by an evil, worthless fuck.

"Can you please tell me what is going on?" Mr. Collins said growing frustrated.

Now came the toughest part. The part Michaels disliked the most. "I am very sorry Mr. Collins, but your wife, Robin, was killed this morning at work."

Mr. Collins's eyes opened wide in disbelief and for a moment just stared at the detective while he processed what he'd just heard.

"What?" he yelled causing his daughter to awake and begin crying. "What? What? What do you mean she was killed?" Mr. Collins stood and raced toward the front door, losing grip of his child who nearly slipped from his arms, while the two cried. "What happened? Jesus Christ No. What the fuck happened?" he screamed.

"Mr. Collins, is there someone I can call to come over and help with the baby, while we talk?"

He tried to compose himself, while the baby squirmed in his arms and screamed in fear. Michaels saw the look in his eyes. The look he had seen many times before. When someone close has been taken from you, it takes part of your body with it. It's a certain look someone gets when they've been told that the one they love is gone.

It's a look that only a few in law enforcement or clergy know.

"Umm, umm, let me, let me see if Robin's mother is home. She lives just a few blocks from here. Oh my God, this can't be true. Let me call her, fuck, where's my phone?"

"Mr. Collins, do you want me to hold your baby and try and calm her while you call your mother-in-law?"

"Ok, ok, do you mind?"

"No problem. Let me have her, and you go in another room and make the call."

Michaels took the now hysterically crying newborn from Mr. Collins, who quickly raced to his bedroom and slammed the door. Michaels could hear him crying and yelling his wife's name. He wiped the tears from the baby's face using the soft cotton blanket she was wrapped in. He walked back and forth from the kitchen to the living room while talking softly to the crying child, like he had done so many times before with his own daughter. Before he knew it, she was asleep once more. With a sleeping baby in his arms, he roamed the hallway until he found the child's room. Hanging on a wall, he saw pictures of Robin and her husband, both with and without their child. Clearly, he could see two very happy people together. He could see the glowing smile and prominent dimples on Robin's face, much different than he had seen just minutes before.

He remembered back to his days as a young father as he laid the infant gently in the bassinet. She shivered as he tucked the blanket securely around her. He stayed there for a moment looking at her and wondering what would become of her life without her mother. He kissed his right index finger and placed it on her forehead. "That's from your mother." With that, he walked from the room and carefully closed the door.

Mr. Collins sat crying on the couch. Michaels took a seat next to him. "Janet is on her way."

"Is that your wife's mom?"

"Yes. Now tell me what happened?" Mr. Collins wiped the tears from his face with his trembling hands and turned facing Michaels. He continued to weep while Michaels told him what limited information he had. He explained he had no suspects, but the motive was obviously robbery and most of the bar's cash had been taken from her while she was doing the morning count. "Dear Jesus, how was she killed? Did she suffer?"

"I don't think she suffered, in fact, I don't think she even saw it coming. She was hit in the head from behind. I'm so sorry sir."

"Oh my God," he shouted placing both hands over the front of his face while he cried. "I'm so sorry." Michaels felt so horrible for this man, knowing his entire life would change so much from this day forward. *This poor man was now all alone in life to raise their baby without her mother,* he thought. Michaels wanted to hug him so bad. He needed it.

"What's next? Can I see her?"

"I am sorry, but you cannot. In all criminal investigations an autopsy must been done in order to rule on the manner and cause of death. Right now, my partner is canvassing the neighboring businesses and I will be talking with all the employees and vendors who may have been there earlier. Someone had to know she was counting money at that time of the morning. Normally in a case such as this, you work from the inside out and that is exactly what I am doing."

"What's today? Friday? What about the Coors Light guy? I forgot his name. He comes by every Friday."

"Yes, we spoke with him. He was helpful in determining the time frame of the murder and was very cooperative with us. Did Robin ever talk about any co-workers, vendors or anyone that threatened her or made her feel uneasy?"

"No, no one. She got along with everyone and she never said anything bad about any of the vendors. Robin was a unique person. She had a way about herself that just made you like her. She was always smiling. It's hard to explain, but if you had ever met her, you would know what I mean." With that, Mr. Collins burst into a lengthy crying spell once more until he lifted his head. "Can I ask who found her?"

"It was one of the other employees. She's the one that called 911."

"Was that Mary?"

"Yes sir, I believe so."

"So now what do I do?"

Before Michaels could answer, the door swung open and in stormed a woman, screaming and crying. It was Robin's mother. Mr. Collins stood from the couch and the two embraced, crying irrepressibly. Robin's mother cried out. "No, no, no, not my baby girl. Please no. What happened? Oh my God. Are you the detective? Did you arrest whoever killed my Robin?" The woman pushed away from Mr. Collins and confronted Michaels.

"No ma'am, we haven't yet. We believe the motive was robbery and the entire Homicide Unit is on the case. The investigation is only hours old, but I can assure you both, we are on it."

Michaels stayed with the two for several more minutes until he said his goodbyes. Robin's mother checked on her granddaughter as Mr. Collins and Michaels walked outside. They stepped out onto the porch and stood side by side. Neither spoke for what seemed like minutes.

"Do you have a cigarette detective?"

"Yes sir."

Surprised by his request, Michaels reached to the inside pocket of his suitcoat and pulled two Marlboros from the box. After having his cigarette lit, Mr. Collins took a seat. Without speaking, Michaels eased down next to him. Mr. Collins hadn't smoked in who knows how long, causing him to cough and labor through the first few drags. The two sat for the next few minutes and enjoyed their cigarettes, looking straight ahead. It was like two old friends who knew what each other was thinking but said nothing. Finishing their smokes, Mr. Collins extended his arm and laid his hand on Michaels' shoulder.

"I need you to find this bastard. You hear me?"

It was a moment neither would forget. Life as a homicide detective was unlike anything he was used to, unlike anything he thought he would ever experience. When Michaels walked to his car, he felt himself overcome with sadness. Strangely, he felt like he did something wrong. He opened his car door and took a seat, looking back at the house where Mr. Collins and his mother-in law were now draped in each other's arms, crying in the doorway. Neither of which could see the tears streaming from Michaels' eyes.

Drying his tears before he made the quick drive back to Clarke's, he hopped from his car and was greeted by Tommy, still standing outside talking with Mr. Powell. "Ronnie, the evening barback's name is Kevin Burley. Mr. Powell is adamant that he was not supposed to be here, but he is due in today at 3 p.m. for the evening shift."

"Oh really? I wonder if he will show up? Did we get all his info?"

"Right here." Tommy handed Michaels a sheet of paper torn from his notebook with all his info written out in his near perfect handwriting. "Burley's only prior is for cocaine possession last year."

"You know, I love fucking dopeheads. It's so nice when you receive information like you just gave me about a potential suspect. Sometimes this shit is just too easy." Since being a homicide detective, Michaels learned most killers make mistakes and if it wasn't by leaving some type of evidence behind, they would surely spout off at the mouth to someone. It looked like this was going to be one of those cases.

"Ok thanks, let me go back in and see how much longer we are going to be so I can get on this guy."

Michaels walked in the bar while Ray and Jeff carried evidence bags to Ray's van.

"How are we coming along Dad?"

"I think we're done here. The body is on the way to the morgue. We got all of our evidence, not to mention a few bloody fingerprints."

After Ray and Jeff departed, Michaels walked to the back room to give it one last look. Robin's body was no longer there and what was once on the desk where she was working was gone. The blood-stained wall and floor were a glaring reminder of the violence that took place. Standing in the doorway leading into the scene, he got a weird feeling, a feeling like he could see the crime taking place. He envisioned the tabletop being used to smash against Robin's skull. Blow after blow he imagined blood flying through the air, onto the walls, the floor and desk. He could hear the noise of the chair crashing as she went limp, face first to the floor, gurgling in her own blood. It was a horrible movie playing in his head.

Mr. Powell was waiting out front on the sidewalk for Michaels. "Is there anything I can do for you detective?"

Michaels handed him his business card. "Please call me immediately if Burley shows or doesn't show for work."

"I certainly will. Is it ok to go in now and clean?" Mr. Powell asked.

"Yes sir, we are all finished. I'll be in touch with you guys as things progress. Remember to call me ASAP about Burley." Michaels scribbled his telephone number down in his nearly full notepad before he walked to his car. Once in his cruiser, he laid his suit coat on the front seat and scratched down what time he cleared the scene. It was 2 p.m. He had already been on the case for six hours, and it had only just begun.

His first stop was Police Headquarters, home of the Evidence Collection Unit. The first pressing task was to see what could be gleaned from the bloody fingerprints on the money and the various papers. Additionally, he wanted to get a mug shot of Kevin Burley for a later photo array to show Mr. Cooke in the event any of the fingerprints belonged to him.

"Hey Dad, do you know which bag has the bloody fingerprints?"

"Jeff already took it in. He's having Ernie look at it." Ernic was one of two Latent Fingerprint Examiners in the Police Department. He was thorough, precise and good at his craft.

"Great." Michaels walked quickly past Ray and into the Evidence Collection Unit's office. Jeff was always thinking and one step ahead of everyone, this was one of the many reasons he was in charge of their unit.

"Young Shithead, Ernie's pulling Burley's prints to compare them to the bloody prints on the paper and money we found in the office," Jeff said.

"Thanks. Can I get someone to print out his mugshot while I'm here?"

"I already have Carol doing that for you now."

"You are the man Jeff Cover," Michaels said with a big smile.

Carol Wilkes, the evening shift evidence tech, emerged from the photo darkroom and handed Michaels two fresh mugshots.

"Is this little fat guy your killer?" Carol asked with a perplexed look on her face.

"He might be. If not, he better show up for work tonight, or he'll be in some deep shit."

Michaels took the photos and sat down at one of the six desks that filled up the tight space. "Doesn't look like some bad ass to me," he said for anyone to hear. "Jeff, where is the black male mug shot book? I want to put together a photo lineup."

Jeff went over to his cluttered desk and handed Michaels a large, three-ring binder full of baseball card sheet protectors, each with a mug shot of a black male who had once been arrested. The binder was jam packed with over 500 photos, chock full of interesting faces.

The plan was to put together a lineup with seven other subjects, similar in age and appearance, to show to Mr. Cooke and positively put Burley where he wasn't supposed to be; at the crime scene. After twenty-five minutes of searching through the book, he had seven good photographs for his lineup to add along with Burley's photo. He would take them back to the office and tape them in a manila folder with numbers 1-8 beneath each to show his witness.

Michaels got up from his chair to return the book back to Jeff's desk, when he saw Ernie walking from the Fingerprint Examination Room. "He's your guy Ronnie, it's him," he said handing Michaels his official report with a big grin.

"Ernie, was it the bloody print on the dollar bill or the piece of paper?"

"Both."

"All right, fucking-A Ernie, that was quick. Great job," Michaels yelled as he shook Ernie's hand in excitement.

He knew how lucky he was to get such a break. A bloody fingerprint is better than a confession. It's so hard to refute, and not something anyone can claim was there just because he worked there, and Michaels knew it.

He stood in the middle of their office reading the report, when he glanced over and caught Ray smiling. Ray was never one to tell Michaels or his older brother, Steve, if he was ever proud of them. He just wasn't that type of father. In fact, he never said the words *I love you* to either of his boys unless they said it to him, but in that very moment, Michaels got the feeling Ray was proud.

Michaels raced to the Criminal Investigation Division, CID for short, in Crownsville, Maryland, located about 45 minutes from Baltimore and 15 minutes from Annapolis. The fellas in the Homicide Unit referred to the aging CID building as The Barn. No one ever knew why, perhaps because of the animals they brought in, or because of the animals who worked there. It was probably both. The guys thought it was ironic that the CID was on the grounds of the Crownsville State Mental Hospital. It's been said, the old red brick building now occupied by detectives, was once the home for the most severely insane.

The old structure consisted of about 50 detectives assigned to the Robbery, Child Abuse, Rape and Homicide Units. The Homicide Unit was buried deep in the rear of the building, for good reason. The tucked away space was rectangularly shaped and was comfortably large enough for the four detectives. Each had their own desk, still allowing for a large walkway directly down the center, used frequently by Tommy for pacing. Tommy had his own office adjacent to the detective's room, with a large desk and two old leather chairs for guests.

Office decorations were something they never worried about. This always seemed odd, given the fact most of them spent more time there than in their own homes. The extent of the office décor consisted of old grey vertical filing cabinets, packed with cases, some old, some new, some solved and some still open. Mounted seven feet up on the concrete wall, was a shelf with an old stereo to play their favorite tunes, sometimes a little louder than some of the others in ear shot cared for. It was unknown if the eight-track player worked, but the radio was just fine, as were the two outdated speakers mounted the same height in opposite corners. The stereo helped to maintain the sanity at times and always seemed to get louder after 4:00 p.m., the time when most of the other detectives and the brass would leave for the day.

Michaels was eager to tell Tommy and the others the news and put together the photo lineup and warrants for Burley. He had a lot to do and it was now 4:30 p.m., eight and a half hours since he first responded to Clarke's Saloon. With his adrenaline flowing he didn't have an appetite, nor was he tired. He was only hungry to lock this asshole up.

Tommy was sitting at Michaels' desk talking to Dredge. Tommy had already called Jeff and got the news about the positive fingerprint hits on Burley.

"What do you need me to do Young Shithead?" Dredge asked.

"Well Dredge, if you could get a description of the place where this dude is living for my search warrant, I'll put together this photo lineup and go show my delivery man."

"I'm all over it son. Donald and I will go over and get a look at his apartment now."

"Young Shithead you're gonna lock this motherfucker up tonight ain't ya?" Donald asked while laughing.

"I hope so."

Detective Donald Hauf was another member of the five-person Homicide Unit. He was a funny, well dressed, hyper guy, with a witty sense of humor who would give a stranger the shirt off his back. He was relentless as a detective, regardless if it was his case or not. He was always there for anyone in the unit, no matter what.

Michaels sat at his desk and began putting his line up together and noticed a phone message from bar owner, Ed Powell. He picked up after one ring.

"Mr. Powell, this is Detective Michaels."

"Just as we suspected, our boy didn't show up for work today. He didn't call or anything."

"Is that normal for him?"

"No, he always calls, even if he is running late. From what we can determine, according to the cash register tapes, it looks as if there is $1,961.00 missing."

"That's helpful, thanks for the call Mr. Powell, let me know if anyone hears from him."

"Will do."

"Tommy," Michaels yelled out from his desk with a beaming smile.

"What?"

"Shocker, dick nuts didn't show up for work today."

"Great, are you leaving soon to show your lineup?"

"Yes sir, just about done."

Before long, the photo lineup was put together, and Mr. Cooke was waiting anxiously at his house for Michaels. He dashed from the office, thinking how wonderful things were coming together and all he needed was Mr. Cooke to pick out Burley. This would be the final piece of probable cause to secure an arrest warrant.

When Michaels pulled up to Mr. Cooke's home, he could see him waiting eagerly at the front door. "Did you get him yet?"

Michaels could only smile, knowing he was so excited to be part of this, but little did he know how much rested on him making a positive identification from the photo array.

"Thanks for meeting me Al, you mind if I come in?"

"Sure, come on in. Honey, this is Detective Michaels, who I told you about."

"Hi Mrs. Cooke. Glad to meet you," Michaels said to the lady standing with Mr. Cooke in the foyer. Michaels immediately noticed a strange look on their faces.

"I've heard a lot about you from my husband. This is so sad. Did you arrest the person who did this?"

"No ma'am, not yet."

"I am very frightened detective. What if that man who my husband saw with Robin this morning, did this? That would make him the only witness and his life could be in danger. Our whole family could be in jeopardy. He could get out on a technicality and kills us?"

"Detective, I ain't scared, but you know, I have a wife and two kids," Al chimed in.

Michaels began to worry. Frequently, this happens to witnesses after they've had time to think and allow others to influence them. He needed this identification. It was crucial.

"Al is there someplace we can sit and talk in private?" Michaels knew he had to get him away from his wife and turn up the heat.

"Yes, let's go in the kitchen, its quiet in there. Honey I'll be right out." The two sat at the kitchen table where there were paper plates with food still on them and full glasses of water. "Let me get these out of the way," Mr. Cooke said pushing the plates and glasses toward the middle of the table. "Frankly detective, I don't know if I want to get involved now. You just don't know what people are going to do these days, especially on all them drugs. My wife is really worried."

Michaels' face tightened, and he could feel his blood pressure quickly rising. He scooted his chair close to the table and leaned toward Mr. Cooke who suddenly had a look of fear across his face.

Michaels gritted his teeth and talked in a low tone so Mrs. Cooke couldn't overhear. "Listen Al, you're a fucking man, right?"

"Well yeah, of..." Michaels didn't allow him to finish speaking. "You just said you had kids?"

"Umm, yes sir a boy and a girl." "Well think of it this way, someone smashed your little girl's skull so hard that parts of her brain were falling out. Knowing this you'd want that motherfucker caught, no matter what. Am I right?"

"Well, yeah I...."

"Exactly. And that's what Robin's family are all thinking right now. Do you understand me?"

"Umm, yes sir."

"No Al, I really don't think you hear what I'm saying." Mr. Cooke could see the anger across Michaels' face. "Look, I don't build a case around just one witness or one piece of evidence. No. When I bring someone to court, I do so when I can put the motherfucker away for as much time as possible. Got it?"

"I see."

Michaels moved inches from his face. "So, I need you to man the fuck up, and look at these pictures and if you don't, we'll take a little drive over to Robin's house and you can tell her widower husband, her fucking mother and her fucking father that you lost your fucking balls and are unwilling to help them. How's that sound?" Michaels reached over and grabbed the back of Mr. Cooke's neck. "So, Al, buddy, what do say? Wanna take a ride?"

Al's eyes opened wide. "No sir, I mean yes sir, whatever you need."

Michaels leaned back in his chair, opened the folder and slid it in front of him. "Good, I have 8 pictures here. I need you to tell me if the man you saw at Clarke's this morning, is in here."

With one quick glance Mr. Cooke said, "That's him. That's him right there. That's the guy. I'll never forget that face," pointing to Burley.

Michaels immediately flipped the picture over and handed Mr. Cooke the pen from his shirt pocket. "Put your initials, today's date and the time on the backside for me please. It's 6:45 p.m." When he finished, Michaels grabbed the folder. "Now that wasn't so hard, was it?"

"Does this mean you're going to arrest him?"

"We're getting there Al, but don't say anything to anyone, ok?" Michaels said in a serious tone.

"Yes sir, yes...yes sir I hear ya. I won't say anything to anyone. You can trust me."

They both stood from the table and Michaels stuck his hand out to shake Mr. Cooke's. As they touched, he could feel his shaking hand, and the moisture from his sweaty palms.

"You did the right thing tonight Al. Thanks. You're a good man."

"Yes sir, I'm sorry. Will you let me know when you get him?"

"Sure Al, I'll let you know."

Back in his car, he yelled out with excitement, slamming his open hand down on the top of his steering wheel. "Fucking A, Woo hoo." He drove back to the office knowing there was still a lot of work ahead. It was now 6:55 p.m. It was going to be a long night. By the time he arrived at the CID, the parking lot was empty except for

Tommy, Dredge and Donald's cars, which was of little surprise. In Michaels' short tenure in the unit, he found it wasn't unusual for the entire crew to work around the clock with little sleep for days following a homicide. During those times, the days seemed to run together, and oddly most would end up forgetting what day it was. Anyone who has ever worked in homicide knows this all too well.

Michaels could hear a Beach Boys song blaring from the office. "Boys, boys."

Tommy popped out of his office when he heard Michaels' voice. "Young Shithead, did he ID him?"

"Sure did. He's mine now."

"Shithead, the description of his apartment is on your desk," Donald said.

Michaels knew how nice it was being part of an exceptional team like he was. Everybody wanted to help all the time, contrary to his days as a narc, where everyone worried about just themselves. Donald appeared from behind his desk wearing only his colorful boxer shorts, crisp white button-down shirt, paisley tie, black dress shoes and black socks. His pants were draped neatly across the nearby file cabinet. Michaels smiled, but by now he'd seen him perform this ritual several times. It was something Donald would do for good luck when they worked a case. Funny thing was everyone in the unit thought it worked, or at least they liked to think so.

Michaels got to work typing the warrant applications for both Burley and his apartment. He was running on pure adrenaline at this point, having no breakfast, lunch, or dinner, just a coffee 14 hours ago.

At one point he stopped to call Mr. Collins to give him an update. The mood in the office was very upbeat. Everyone was visually excited that another homicide was soon to be solved. Though the rear outside door was open for ventilation, smoked filled the unit's area. The guys were laughing and cutting up. Michaels alerted them he was about to make a call. He surely didn't want Mr. Collins to hear their laughter in the background.

Calling the number, he wondered what Mr. Collins was doing since they last spoke. He picked up on the third ring. "Mr. Collins? Detective Michaels."

"Yes sir." he could hear the gut-wrenching sadness in his voice. In fact, he could tell he'd still been crying. After a brief silence, he told him about the ID made by the Coors Light vendor, the bloody fingerprints at the scene, and the suspect employee not showing up for work. "Did you arrest him?" Did he say why he did this to my wife?" he sobbed harder.

"No sir, not yet. I am working on getting warrants, so we can look for evidence when we arrest him. We should be hitting his apartment by 10 or 11 tonight, so I'll call you first thing in the morning."

"Can you call me tonight? I want to know why the bastard did this to my wife. Hell, she would have given him the money. I hope he dies," he yelled out in anger. Michaels could hear him slam his fist on a table. "I'm sorry detective. I really appreciate you calling me."

"No need to be sorry. I understand. That's no problem, it's the least I can do. I'll call you as soon as I can."

Michaels hung up and sat staring at the wall for a few seconds. His emotions were getting the best of him and he needed to pull himself together. He didn't know what was coming over him or why. He wondered if it was because he held their little baby, a child who would never know her mom. For some odd reason he felt connected to these people. He didn't know how long he was staring, but everyone in the unit was watching him, and he had no idea.

"You ok Shithead?" Dredge asked.

He lifted his head slowly like he was in a trance. "Yeah, woo, that really got me."

"Cream and sugar in your coffee?" Dredge asked trying to change the topic quickly.

"Yeah, thanks." He composed himself and began typing. There was too much left to do. After working vigorously for 45 minutes, he finally finished both documents. Dredge and Donald would take the Arrest Warrant Application to the Commissioner's Office and wait for the warrant to be issued, while Michaels would take the Search & Seizure Warrant to a judge for a signature. Michaels reached out to Judge Bruce Williams, who he used frequently during his narc days. The judge was fond of Michaels, respected and trusted him, and his home was close to the CID building. It didn't matter if it was 3 p.m. or 3 a.m., Judge Williams would always welcome him into his chambers or his living room. It didn't matter.

It did not take Michaels long to get back to the office with a signed warrant for his suspect's apartment. Tommy had already lined up members of the SWAT Team to meet at a mall located a block from the residence. "Signed motherfuckers," he said, slamming the folder on his desk.

"Eat some pizza Shithead," Tommy ordered. "Donald called and said they are on their way back with your 1st Degree Murder Warrant."

"Great, and I'm starving too. Thanks Tommy."

Michaels looked over and saw two large pizza boxes on Detective Mark Howes' desk. Mark was the last of the detectives in the unit. He was on vacation but was due back the following week. One thing for sure, if Mark had been in the office, he would have been pissed off had he known his desk was being used as a buffet table.

Mark Howes was a bit prim and proper, always perfectly groomed, wearing high dollar suits. He spoke in a somewhat joking, yet serious and condescending manner to everyone. His nickname was Poodle because of his kinky, curly hair. He too was an awesome detective. Besides being very tenacious with great instincts, he was funny as hell. A good sense of humor seemed to be a prerequisite for being in Tommy's close-knit unit. Currently a student at the University of Baltimore Law School, Mark was destined to be a kick ass lawyer one day. To add to his persona, he placed yellow evidence tape on the floor surrounding his desk, telling everyone to *stay out of his duly assigned work area*. He was arrogantly pretentious, but loveable.

Michaels grabbed two slices of pepperoni pizza and one of the cold Cokes from the vending machine and sat at his desk. He had been going 100 miles an hour nonstop for 15 hours, now all that was left was to find Burley, put cuffs on him, question him and search his apartment. Those tasks alone would take at least 4-5 hours depending on if he confessed and how much, if any, evidence would be found at his apartment.

By 10:30 p.m. Tommy, Dredge, Donald and Michaels drove to the mall located a block from Burley's apartment. They met with the sergeant of the SWAT Team and gave him the low down on the case. Members of the entry team did a quick drive by of the apartment, so they knew exactly what door to hit. At the time of the drive by, they saw a light on inside and a least one person moving around. This was a good sign.

The specially trained tactical officers approached the apartment in their fully blacked-out Suburban, packed with six heavily armed cops. They were bad asses, and they knew it. Those from the unit followed behind in two cars with their lights out. Their vehicle came to a quick stop fifty yards away and the team slipped quickly from the rear door without making a sound. The first man carried the solid steel battering ram for easy entry, nicknamed, *the key*. The unit waited and monitored the radio, listening for the *all clear* notification.

Dredge and Michaels sat in Dredge's car behind Tommy where he and Donald waited with their windows down. Suddenly, they heard a loud metal crashing noise as the front door was slammed opened by the 75-pound key. Several of the Team members were heard shouting the words *Police, Police Get down on the ground*. In less than two minutes, Tommy received the *all clear* message to start in.

Approaching the apartment, neighbors were standing in their partially opened doorways peering out. This commotion was nothing new to anyone who lived there. It was a frequent flyer stop for the SWAT Team. The door had a large gaping hole where the door knob used to be, now in pieces all over the floor. Inside, two members of the SWAT Team stood over Kevin Burley lying on the living room floor, with blood seeping from a fresh wound on his forehead. His hands were tightly secured behind his back with a thick durable set of zip ties. At the other end of the living room lay a skinny black female, face down, sporting the same type of restraints drawn tightly on her wrist behind her back.

"What happened here? Somebody didn't cooperate with the police?" Michaels said sarcastically looking down at Burley.

One of the SWAT Officers standing guard over him chimed in. "You may want to look in the bathroom. Genius here locked himself in and tried flushing money down the toilet. We kicked the door in, and your boy was, how can I say, less than cooperative."

"I didn't do anything, you just hit me," Burley refuted lifting his head up from the rug.

"Shut the fuck up asshole," the officer said burying his boot between his shoulder blades.

"Flushing money? Now why in the world would you flush money, when there is dope all over this shit hole? I wonder what we are going to find on that money. Maybe someone's fingerprints perhaps? Mmm, I wonder," Michaels offered as a smartass.

The bathroom door dangled by one hinge and the knob was compressed into the door from the brute force of a #12 size boot. The dirty bathroom floor was riddled with $20 bills, some with dried blood on them, and others submerged in the toilet.

Michaels shook his head and walked back to the living room. Scanning the apartment, he could see a few rocks of crack, a pipe and an ounce of fresh pot sitting on the coffee table in front of the faded plaid couch.

"Somebody was having a little party I see," Michaels uttered to everyone in the room.

"Hey Shithead, take a look at this." Michaels knew it had to be something good for Dredge to call him over. It was more money, and this pile had even more signs of dried blood.

"Holy shit," Michaels said in amazement to Dredge.

"How much did they say was taken?"

"A little over $1,900 I think."

"There isn't a whole lot missing then, probably just enough to buy the dope on the table and what they've already smoked up."

"Thanks for your help brother," Michaels said to Dredge, both gazing in astonishment at the overwhelming evidence. "You know Dredge, solving a murder is like seizing 20 kilos of cocaine. It's a great feeling."

"I know son. It is a good feeling."

Shortly after entry was made, Evidence Technician Carol Wilkes arrived. She began systematically photographing the rooms in the dingy one-bedroom apartment. Following the photographs, she packaged up the dope from the table, the blood-stained money from the bathroom and dining room, more money taken from Burley's pockets and the bloody t-shirt found stuffed inside the kitchen trash can.

Michaels lifted the female from the ground and told Donald to join them outside. The two walked the twenty something year old to the front of the building.

"What's your name?" Michaels asked her.

"Sondra. I was only smoking pot. I wasn't doing the crack." It was obvious she thought the dope was the reason for busting the door down. Boy was she wrong.

"Are you Kevin's girlfriend?" Donald inquired.

"No, I just met him last week at the bar."

"What bar?" Donald asked her.

"Clarke's, where he works."

"This is Detective Hauf and he is going take you to our office and get a statement. Depending on how cooperative you are, will determine if he arrests you or not. Do you understand me?" Michaels said.

"Yes, but can you take these off? My wrists hurt."

"That's up to this detective," Michaels said looking in Donald's direction.

"You are going to cooperate right? I'm in no mood to fuck around tonight," Donald asked.

"Yes, yes, but I was just smoking pot."

Donald had one of the SWAT members stationed outside cut off the zip tie from her wrists. He grabbed her by the arm and whisked her into his car and sped off.

When Michaels re-entered the apartment, Burley was sitting on a dining room chair someone had pulled to the middle of the living room. He was slumped forward with his head nearly in his crotch. He knew his shit was weak. Someone obviously told him we were homicide detectives, not narcs. Tommy pulled Michaels into the kitchen to talk. Dirty dishes were piled in the sink and on the counter and roaches were feeding on the crusty food at the base of the trash can where the clothes had been stuffed.

"You and Dredge take this asshole to the CID and I'll stay here with Carol, so we can finish up."

"Has he said anything?" Michaels asked.

"He asked to see the warrant and I told him he would get a copy of everything. That's it," Tommy answered.

"Ok, then we're out of here," Michaels said and walked to the living room. "Get up Kevin. We are going to take a little ride. Come on Dredge."

Michaels grabbed Burley's arm firmly and lifted him forcibly from the chair. "Can one of you guys cut these off his wrists please so I can cuff him?"

The SWAT Team sergeant pulled a pair of snips from his bullet proof tactical vest and cut them with one quick sweeping motion. Michaels re-cuffed him behind his back with his old pair of handcuffs passed down to him by Ray. The young detective always thought it was cool to be using his dad's cuffs.

Dredge and Michaels walked Burley to the parking lot where Michaels secured him in a seat belt in the back seat and locked the door. Michaels rode shotgun as Dredge drove, who wasted no time pulling from the apartment complex and onto the main drag. Not a word was spoken, and Michaels began wondering how the pending interview would go with the newly cuffed suspect

"Dredge, are you and your son going to the mountains to deer hunt again this year?"

"Yeah, he's all excited. He got his first buck last year, you know."

"That's right. Mel and I are going again, except this year Mel's got a small camper, so we are upgrading from freezing our asses off in a tent."

Without warning, Michaels caught a glimpse of Burley's foot swiftly lunging forward, kicking Dredge squarely in the back of the head. Like a rag doll, his head jolted forward striking the steering wheel, instantly losing consciousness. The car crossed into the opposing lane of traffic, narrowly missing an oncoming U-Haul truck, then slammed into the steel guard rail adjacent to the shoulder. The sound of glass breaking and metal on metal screeching was all that could be heard. When the car struck the rail, it spun backwards making it tip onto the two driver's side wheels, nearly rolling over, then bouncing down to a stop on all four tires.

When the car came to a stop, Burley began ramming his shoulder into the door, but was unable to apply enough force for it to open. Dazed from hitting his head on the passenger window, Michaels could hear the noise coming from behind and he knew exactly what it was. He unfastened his seatbelt with his left hand while he reached to his waistband for his .38 caliber Smith & Wesson. The holster was empty. The gun had fallen from the aged holster during the wreck. The banging intensified. Burley was now leaning back in the seat, using all his might and kicking the door with both feet.

Michaels had the wherewithal to open his door in an attempt to stop his suspect from escaping. Without a gun, he knew it was going to be a one on one battle to prevent this mad man from getting free. With no radio or weapons and an unconscious partner, he knew it was on. He flung his door open and while climbing out he noticed his handgun wedged between the seat and the floorboard. He reached down and tugged at the gun. It barely moved.

Pulling with all he had Michaels saw the back door fly open. With one last pull he freed the weapon and stumbled to the back side of the car where the rear passenger door was open. Burley was frantically shaking his upper body back and forth attempting to free himself from the seatbelt now entangled in his handcuffs. Struggling, he looked up at Michaels when four loud shots rang out, each accompanied with a bright blaze of muzzle flash from the gun clenched in Michaels' hand. All four bullets pierced through Burley's grey colored t-shirt and into his upper chest cavity. He moaned while blood poured from his mouth, causing him to choke up bright red bubbles of blood from his lungs. *Now the blood that would soak his clothes would be his own,* Michaels thought.

Michaels watched while his body went limp and void of life. Immediately, he turned his attention to Dredge. "Dave, Dave, are you ok? Dave," he yelled running to the driver's side door, now buckled inward and slightly open. Dredge came to and wiped the blood dripping into his eyes from the gash on his forehead. "Are you alright brother?" Michaels asked while putting his trembling hand on Dredge's shoulder.

"Oh fuck, my head. You ok? What happened?" he asked, blinking rapidly trying to compose himself.

"Burley kicked you in the head and we crashed into the guardrail."

"Man, my head is killing me. Are you ok?"

"I'm a little sore, but he's not," leaning his head in the direction of the rear seat.

"What happened to him?" Dredge asked too sore to turn his head.

"I shot that piece of shit. He tried to kill you and then tried to escape."

"How is he?" Dredge asked rubbing his forehead.

"How is he? He's fucking dead, that's how he is," Michaels said pointedly. "Where's your radio so I can call this in?"

"Umm, under my seat."

Michaels found the radio laying on the back floor where it had slid from the crash. With his hands still trembling from stress he keyed up the radio.

"Detective 132 to Dispatch."

"Go ahead."

"Be advised, I've been involved in a departmental shooting on College Parkway near Shore Acres Road. Please notify Sergeant Suit. We are going to need a few patrol cars, the Evidence Collection Unit, a tow truck and an ambo for Detective Hart please."

"Do you need a second medical unit for the suspect?" the dispatcher said with his voice cracking.

"Uh, that'll be a negative radio, just the on-call Medical Examiner."

"10, 10-4," the Dispatcher stuttered.

In seconds, Tommy was on the radio calling Michaels with an unusually worried sound to his voice. "Detective 130 to 132."

"Yes sir."

"You ok Ronnie?"

"Yes sir, Detective 131 is a little banged up. We have an ambo en route for him."

"I'll be right there."

Michaels retrieved a blanket from the trunk and placed it across the rear doorway to cover Burley's body, hiding it from the slow driving onlookers.

In record time Tommy arrived, skidding up to the scene with his lights and siren blaring. His driver's door swung open before the car came to a complete stop. Michaels walked over, and Tommy shot out from his car. Sirens could be heard coming from all directions.

"How's Dredge?" he said walking briskly to where he was leaning against the guard rail holding gauze from his first aid kit on his head.

"He's dazed. His head has a nice gash in it."

"Dredge. Talk to me."

"My head hurts. I'll be alright if I could just get this to stop bleeding."

"Ok, we'll get you taken care of." With that Tommy turned and walked to the back of the car and lifted the blanket concealing the body. He nodded his head as if he was giving his approval and lowered the blanket.

"What happened, Ronnie?"

"The fucking asshole kicked Dave in the back of the head. He lost control of the car and we smashed into the guard rail. He then kicked the door open to escape. When I got out, I ordered him to stop but he came at me, so I shot him."

"How many times did you shoot him?"

"Umm, let me see." Michaels unsnapped his holstered handgun and opened the cylinder. He could tell from the firing pin impressions on the base of the shell casings that four rounds had been fired.

"Four times, yep four. Wow, that happened so fast."

"I'm going to need your gun and I'll have Donald interview you when we get to the office. Sit in my car and don't say a word to anyone. I'll take it from here."

"Got it." Michaels turned and began walking toward Tommy's black unmarked Crown Vic when he could see an ambulance and two marked police cars race up to the scene.

"And hey Shithead" Tommy yelled over the siren noise, "Good job."

Michaels nodded and gave him a quick thumbs up before he climbed in the front passenger seat.

Before long the scene was lit up with emergency vehicles and several members of the upper command staff. Dredge was eased into the rear of an ambulance by two paramedics and taken away. Evidence Technician Wilkes had finished up at Burley's apartment and was now on location photographing and taking measurements. In his unique protective way, Tommy kept all the brass from Michaels, who everyone could see through the front window of his car. To most cops this scene would seem chaotic. There were LED lights flashing, traffic being diverted by cops yelling at people, high ranking staff milling about, an injured detective being treated by medical personnel, a flashing camera and, of course, a dead murder suspect laying in the back of a car. But none of that fazed Tommy. He was in complete control, walking around the scene with purpose and a sense of calm, giving direction to several people and answering some of the idiotic questions from the brass.

"Well look who's here. Long time no see Doc. What's it been, 15 or so hours?" Tommy yelled out when he saw Doc Johnson walk up with his clipboard and camera.

"Hi Tom. I was told this was a police shooting?"

"Yeah, this is the guy who killed the girl at the bar this morning. Ronnie and Dredge were taking him to the office, when he kicked Dredge in the back of the head and Ronnie had to shoot him."

"How's he doing?"

"Who? Ronnie or Dredge?"

"Both."

"Dredge is on his way to the hospital and Ronnie is in my car. He's fine. I'm just keeping him away from everyone."

"Good idea. Ok let me see this asshole."

"Doc if you don't need me, I want to get Shithead out of here before the press arrives. Can you stay until Carol is done and the ME van arrives?"

"Sure Tommy, get out of here and take care of that boy. Hey, and tell him I said *Good job.*"

"Will do. Thanks Doc."

Back at the office Sondra was sitting in a chair next to Donald's desk sleeping. Donald walked from the coffee room when Tommy and Michaels strolled back to the office area. Without his radio on, Donald had no idea what had transpired in the last hour.

"Hey boys, fresh coffee in there if you want some." Sondra leaned up in her chair and rubbed her eyes. "Young Shithead, she knows nothing about the murder. She said your boy contacted her out of the blue today around 8 a.m. Said he was going to go buy some pot if she wanted to party with him. He showed up at her house with a lot of money in a plastic bag. They drove around Annapolis to some of the hot spots where he disappeared from the car for a while. She said he seemed very jumpy and hyper. I put her statement on your desk."

"Thanks brother," Michaels said as he picked up the three-page typed statement and shoved it in his accordion case folder. Donald grabbed his car keys and announced he was taking Sondra home.

"Not so fast young man," Tommy bellowed from the coffee room. "I need to see you in my office. Ronnie, ask her if she knows where any of Burley's family lives."

"Yes sir," Michaels answered knowing another death notification had to be made by somebody, but this time not him.

Donald plopped down in the large leather chair in front of Tommy's desk with his coffee in hand and Tommy shut the door. "What's up boss?"

"Ronnie had to kill Burley tonight and I need you to interview him."

"What? Are you fucking with me?"

"No, Burley kicked Dredge while he was driving, they crashed, and he came at Ronnie while he was trying to escape. I am dead fucking serious."

"Damn."

"Make sure you cover everything in his statement, how he was in fear for his life, how he ordered him to stop, hell Donald, you know what I need."

"I got it. I got this boss. I'll take care of Young Shithead. If he's ok with it, I'll just tape record it and have the secretary type it up in the morning."

"What time is it anyway?" Tommy said pulling his shirt sleeve back to see his watch. "God damn it's 12:30. Ok, you can use my office to interview Shithead and listen to me, when you are done, wait here for me. Do you understand?" he said adamantly.

"You got it."

Tommy got up to see what Michaels had learned about Burley's next of kin. "Well, anything?"

"The only thing she knows is that today he said he was going to Georgia to live with his parents. She doesn't know much because they just met."

"Ok. Donald is going to interview you in my office. I'm going to run this young lady home, then go check on Dredge."

"Roger that. I promised I'd call Mr. Collins and give him an update when we arrested Burley. Is it ok to give him a shout before he hears about this on the news?"

"Yeah, yeah, good idea. Give him a call and then get that interview done. When you are finished, you are not to leave. Do you hear me?"

"Is there something wrong?"

"No. Just do not leave."

"Yes sir. I hear ya."

"Come on young lady, I'm taking you home."

"Did Kevin kill someone? Did he get arrested?" Sondra asked.

"Yeah, something like that, let's go."

It seemed like many days had passed since Michaels first knocked on the door of the Collins residence and changed the lives of an entire family. He was sure the news he was about to convey would give Mr. Collins a sense of relief and justice. Michaels called Mr. Collins' cell phone. It rang and rang and rang. There was no answer. The man, he thought, had to be wiped out and completely exhausted.

"Fuck," he yelled out terminating the call and hitting redial.

"You ready Young Shithead? Let's get this over with." Donald said pulling his tape recorder and a blank tape from his desk.

"Mr. Collins?"

"Yes."

"This is Detective Michaels. I'm sorry to call so late, but I promised you an update."

"Did you arrest him? Did he say why he had to kill her?" he said speaking very softly.

"Umm, well yes and no. You see when we arrested him, he tried to escape, and I had to shoot him. He's dead Mr. Collins." There was silence on the phone. Michaels waited for him to respond.

"Oh my God. Thank you, Lord. Thank you, detective. Thank you so much. Are you alright?"

"I am, but my partner's not. He got kicked in the back of the head and hit it on the steering wheel."

"Oh my God. I hope he's okay."

"He will be. He's a tough old bird. So obviously this case is done, and you won't have to ever worry about going to court or facing this asshole, excuse my language."

"Oh no apology necessary, he got what he fucking deserved. I just can't believe all of this. Everything is going in slow motion and I'm just waiting to wake up from this nightmare. I'm waiting for Robin to walk through the front door." He attempted to talk while he cried. "I can't believe I'm never going to see her again. We had so much we wanted to do together. What am I going to do with our daughter? Robin so loved being a mother. She loved our daughter so much." Mr. Collins continued sobbing, struggling to hold his emotions in check. "Thanks for the call. I'm sorry detective. I have to go." The phone went silent.

Michaels joined Donald in Tommy's office and closed the door. Donald conducted a detailed interview of the entire case beginning with Michaels arrival at Clarke's Saloon to the near tragic events which caused the shooting death of Kevin Burley. Because the interview was tape recorded, the two conducted themselves professionally. The interview lasted for two hours, and by 3 a.m., it was complete and officially ruled a justifiable homicide by Detective Donald Hauf of the Homicide Unit. Now all that was left was for Donald to interview Dredge as soon as Tommy brought him to the office. Before long they arrived.

"We're back," Tommy announced as he and Dredge walked into the office. Dredge followed, wearing a padded Velcro neck brace with a large white bandage covering most of his forehead.

"How are ya brother?" Donald asked.

"I'm good. Just a little headache that's all."

"I take it you guys are all done. All good?" Tommy asked directing his question to Donald.

"Yes sir. It's justifiable. No doubt." Donald said with conviction.

Dredge sat at his desk and lit a cigarette. Michaels was sitting across from him. Dredge took a long draw from his cigarette and blew it out slowly and turned his head in Michaels' direction.

"Thank you son, for tonight."

Knowing Dredge was a man of few words, Michaels simply answered, "No problem Dave."

"Dredge, you up for giving me a statement tonight?" Donald inquired.

"Not really," he chuckled. "But we might as well get it over with."

"Is it ok if I tape it? I'll have the secretary type it up when she comes in? It'll be a lot faster."

"Like I said, not really, but can you give me a little bit?"

"Sure brother take your time. Whatever you need. Can I get you a coffee?"

"I'd love one."

Donald got Dredge a coffee and the four sat and talked about the case for what turned out to be two hours. It was the longest day ever for Michaels since being in the unit. The ups and downs of the day, the plethora of emotions and the adrenaline that rushed through his body as he killed his first human being.

Eventually, the two went into Tommy's office and for the next hour Donald comprised a thorough shooting defense for Michaels. With an excellent working knowledge of the law, Donald formulated a neat package of questions that along with Dredge's answers would ultimately go before the State's Attorney's Office for a final decision regarding the justification of the shooting.

"Come on grab your coats," Tommy said to his detectives with a sound of urgency in his voice. Again, he wasn't asking, he was telling but no one knew where they were going. They all looked at one another and followed him from the building like sheep.

"We are taking my car. Get in."

Now almost 9:00 a.m., he sped from the CID parking lot like he was in a rush to be somewhere. He made a left onto the main drag, traveling at 60 miles an hour for a whopping 15 seconds, until he turned abruptly into the lot of Sonny's Bar and slammed on his brakes. Totally befuddled, they followed their sergeant into the dingy, poorly lit bar like good soldiers. Before you knew it, everyone took a seat and drinks were ordered. It was celebration time.

Now of course, they were the only ones there, along with Sonny, the frail Asian owner, who the bar was named after. The guys couldn't believe they were drinking at 9 in the morning, but the cold beverages tasted especially good.

Everyone ordered their favorites, Tommy and Dredge both with vodka on the rocks, Donald with his all-American Budweiser bottle and Michaels with a cold can of Miller Lite. It was simple, Tommy was proud of his unit and thought it was time for a cocktail regardless of where the sun or moon was. Tommy figured since his guys had been through so much, a drink would serve as a great ending to a busy day. Now with barely any food, except for a few slices of pizza, the buzz from the alcohol came on quickly. They all had an exceptional time laughing and reliving the moments in the case. It was the truest sense of teamwork, and this time it cost someone a life.

"I'd like to make a toast," Tommy said standing from his bar stool and raising his glass. "I'm so proud of all you sons a bitches and Ronnie, way to take care of things tonight. You acted quick on your feet and you did your job. Outstanding. Cheers to the best bunch of detectives ever."

After a straight hour of drinking, Michaels eyes darted over to the door when it opened. His jaw dropped when he saw two armed men wearing suits walk in. In an instant, he saw his career flash before his eyes. It was Captain Donoho and Lieutenant Tank, the top commanders of the Criminal Investigation Division. "Oh shit, we are cooked," he mumbled to Dredge sitting next to him who hadn't noticed them yet. *We are all done,* he thought to himself. He knew they would be suspended, and God knows what else. Michaels knew his day was about to get worse.

"Young Shithead," Lieutenant Tank yelled out with a surprising smile on his face.

"Well done boy and good work gentlemen," Captain Donoho said lifting his hand high in the air to slap Michaels a high five. "Are you two alright?"

"Yes sir and thank you sir, sirs," Michaels said barely able speak from his nerves. Before they knew it, the two senior members were drinking beers, toasting the Homicide Unit and celebrating along with them. Come to find out, Tommy invited them to the bar. It was old school leadership rarely seen. It was priceless.

After three hours, the entire unit was drunk, tired, starving and it was time to go home, at least for one detective. "I'm done," Michaels announced to everyone in the bar, which was still only those from the unit. He pulled out his cell phone and put a call to his dad for a ride. He said nothing to Ray about the shooting and he didn't know what had been released to the press. There was no way he was about to get behind the wheel of a car with the way he was feeling.

The Captain and Lieutenant only stayed for two beers and by this time they were gone. Everyone thought how cool it was that they would stop in for a beer, driving their unmarked police cars, with another parked out front.

Not long after the call, Ray strolled into the bar. "Hey Ray," Tommy yelled out in a slur, helping himself from the bar stool and putting his arm around Michaels. "Ray, Ray, Young, Young, Shithead, I mean your son, did a real good, good job tonight."

"Hi everyone," Ray said with a big smile on his face. "Christ, what happened to you Dredge?"

Before Dredge could utter a word, Tommy interrupted him. "Ray, Ray, your son, kill, killed that ffff-fucking piece of shit tonight. The one who killed that lady this morning. I'm so proud of this son of a bitch. I'm proud of all of them," Tommy then planted a slobbery kiss on Michaels' cheek.

"What? When Ronnie? Are you ok?" Ray turned to his son.

"Ray, it's a good shooting. Our suspect did this to me," Dredge said pointing to his bandaged head and neck. "He was trying to escape, but Young Shithead took care of business."

"Let's go Pop. I'll tell you in the car," Michaels said walking toward the door desperately wanting to leave.

"See ya Young Shithead" rang out from the crew while Ray and his intoxicated son left the bar.

"I'll have someone drop your car off at your house." Tommy said.

On the drive home, Michaels filled Ray in on everything since they last saw each other over 24 hours ago. He couldn't believe they were already into a new day. In Ray's unique quiet way, he took it all in and said, "Good job." That would be the most Michaels would ever get from the man he was always trying to impress. A short time later, Michaels was dropped off at his house and worked his way inside.

He flicked the lamp on from the wall switch and dropped his keys in the decorative ceramic bowl on the table. His townhouse had two bedrooms upstairs, one for his daughter and the other a guest bedroom, but sadly both were rarely used. On the ground floor was a third bedroom that Michaels slept in, along with a separate living room, dining room and kitchen. If he wasn't eating at the dining room table or fixing a meal in the kitchen, he spent most of his waking hours on his favorite recliner in the living room where the television and sound system were. He enjoyed the sitcoms of Cheers and Seinfeld to keep his mind off work and make him laugh. If it was music he yearned for, his taste ranged from classic rock to the dance tunes of the Saturday Night Fever soundtrack. He had good taste for a single man, as you could plainly see from the matching country décor in his home, kept neatly arranged. It was now time to unwind from the emotional roller coaster he had been on.

Several hours had passed when the sound of Michaels' cell phone could be heard ringing from within his coat pocket, startling him. He awoke in his recliner, still dressed in his suit pants and wrinkled shirt. His tie, shoes and coat were strewn about the floor. He had no recollection of the drive home or how he ended up passed out in his recliner. It was now 6:00 p.m.

He didn't bother trying to focus on the caller ID, "Hello."

"Hi Ronnie. Do you have a second?" It was his ex-wife, Stacey.

"Yeah, sure. What's up?"

"Are you ok? You sound like you just woke up."

"As a matter of fact, I did. Stacey, what's today?"

"What do mean? What's today?"

"I mean what day of the week is it?"

"Have you been drinking?"

"Jesus Christ no. I've been working a homicide. It's Tuesday, right?"

"Yes Ronnie."

He rubbed his eyes and pounding head. "Damn, it's 6 p.m. already? Fuck."

"I was wondering if you were going to get Nicole tonight for dinner. She hasn't seen you in days and she's been asking why you haven't called." His heart sank.

"I'm sorry. I've been busy. Yes, tell her I'll pick her up around 6:30 p.m. I gotta take a quick shower."

"Well don't forget," and she hung up.

He shuffled to the bathroom to clean up. He loved his daughter so much, but it always seemed like his job kept him from her, which was exactly the reason his marriage to Stacey ended. It wasn't that he didn't have a good wife. She treated him great, in fact, she put up with more shit than most, but he just gave more time to his job than he did his home life. Though his priorities ruined his marriage, he knew he ended up with a beautiful daughter who he loved tremendously. This evening they would enjoy their two-hour long dinner together.

Runaway Murder

For the next two weeks, the unit worked three drug related near fatal shootings, one questionable suicide and a vehicular manslaughter where a very angry wife plowed over a not so faithful husband and his girlfriend, killing one and landing the other in shock trauma.

The phone rang like it always did at the most inconvenient time. It was a little after 3:00 a.m. and the person on the other end was talking to Michaels like he had been awake for hours.

"Whoa, whoa, slow down."

It was a police dispatcher on the midnight shift who was wide awake and talking a little too fast for Michaels' brain at that hour. He held the phone aside and took a minute to wake up and glanced at the clock to see the damage. Alert in record breaking time, he put the phone back to his ear to hear the news.

"We got a homicide," she said excitedly. "A girl's body was found in the woods off of Pasadena Road. Sergeant Suit said he would meet you at the scene and Detective Hart has also been notified." He ended the call quickly and tripped to his closet.

There was no need for a suit and tie, jeans and warm clothes would have to do at this hour. It was a bitter cold January morning with the temperature hovering around 5 degrees and the ground solid as ice, which was all too common in Maryland's suburbs. He arrived at the scene just before 3:45 a.m. Using his brand-new empty notebook, he made his normal notations regarding his arrival time, weather conditions and temperature. The body was said to be in a vacant 3-acre wooded plot, part of which was a densely overgrown deserted little league ball field. The field was adjacent to the road where he had parked next to the patrol sergeant and officer, who were waiting in their heated cars. It was difficult to recognize the playing field from the road. It was now blanketed with small trees and scattered trash. From the number of empty beer cans, this was obviously a well-known secluded spot for late night rendezvous and partying. Thanks to a young couple looking for a place to unleash their hormones, a dead body was discovered.

This victim was on the cold hard sand next to an old concession stand, a short distance from where he had parked. He was escorted to the body by a female officer who maintained the Crime Scene Log and was still amazed by the whole death thing. As they approached the site, he could see the victim laying on her back, stretched out, with both arms extended above her head. She was completely nude, wearing only what looked to be a thick blue necklace.

"Thank you officer I'm good from here," Michaels told her.

He could see the victim was a white female with medium sized breast and a full complement of pubic hair. From her appearance he guessed her age to be about sixteen to twenty years old. Once closer, he could see that what he thought was a necklace wasn't. It was a purse strap tied loosely around her neck, most likely used as a strangling device. Her right cheek was red with blood and freshly exposed tissue. It was apparent from the wound that a small animal had been feeding on her. Only inches from her head was an imprint in the soil where something the size of a fox had laid. Standing above the victim, a cold feeling ran through Michaels. *Homicide is so unforgiving, so final*, he thought.

Nearly an hour passed when Evidence Technicians, Jeff and Carol, joined Michaels. Like always, he loved having Jeff at a scene. He was a wealth of knowledge when it came to gathering evidence and discovering clues. Close behind them were Tommy and Dredge.

"Who is she?" Carol asked.

"Well Carol, she didn't have her fucking driver's license in her mouth, so how in the fuck am I supposed to know?" Michaels said in a condescending tone. "Hell, I've only been here five minutes myself."

Tommy handed Michaels a coffee and asked what he needed. He could see the first thing was to get Carol away from him.

"A search team to comb these woods for starters would be good," Michaels requested. Tommy knew it was one of the first things that had to be done so he volunteered Carol to coordinate the search and before you knew it, Carol and Tommy were gone. As a sergeant, he was the master of keeping his guys happy so they could perform at their best.

By this time, Jeff was kneeling next to the body looking for clues. Dredge and Michaels lit up, drank their coffees and watched Jeff at work.

"Look at this Ronnie," Jeff said.

Dredge and Michaels both bent down on each side of the body. Jeff pointed out a conspicuous ligature mark on the victim's wrists. It was obvious she had been bound with a small cord or string that left visible marks where it was tied tightly to her skin. Oddly, whatever was used was nowhere in sight. The purse strap around her neck was tied in a knot but wasn't tight against her skin. The strap left obvious marks on her neck where her attacker must have twisted and torqued it tightly to strangle her.

They examined her head as best they could prior to a closer exam at the morgue. Her hair was matted with dried blood, but they could see at least two large incisions on the top and side of her skull. The holes looked deep and approximately 3" x 3" wide. *Someone had hit this poor girl very hard*, Michaels thought to himself. It reminded him of the Collins case.

"Shit, someone must have really wanted this girl dead. Fuck, whoever did this smashed her skull, strangled her, bound her wrists, stripped her of her clothing, and most likely raped her," Jeff said to anyone listening.

When Dredge stood up, he looked up at the concession stand, where the roof extended over like an awning all the way around the top by a foot. He couldn't believe what he was seeing. "Jesus Christ, look at this," he said in amazement. "That's blood up there," pointing to the top of the stand.

"Holy shit it is," Michaels said as the three stared upwards. Several drops were spattered across the underside of the roof, angling in a direction away from the body. More blood was on the side of the stand, three feet from the ground and all the way to the top.

"Damn, whoever hit this girl hit her hard, real hard, for blood to be that far away," Jeff said.

Like always, Michaels began to visualize the brutal murder happening before him. It helped him with the placement of evidence, but it haunted him still the same. "It must have been a horrifying nightmare for her, like something you'd see on a late-night cable show," he said. He felt so sorry for her and he didn't even know her name.

Jeff photographed the entire area, vacuumed her body with a special device used to collect hairs and fibers, then swabbed the outside area of her vagina. Next came the waiting game for Doc Johnson before they moved the body and continue with their on-scene investigation. Jeff was hoping there would be some clues left behind to help identify the person or persons who had done this. He knew all too well how common it was in a homicide or crime of violence for the *transference of evidence to* take place.

Now daylight, Jeff and the detectives could hear the search team at work. Michaels took a break from the dead body and walked around the immediate area where no one had been. There were broken bottles, beer cans and trash everywhere. A small dumping ground for everything from an old small block engine to a human being. How convenient. As an avid hunter, Michaels was quite familiar with searching for signs of disturbance in the woods. He had done his share of tracking wounded deer on more than one occasion with his best friend, Mel Foster.

About 20 feet from the body was a section of woods made up of mature, towering pine trees. There seemed to be less and less trash the further he walked, with a few downed timbers to climb over. About 100 yards into his search, something caught his attention. Moving closer, he could plainly see a pink cloth partially covered with pine needles and dirt speckled across it. The spot where the soil had been brushed from was fresh. He was careful not to move anything without having it photographed first. Squatting next to the item, he hoped it wasn't just another piece of trash. The fact that someone or something had attempted to cover it kept him optimistic.

Without moving a thing, he could make out the cloth to be a long sleeve shirt. *This looked good,* he thought. *Someone must have tried to hide a piece of her clothing.* The more he looked at the sweater and how it was sparsely covered, it dawned on him who the culprit was. This half-ass concealment was done by an animal. It was obvious. He theorized the animal which fed on the deceased had carried off an article of her clothing covered with her scent, to a spot in its territory where it could be hidden. It reminded him of an old Collie his parents had when he was a kid. The dog would kick a little dirt on her bone, then act as if it was undetectable by anyone but her. That is exactly what has happened here.

He continued his brief search, but quickly returned to the body to tell Jeff and Dredge of his find. "I got something back here boys," he said to them in excitement.

"What is it?" Jeff said as he pulled the camera quickly from his eye.

"I think I got her shirt."

"I'll stay here with the body Jeff, go ahead," Dredge said.

"Let me see what the boy found." Jeff scrambled around packing his equipment to take with him. His camera was swinging from his neck while he was lugging a nylon sack full of evidence bags, and who knows what else.

Jeff, a former Department of Natural Resources Officer, agreed with Michaels' animal concealment theory. He, too, had a considerable amount of experience and training in the woods and with animals. After taking measurements and several photographs, he gently laid the garment out on a large piece of paper he had spread open on the ground. They could see it was a long sleeve shirt and a girl's sweater turned inside out. Jeff snapped several pictures and then examined the garments closer. There was dried blood around the neck areas, and several feet of string protruding from the sleeve.

"This string is the same width as the marks on her wrists," Jeff pointed out. The thin cord was still tightly knotted. Jeff cranked off some more pictures and lifted it carefully.

"It's been cut," Jeff said, holding it in his hands. In total silence, they stared at the clothes and string. Though they never spoke, Michaels believed Jeff was seeing the brutal murder taking place just as he was.

They made their way back to Dredge and Tommy who were standing near the body and talking with Carol. The search team was now getting closer to the area where the body lay. Jeff opened the evidence bags, so Tommy and Dredge could see their latest find.

"What's that?" Dredge questioned.

"It's her shirt and sweater and the string that bound her wrist. That's what that is," Michaels told them.

"Shithead, so far the search team has come up empty. No purse, no pants, no socks, no shoes and no murder weapon."

"Shit, but there is still plenty of woods to go," Michaels said with optimism.

Michaels desperately wanted to find these items, but first and foremost, he needed to know just who she was.

"Hey fellas."

"Doc, good to see ya," Tommy said.

"What do we have here?"

Michaels spoke up. "Doc, she has a few large cuts to her skull where she was hit with extreme blunt force. She's got ligature marks where she had been bound and a purse strap tied around her neck which looks like it was used to strangle her. To me, it looks like the cause of death would be trauma to the head and maybe the strap was used as a come-along or a temporary strangling device. Who knows?"

"Let me take a look."

Doc dawned his rubber gloves and carefully separated her dried blood-caked hair. Those are some deep wounds. I agree, these would most likely cause her death." He took a few pictures of the victim. "Do you all have what you need? Are we ready to turn her over?"

"I am Doc, if these guys are," Jeff said.

"Let's do it," Michaels added.

Also wearing rubber gloves, Jeff placed a large sterile blue evidence blanket on the forest floor. Jeff and Doc slowly rolled the rigid body onto her stomach. Dotted across her entire back were six, small circular burn marks like those inflicted by a cigarette. No one could believe what they were seeing. It was evidence of a torture.

"Oh my God," Michaels said in surprise.

"Jesus," Tommy uttered.

Doc was steadily pulling pictures from his camera, while they self-developed in his hand. Dredge said nothing, rather lit up another cigarette and turned away so as not to see the wounds anymore. Once Jeff had finished with his measurements, he used his special vacuum on the backside of the victim, then swabbed the outside of her anal cavity.

"They're telling me on the radio the ME crew is here with the van. Are you ready for them?" Tommy asked.

"Go ahead guys. You all can leave. I'll stay here and help them and then I have a few more things I want to do," Jeff said.

"Thanks brother, I need to find out who she is and who didn't like her," Michaels said and with that everyone, but Jeff, made their way to their cars.

Given the nature of the scene, Dredge and Michaels were hopeful that semen would be found in her. With the body removed, Jeff collected the soil in the immediate area in hopes of finding hairs belonging to the attacker or attackers. Carol took samples of the blood stains on the concession stand with a sterile swab.

Back at the CID, Michaels immediately got his hands on a stack of 110 Missing Persons Reports. The Police Department didn't have a Missing Persons Unit, rather, nothing more than an energetic evening shift cadet who would call and see if the person of interest had returned home. One thing for sure, nobody was aware of any critical missing person cases that were anything more than a symptom of a marriage gone bad.

Michaels started by sifting through the pile, separating boys from the girls, blacks from whites and discarding anyone too old or too young. After that, he was left with 44 missing women, who ranged anywhere from 12 to 30 years old. Now he had the painstaking task of calling each to see what, if any, information he could gather. Many of the calls were received by voicemail, at which time Michaels left a friendly message in his serious detective voice. From the other calls, he learned the once reported missing person was now home and they had just forgot to notify the department. The line he heard repeatedly was *Oh we forgot to call, she's been home for days*. This was good for them, but his leads were vanishing. After about 20 calls he began to worry. Nothing was panning out. He knew he needed to identify his victim, if he was to have any chance of solving this one.

"Man Dredge, I hope this wasn't a dump job from another county," Michaels said to Dredge who was writing up a shooting case from the previous week.

"Did you put a teletype out to all agencies, alerting them of her discovery and description?"

"Shit, no not yet."

"I already did," Tommy blurted out as he walked from his office.

"You are the man, thank you," Michaels said.

Michaels decided it was as good a time as any for a smoke break. He opened the door at the rear of the office for ventilation and stood at the top off the metal stairwell. It was already dark and temperatures were dropping. The night was clear, and the cold air felt good on his face. It had been a long day. The phone rang at his desk. It was Stacey.

"Homicide, Detective Michaels."
"Hi Ronnie."
"Hi."
"Hold on somebody wants to talk to you."
"Hi Daddy."
"Hi Honey. What are you doing?"
"Are you coming over tonight?"
"Aww, no baby I can't. Daddy is working right now and when I'm done, you'll be asleep. How about you and I get a pizza tomorrow night?"
"You promise?"
"Yes Honey, I promise. I love you. I miss you."
"I love you too. Bye."
"Bye."

"What did you just promise Ronnie?" Stacey asked in a nasty tone.

"We are going to go out for pizza tomorrow."

"Don't forget. Don't you dare let her down."

"I won't. I gotta run. Bye."

He finished his cigarette and started back on the reports, getting more anxious as the pile grew thinner and thinner. Periodically throughout the evening, Michaels' desk phone would ring. Most of the calls were people returning their messages, simply telling him the person he was inquiring about was no longer missing. However, one of the callers confirmed her daughter, Kathy, still had not returned home. He quickly thumbed through his dwindling stack and found the report. The missing 15-year-old was Kathy Jarvis. He could hear the worry in the caller's voice. She said her daughter frequently ran away, but this time it was for much longer than normal and more importantly, no one had heard from her. Unlike most of the other reports, there was no photograph attached, just a written description and it was spot on. He knew he had to delve further.

"Ma'am, I'm sorry to interrupt you. Would it be alright if I come over and speak with you?"

"Well yes, you sure can."

"I'm about 30 minutes away. I'm leaving now. Is the address on the report correct?"

"Yes, it is. I'll see you soon," the woman said eagerly.

Michaels told Dredge and Tommy what he had. "Take one of the Polaroids with you," Tommy said as Michaels rushed to put his coat on.

"What?"

"Take a picture of your victim with you I said."

"Tommy, half her face has been eaten off by an animal. Are you kidding me?"

Dredge leaned back in his chair to watch the fireworks between the two.

"No, I'm not kidding you. If you don't need to use it, don't. But you need to be 1000% sure it's her before you start working this case."

"Man, I don't want to do that." Michaels grabbed one of the gruesome pictures from his case file and shoved it in his inner suit coat pocket along with his notebook.

"I'm out of here. I'll call you Dredge," he said as he walked briskly from the building.

He hopped into his car and drove to the small middle-class neighborhood of Glen Burnie. The home where the Jarvis family lives was built in the sixties on a quiet suburban street. Parked in front was an older Chevrolet Blazer. He walked up the steps and the door opened before he had a chance to knock. There stood a woman with an obvious look of concern across her face.

"Hi Detective Michaels, I'm Ruth Jarvis, Kathy's mother. Come in please."

He followed Mrs. Jarvis into the living room where they sat next to one another on the couch. He reached into his suit pocket and pulled his notebook out to begin writing. Mistakenly, he also grabbed the unsightly Polaroid. He watched as the photograph slipped from his hand and spiraled to the floor. In an instant he thought how tragic it would be if Mrs. Jarvis were to see the picture before they even had the chance to talk. Frantically, he reached down and jerked the picture from the carpet. She watched as he nervously shoved it back into his pocket, averting a disaster.

She reiterated that her daughter was a frequent runaway, who would normally be gone for a few days, but would call home religiously.

"How often would she run away Mrs. Jarvis?"

"Oh my, probably every two weeks or so. I've tried punishing her, but then she would just runaway more. She's a defiant one, I'll tell you that."

"Do you know where she would go?"

"Oh, here and there, mainly with boys."

"I see. Do you know her boyfriend's name and where he lives?"

"Kathy doesn't have a boyfriend detective. I hate saying this, but my daughter gets around, if you know what I mean?"

"In the police report, it looks like she has been gone now for 10 days?"

"Yes sir, it was the first of January, New Year's Day. How could I forget?"

He scribbled in his notebook when Kathy was last seen and what she was wearing, when something unexpected happened. While in midsentence with Mrs. Jarvis, he stopped abruptly and looked at the teenaged girl walking down the steps from the second floor of the home.

OH MY GOD, he thought to himself. It was his victim. She was alive, fully dressed and uninjured.

"Mary, come over here, I want you to meet Detective Michaels from the Missing Persons Unit. He's going to help find Kathy."

Still in shock, he had a difficult time speaking, while he stared in amazement at his victim's identical twin sister walking toward him. It literally made the hairs on the back of his neck and arms stand up, while a cold chill rushed through him. This was something he was not ready for. It was an immediate confirmation of his victim's identity. No photos were needed. Mary's teeth were crowded and twisted just like the victims. Her hair was the same color, same style, as were her eyes and the rest of her body, except, she was alive. *I am about to hear my victim speak*, he thought to himself as Mary sat in the chair next her mother. He was still looking at her, trying to comprehend who or what he was looking at.

"Hi, I'm Mary," she said in her squeaky high-pitched flirtatious voice.

Struggling to speak, he managed to formulate a question. "Hi Mary, do you have any idea where your sister may be?"

"Who knows, she fucks…"

"Mary, watch your mouth," Mrs. Jarvis interrupted.

"Well it's true Mom and you know it. My sister will sleep with just about anybody."

The three sat and talked about Kathy for several minutes. Because of her lifestyle, Kathy would make this case harder to solve than normal. Kathy was 15 years old going on 21. She was an attractive, well developed white female, in need of a little dental work, who knew all too well how to use her body and survive on the streets. Running away from home was an all too frequent occurrence for Kathy. Her parents and sister had lost count of the number of times she had left unannounced. This time would be her last.

"Detective, was that a picture you brought with you?"

"Um yes ma'am, but it's not something you need to see."

The calm, mild manner mother quickly got irritated. "Is it of my daughter?" she insisted.

"Mrs. Jarvis, I am not in the Missing Persons Unit. I'm a homicide detective."

Mary shot up from her chair. "Homicide?" she yelled. "Why the hell are you here? Is my sister dead?"

"Why didn't you tell me you were with homicide?" Mrs. Jarvis asked.

He knew this was going to be tough. He assured her he did bring a picture, but it was only a picture of a ghastly body, not something she needed to see. She insisted he show her the picture. To his surprise, Mrs. Jarvis reached out and grabbed his wrist and squeezed. She looked him square in the eye. "I need to see the picture detective. If my daughter is dead, I need to know."

He reached inside his jacket, pulled out the picture and hesitated before he handed it over. Mary grabbed it from his hand. She and her mother looked at the gruesome site and both immediately began sobbing.

"Oh my God, it's her Mom."

Mrs. Jarvis took the picture. Tears fell from her eyes onto the photo. From the look on her face, you could tell this was something she had expected.

"What happened to her cheek?" Mary asked.

"We believe that was from an animal. You see, she was found in a wooded area in Pasadena."

Mrs. Jarvis handed the photo back to Michaels. She pulled Mary into her arms and the two cried while he sat quietly watching them.

After several minutes, Mrs. Jarvis and her daughter took a seat on the couch next to him. While the two continued crying, he was able to ask some important questions, like who were Kathy's friends and enemies? And most importantly, what occurred on the date of her disappearance. What he learned was beyond unusual. Probably one of the most bizarre runaway stories imaginable. It was obvious that Mary had more information than she led her mother to believe. Mary explained that on New Year's Day, Kathy called to order a pizza from a local Pizza Palace where she had ordered from several times before. Thinking she knew the number from memory, Mary said Kathy called from the house phone. Little did she know, she was calling the devil himself.

Mary went on to say Kathy had called the wrong number but instead of hanging up, she engaged in a lengthy conversation with the stranger who answered the phone. This was the first Mrs. Jarvis had ever heard of such a story, and it shocked her. Mary claimed they talked on the phone for a while and the man invited her to his home and to no surprise, Kathy accepted.

"Mary, my God, why didn't you tell me about this? We could have told the police."

"It was just my sister being a whore again Mom. It wasn't something you needed to know, and I thought she'd be home soon after, you know."

Kathy agreed to meet the person on the other end of the phone and left wearing her blue coat and purse. That was the last anyone had ever seen or heard from her.

At the time of Kathy's disappearance and subsequent murder, their home phone was not equipped with caller ID or any other features that could identify who she called on that particular evening.

"Can either of you describe Kathy's purse?"

Mary quickly piped up. "Yeah, I bought it for her for Christmas. It was a regular size purse. It was dark blue with black stitching." He knew the purse she was describing matched the strap tied around his victim's neck.

Almost an hour later, he left the Jarvis' home after first obtaining a school picture of Kathy for his investigation. Before he left, he handed his business card to Mrs. Jarvis who was still weeping. She wrapped her arms around him and said, "thank you." Michaels returned the hug. "I'm sorry Mrs. Jarvis," he said. She then followed him out into the cold to his car.

"Thanks again detective. I'm sorry I couldn't help you more."

"Mrs. Jarvis, no apology needed. I'll stay in touch with you. If you think of anything, please call me."

He climbed into the driver's seat and with his door still open she had one final question. "Do you think you will find who did this?"

Looking up at Mrs. Jarvis, who was wiping the tears from her eyes, he said, "Mrs. Jarvis I can tell you I will do everything I can to solve this case for you and make whoever did this be held responsible. That ma'am I can promise you." The crying Mrs. Jarvis thanked Michaels, closed his car door and watched as he drove off.

Driving back to the CID he threw his notebook onto the passenger seat. *That was a horrible death notification* he thought. He had seen, for the first time, what looked to be his victim alive. Frankly, it made no sense to him that he was giving a death notification about someone who was standing right in front of him. It wasn't right. It wasn't normal. Knowing the bond between identical twins and of course a mother, this notification seemed to be magnified and it hurt him deeply to be that person once again to break the news. He rushed back to the office to tell Tommy and Dredge what he had learned. Now the challenge will be to find the monster who took Kathy's call that evening. *What piece of shit would invite a total stranger, not knowing what she looked like or how old she was, to meet him? And what 15-year girl would do the same thing?* Michaels pondered.

When he returned Donald, Mark, Dredge and Tommy all gathered in the sergeant's office. They, too, were surprised to learn of the circumstances leading to Kathy's disappearance.

"Well that was a good first step. This could have been a lot harder if we didn't know who she was," Tommy said as he blew smoke straight up in the air.

"Now we just need to figure out where she went that evening," Mark said.

"That will be like finding a needle in a haystack," Donald added.

"Young Shithead good work tonight. Get out of here. I'll see you in the morning. Give Mark that photograph of your victim. I'm going to have these guys make up a poster for you to hand out tomorrow and I'll get something out to the newspapers," Tommy said.

"Shithead, before you leave, do you know what pizza place your victim intended to call?" Mark asked.

"Yeah, it was the Pizza Palace on Ritchie Highway in Glen Burnie. Why?"

"I'm going to change a few of the numbers around and do a little digging. I want to see if any registered owners of telephone numbers similar to the business have a criminal record."

Mark's suggestion came as no surprise since he also was a former narcotics detective. "That's a great idea Mark. Thanks brother."

"Good idea Poodle. While he's doing that Donald, you start working on a flyer for Ronnie," Tommy ordered.

"I'm on it. It will be on your desk in the morning Shithead."

"Thanks Donald."

Michaels drove home that evening wondering how he was going to solve this one. He knew he needed a witness and he needed one bad.

The next day Dredge and Michaels drove back to the crime scene to canvass the homes in the adjacent community. With them they had a stack of Information Sought posters with Kathy Jarvis's picture on the front along with the telephone number to the Homicide Unit prominently displayed. By now, most of the residents heard the news of the girl's body found in the woods nearby. Though concerned, none of them had any information which could help. Located about a mile from where the body was found was a local tavern. They would try there next.

They walked into the unlocked door of the tavern with a stack of flyers. The establishment was not yet open, but there was a car out front, which they figured belonged to an employee.

The bar was dimly lit. "Any one home?" Michaels shouted.

A female with a scratchy smoker's voice yelled out. "We're not open." She entered the bar area and saw Dredge and Michaels wearing their overcoats.

"You must be cops."

"Yes ma'am, we're with the Homicide Unit. I'm Detective Michaels and this is Detective Hart. I don't know if you heard about the girl found dead in the woods just up the street yesterday, but we are investigating her murder." Michaels conspicuously had his badge in his hand while he was talking.

"I saw that on the news. That's a shame. What can I do for you? My name is Barb. Have a seat?"

The three sat down at a high-top roundtable. The place smelled of cigarettes and freshly applied bleach. The bar was a hangout for locals to shoot pool, throw darts and occasionally fight.

"Have you ever seen this girl before?" Michaels said as Dredge handed her a flyer. She examined it closely, looked at the bar, then looked back at the flyer.

"Yes, she was in here a few days ago. It was either Friday or Saturday. No, I took off Saturday, it had to be last Friday night."

"Today is Tuesday, she was found yesterday," Michaels said.

"Was she the one they found murdered?"

"Yes."

"God damn. I remember asking her for ID, but she said she didn't have it with her, just like everyone says. I told her I couldn't serve her without ID. She seemed worried or scared, but I just figured she was underage."

"What did she order?"

"She didn't. I didn't give her the chance. You must be 21 to even be in here, so I hit her up for ID first."

"Was she with anyone that you remember?" Dredge asked.

"Yeah two guys, who I've never seen in here before."

"Can you describe them?" Dredge asked.

"One was a real asshole. He got all pissed off when I wouldn't serve her. He was one of those guys who liked showing off his muscles. Probably on steroids. He was about 22, short brown hair, wearing a real tight short sleeve shirt to show off his arms in the dead of winter. I think he had jeans on."

"And the other guy?"

"He didn't say anything. He was a frumpy looking dude, about the same age, kind of fat. He had some faded, dirty Pink Floyd t-shirt on. I'm not sure what kind of pants, probably jeans. He looked dirty. You know what I mean? Like a guy who didn't wash much. I guess that's from all my years being a bartender. They didn't stay after that. They left, like they had someplace to be."

"I'm going to give you my card. If either of them ever comes in again, will you call me?"

"Sure. Do you think they killed her?"

"We don't know, but your information was helpful. Here's my card. I put my cell number on the back," Michaels said.

"Do you think you could sit down with one of our detectives, who is an artist, and describe these men to her?" Dredge asked before they left.

"Umm, not really. I really didn't look at their faces much, just the girl's."

They both knew how crucial it was to identify the two men seen with Kathy, since her disappearance was such a mystery, and no one knew of her whereabouts. Those two men were the key to solving this case.

"Well you've been a big help Barb. Thank you."

"Sure, come in for a beer anytime on me. I work Tuesdays, Wednesdays, Fridays and Saturdays. And I'll hang these flyers in the bathrooms and by the pool tables for ya."
"Thanks."

"Good luck."

They climbed back into the car and headed to the office. "So now we know there are two guys involved here Dredge, just not local enough to frequent this place." Dredge nodded his head in agreement and the car was quickly filled with cigarette smoke.

Several days had passed with no credible leads coming in on the Jarvis investigation. Michaels was running into one dead end after the next and then it happened.

"Homicide, Detective Michaels."

"Is this the Homicide Division?" The seemingly stoned voice on the other end asked.

"Yes, this is Detective Michaels, what can I do for you?"

"Yeah, I was shooting pool the other night at the Earleigh Heights Tavern, and, and, I saw this poster on the wall with some girl's picture on it. It said she was found dead. Is there any kind of reward?"

"Yes, up to $10,000 is being offered by Metro Crime Stoppers for information leading to the arrest in this case. What can you tell me about this sir?" Michaels anxiously asked.

"How do I get the money?"

"How it works is, you tell me the information, and then I will give you their tip line number. You call them after you get off the phone with me and they will assign you a special number." He opened his notebook to a blank page and with pen in hand he was about to start writing when the phone went dead.

"Fuck," he said slamming down the phone.

"Did they hang up?" Dredge asked.

"Yeah, motherfucker."

"Maybe he'll call back or call Metro Crime Stoppers."

"What do you have Ronnie?" Tommy asked peering out of his office after hearing the noise.

"Some guy called apparently with information and he wanted to know if there was a reward. When I said there was through Metro Crime Stoppers, he hung up.

"Maybe he's calling them."

"That's what Dredge said."

"Well, I've had enough. I'm getting out of here guys." Michaels slipped his overcoat on and made his way to his car. He wondered if he would ever solve the Jarvis case and today's tease was just that, a tease from someone either high or drunk. Barely out of the parking lot, his radio sounded.

"Detective 130 to 132." Michaels heard Tommy calling him. *I just left. What the hell could he want?* he thought.

"Detective 132 go ahead."

"Come back to the office Ronnie."

"10-4," he answered. *Could it be another homicide?*

Michaels made his way into the office and Tommy handed him a piece of paper just faxed in from Metro Crime Stoppers. The information contained in the body of the document from Tipster #0545 was well worth the trip back to the CID. According to the caller, Kathy Jarvis had been staying with a subject by the name of Guy Allen in the Southdale Apartments, along with another subject, known only as Mark. Michaels knew these apartments were located about 5 miles from the Jarvis home, close enough for Kathy to walk, hitch hike or be picked up. The caller claimed to have no more information. This is a call every homicide detective loves to get. It's a piece of information that gives an investigator the smallest lead and often helps solve the case. This was that call.

"Damn Dredge not only do we know who our victim is, now we know where she was staying, who she was staying with, and maybe where she was just before she was killed. This is good stuff."

"Are you going straight to the apartment complex tomorrow instead of coming here first?" Tommy inquired to Michaels.

"Hell no, I'm going there right fucking now. Dredge I'll give you a call." And with that, Michaels drove his four-cylinder cruiser as fast as it would take him to the Southdale Apartments, located about a half hour from the CID.

He pulled into a parking space reserved for *Maintenance Vehicles Only* in front of the building where the leasing sign was displayed. Not sure exactly what time their office closed, he ran down the stairwell where the arrows pointed. A man in his mid-thirties was walking from the model apartment carrying a briefcase and inserting a key in the deadbolt.

"Excuse me sir, are you the manager?" he blurted out.
"Yes, but we are closed for the day. We open at 9 a.m. tomorrow." Obviously in a hurry to leave, the man was trying to blow off Michaels, who wasn't about to settle for that.

By now, he had his badge and ID in hand and had it positioned uncomfortably close to his face.

"Sir, I'm Detective Michaels from the Anne Arundel County Police Homicide Unit and unless you want to get locked up tonight for Obstruction of Justice, I'm going to need you to unlock this fucking door so you and I can go inside and chat. Do I make myself clear?"

He put his credentials away and replaced them with his handcuffs from his waistband.

"Ah, ah, yes, yes let, let me do that," the man stuttered nervously fumbling through his key ring trying to find the correct key.

Now inside, Michaels took a seat in front of the desk the gentleman sat behind.

"Sir, like I said, I'm Detective Michaels from the Homicide Unit, and you are?"

"My name is John White."

"Are you the manager?"

"Yes sir."

"That's great. John, there is an easy way and hard way to do what I'm about to ask. The hard way is to pick up an Obstruction of Justice charge, then when you get out of jail, I'll have you served with a Grand Jury Subpoena forcing you to bring all your records down to Annapolis and testify before the Grand Jury. Or, what I prefer, is simply tell me the information I need to know and then jump in your car and go home. Which one sounds good to you?" Michaels said tapping his notebook on the desk in front of him.

"The latter sounds good," White said with his voice cracking.

"That's what I thought. Now John, I'm investigating the murder of a young girl whose body was found a few miles away. It is my understanding she was staying in one of your apartments for a short time with a fella by the name of…" Forgetting the name of the subject, Michaels opened his case file and looked down at the Metro Crime Stoppers Tip Sheet. "Guy Allen and another person known as Mark. Do any of these names ring a bell?"

"Yes, I'm very familiar with Mr. Allen. He owes us money for two months' rent and then he broke his lease without giving us proper notification, like his contract requires. Our corporate office is handling everything now, you know, like suing him for the money and all that stuff."

Frustrated with the news he just heard, Michaels looked up from his notebook. "Shit, when did he move out?"

"A few days ago, but we are really not sure exactly when. You see, we didn't find out until Maintenance went into his apartment to change the furnace filter, that's when we realized he broke his lease."

"Who else was on the lease with him?"

"No one, and I never saw him with a girl either, just a guy here and there.

"Did you ever see him with a muscular fella?"

"Yeah, yeah, I have. One time he kept staring at me, like he was mad at me for looking at him. Strange dude."

"I need to take a look in his apartment."

"I can take you there, but it's been cleaned up, repaired and ready to be rented. It has a coat of fresh paint on the walls and new carpet. He really trashed the place. You know what was odd? One of my maintenance guys told me one of the walls in the master bedroom closet had to be completely replaced. He said there were two big holes in the wall. Each was about the size of a softball where it looked like something was mounted. You see, corporate doesn't like these apartments empty any longer than a few days."

"God damn it."

"I did take pictures of it before they fixed it for corporate."

"Do you have those pictures here? Let me guess, corporate has them."

"One copy has been sent off, but I have my set for court. Let me get them."

Michaels was intrigued by what he was about to see. Mr. White pulled a manila folder from a file cabinet and pulled out 10 pictures taken of various rooms in what was once Guy Allen's apartment.

"Here you go."

Michaels carefully examined each. "Damn, they did trash the place, what a pig."

Photographs were taken of each room, the damaged walls and burn marks on the carpet. There were beer cans, liquor bottles, empty cigarette boxes, burnt cigarettes and remnants of trash from various fast food chains scattered everywhere. In the master bedroom was more clutter. In the large walk-in closet, there was an old wooden chair in the corner with one of its front legs broken off. The broken piece laid splintered just a few feet away. On the wall directly in front of the closet entrance were two gaping holes. From the looks of the damaged sheetrock, something had been pulled from them. The holes were almost level with one another, approximately 3' apart and about 4' off the ground, like it once had hardware used to restrain someone.

"Detective, I'm sorry, but are you going to be much longer, it's my wife's birthday?"

"I'm going to take these with me. I'll make duplicates and return them tomorrow. Thanks for your help John. Here's my card. I'll just need a copy of Mr. Allen's lease and you can get home to your wife."

Michaels was in his car trying to get someone from the unit on the phone. "Homicide, Hart."

"Dredge it's me."

"Shithead, what's going on?"

"Why are you still there?"

"We got to talking, you know. How'd it go at the Rental Office?"

"Unfuckingbelievable Dredge, that's how it went." I need you to run this person's name and find out everything you can on him please."

"Give me his info."

"His name is Guy Allen. He is a white male, 24 years old with brown hair and brown eyes, around 5'7-5'9, 220 pounds or so. He sounds like the frumpy fat ass the bartender told us about. I'm on my way back."

Michaels liked how the puzzle pieces were coming together, slowly but surely. He kept having flashes in his mind of Kathy's body lying nude in the woods with her face partially eaten. He wondered if he was going to be putting handcuffs on someone soon. Thinking back to the interview with his victim's sister, Kathy was said to be someone who could handle herself in a fight, a wiry, short tempered girl who would fuck or fight nearly anyone. Knowing this, Michaels surmised his victim would not be easily handled by one person, especially by a fat ass frump like Allen.

When he got to the office, Dredge had a complete workup prepared, including a photograph of Allen and his last known address, which turned out to be his mother's home in Arnold, Maryland.

"Here you go Shithead," Dredge said handing him a manila folder.

Michaels examined the picture. His first assessment was that he was a typical slob who would have a tough time ever getting a girlfriend. "I can just picture this asshole thinking he's got some young chick on the phone and trying to con her over to his apartment. That would be the only way he'd get laid." His prior arrest was only a minor marijuana charge. No crimes of violence, but he still liked what he was seeing. It was time to go pay Guy Allen a visit.

Dredge and Michaels went together on this one. Knocking on the door, they impatiently waited for someone to answer. When Guy opened the door, he displayed an obvious look of surprise with both eyes bugging out like a deer in headlights. *Fucking pedophile* was the first thought that entered Michaels' mind. He was wearing a dirty grey pair of sweatpants, holey socks and a wrinkled Budweiser t-shirt. His receding hair was uncombed, like he had just climbed out of bed.

"Guy Allen, I'm Detective Michaels and this is Detective Hart," Michaels said giving him a quick glimpse of his badge and credentials. Instead of waiting for an invite, both brushed passed Guy. The three stood in the middle of the living room, well-lit by a lamp on an end table.

Just as planned, Guy was surprised that Michaels not only recognized him, but knew his first and last name. The detectives enjoyed watching the actions of guilty people. It's comical at times. Face it, two well-dressed detectives barge their way into your home and you never question what they want or why they are there? In these instances, Michaels learned to strike while the iron was hot.

Their tactic was not to give the person time to think or get comfortable in his own home, but instead they begin firing off a series of questions in such a way to lead him to think they already knew the answers.

"I know it hasn't been long, but exactly when did you move back in here Guy?"

Both Dredge and Michaels could plainly see him struggle to speak from the nerves that overtook him. He stuttered and stammered until he could spit out some words. "Umm, I, I don't know, about a week I guess," he said moving his head side to side, looking at the carpet beneath his feet. His answer was good, both detectives thought, putting him out of the apartment and into his mother's address immediately following Kathy's murder.

"And what was your address at the apartment?" They could tell this question really got to him. His body was shaking, and his face turned pale. Michaels was waiting for him to pass out. You could tell he didn't want to answer the question and Michaels and Dredge knew they had the right person. Either their killer, or an accomplice was standing just 2 feet away about to piss his pants.

"Ah, I don't remember. I didn't live there long."

"That's ok Guy, I have it right here." Michaels reached into his suitcoat and pulled out his notebook. He flipped it open.

"Let's see, does 7887 Bay Circle, apartment 101 sound familiar?"

He became very fidgety, rubbing the back of his neck repeatedly, looking around the room like he was waiting to be rescued. They knew all too well that when one's blood pressure and stress increase in dicey situations like these, heat commonly rushes to a person's neck causing an increase in temperature, thereby making one subconsciously rub the area to displace the heat. It's a tell sign any good investigator knows and looks for at key moments.

His mouth was now void of any saliva or the slightest bit of moisture. "I guess that's it. Why do you wanna know where I lived?" he struggled to ask.

Neither gave him the satisfaction of answering his question, after all, it was their interview not his.

"Who lived there with you Guy?" Michaels asked as Dredge stood behind his partner documenting the interview.

"Well nobody really. I was always there by myself most of the time." It was obvious Guy didn't know what the detectives knew and surely didn't want to get caught in a lie. "A buddy stayed with me for a little bit, but nobody else," he said adamantly. "What's your friend's name?" Michaels asked like he was just making conversation. Again, Guy's emotions were blatant. He was a horrible liar.

"What friend?" he mumbled.

"You just said a buddy lived with you, fuck, I feel like I'm pulling teeth. What's his God damn name?"

"Um, ah, Mark."

"And does Mark have a last name?"

"Flores, but he wasn't on the lease. He really wasn't a roommate. I mean, you know, he just stayed there sometimes."

Michaels continued to talk, brushing over the roommate topic and onto the bombshell questions without warning. "Did you have a lot of girls at your apartment?"

Dredge was steadily taking notes. This was the question that nearly floored Guy. Now, after being in his house for 15 minutes and faced with the latest question, Guy finally got up the nerve to timidly ask the question. "Why are you asking me these questions?"

Dredge spoke up. "Look Guy, we are just trying to conduct a God damn investigation, so would you just cooperate?" he said with a raised voice. *This was a great question,* Michaels thought knowing Guy had been cooperative thus far.

Just as Guy began to answer him, Michaels produced the 5"x 7" colored school picture of Kathy from his coat pocket. Dredge lifted his head from his notebook as he too was surprised. "How long have you known this girl?" What little blood was left on Guy's face was now sucked away. He was white as a ghost and he could barely contain his hands from shaking.

"I, I, I, I don't know her." *Oh my God,* Michaels said to himself. *Was that the best he could do?*

"So, you're telling me you do not know her?"

"Nope." His answer was short and suspicious.

"That's funny Guy, we got information she was staying with you."

"No. I don't know her I said." It was obvious he was lying, and he knew the detectives weren't buying it.

"You're telling us you've never seen this girl in your life? Bullshit."

"Um, no, no sir." He was still trying to appear and sound believable.

Michaels wanted to see his room. He wanted to see how he lived and if there was anything belonging to Kathy in plain sight. He wanted to see how a 24-year-old, unemployed bum, who still lived with his mother in the basement of her split foyer, who found 15-year old girls attractive, lived.

"This is a nice house," Michaels said walking away from Dredge and Guy toward the kitchen. "Are your parents' home Guy?" Michaels said with his back still to him.

"No, my father passed away last year, and my mother works at the senior center down the street."

"Will she be home soon?"

"No, not for a while."

Michaels continued to meander down the hallway deeper into the home. "What did your dad pass away from?"

Guy looked at Dredge, who stood steadfast in the living room with him.

"He had a bad heart."

"Sorry to hear that. Where's your room?" he asked nonchalantly.

Michaels wanted to search his room. He was a master at getting consensual searches from his days in narcotics. He figured since he and Dredge arrived unannounced, he had no time to move, destroy or hide anything.

"Why?" he mustered up the nerve to ask.

"Guy, Jesus Christ, he just asked where your room was, why are you acting like you have something to hide? You don't have anything to hide, do you?" Dredge was setting him up. The hook was dangling in front of him and he took it.

"No, no I don't have anything to hide. No."

"Of course you don't, so show him your God damn room."

Once again Guy had difficulty swallowing because of his nerves. Without saying a word, he walked down the small flight of stairs with Michaels and Dredge close behind. He entered his room and Michaels watched Guy's eyes swiftly scan the entire area as if to be looking for anything incriminating.

"Guy, I saw an asthma machine upstairs. Does your mom let you smoke in here?" Michaels had not verified if Guy smoked cigarettes, but he wanted to do so given the marks on Kathy's back.

Finally, a question he didn't fear, Guy opened the broken drawer on the nightstand next to his bed and pulled out a half empty pack of Newport cigarettes.

The room was a total shit heap with piles of dirty clothes spread about. There were rolled up socks and stretched out dirty underwear on the unmade full-size bed, with unwashed, discolored sheets. The pillow on the bed had no case and looked like it belonged in the dump with greasy, dirty hair stains.

Many times, someone who commits a violent sex act or murder will keep something that belongs to the victim to serve as a reminder. That item, whatever it may be, was what Michaels and Dredge were looking for, something that belonged to Kathy. They knew from the purse strap around Kathy's neck, the rest of the purse and its contents were missing.

There was nothing obvious that belonged to the victim in the open. In such a brief time together as partners, the two detectives worked excellent as a team. Dredge made small talk to distract Guy, while Michaels looked around the room, opening his closet door and looking at the mess on top of his dresser. Though nothing incriminating was found, they got the distinct feeling Guy had something to hide.

"Here's my card. If there is something you need to tell me, call this number. If not, I'm sure we will be talking again real soon." Guy didn't seem happy with that news, but *too fucking bad*, Michaels thought to himself.

When Dredge and Michaels returned to the office, a call came in from the Evidence Collection Unit. "Homicide, Detective Michaels."

"Shithead," the voice yelled on the other end.

"Hey Jeff, what's going on brother?"

"How's it going?"

"We think we just left the person who Kathy may have been staying with."

"Really, how did that go?"

"We got a peek in his room but didn't see anything. He was noticeably nervous, with something to hide. Before I forget, I got my hands on about 10 pictures of the apartment where our victim may have been that I need duplicated and enlarged. Can you do that for me please?"

"Yeah, just drop them off. Hey, the reason I called was to let you know that the FBI Lab found a Caucasian hair on your victim's body, but no semen."

"No semen? Shit, how can that be? Fuck."

"She may have showered is all I can think."

"I'll work on getting a DNA sample from the asshole we talked to today, and there may be a second subject as well."

"Just let me know when, so I can have a tech meet you there."

"Will do brother. I'll leave those pictures on your desk. Thanks."

"I'll get right on it." And they both hung up.

Michaels looked at his watch and bolted from the CID. He was late but managed to pick up Nicole a little past 6:45 p.m. Stacey stood in the doorway as he ran up.

"Sorry, I got tied up." She shot him a nasty look when she opened the front door.

"I was just getting ready to call you."

"There's my beautiful daughter. Hi Nick," he said as he saw her running to the front door. "Are you ready to eat some pizza-pie?"

"Yaaa, let's go," she said as she reached out to hold his hand.

The two had a wonderful time coloring placemat at their favorite Italian restaurant and chowing down on pizza. They always had to ask for extra crayons and a placemat for Michaels. They had a little tradition of collecting and coloring them at various restaurants. It was their special daddy/daughter thing. He loved being with her, especially when she would hold his hand walking to and from the car. It was a reminder that someone relied on him and her precious touch made him feel loved. Better yet, being around her made him feel young again, acting as goofy as he wanted, and she loved it.

They ended their evening with big hugs and butterfly kisses in the car, another one of their things. Hand in hand they walked to the front door where Nicole was swept off her feet for a final hug and kiss goodbye.

"I love you Honey."
"I love you Daddy."

"When are you getting her next Ronnie? You know this is getting really ridiculous."

"I don't know Stacey. Shit, I'm in the middle of homicide. I just can't pack up and leave after 8 hours, not in this job. I'll call you."

"Yeah, that's what you said about the other job." The door slammed in his face.

After the day he had, he wanted a stiff rum and Coke. Making his way into his townhouse, he flipped on the lights and spotted his half full glass of rum next to his recliner where he had passed out the night before. He grabbed the glass, dumped out the watered-down drink and topped it off with a fresh double mixture. He threw his suit jacket on the couch, ripped off his strangling tie and flopped onto the chair, like he had just finished a marathon. It was late. Another long day of putting pieces of a puzzle together, attempting to solve his latest murder. It was a lot of stress and he felt bad because he had not talked to Mrs. Jarvis today to fill her in. Sipping on his beverage he sat quietly, wondering what it must be like losing a child, and what Mrs. Jarvis was doing.

Almost in a trance, he thought back to when he first told her of her daughter's death and how he distinctly remembered the look of despair in her eyes. He recalled seeing the life pulled from her body and how bad he felt delivering such life-changing awful news. But mostly, he would never forget the numbing feeling when Kathy's identical twin sister walked into the room, and how his knees weakened, leaving him without words. Like other homicide cases, he felt it was his sole responsibility to solve the case for the family. He knew they were relying on his tenacity, prowess and talent for justice. *That pressure is an unbelievable burden to place on one man's shoulders. It ages you. It's the type of stress that few have experienced,* he thought.

He remembered getting up two more times and fixing himself potent drinks, the last of which contained barely any soda. It was just what he needed to relax and pass out. He awoke the next morning still in the recliner and dressed in his badly wrinkled clothes, with an empty glass on the table next to him.

Before Michaels got to the office the following day, Dredge had already completed a full work up on Mark Flores. He was a white male, 25 years old, 5'6", 210 pounds and had managed to rack up six assault charges over the last 3 years.

"Looks like we have a fighter here Dredge," Michaels said perusing through the arrest records. "What I can gather from his mug shot and his description, I think he's going to be the muscle man in the tavern that night with Kathy."

Tommy was in his office with both feet crossed on top of his desk, cigarette in one hand and a coffee in the other, talking to Lieutenant Tank.

"Well good morning Shithead," Tommy said.

"Good morning Lieutenant. Good morning Sergeant," Michaels said respectfully.

"Tommy said you think you found where your victim was staying?"

"Yeah, I think I have them both identified. One guy is a soft mommy's boy and the other looks like a steroid user who likes to fight. Dredge and I are leaving now to have a little chat with the muscle head."

"Sounds like a plan to me. Good luck."

"Just hold on a second Shithead, let me get my coffee," Dredge said. He was the master at putting the brakes on Michaels.

"Let me get a cup too, while I wait for your old creeping Jesus ass," Michaels said causing Lieutenant Tank to spit his coffee onto the floor in laughter.

"Dredge, before we leave, I need to call Kathy's mom."

Michaels sat at his desk and took a deep breath as he flipped through his notebook to find her number.

"Mrs. Jarvis? Hi, this is Detective Michaels." She sounded relieved to hear from him. I called to give you an update about what has been going on for the last couple of days."

"Yes, thank you so much for calling. I've been wondering."

He gave her a full low down of the interview with the manager at the apartment complex and with Guy, including the visit to his current home. She was all ears and it seemed as if she was waiting for him to say he had made an arrest, but unfortunately, he did not.

He went on to tell her about Guy's acquaintance, Mark, and their immediate plans to interview him and gather DNA evidence from both. As he was about to hang up, she thanked him in a very sincere tone for calling. He thought of how sad it was to hear her speak. He got the feeling that she had not left the room where he last saw her several days ago. Oddly enough, he could tell from the hollowness in her voice, that a part of her was now missing. When he hung up, he wondered momentarily how he would react if he lost Nicole, his only daughter, that he barely was able to hold on to.

"Hey Shithead, let's get a bite to eat first," Dredge said picking up the pack of cigarettes from his desk. "Are you alright boy?"

Michaels forgot Dredge was sitting across from him while he was on the phone. "Yeah, I'm fine," he said pushing out a large exhale. "I'm ready when you are."

"I'll drive today son. You're driving makes me sick."

Laughing Michaels said, "Oh, he speaks. I guess you're probably done talking for the day, aren't you?" Dredge looked at him and smiled and they walked from the building.

Their meal seemed like it took forever, and Dredge's driving made it seem even longer. When they finally made it to the address, Michaels was already knocking on the door before Dredge barely got out of the front seat. Mark had obviously been expecting their arrival. There was no doubt Guy had warned him.

"Mark? I'm Detective Michaels and this is Detective Hart. Do you mind if we come in and talk to you?"

"I'm getting ready to go to the gym."

Mark looked much different than Guy. He had all the telltale signs of being a steroid user. He had an aggressive scowl on his face, like he was pissed off about something, and was abnormally muscular. He dressed much different than his fat ass friend. He had on a dark blue athletic suit with white stripes down the arms and legs. His white tennis shoes seemed new. His hair was neatly combed, and it was apparent he took care of himself, both with his grooming and his fitness. He immediately gave both detectives the feeling he did not want them there. He wanted them to leave and to get away as fast as possible.

"Why do you wanna talk to me?" *This dude was much more forward than his friend,* Michaels thought to himself, so he immediately threw Guy under the bus.

"I understand you are friends with Guy Allen?"

"Yeah, what about him?" he said in a disrespectful tone.

Michaels wasn't going to beat around the bush. He knew he had to meet aggression with aggression. "How often would you go to his apartment?"

"I've been there a couple times. Why?"

It was obvious he was lying. His responses were short, and he kept looking at the door. "Is this going to take long? I really need to get to the gym."

Dredge was standing slightly behind Michaels right side while he was talking to Mark. He couldn't see what he was doing, but he assumed he was taking notes like usual. Michaels noticed Dredge step forward toward Mark with his finger pointing at him. "The gym can wait. Do you hear me?" Dredge was pissed.

"Well I don't know why you guys want to talk to me. Maybe I need to get a lawyer." By now it was obvious he too had something to hide. They knew they were on to something.

"Answer the man. When was the last time you were in Guy's apartment?"

"I do not know. He doesn't live there anymore. Are you done?"

You could tell Dredge and Mark didn't like each other. Dredge took a step closer to him.

"No, I'm not. So think. It can't be that hard unless you're a fucking idiot. Was it a couple of days, one week, two weeks or three weeks?" Dredge continued with his questions and Mark was getting noticeably upset. He puffed his chest out and took on a fighting posture. Dredge stood nearly the same as Mark. All hell was about to break loose.

"Leave now. I want a lawyer," he yelled. When he uttered those words, Michaels also stepped closer to Flores. There were hoping he would take a swing at one of them, so they would have a reason to lock him up and beat his ass.

Dredge sounded like Arnold Schwarzenegger when he stuck his finger in the punk's face. "We'll be back."

Mark stood there as they turned away. For once Dredge was now walking faster than Michaels. Once in the car, Dredge slammed his door. He was on fire. "Fucking Asshole," he said. He quickly shoved a cigarette in his mouth and angrily flicked his lighter.

"I thought he was going to take a swing at you Dredge." He grunted like a bear and Michaels assumed he agreed.

Now the puzzle was very clear. They could easily see Mark was the aggressor with Kathy especially if she resisted any of his sexual advances. Mark was the type who not only resisted authority but wouldn't accept being turned down by a 15-year-old runaway. Driving back to the office, Michaels pictured Mark with his hands holding on to the purse strap tied around Kathy's neck. He could see him holding it like a horse bridal, twisting it while she was restrained in the closet until she would succumb to his and Guy's perverted desires. Then, he imagined Guy, the little fat fuck, jerking off and burning her with his cigarette trying to get some cheap thrill while Mark violently raped her.

"We need to get their hair," Dredge mumbled under his breath as if he was talking to himself.

"I'll start working on that as soon as we get to the office."

At the CID, Dredge and Michaels sat down in the chairs in Tommy's office. "How did it go boys?"

All three of them simultaneously lit cigarettes. Clouds of smoke filled the room. "He is a fucking asshole," Dredge said pointedly.

"Put it this way" Michaels interjected. "This motherfucker was completely different from his little fat fuck buddy. His high school yearbook probably says, most likely to kill."

Everyone laughed.

"What's next? Are you getting warrants for their DNA?"

"Yeah, I'm going to start working on that in a few minutes."

By now it was nearly 3:00 p.m. and Hauf and Howes strolled into the office. "What's going on with your case Shithead?" Donald asked as he filled the doorway of Tommy's office.

Before Michaels could even answer, Donald asked for a cigarette. Michaels updated them on the interviews with Mark and Guy, the near confrontation and the plans to obtain search warrants for their blood, hair and saliva.

"Cool. Need any help?"

"We might when it comes time to bring these guys into the hospital to make our extractions, if you know what I mean?" Michaels said with a smirk on his face. "I'll let you know."

Michaels walked back to his desk to start working. Dredge followed and gave him the notes he took while Michaels was talking to Guy on the previous day. They were impeccable. His handwriting was perfect. Each letter was the same height. You could tell he pressed down hard with his pen as each letter was dark and legible. Michaels always joked with him saying *he couldn't type as neat as Dredge wrote.* Michaels scanned the notes and to no surprise they contained every detail of their conversation.

The four sat at their respective desks, all quiet and busy with something, when Tommy walked from his office and made an announcement. "Let's eat."

The commander had spoken, and it was time for them to depart. They climbed into Tommy's car and drove to a seafood restaurant near the Annapolis Mall.

As usual they chowed down, talked about their cases and laughed their asses off. When finished, the four walked through the restaurant weaving through the occupied tables. Michaels could hear a few youngsters and their parents laughing harder than normal as he passed by. Their laughter got louder, and he noticed people at the other tables laughing as well. He wondered *what the hell was so funny,* but he brushed it off. They were now off to the Annapolis Mall.

In Tommy's car, Dredge occupied the front passenger seat and the rest were in the back with Michaels jammed between Donald and Mark. Once at the mall, the guys each helped themselves to a coffee from one of the small shops.

Coffee was a big deal in the morning and after dinner for the unit. It was a ritual. As they drank, talked and walked, Michaels again heard giggles from behind him. This time the amusement came from four teenage girls.

One of the girls called out. "Excuse me sir," the young blonde said while briefly suppressing her laughter. The guys stopped and turned toward the girls. "Your pants are ripped," the brave girl said pointing at Michaels, while the other three girls walked off laughing hysterically.

He immediately thought, *Oh my God. That had to be why everyone was laughing in the restaurant.*

He reached to the seat of his pants, expecting to feel a small hole but to his surprise his entire hand fell through the crotch of his pants. Somehow during the course of the day, the seam of his pants had worked its way out from the top, near the belt loop, all the way to the bottom of the zipper. This wasn't just a hole, this was a complete wardrobe malfunction. While he felt the monstrosity of the hole, Tommy and company gathered around to see. Their laughter echoed throughout the food court. Michaels was so embarrassed knowing he had walked through a restaurant and a mall with his whitey-tighties showing. In haste, he stripped off his suit coat and tied it around his waist to cover his partially exposed rear end and by now he was laughing along with them. It was so funny, many of the mall patrons couldn't help to notice the guys in tears. Their laughter continued the entire drive back to the office. This would be one of those days that would be talked about for years to come.

At the office, the laughter and Michaels' plans to prepare the search & seizure warrants were aborted. He needed to go home for the evening since he couldn't bear to stay at work in his clothes or lack thereof.

"Dredge, I'm out of here. It may be ok for Donald to walk around in boxer shorts, but I'm not parading around here in my custom hospital gown."

Still laughing, "Ok son, I'll see you tomorrow."

He made it home at 11:30 p.m., just in time to watch the Johnny Carson Late Night Show and fix a cocktail. He peeled off the pants of his expensive suit and piled them near the front door to be dropped at the cleaners for repair. He finished off the half gallon of rum by making the first drink a little stronger than he normally cared for. He took a sip, causing his head to shiver.

He sat in his recliner for the next couple hours enjoying several cocktails, watching a variety of mindless programs and before long, he was drunk and had smoked way too many cigarettes while periodically laughing out loud about the night. Lately, he had been drinking and smoking a lot more than he should have been from the stress he was putting himself under. Drinking, he thought, would allow him to escape his pressures and put him at ease. With his living room full of smoke and the smell of rum in the air, he was able to make it to his bedroom and pass out not long after his head hit the pillow.

It was 7:00 a.m. when his alarm clock went off. He took a shower and got himself dressed after first inspecting the crotch of the pants he was about to wear. It seemed unblemished. *Thank God.* When he arrived at work no one from the unit was there. It was a wonderful time to take advantage of the silence and begin working on the warrants for Allen and Flores. Tommy rolled in first about an hour later. He told Michaels how the unit all went out to their favorite drinking hole, Kaufmann's Restaurant, after he had gone home last night.

Michaels worked most of the afternoon on the warrants, with high hopes they would produce the results he needed to arrest both suspects. If signed by a judge, this would allow him to take by force, if necessary, blood, hair and saliva from Guy Allen and Mark Flores. Finally finished and on his way to court, he noticed Dredge walking slowly across the parking lot. He looked like he had been run over by a train.

"Rough night Dredge?" Michaels said sarcastically.

"Good morning Shithead," he muttered not hearing a word he said.

"I'm headed to the courthouse to get the DNA warrants signed for these two fucking assholes."

"You're done? You're a wild man. See you when you get back."

After a quick visit to Judge Bruce Williams, he had two signed search & seizure warrants for the personal fluids and hair of Allen and Flores. Michaels was excited, hoping one of their hairs would match the hair found on Kathy's body. He rushed back to the office.

"Bamm, signed boys."

Dredge was leaning back in his chair. Tommy darted from his office and picked up the phone on Donald's desk.

"Ray," he yelled to the person on the other end of the phone. It was obviously Michaels' dad.

"Can you meet us at North Arundel Hospital at 6:30 p.m.? We have two guys we're bringing in."

Michaels' cell phone rang, and he could see from the caller ID it was Stacey. He ignored her call. He didn't have the patience or desire to hear her shit, especially now.

Tommy assigned Donald and Mark the task of picking up Flores and Dredge and Michaels the chore of bringing Allen in. Both were to be brought to the hospital at all cost. Tommy figured it would be best if Dredge was not in the same room as Flores, but little did we know who else would clash with him.

When Donald and Mark arrived at Flores' address, his mother answered the door. Donald introduced himself and asked to speak with her son.

"Can I ask what for?" she questioned.

"Are you his mother?" Donald asked politely.

"Why yes I am."

"We have a search & seizure warrant for your son in connection with a murder investigation," Donald said bluntly.

No sooner did those words come from Donald's mouth when Mark Flores appeared from behind the door. "It's ok Mom. Call my lawyer." And surprisingly he walked outside with the detectives and got into the back seat of Donald's car without resistance. Flores said nothing during the 15-minute ride to the hospital, but the night was still young.

As Dredge and Michaels pulled up to Guy's address, they noticed him walking from the front door in a hurry. "Muscle head must have called him," Dredge speculated.

Michaels slammed on the brakes, threw the car in park and jumped out. "Hey Guy."

Guy glanced at both detectives and took off around the side of his home and out of sight.

"Motherfucker," Michaels yelled out and he took off after him.

By the time he reached the backyard, Guy was nowhere in sight. From the sounds of the nearby dogs barking, he quickly determined his direction. Still in great shape, Michaels scaled the fence of the adjacent yard with the tiring and obese Allen in sight.

Michaels yelled out to him. "Guy you better stop, I have a warrant for you." Little did he know it was a search & seizure warrant and not an arrest warrant. Now completely out of breath, bent over coughing and gasping for air, Guy stopped at the base of the next fence.

"I, I, I, give up. Don't shoot."

In seconds Michaels made it to the same yard where Guy was doing his best not to throw up.

"Let me see your hands, you fat fuck."

Unfortunately for Guy's sake, he was so busy trying not to get sick, he couldn't seem to get his hands up quick enough before Michaels pelted him in the jaw with a stinging right cross punch. Down went Guy into the tall uncut grass, moaning as he landed face first on the ground. Michaels pounced on him and quickly had both hands secured behind his back in handcuffs.

"You fucking dumbass. Did you actually think you could out run me? Guess what asshole? I have a warrant to take your DNA. You're coming with me to the hospital. Now get your fat ass up." Michaels grabbed Guy by one arm and yanked him to his feet. The right side of his face was covered in dirt and grass. Blood dripped from his cut lip where Michaels' fist landed.

"I'm not under arrest?"

"Not yet, but you do have to come with me. Got it? Now let's go."

By the time they made it back to Guy's house, Dredge was leaning against the hood of the Reliant smoking.

"Dredge, look who I found."

"Awww, did someone fall down?"

"Yeah something like that."

"Why did you hit me?"

"Shut the fuck up and get in the car," Michaels said opening the rear door shoving him in.

Even with the short chase, both teams of detectives arrived at the hospital at the same time. Tommy was waiting in the parking lot talking to Ray by the Evidence Collection van. A nurse, who had already been prepped, had two exam rooms set aside. Luckily, neither of the suspects saw the other. Flores was taken into one room and Allen into another.

"Hey Dad."

"Hey Ronnie. Is this your case?"

"Yeah, they're suspects in the Jarvis case. We need their DNA samples."

"That's what Tommy just told me."

"As you know, the State Police Lab likes a minimum of 25 hairs from their head, arm, pubic area, and legs. The nurse will take their blood and do the swabs."

"No problem. Let's get to it."

Ray and his son went into the exam room where Guy sat slumped over in a chair with a swollen bloody lip.

Ray took control. First, the nurse took three vials of blood from Guy's arm and swabbed the inside of his mouth with a long Q-Tip. The little pussy grimaced as she put the needle in his forearm and gagged on the swab.

"Now I need you to pull at least 25 hairs from your head, arms, legs and pubic region," Ray said in his own intimidating way, towering above him.

"Why so many?" Guy said in a scared, squeaky tone.

"Because that's what the judge ordered."

"Can't you just cut them?" he begged.

"Nope we need the roots. So, either you do it or I will do it for you." Everyone in the room could see Ray was getting hot and his patience was wearing thin.

Guy reluctantly began pulling hairs from his head, making pathetic noises of discomfort and pain on each pull.

"You need to move a little faster. I don't have all night," Ray warned.

"I'm going as fast as I can."

"Go faster," he said stepping closer to Guy. Within 20 minutes, they were finally done.

"You can leave now," Michaels told him.

"How am I supposed to get home?"

"I don't know. Call your mommy, or better yet, walk," Michaels said while escorting him from the emergency room doors.

"Guy...the next time you see me, I'll be putting these on you," Michaels said swinging his handcuffs, wearing a shit eating grin.

By the time Michaels made it to the second exam room, Donald was already inside with Ray, Flores and the nurse. Suit and Dredge were standing directly outside. The nurse informed Flores that she was going to draw three tubes of blood from his arm and swab his mouth. You could tell he did not want to be there. His face was red, and he was grinding his teeth in anger.

"I don't know why I have to do this," he said in a nasty tone.

At that point, Ray stood about 2 inches from his face and let him know the rules.

"Because we said so young man. And under no circumstances will you leave this fucking hospital until we are done. Do you hear me?"

Michaels had seen his father pissed before and he knew this was not going to end well if he didn't cooperate. Without warning, in walked Dredge and Tommy. Mark looked up at Dredge and the two exchanged foul looks.

The nurse stuck the needle in his arm and obtained the three tubes of blood while Flores and Dredge stared at one another. Everyone could feel the tension rising in the room. Now it was time to pull some hair.

Ray wasted no time explaining, in no uncertain terms, what was going to happen to Flores if he didn't cooperate with the next step. "I need a lot of hairs from your head, your crotch, your arm and leg, and if you don't do it right the first time, I will do it for you and trust me, you don't want that."

Flores reached to his scalp and tried to pull two or three hairs. He tried to maintain his toughness, but he couldn't sustain his act. He was quick to say he was not going to do it and that's all the boys needed to hear. It was on.

The nurse dashed from the room. Just about the entire Homicide Unit was in this small exam room holding down the screaming, steroid-using freak, while Ray took great enjoyment yanking more hairs than necessary from his body. Donald had Flores' arm twisted behind his back in such a way that it was about to snap. With help from Mark and Michaels, Tommy was barely able to get a pair of handcuffs on his large wrists behind his back. The muscle head yelled from hairs being violently removed and the hurtful compliance moves placed on him. Now it was time to take the hairs from his pubic area. Without hesitation Ray reached down the front of his Adidas athletic pants and yanked the biggest clump of pubic hairs ever seen.

"Owww, he screamed. "Motherfuckers." His voice could be heard throughout the ER.

Within minutes, the evidence they needed was retrieved. Flores was lifted from the cold tile floor where the extractions took place and slammed in the chair that had fallen over. Dredge leaned over him and stuck his right index finger firmly against his forehead and between his eyes. "Now let's get something straight you piece of shit." Flores' face was blood red in anger, and he growled at Dredge like a wild dog. "We're going to take these cuffs off and let you walk, and if you so much as make one fucking noise, you're going to regret it. Do you fucking understand me?" Flores' jaws clenched as he slowly nodded his head in agreement. Once uncuffed, he stormed through the ER doors and out of the hospital like a caged animal being released.

"Way to go Ray," Donald said laughing. Ray just smiled and finished packaging the evidence.

Once Dredge was finally dropped off at the CID, it was late, and Michaels drove home. He noticed that Stacey had called several times during the ruckus at the hospital. By now it was 10:00 p.m. and he wasn't going to call and possibly wake her. That was a call that could wait until the morning.

He stayed up for hours downing one rum and Coke after the next trying to clear his mind so he could sleep. He took his drink into the bedroom and smoked his last cigarette for the evening. He tossed and turned for 2 hours, replaying different scenarios in his head about how Kathy was murdered at the hands of his suspects. The visions were all too real. It was troubling visualizing how she must have been tortured sitting in that wooden chair in Allen's closet. Staring at the clock he finally got up and searched through the bathroom medicine cabinet and found an old bottle of sleeping pills. Knowing he had to get up in just a few hours, he needed something to help him sleep to avoid being miserable the next day. Though the directions said *take one tablet before bed,* he put three in his mouth and washed them down with the last sip of the drink.

He spent the next few days going over everyone's notes so he could begin writing his report. Report writing in homicide was a tiresome task. Homicide reports required much detail and it is often what a defense attorney relies on to have a case overturned or to confuse a detective later in testimony. Fresh out of leads, this was an appropriate time to write, waiting for the results from the lab on Flores and Allen.

A week went by before he finally got the call from Jeff Cover. The lab results were in. "Young Shithead."

Recognizing Cover's voice, Michaels answered back like always. "Jeff Cover, Jeff Cover, Jeff Cover. Tell me some good news Jeffrey."

"Wish I could man sorry, neither of your guys' hairs match the one found on Kathy."

"Fuck."

"Yeah, and it gets worse. We don't have any DNA to compare theirs to. Hell Ronnie, the hair could belong to one of us for all I know. It might not be a bad idea to get samples from anyone who was at the scene, just so we can exclude or include ours."

"That wouldn't be a bad idea. Damn it Jeffrey, thanks but no thanks for the call," Michaels hung up disappointed and upset.

Dredge had been looking at him while he was on the phone. He could tell what the news was from what he heard.
"Nothing?"

"Nope. Let's see, we don't have any semen, the hair found on her doesn't belong to Allen or Flores, we have no witnesses, the evidence from the apartment has all been destroyed, fuck, which means we either need a confession or one real good witness to come forward. This is not good. Shit, now I have to call Mrs. Jarvis."

Reluctantly, he called Mrs. Jarvis to give her the news. She answered the phone on the first ring, like she had been sitting next to it waiting, since his last call.

"Hello."

"Hi Mrs. Jarvis, this is Detective Michaels again."

"I know."

"I'm really sorry, but I don't have good news. We didn't get a match on the hairs. That means we have no physical evidence in this case." He could hear her sobbing as he spoke when she interrupted him.

"You know, my Kathy wasn't perfect, but she was a good-hearted person and I miss her."

"Yes ma'am, I am sure you do, and I am confident our two suspects killed your daughter. There is no doubt in my mind, so I'll keep at this. I'm sorry Mrs. Jarvis. If I get anything else, I'll be sure to let you know."

"Thank you so much."

About to hang up, he could still hear her crying and hearing that made his heart sink.

A few weeks had passed since anyone in the unit had a new case. Michaels' only open case was Jarvis and despite using the media and distributing flyers throughout the county, nothing new trickled in. It was as if no one cared.

He arrived at the CID at 2:30 p.m. to start the evening shift but was surprised with some interesting news from Howes. "Shithead, I got something you're going to like. You owe me son, big time."

"Oh yeah, now what Poodle Head?"

"Remember several weeks ago I asked for the name of the pizza joint where Kathy intended to call on New Year's Day?"

"Yeah, What about it?"

"Well, I got subpoenas for any phones listed to Guy William Allen and to his mother, Jean Marie Allen."

"Yeah and?....Stop fucking with me Mark, get to the point."

"There were no phones listed to Guy Allen, but two listed in his mother's name. One of the phones had an incoming call received at 4:30 p.m. on New Year's Day from the Jarvis's home phone. The cell number listed to Mrs. Allen is one digit off from Pizza Palace's number. He's your man." Mark handed Michaels a small stack of papers containing the records.

"Mark, you are the fucking man." Michaels ran over to his desk and started hugging him.

"Yeah, yeah, I know. Get away from me," he said while laughing.

Michaels sat down at his desk with a big smile. "It's arrest warrant time."

"Shithead, what's going on?" Tommy asked while he and Dredge strolled into the office.

"Listen guys, Mark got subpoenas for phone records listed to Allen's mother, and it shows one of her phones receiving a call at 4:30 p.m. on January 1st from the Jarvis' home phone. Come to find out that very same phone is only one digit off from Pizza Palace's number, where Kathy was trying to call. Isn't that fucking great news?"

"That's outstanding Shithead, probably not enough for an arrest warrant, but you're getting closer. Now you need to show Guy was in control of the cell phone that was called," Tommy said.

"You don't think I have enough?" Michaels inquired.

"You do realize our new State's Attorney is a fucking pussy and he wouldn't approve an arrest warrant at this point," Dredge added.

"He's too fucking busy sexually harassing his staff to figure out how to win a case. No wonder they hate him. Dredge, how about you and I pay Guy a visit tomorrow and see if we can get him to flip on Flores?"

"You got it son."

By 10:00 p.m. Dredge and Tommy called it a night and invited Michaels to join them for cocktails at Kaufmann's Restaurant. He declined and instead continued writing the Jarvis case until he left for home at 11:45 p.m. This news reinvigorated his drive to solve the case.

On the way home, Michaels approached the Earleigh Heights Tavern where Kathy Jarvis was last seen with Allen and Flores days before her body was discovered. Approaching the tavern, he thought to ride through the packed parking lot in hopes of catching someone getting high or doing something wrong. With an arrest, he assumed, maybe he could solicit information about the Jarvis murder. *Somebody from the bar had to know something*, he figured, but things didn't quite work out that way.

Michaels' car squealed to a halt near the bar's entrance.

"Stop, Police," he yelled at the top of his voice, jumping from his cruiser. Positioning his body across the hood, he took aim at the middle of a man's back who was walking slowly away from the bar toward the road. He was armed with a rifle equipped with a long banana style clip extending from the bottom of the weapon. The entire occurrence was surreal and moved in slow motion. Michaels was surprised how steady his aim was, holding tight on the armed moving target.

"Drop the gun, he yelled." Ignoring the demand, the subject kept walking. "I said drop the gun," he shouted once more.

Michaels couldn't believe there was no one else in the parking lot. He could see the gunman was a white male, wearing faded blue jeans and an old flannel shirt. He shouted the commands once more and the gunman stopped. The sights from his handgun were fixed on his upper torso. "Drop the gun or I will shoot you."

The man looked over his right shoulder toward Michaels. Quickly, Michaels thought to himself, *if he turns clockwise, his gun barrel will cross my path and I will shoot him. If he turns to face me in the opposite direction, I won't shoot.* The gun toting man turned in a counter-clockwise direction and faced Michaels with the rifle pointed to the ground. "I'll tell you one more time, drop the gun or I'm going to shoot you."

The man slowly took one step directly toward Michaels, then a second. Michaels squeezed down on the trigger of his handgun. His aim was true and steady on the center of the man's chest. He was about to die. Then without warning, the man bent forward and laid the rifle to rest on the asphalt in front of him. "Turn around and get on your knees. Then as fast as the incident unfolded, it ended, and no shots were fired.

He reached into his car and grabbed his handcuffs hanging from the steering column blinker lever. He holstered his weapon and cuffed him from behind while the suspect remained on his knees. "Get up." With one hand firmly on the cuffs, he jerked the man to his feet and escorted him and his weapon to his car. When he opened the door, his portable radio fell to the ground. The radio had slid across the passenger seat and fell between the seat and door when he abruptly stopped. Because he never called out his location to dispatch no one had a clue what he was doing or where he was. Now that the incident had ended, Michaels' hands were shaking. Just seconds ago, he was about to kill someone and was steady as a rock and now adrenaline surged through his veins and was in full control. With the radio trembling in his hand, he calmly keyed up the microphone.

"Detective 132 to radio, I have an armed subject in custody in the parking lot of the Earleigh Heights Tavern. Can you start me a patrol car please?" The dispatcher responded back with a sound of urgency in her voice.

"10-4. Do you need radio silence?"

"Negative, just one car for transport please," he said as calmly as possible. A nearby patrolman responded swiftly with his lights and siren activated to the lot.

For the few minutes he waited for the officer, he talked to the gunman who was now seated next to him. "What the fuck were you doing man? I almost killed you. What's your name?"

"I'm sorry sir. My name is Tim. I was in the bar earlier and this guy sucker punched me for talking to his girlfriend. I live in the trailer right there," he said motioning to a mobile home behind the bar. "I got my gun and I was waiting for him."

"Man, you are lucky to be alive, do you have any idea?" he yelled.

"Yeah, I'm sorry. I'm really sorry. Thanks for not shooting me."

By now the patrol car had arrived and the officer took custody of the prisoner. It was just after midnight and small groups of people began trickling from the tavern. He sat in his car for a few minutes to get his shit together. He was dumbfounded. He was either about to be involved in a gun fight or was about to execute his second human being had he taken one more step. *I most likely prevented a murder. This dude was lying in wait to kill another person. It had all the ingredients for a first-degree murder case.* He retrieved the rifle from the back seat and removed the fully loaded high caliber 8" banana style magazine and the one chambered round.

By the time he made it to the nearby police station to prepare the paperwork, his shaking subsided. The 22-year-old was charged with Reckless Endangerment among other violations. Come to find out the crime of Reckless Endangerment had just gone into effect as a new law in

Maryland at midnight. Since this untimely circumstance occurred at 12:05 a.m., Michaels was the first law enforcement officer in Maryland to charge someone with this crime.

After completing the paperwork, he made several entries in his notebook. He looked up at the clock on the wall, it was 1:40 a.m. and time to go home.

When he arrived home, he didn't even remember driving there, which was no surprise considering the rollercoaster of emotions he had just gone through, and to think, Tommy and Dredge had no idea what had happened. He flipped on the lights and threw his keys on the dining room table along with his suit coat. He needed a beer. *I wish I had someone here to talk to,* he thought. With a cold Miller Lite in hand, he dropped down in his recliner. Thoughts raced through his mind. *Wow, what a day.*

He was the first to arrive at the office the next morning. This would be the day to bring in Guy Allen and hopefully break him and the case wide open. Knowing Mark Flores had already lawyered up, there was no chance of interviewing him unless his attorney would allow him to speak with us, and he knew that would never happen. Without any viable physical evidence, today would be the day for Dredge and Michaels to team up and craft their best interrogation.

"Good morning Shithead," Tommy said holding onto his coffee like it was a precious brick of gold.

"Top of the morning to ya sergeant." Michaels did in his best Irish voice.

"You're here awful early Ronnie."

"Yeah man, big day today. Dredge and I are going to bring that fat fuck Allen in."

"Do you think he'll go for it?"

"I do. He's a soft little pussy, probably a pedophile, and who knows what else he's done that we don't know. We must either make him believe Flores is cooperating with us, or that it is in his best interest to come forward first. I don't think he's our killer so this shouldn't be that hard. I know the guilts and the thought of jail are eating him alive. When I show him the phone records, he's going to shit."

"I hope your right. Look who it is. Good morning Dredge, you big bag of fuck," Tommy said.

"What's going on? Why are you boys so damn chipper this early in the morning?"

"Cause as soon as you wake your old ass up, we are going to bring Allen in and get him to give up Flores today."

"Oh, we are? Are we?"

"Yup, that's the plan, you big penis looking bitch."

"By the way Tommy, I had a close call last night in the Earleigh Heights Tavern parking lot. I almost shot a man that was walking around with a loaded rifle."

Tommy walked over to Michaels' desk. "What the hell happened?"

"A guy got hit in the face for talking to some dude's girlfriend, so he left the bar, got his assault rifle and was all set to kill him when he came out, I guess."

"Damn Shithead. It sounds like you prevented a murder. Good job. Did you lock him up or did a uniform? Tommy asked.

Michaels chuckled. "I did. No one even knew I was there. When I saw the guy with the gun I slammed on my brakes, and my fucking radio slipped off my seat and fell between the passenger door. He's lucky he put the gun down, that's all I can say."

"Damn son."

By 10:00 a.m. Michaels was crawling out of his skin waiting on Dredge. After repeated requests, Dredge finally gave in to the young hyperactive detective and off they went to the Allen address. During the drive, neither talked but instead just smoked and drank their coffees. When Michaels pulled up to the address, they both flicked their cigarettes to the ground as they headed toward the front door. They noticed the picture window curtains being pushed aside, and Allen's head appeared with a petrified look.

As fast as they opened, the curtains fell back into place as he darted out of sight.

"There he goes Dredge, he's running again. I'll go outback," Michaels said running around the left side of the residence just as he had done once before. Casually, Dredge continued to the front door and knocked. There was no answer, but he could clearly hear commotion inside the home.

"County Police, open up," Dredge yelled out knocking harder with his fist. Without an arrest warrant, they knew they weren't allowed to force their way in.

With Michaels behind the house, Dredge walked to the window of Guy's bedroom which was located in the front. He crouched down and peered inside and was not prepared for what he was about see. Guy was sitting on the floor leaning against his bed with a look of horror and panic on his face. With a knife placed against his left wrist, he gave it a quick stroke and blood squirted on his face, arm and t-shirt. He thrashed at his wrist once more and the sharp blade made a larger cut. Blood gushed from both gaping incisions. Dredge could not believe his eyes. He was committing suicide right in front of him.

"Dredge, Dredge," Michaels yelled walking toward the front of the house. "Can you see him?"

Dredge stood up fast and walked from the window before Michaels could reach him. "No, I don't know where he went. I can't see him. Oh well young man, let's get out of here. We'll get him another time."

"You alright brother?" Michaels asked.

"Yeah, yeah. Let's leave and let things calm down and come back later."

"Let me knock on the front door first."

"I already did. Come on son, let's go."

"Did you knock on his window?" Michaels said walking in the direction where Dredge had just left.

"Yes, I did several times, now let's go," Dredge insisted.

"Fine, but I want this fucker today."

"I know. Don't worry, we'll get him. Just be patient. It'll all work out."

In the car Michaels was fuming. "I bet he thought we were there to arrest him. That fat fuck."

"Oh, no doubt," Dredge mumbled.

As usual the two said very little on the drive back to the office.

"Boys, boys, how'd it go?" Tommy shouted when he saw them approaching the office area.

"Fucker saw us through the window and wouldn't let us in. That's how it went. He knows his shit is weak. He knows he's fucked and eventually his ass is going to jail for this. I'll get him. You watch. I'll hunt that motherfucker down, if it's the last thing I do." Michaels dropped in his chair and let out a big sigh. He was pissed.

"Young Shithead, you need to chill. You'll get him," Tommy said sitting at Hauf's desk.

"I'm good. I don't like the fact that he wouldn't open the door. I told Dredge he probably thinks we got a hit on one of his hairs or the fluids we took at the hospital and we were there to lock him up. I just hope he doesn't lawyer up on us in the meantime. That's what I'm afraid of."

Dredge sat quietly at his desk and offered nothing to the conversation.

For the next several hours, Tommy and Dredge had to constantly pull the reins back on Michaels who wanted to stake out Allen's home with hopes that Guy would appear outside. Then a call came in from the Dispatch Center. It was a supervisor for Tommy.

"Sergeant Suit."

"Hi Sergeant, this is Rosemary. We have units responding to 912 Church Road for a subject found DOA by his mother. It may be a suicide, but we haven't received word yet."

"What did you say the address was?"

From the sound of his voice, Dredge and Michaels were now both focusing on Tommy jotting something on a piece of paper.

"Thanks," and he hung up. "Shithead, what's the address where Allen lives?"

"912 Church Road. Why?"

"They got a DOA there. A mother found her son dead. It's an apparent suicide."

"What the fuck? We just left. Are you serious? Come on Dredge let's go."

With Michaels driving, the two left the building and raced to the address. Dredge said nothing.

Standing outside the Allen home were two patrolmen talking, one of which was Michaels' good friend, Sergeant Richard Speake. "Uh oh, the big guns are here. Is that Detective Sleuth himself, Ronnie Michaels? You guys handle suicides now? That's great, can we leave?"

"Ha-ha dickhead. I mean Sergeant," Michaels said jokingly. "No, you can't leave. Always an asshole, aren't you Richard? Congrats on your promotion by the way. I haven't seen you since you put those stripes on. Way to go. You are the first out of our academy to get promoted."

"Thanks Ronnie, but didn't dispatch tell you? This is a suicide. Hi Detective Hart."

"Hi Sergeant."

"The mother found her son in his room when she came home from work. It looks like he cut his wrist with a butcher knife. She said he's been acting really strange lately, like he was pre-occupied with something."

"What's his name?" Michaels asked excitedly.

The sergeant yelled over to the officer standing by the front door. "Hey Porter, what's your victim's name?"

The anticipation was killing Michaels. *Could this have been an early death sentence?*

"Guy Allen," the officer stated.

"This must have just happened. We were here three hours ago, and we saw him look out the front window. He wouldn't open the door."

"What? Ya'll know the victim?" the sergeant asked.

"Fuck yeah. He's one of our suspects in a murder we're working. Was he found in his bedroom?"

"Yeah, on the floor. He must have been leaning against the bed when he cut himself."

Michaels looked over at Dredge who was standing on the sidewalk smoking a cigarette. "Didn't you say you looked in his window?"

Dredge took a big drag from his cigarette and looked at him with a peculiar blank look on his face. Cold chills ran up the back of Michaels' neck. "Yup."

"Could you see in?" the sergeant inquired.

"Not really. It was hard, you know, with the glare and the dirty window."

Michaels walked to the window of Guy's room. What he clearly saw was the body of Guy Allen laying partially on his left arm, completely covered in blood. He looked over at Dredge who was staring at him. He knew what his partner had done.

"Come on son. You ready to go?" Dredge said calmly.

"Sure, just one thing. Officer Porter did he leave a note?"

"No sir. No note was found."

"Thanks. Hey, it was great seeing you again and congratulations." Michaels looked over at Dredge who was already walking toward the car.

"Catch ya later Ronnie."

In the car Michaels looked over at Dredge who was peering out the window. Sergeant Speake was bent down in front of Guy's window looking in.

"Let's go," Dredge ordered.

"Are you alright?"

"Can we get back to the office? I got shit to do."

"Sure partner. We're out of here." Driving to the office, Michaels sensed the uneasiness in the air and felt a need to talk. "Well, there's one down. I knew it. He didn't want to go to jail. Guilty motherfucker."

Dredge sat looking out the passenger window taking long draws on his cigarette. Michaels didn't want to ask him any questions about what he saw or didn't see earlier through that window. *Some things are better left alone.*

Back at the CID, Mark and Donald had arrived for the evening shift and both along with Tommy were gathered in the Homicide Unit's area.

"Well?" Tommy asked before Michaels or Dredge could get seated.

"Charged, convicted and sentenced to death. Guy Allen is dead," Michaels said proudly.

"I guess the thought of jail was too much," Donald said.

"Hell, I wish they could all be that simple. But now without any physical evidence and the second guy with a lawyer, I'm fucked unless some mysterious witness comes forward."

"I thought for sure this Allen fella was going to give up Flores," Tommy said.

Dredge sat quietly with a blank look on his face. "You ok Dredge?" Donald asked.

"Yeah just tired, that's all."

"Let me give Mrs. Jarvis a call," Michaels said picking up his phone and looking at Dredge.

"Hello Mrs. Jarvis, did I catch you at a bad time?"

"No detective. How is everything?"

"Mrs. Jarvis, as you know I have two prime suspects. There is no doubt in my mind they both had something to do with Kathy's death. Well today, the suspect who I believe your daughter called by accident, killed himself."

"Oh my. Why would he do that?" her voice trembled. He could hear her begin to cry.

"My partner and I went to pick him up today so we could interview him to see if he would give up his cohort. He saw us through the window when we pulled up and my theory is, he thought we were there to arrest him, so he committed suicide."

"Who found him?"

"His mother did ma'am."

"That is so sad. I'll bet she's a mess. I'll keep her in my prayers. So where does that leave things?"

"I'm afraid to say, not where I would like to be since the other suspect has already requested an attorney. You see once that happens, we're not allowed to speak with him unless his attorney is present. So, given the lack of physical evidence, we need a witness. I will keep advertising the reward in hopes of enticing someone to come forward."

"Detective Michaels, I really appreciate you keeping me informed. You're a good person and I trust you'll do the right thing."

"Thank you, Mrs. Jarvis. You can call me anytime and I'll be in touch. Goodbye"

"Goodbye detective."

Working Man

The cold months of winter passed with only a handful of stabbings and a police shooting. The dog days of summer had set it. It was a blistering hot August day and the temperature was already 90 degrees by 7 a.m. The humidity made matters worse. Michaels was on day shift and had been waiting at the county garage for over an hour while the mechanics added Freon to his air conditioner. He was about to start to the office when he heard the obnoxious beeping sound from his cell phone. He looked at the number, and it was the Dispatch Center. He knew that meant somebody was dead or about to die. It was rarely anything else.

"Detective Michaels here, you rang?" he said in a friendly voice to the female answering the phone.

"Yes detective, Sergeant Suit wants you to respond to 8500 Dorsey Road in Hanover for a deceased male discovered at a construction site.

"Oh good, on my way." Michaels said sarcastically.

The construction site was 15 minutes from the county garage and the drive was cooler now that the much-needed air conditioning was working. The weatherman on the radio said it was 105 degrees with the heat index. It was hot. At the scene, he saw a marked police car parked next to an ambulance and several people standing around a body covered with a sheet. When he stepped from his car it was like walking into an oven and there was no way he was putting his jacket on. He jotted his arrival time in his notebook and walked to the group standing around the body.

"Good afternoon gentlemen, I'm Detective Michaels from homicide. Hot enough out here for everyone? What do we have?"

"The deceased is a new employee who has only been working here for a few days. He's a 39-year-old white male who lives in Baltimore City who is new to the whole construction line of work. It looks like he died of heat stroke according to the paramedics." the officer stated while reading from his own clipboard.

"Detective, I'm Frank Blucher, the foreman here. The guy's name is Ken Jenkins and he's only been working as a laborer for the past three days. I had him moving metal beams all morning to the back of the site. We don't know when he collapsed. I told everyone at the start of the shift to stay hydrated because of the heat, but I guess he didn't listen."

Michaels bent down and pulled the sheet back. The man's eyes were closed, and his skin was abnormally red. He was dressed in jeans, a white shirt and new Timberland boots. His lips where white, dry and crusty, almost as if they were about to crack. There were no obvious signs of injuries on him.

"When I hired him, he said he had just lost his job at the Port in Baltimore where he worked for 10 years. He practically begged me for a job. He said he had 3 kids. I figured he'd work his ass off for us and now look."

"Is Doc Johnson on his way?" the profusely sweating Michaels asked the officer.

"Right here," Doc said approaching the men from behind.

"Hey Doc, how's it going? You got here fast."

"I had just finished delivering a baby boy at North Arundel Hospital when I got the call."

"And there you have the circle of life. He giveth and he taketh," Michaels preached.

"Yes, he does. He sure does."

Doc squatted down next to the deceased with his favorite camera in hand. He reached down and lifted one of the eyelids. You could see the pupil was dilated and the whites of his eyes were blood red. "He's got all the signs of heat stroke. Let me get a few pictures and we can get him to the Medical Examiner's Office. And don't say anything about my camera."

"Nope, not a word Doc. I'm just surprised they still make film for that. You know I saw one of those on the What's it Worth Antique show on T.V."

"Funny. Hey, it still does the job youngster, now get out of my way," Doc said laughing under his breath.

Michaels made several notations before he headed back to his car just in case the ME's Office determined the death was something other than heat stroke. He noted the witnesses' names, what the deceased had been doing at the time of his demise, the temperature, the condition of the body, especially his pupil. All signs pointed to heat as the killer of this hard-working family man.

In the comforts of his cool car, Michaels called Tommy at the office. "Young Shithead, what do you have?"

"I'm headed to Baltimore City to do this death notification. Everyone, including Doc Johnson, thinks its heat stroke. This poor guy has only worked here for three days and to top it off he is new to construction work."

"How old is he?"

"He's 39, married with 3 young kids. This is really going to suck."

"You don't have to do this one Ronnie, I can have the patrolman make the notification."

"No Tommy. I don't want this young guy doing it. This is going to be a tough one. I'd feel better if I did it myself."

"Do you want to take someone with you?"

"Nope, I'll take care of it."

"When you're done just go home."

"Will do."

The address he had for Mr. Jenkins was a row home in a low-income section of Baltimore City. Driving down the narrow streets, he could see most of the neighborhood was without central air conditioning and only a few had window units. When he turned onto the victim's street, he slowed for the slew of kids cooling off in the water gushing from the fire hydrant. It amazed him how happy the children seemed from the simple pleasures of the lukewarm spouting city water. He wondered if any of those children belonged to the deceased.

The front door and all the windows were open in the house. He walked slowly up the steps and could hear several people inside through the open door. He knocked on the rusty frame of the metal screen door and someone from inside shouted, "Come in."

In the living room there were two shirtless adult men and a young boy about 8 years old sitting on the couch and one adult female wearing a faded pair of cut off jean shorts and a tank top, sitting on the steps leading upstairs. The house was unbearably hot, but they seemed unfazed. In the corner of the living room was a fan oscillating, only merely redistributing the stifling air. Everyone stopped talking when Michaels stepped into the room. Without his jacket, his badge and gun were visible.

"Sorry to bother you folks, but I'm looking for a relative of Mr. Kenneth Jenkins."

They all spoke over top one other, making it difficult to decipher who was who, but he was able to make out the female sitting on the steps was his sister.

"Ma'am is there somewhere we can speak in private?"

He was reluctant to make this notification in front of the young child and others in the tight space, knowing many times parents prefer to do it themselves in their own way, on their own terms.

"You can say whatever you have to say in front of them. We're all family."

"Ma'am I need to tell you something very private. May we please go into another room?"

"Detective, I said we're all family, whatever it is you need to say, just say it."

He looked down at his shoes. He knew his words would sweep through the room like a tornado.

"Well?" she insisted.

He took a deep breath and looked at everyone in the room with their eyes piercing him. "I am sorry to have to tell you this but your brother, Kenneth, died from heat stroke at his job."

Just as he expected, the room erupted with blood curdling screams and hysterical crying. One of the males tried to hold the young boy who fell to the ground crying and pounding his fist on the floor. Every person in the room lost control. It was pandemonium.

Normally during a death notification, the detective hopes at least one person in the room will keep it together, but that was not the case today. People were yelling "NO, NO, NO," while others were pacing the floor, crying out of control. There was nothing he could do but stand there, helpless, as they tore the room apart. At one point the young boy ran out of the front door screaming for his brother and sister with his aunt chasing behind. Michaels didn't know what was happening outside except more yelling and crying could be heard. He quickly got the sense of just how close knit the neighborhood was.

The hysteria inside calmed somewhat after 15 minutes. Michaels stayed and explained the process and answered what questions he could. After an hour, he finally left the residence. Outside he could see and hear neighbors crying and hugging one another. *I feel like I had just destroyed an entire block. Before I arrived, people were playing in the street, laughing on their porches and enjoying each other in their living room, regardless of the temperature. Then I show up like the Grim Reaper. It's no wonder the majority of my suits are black. I shouldn't be driving a police car. I'd be better suited in a fucking hearse carrying a big fucking sign that says run if you see me. That's how I feel.*

By now it was well past quitting time and he was back in his car driving home.

"How was it?" Tommy asked as he answered his phone. It was like he sensed something.

"Bad"

"Real bad?"

"Yes"

From his days as a homicide detective, Tommy had done his share of notifications, so he knew exactly what his newest detective was experiencing. "Ok pal, see you tomorrow. Take it easy."

"Yes sir."

Driving from the city, he remembered he had been invited for spaghetti dinner by his mom. Considering what he had just gone through, he was especially glad since he wasn't in the mood to fix something to eat or sit alone at a restaurant. His parents lived not too far from his own townhouse. Bev and Ray had a nice ground level two-bedroom condominium. Beverly worked at the North Arundel Hospital in the billing department. There were two things you could count on with Beverly. She didn't take any shit from people and she adored her two sons. With a maiden name of DiMaggio, the 5'3" Italian would stand up to anyone which was where her younger son, the detective, got his energy and spunk.

When he got to their condo, Beverly greeted him at the door with a warm hug and a kiss on the cheek. "Hi Hun. How are you? I smell smoke on you. Are you still smoking?" she asked like he was in high school.

"Sure am, like a house on fire. My God it's hot. Hi Dad" he said walking into the cool living room. Ray was relaxing on his recliner holding a full cocktail glass in his hand. "Hi Ronnie. How are you? What would you like to drink?"

"I'd be better if it wasn't hot as balls outside. I'll take a beer if you have one. God knows I need it after the terrible heartbreaking case I just had."

Beverly went to the kitchen and returned to the living room with a cold Miller Lite. "What happened?" she asked always intrigued by his work. He was now sitting on the chair next to Ray. Beverly sat eagerly on the edge of the couch waiting to hear the story.

"I just had a horrible death notification. This poor guy, married with 3 young kids had just been laid off at the Port, died of heat stroke at a construction site. He lived in the city just over the county line. When I went to do the notification, I ended up telling a whole room full of family, including a young child. It was bad. Everyone went berserk."

"Oh man. What did you do?" Beverly asked.

"That's just it. There is nothing I can do except sit there while they cry, scream, sometimes faint and then hug you. Someone who they have never met, they clutch onto you like you are connected in some way to the one they lost. It's hard to explain. It's really weird." Beverly saw her son's eyes well up. He quickly tilted the beer can to his mouth to hide what was happening to him. "Ronnie, are you ok?" Beverly asked while Ray sat quietly sipping his cocktail.

"Yeah, yeah, I'm fine. It was like I turned the entire neighborhood upside down. I left there feeling like I caused this guy's death. All was fine in their lives, hell, all was fine on their street, until I arrived."

"No son, it's not your fault. God put you there because he knows you are the best one to deliver that message for him. He has taken one of his children and you are his messenger to the surviving loved ones. So no, it's not your fault. You are doing God's work, remember that."

"Thanks Mom. I guess that makes sense. Damn is it time to eat yet? I'm hungry."

Michaels pondered for a moment thinking about what she had just said. He still battled in his head wondering *Is this a larger task assigned from someone far greater than my sergeant?* Not realizing his sudden silence, Ray and Bev watched their son while he stared at his beer can. He put the can to his mouth and after four big gulps, it was gone.

"Dinner should be done. Ronnie, do you want a glass of red wine with your pasta?"

"Ray, do you want a glass too?"

"Sure, I'll pour us all one."

The three of them sat down and enjoyed their meal, talked and polished off the large bottle of Merlot. He stayed at his parent's condo for three hours. He hadn't visited them in a few weeks, so they used the time to catch up on everything from work, to who was suffering from what ailment, to whose marriage was about to end. By eight o'clock it was time to leave. Somewhat tipsy from the wine and beer, he gave them both a hug and said, "I love you." This was one of those few times Ray said he loved him in return, which he assumed was because his father had been drinking, but he still liked hearing those rarely spoken words.

When he arrived home, he was glad he had turned his air conditioning down before he had left that morning. It was a much-needed relief from the heat outside. He took off his gun and badge and laid them on the table next to his recliner. Tired and buzzed, he got himself a beer, turned on the TV and switched through the channels to find something that would make him laugh. He needed to laugh. Eventually, he caught himself daydreaming about his trip to the city, not realizing he had already surfed through the entire compliment of channels several times.

What he had experienced that day was weighing heavily on him. He stared at the cast of his favorite sitcom on the screen but couldn't erase the picture of the little boy crying on the floor, screaming hopelessly for his daddy. He stayed up and finished his last nine beers, then managed to stumble down the hall to his bedroom where he quickly passed out.

A Note Won't Do

It was near the end of October and the weather was getting cool. This was the time of year for Michaels and long-time friend, Mel Foster, to deer hunt. Michaels had been a zealous hunter since Ray gave him his first Daisy Red Rider BB gun at the tender age of 7. All his childhood and adult life, Michaels loved being outside regardless if he was hunting, fishing or camping. The woods and water put him at ease and lately he needed it more than ever.

Mel was four years older than Michaels. They met through his brother Steve when Michaels was 13. Mel and Steve worked together at a florist shop. Steve wasn't a hunter, but Mel was, which was how their friendship spawned. Mel, or Elmer, as Michaels sometimes called him, had an enthusiastic sense of humor and could repair just about anything. Besides being a good cook, he was a hard worker and would do anything at any time for a friend. Michaels would never forget the time Mel got out of bed and drove an hour away to pick him up simply because he asked. He often recalls how he had found himself needing to abruptly bail from a bachelor party bus that was out of control at 2:00 a.m. with a bunch of drunk cops. He needed a ride home and he called his buddy and without hesitation, Mel was there for him. He was truly one of kind.

Michaels worked day work on this Friday and Mel was set to stay the night at Michaels' house in the extra bedroom. The plan was to leave around 4:00 a.m. and travel over the Bay Bridge to their hunting property on the Eastern Shore. They were leasing some awesome land and it was the home of some monster bucks. Mel came over at 5:00 p.m. carrying marinated deer tenderloin steaks bound for the grill along with 100 proof rum.

The two stayed outside most of the evening grilling and drinking. The rum was Mel's favorite and Michaels' too, if he wanted to forget part of the night. They had an enjoyable time laughing and strategizing about how and where each of them were going to hunt the next day. Their day trip would be a much needed get away for the stressed-out detective. By 10:30 p.m. they were drunk, and Michaels made his typical announcement when it was time to call it a night.

"I'm done," he said with his melting face and red eyes.

Mel staggered to the spare bedroom and Michaels collapsed on his bed, both knowing the alarm would sound before they knew it.

The two hadn't been asleep long when they were startled by a loud bang at the front door. Michaels nearly fell as he struggled to put on a pair of jeans. After several attempts, he squinted to read the clock. It was 3:00 a.m. He faltered down the hallway as the knocking persisted.

"Alright, alright, I'm coming. Jesus Christ," he yelled out.

He cracked open the door to see his life-long friend, Gary Webb, standing in the doorway in uniform. Gary was an officer on the Police Department who worked the midnight shift in the Northern District.

"Hey Ronnie, sorry to wake you. Can I come in and talk to you for a second?"

"Fuck Gary, yeah come on in. What's going on?"

"Hey Melvin," Gary said when he saw Mel coming down the stairs to see what the commotion was. "You guys going hunting in the morning?" Gary questioned while looking at the gear piled by the door.

"That was the plan. What the fuck's going on?"

"How well do you know your neighbor?" Gary asked Michaels as he pointed to the adjoining townhouse wall.

"Who, Darlene?"

"Yeah."

"I've known her for years. She cuts my hair."

"Does anyone else live with her?"

"Yeah, she lives with her mom and brother. Why?"

"Her mom was killed in a car accident tonight. Some asshole, doped up on PCP, ran into the back of her while she was stopped at a traffic light near Furnace Branch Road. He never touched the brakes and her car caught fire and exploded. The body was burned really bad."

"Oh shit, she and her mom were so close. How'd she take it?"

"That's why I'm here Ronnie. No one is answering her door. I was going to leave a note for her to call Northern, but I was hoping you might have her telephone number."

"What time did this happen? It's 3:00 a.m."

"It happened when I came on at 11:30 p.m., but it's taken this long to identify her because of the condition of the car and the body."

Michaels opened the door and saw both Darlene's and her brother's car parked side by side. Darlene was a year younger than Michaels and her brother, Roger, was a year younger than her. Roger was a big guy. Michaels never knew what he did for a living, but he was always cordial to him. There was no way he was going to let them find out about their mother's death in the morning. *No way. A note just won't do*, he thought.

"Did you knock hard Gary?"

"Hell yes. I've been pounding on their door for the last 5 minutes. I'm surprised you couldn't hear me."

Michaels searched for her number in his cell phone and called. The phone rang and rang but no one picked up. Mel ran upstairs and placed his ear against the adjoining wall.

"No wonder they can't hear the fucking phone. They have music playing," Mel said.

Michaels went outside and began pounding on the door. After several minutes his knuckles were bleeding. "Gary, you can leave, I'll take care of this." He continued knocking on the door while simultaneously calling her phone and shouting her name.

"Ronnie, thanks. If you get through to her and she wants to call me, you know the number."

"You got it Gary, see ya."

Michaels couldn't believe no one inside could hear the intolerable banging sound. He was so loud, neighbors were watching from their doorways. *God knows what they must been thinking,* he wondered.

Mel stuck his head from the door and suggested he try getting their attention by knocking on the adjoining wall upstairs where the music was originating. Michaels told him to pound away, now hard up, but not willing to give up. Mel went upstairs and proceeded to wail away on the wall while Michaels continued the same out front. Darlene finally answered the door, barely cracking it open.

"Ronnie, what are you doing?" she asked half asleep.

"I need to come in."

"No, I'm sleeping. What do you want?"

Irritated, he repeated himself. "I need to talk to you."

"I'm not dressed, you can't come in."

"Then get dressed. I need to come in and talk to you now. It's very important."

"Hold on. Let me get my robe. Give me a minute." She closed the door and returned shortly, allowing him in.

"Now what's going on?"

"Darlene, I really hate having to tell you this, but I thought this would be better coming from me rather than a stranger."

"What Ronnie? What?" she said with a look of panic in her eyes.

"God, I don't want to tell you this. I'm so sorry, but your mom was killed in a car accident tonight on Ritchie Highway."

When those horrible words slipped from his mouth she screamed. "No, no, no, Mommy." She continued to scream the same words while running up the stairs. He didn't know where she was going but assumed to her mother's room to see if she had returned home. She continued to cry and shout. "Mommy, Mommy, Mommy," repeatedly as she came downstairs. Still crying, she tried to ask him what had happened, when Roger came running half way down the stairs shouting.

"What the fuck is going on? What's going on? Why are you crying?"

"Mommy's dead, mommy's dead Roger."

Roger lost it. He began yelling. "What? No way, No FUCKING way." Michaels was sure Mel could hear him through the wall. Violently, he began hitting the wall with his fist putting three big holes in the sheet rock. The force from his clenched hand knocked a picture from Michaels' wall on the opposite side.

Michaels always figured notifications were tough enough when he didn't personally know the victim or their family, but in this instance, it was much worse. He knew them both. The chaotic outrage from Roger lasted for several minutes. After beating on the wall, he commenced to banging his head. Darlene ran up the steps and hugged him. They both clutched tightly to one another and cried. Standing alone in the middle of the living room, he could only watch the brother and sister experience their greatest sorrow. He couldn't imagine how it would have been had they found out several hours later by phone, from a stranger working the front desk at the station.

Eventually the three sat at the kitchen table while Darlene made a pot of coffee. As expected, they wanted to know every detail. All of them. What little Michaels did know wasn't going to be easy to say. For a moment, he contemplated withholding the cause of death, but soon changed his mind. These people, he thought, trusted him and he owed them the truth. The tears continued to flow while he vaguely explained how the accident occurred. Darlene told Michaels that their mother, Edna, was on her way home from visiting her friend who was sick with the flu. Sensing the vagueness in Michaels voice, Roger asked about the condition of her car. He had to tell him, knowing he would eventually find out. Michaels took a sip of his coffee and placed the cup slowly on the table. Roger and Darlene looked at him, anxiously waiting for him to answer.

"Ronnie, what's wrong? Why won't you tell us about her car?" she asked.

Michaels reached out with both hands and placed them on their arms. "The car's gas tank exploded on impact from the force of the other car."

"Oh my God," she screamed.

"Motherfucker," Roger shouted. "Jesus fucking Christ. Did she at least get pulled from the car?" Roger said with tears pouring from his eyes. "Don't tell me she burned to death," he cried out. Michaels did not speak, and Roger knew the answer.

Their crying increased, hugging one another again. Michaels could only sit, watch and listen.

"If it's any consolation, the investigator on the scene believed your mother never suffered. He said the impact would have killed her instantly."

The conversation at the kitchen tabled turned from Edna to the driver of the other car. They wanted to know his name, age, and where he lived, none of which Michaels had. They wanted to know if he was charged, which he assured them he had been.

"Let me call my friend, Officer Webb, and see exactly what he was charged with. Can I use your phone?"

"Yes. Help yourself."

Michaels walked to their phone on the kitchen wall and glanced at the nearby clock. It was 4:30 a.m. The person responsible for the crash was a known loser to the guys at the station named Billy Golas. He said the officers in the district would frequently find him in abandoned buildings fucking skanky whores of both sexes. When Michaels heard the name, he was stunned.

"Are you fucking kidding me Gary? What's his description and date of birth?"

By now Roger and Darlene turned in their chairs watching and listening intently. He hung up without saying goodbye to Webb.

"What, Ronnie? Do you know who it is?" she inquired.

He sat down at the kitchen table. "He's a worthless piece of shit named Golas, who I locked up last year for selling me PCP. He's a real burnout."

Roger jumped up and his chair flipped across the floor. He slammed his fist on the table, causing their coffees to splash. "And he's not in jail? Why isn't he in fucking jail? Jesus fucking Christ."

"He only got a few weekends, that's all. The State's Attorney took a bullshit plea because he was too incompetent to try the case. Either way, it's critical we tell the State's Attorney's Office Monday." Both Darlene and her brother's emotions switched from sorrow to pure anger. Like Michaels, they could not believe what they were hearing.

He stayed and talked with them for another hour explaining how Edna would first undergo an autopsy before she could be released to the funeral home of their choice. He always made it a practice during a notification, just as he taught the recruits in the police academy, never refer to the deceased person as *the body* or *the remains*, but by their name. After all, it was their loved one you were talking about, not a science project. The other point he stressed was never be in a rush to leave. In this instance, especially since he knew everyone, he stayed longer than normal to console them. By now it was close to 5:30 a.m. and his job as a friend and a cop was done. Darlene and Roger both gave Michaels intense hugs and simultaneously thanked him. Those words meant a lot.

"Take care of one another guys. I'm next door if you need me," and he walked out.

Mel was fast asleep on the couch and awoke when he heard the front door shut. "How'd it go? I could hear them screaming and banging on the walls. Shit, even one of your pictures fell and the glass broke in the frame. I put it on the dining room table."

Poor Mel had been waiting patiently when he could have left, Michaels thought to himself. "Thanks brother. I'm sorry there's no way I can hunt now."

"Yeah I figured," Mel said as he gathered his hunting gear.

"Sorry Elmer."

"No problem Fudd."

Michaels helped him carry his bow and backpack to his truck while the sun creeped up on the horizon. It was going to be a beautiful day for someone, just not for

Darlene and her family. The two best friends said their goodbyes and Michaels stopped and looked at Darlene's door before he opened his own. He could only imagine the sadness which had now overtaken their lives because of his brief visit.

He laid in his bed and let out a loud sigh. He thought how awful it would have been for Darlene and Roger if someone else had informed them of Edna's death. He lit up a cigarette and smoked only half before it was snuffed out. Drained from the jumble of emotions he had just experienced, his eyes shut.

Stone Cold

It had been three days since Michaels broke the news to his neighbor. He was driving to work smoking a cigarette when he noticed a missed a call from the Dispatch Center. He reached for his phone and called the number.

"Channel five," the man said, who answered the phone. Michaels didn't recognize the voice.

"Hi this is Detective Michaels, someone called me."

"Yes, Sergeant Suit said to meet him at 5566 Blue Herring Ct right away. We got a body discovered."

"Can you tell me where that is?"

"Let me check, umm it's in the community of Chase Landing off Eagles Way in Pasadena. He wants you to let him know when you're on your way."

"Alright, will do thanks." He hung up and reached for his portable radio on the passenger seat.

"Detective 132 to 130."

Tommy answered quickly. "Ronnie, do you have the address?"

"Yes sir."

"See you when you get here." Michaels pushed his foot down on the gas pedal.

When he pulled into the densely populated townhouse community, he easily found the address from the overwhelming number of emergency equipment, police cars and people gathered in one area. Just like every other crime scene, detectives in the Homicide Unit were never the first to arrive but always the last to leave and the ones who remembered the longest. Tommy and Dredge were waiting for Michaels outside the townhomes. They were both talking with very somber looks on their faces. It was cold outside. Of course, those from the unit all donned their trench coats. It was going to be a long night.

He parked near the fire hydrant where his partner was standing. He flipped open his notebook to a clean page and jotted down the address and arrival time. He walked up to Tommy and Dredge who barely acknowledged him. Something was terribly wrong. He could tell from the way they were acting.

"What do we have?"

"We got a body wrapped in a bedsheet stuffed in a drain pipe a few yards from the beach. It was found by a couple of kids coming home from school. We got a young girl sitting at Eastern District Station that's involved somehow. She lives at this address and knows something, but her story keeps changing. Her brother called 911 after she told him her friend was killed. That's all we know so far. Detective Lowe is standing by with her. Ronnie, I need you to go talk to them and find out what happened and get back to us ASAP," Tommy said.

"I'm on it. Do we know who the victim is?"

"Yes, we believe her name is Jenny Chambers. She's 11 years old."

As Michaels was about to leave, he noticed a car coming down the road at a high rate of speed in their direction. He reached for his gun, not knowing what was about to happen. The car pulled in front of the residence where everyone was gathered and slammed on its brakes. The doors swung open and two very concerned parents emerged.

"Where's my baby? Where's my baby? the woman yelled while she and her husband ran through the crowd toward the townhome where Dredge and Tommy stood. They were the parents of Jenny Chambers. "Where's our daughter? Where's my Jenny?" the mother screamed.

Michaels intercepted the parents before Tommy got to them. The mom was running toward the front of the townhouse where the police were keeping anyone from entering. One of the patrol officers standing on the sidewalk stepped in front of the mother and denied her access into the home. Michaels walked up behind the Chambers'. "Folks, folks can I talk to you? I'm Detective Michaels." He took them both over to his car and away from the growing crowd.

"Where is our daughter detective?" Mrs. Chambers pleaded while tears streamed down her face.

"Can you tell me your names please?" The father stepped forward and shook Michaels' hand.

"I'm Rob Chambers, Jenny's father and this is my wife, Kelly. Can you tell us if our daughter is ok?"

"First, I want to tell you both that I just arrived too and we don't know much yet."

"We haven't heard from our daughter and she was supposed to walk home from school with Paige, who lives there," Mrs. Chambers said pointing to the townhouse under guard.

"Has anyone heard from Paige?" Mr. Chambers asked.

He purposefully avoided his question and asked them to describe Jenny and the clothes she was last seen wearing. Mrs. Chambers quickly spouted out Jenny's height and weight, then after fumbling through her purse, pulled out a school photo from her wallet.

"Here, this is my Jenny." She paused and looked at the picture in her trembling hand before she handed it over. "She left for school at 6:30 a.m. like she always does with Paige. I remember, today Jenny was wearing a light blue sweater I had bought her and a pair of blue jeans. She was wearing her light brown winter jacket with fur around the hood and brown boots. I told her how cute she looked." She turned and began crying in her husband's arms.

Since Michaels had not seen the body, he couldn't confirm if it was their daughter laying in the pipe.

"Could you both wait here please? I'll be right back."

"Yes," Mr. Chambers said.

He walked to the front of the townhome to get the full description of the victim. He saw Dredge talking to Ray and Jeff. The crime scene was inside a modest community, part of which backed up to a secluded cove of water, lined with a narrow beach. The border of the cove was partially filled with cattails and debris from a larger body of water, where locals enjoyed boating and other recreational activities.

"Hi fellas."

"Hey Ronnie," Jeff said in a depressing tone.

"Has anyone seen the victim? I have a mother and father at my car whose daughter is missing, and they gave me this picture."

Dredge took a big drag from his cigarette and answered his question with smoke pouring from his mouth.

"The paramedics who arrived first, uncovered the victim slightly to check for vitals, otherwise, none of us has seen her."

"I have a good description of her clothes too if that'll help."

Dredge snatched the picture from Michaels' hand. "Let's go take a look. Bring your camera Jeff. You guys stay here," Dredge said to Ray and Michaels.

Dredge took two slower, deliberate drags from his cigarette then stomped it out on the ground. It was no surprise Jeff already had his camera out snapping pictures while he walked toward the beach where a uniformed officer stood near a drainage pipe submerged into the ground.

"Is this your case?" Ray asked his son.

"No, thank God. This one belongs to Dredge."

"I think it's going to be her Dad. I think it's the daughter of the two parents that just pulled up."

Michaels looked over his shoulder and saw Mr. Chambers holding his wife in his arms. From the look on his face, he could tell they were getting impatient and wanted answers.

Dredge and Jeff walked back up the slope toward Ray and Michaels. Dredge reached in his pocket and retrieved another cigarette. He had a very strange look on his face, one Michaels had never seen. He looked extremely sad. He smoked his cigarette and looked back in the direction of the water where he had just come from.

"It's her." It's definitely her," Jeff said quietly.

He handed Michaels two close-up pictures of the victim's face and neck. They were dreadful. The prominent marks across the front and sides of her neck were a painful scarring of the violence it took to kill her. For a split second, Michaels thought of his own daughter. He looked at Dredge who was still staring at the creek. This one got to him, he could plainly see, so he spoke to him using his real name.

"Dave, do you want me to tell the parents?" He didn't say a word, only continued taking long puffs of his Merritt and blowing them out forcefully. He gave him a moment.

With his back turned, Dave quietly answered. "Yeah please. Would you mind telling them for me?"

"You got it."

With worried looks and tears on their faces, the Chambers saw Michaels walk in their direction. Michaels could feel his heartbeat faster the closer he got. Their beautiful daughter was dead, wrapped in a bed sheet and shoved into a casket that was nothing more than a cold, dirty, cement pipe. Mrs. Chambers pushed herself from her husband's chest and ran toward Michaels. She must have read the look on his face. Her body melted into the ground while she fell at his feet, bursting in tears.

"Where's my Jenny? Where is she? Please tell me she's ok? Please, please." Don't tell me she's gone."

The neighbors standing outside drew their attention to the hysterical mother begging for answers. This was surely not the place where Michaels wanted to deliver such a horrific death notification. Mr. Chambers and Michaels helped her to her feet.

"Let's walk over and get in my car so we can talk."

While they walked, Mrs. Chambers grabbed Michaels by the arm and stopped him in on the sidewalk. "No, tell me where she is. I need to know now," she yelled.

Michaels looked them both in their eyes and pleaded once more. "Can we please get in my car?" Mr. Chambers stood behind his wife as she stared at Michaels. He knew what Michaels was going to say before he uttered a word. He placed both hands on his wife's shoulders. She was not about to take another step. "Just tell me. I need to know where my baby is. Please."

Michaels swallowed once more. "I am very sorry, but your daughter is dead."

Mrs. Chambers dropped to her knees on the sidewalk and screamed. "*NO*". Mr. Chambers practically fell on top of her while they both cried. Michaels knelt beside them, putting his hand on Mr. Chambers's shoulder.

"I am so sorry," Michaels said as he noticed Ray, Jeff and Dredge watching him.

For the next several minutes Michaels stayed with them as they cried. The time came when the Chambers wanted to see their daughter and wanted to know how and why she was killed.

"Where's our daughter? I want to see her. I need to see my baby. Where is she detective?"

"I'm sorry Mr. and Mrs. Chambers but you cannot see her yet. She is part of a crime scene that we have to process for clues."

"Detective, I need to see my daughter now." Mrs. Chambers darted in the direction of the beach screaming her daughter's name. Mr. Chambers gave chase, quickly catching her and grasping onto her arm to stop her attempt to see their daughter's cold, dead body. Michaels joined them a few yards from where they originally stood, both laying in a pile on the ground with their clothes covered in dirt.

"Mrs. Chambers, you have to listen to me. Look at me," Michaels said squatting next to them. By now all who had gathered were watching. "You want us to find your daughter's killer, don't you?"

Mrs. Chambers lifted her head up with grass and dirt embedded in her hair and face. She cried uncontrollably and mumbled the word. "Yes." The three stood up and by now Dredge had joined them.

"Mr. and Mrs. Chambers this is my partner, Detective Dave Hart, with the Homicide Unit. He is the primary detective for your daughter's case. He is the best. He will finish filling you in. You are in good hands, trust me."

Mr. Chambers reached out and shook Michaels' hand. "Thank you, detective."

"I am so sorry guys. Don't worry, we will get the bastard who did this."

Michaels walked over to his car and was about to leave when there was a knocking sound on his window. It was Dredge. "Can I talk to you for a second?" His eyes had an unforgettable look of gloom about them.

"Yeah brother. What's up?"

"Just want to say thanks. I just couldn't do it."

"No problem. That's what partners do right?"

"Yeah. Thanks."

Before he left, Michaels noticed Tommy in a heated discussion with the Eastern District Commander, Captain Mike Gibbons. Tommy's arms were waving in the air and the two looked as if they were ready to exchange blows. He couldn't wait to hear what that conversation was about.

Michaels made it to the Eastern District Police Station to interview the witnesses. "Hi Detective Michaels," the Booking Officer said sitting behind the front desk. "Detective Lowe is in the back with your witnesses."

Michaels was buzzed in through the secure door and walked to the rear of the station. There was a young boy sitting in a chair next to one of the platoon lieutenant's desk. In a nearby interview room sat a petite girl with a black and blue swollen shut left eye, crying in her hands and shaking out of control. Next to her was Detective Bonnie Lowe, from the Sex Crimes Unit. A talented detective with over 20 years on the job, Bonnie was tasked to sit with the young witnesses to keep them calm and she did just that. Bonnie whispered softly in the young girl's ear, then she excused herself to speak with Michaels.

The two walked down the hallway out of earshot. As no surprise, Bonnie had comforted both witnesses, especially the badly battered girl. Thanks to Bonnie and her interview skills, the girl was now willing to talk.

"Ronnie, she keeps saying, *he said he would come back and kill me. He will kill me.* I only got bits and pieces from her so far because she is so traumatized. I can tell you that the person who killed her friend, let her live. That I know for sure."

The Booking Officer stuck her head into the hallway where they were talking. "Excuse me detectives, the children's parents, Mr. and Mrs. Dodd are here."

In the lobby were two very nervous parents in their early 40's, pacing back and forth on the other side of the bullet proof glass. Michaels walked through the door and introduced himself. "Mr. and Mrs. Dodd, I'm Detective Michaels. Your children are here and safe."

"Oh, thank God, can we see them? Are they hurt? Mrs. Dodd asked.

"Folks, I need you to help me with this. I just got here so I haven't had a chance to talk with your children, but another detective has been here trying to make them feel at ease. First, what I know so far is your daughter is lucky to be alive. Both parents held on to each other's arms and tears began to flow. Her friend, Jenny Chambers, was murdered today."

"Oh my God, what happened?" Mrs. Dodd cried out. "Is our son ok?" Mr. Dodd asked.

"Yes, your son, Johnny is alright. Paige is still very frightened. She knows something about the murder, but we just don't know exactly what. Right now, we are not sure how Jenny was killed."

"Dear God, our poor little girl. We need to see her," Mrs. Dodd said.

"I need to tell you this first, so you can prepare yourself. Whoever killed Jenny hit your daughter in the face and blackened her eye. She is severely devastated and clearly in fear for her life."

"God damn motherfucker. I'll kill him. I'll fucking kill him," Mr. Dodd shouted out as he clenched his fist and paced the floor.

"You will need to get her eye looked at when I'm done. Right now, she has an ice pack on it to keep the swelling down but it's pretty bad."

"Fuck," Mr. Dodd yelled out.

"She told your son something about the murder and I need to find out what she said. So, I need you to give me a number I can reach you after I talk to them. Please." There was a moment of silence while Michaels stared into Mrs. Dodd's eyes.

"Can we at least see them so they know we are here?"

"Yes, of course you can. Mr. Dodd, please listen to me. I need you both to stay calm when you see Paige's face."

"I can only say we will try. That's all I can say," Mrs. Dodd said.

"I'll try," Mr. Dodd said under his breath, staring at the ceiling.

"Great, and then I need you to tell them it's ok to talk to me. Will you do that?"

"Yes, I'll do that. They'll talk to you. We've got to find this person. Who would do such a thing?" Mrs. Dodd assured him.

He walked them to the back of the station where their children waited. Seeing their parents, they jumped from their seats and ran into their arms. The four hugged and the children's emotions released in tears. As difficult as it was, both parents tried desperately not to draw attention to Paige's swollen, badly bruised eye.

"Are you guys ok?" Mrs. Dodd asked.

"Can we leave now? Can we? I want to go home," Paige pleaded never once mentioning her injury.

Mrs. Dodd stopped hugging her children and positioned them both in front of her so they could hear her words. "I need you both to listen to me. Your father and I need you both to talk to these nice detectives and tell them everything you know. You must tell the truth so we can catch whoever hurt Jenny. There is nothing to be afraid of anymore Paige, we are all here now. Do you guys hear me?"

"Yes Mommy," Paige said.

"Yes," Johnny responded.

"We will see you in a little bit and we will get something to eat when you're done," Mr. Dodd said to his children. With that, they exchanged one last group hug and Mr. and Mrs. Dodd raced to the front of the building where they shoved the doors open, both bursting into tears in the parking lot.

Michaels decided to first interview Johnny. The longer Bonnie was with Paige the more relaxed she would be and easier to interview. Before he took Johnny to the squad room, he opened the door slowly to the room where Paige and Bonnie sat. Paige still had an unforgettable look of fear on her face as the tears dripped onto her lap. Sitting close to her, Bonnie had her arm around her shoulders and was telling her softly, "Everything will be alright. You're safe now. Nothing will happen to you." Michaels knew how fortunate he was to have someone as experienced and compassionate as Bonnie there to help.

"Hi Paige. Can I get you something to drink, like a soda or water?"

With her head hung down she nodded and barely mumbled, "Yes, a Coke please."

Michaels went to the vending machine outside the squad room and retrieved two drinks and potato chips for her and her brother.

"Here you go Paige, one ice cold Coke and some chips in case you're hungry. I'm going to talk with your brother while you and Ms. Bonnie hang out, and then you and I will talk ok?"

"Yes sir," she said lifting her head to take the drink from his hand. "Thank you."

Michaels couldn't believe how horrible she looked. *Only a fucking monster could do such a thing to such a precious little girl like her,* he thought.

He took Johnny to the adjacent unoccupied squad room. "Have a seat buddy." They both sat next to each other in old wooden chairs with flip up desk attachments for the officers to use at lineup.

"Thanks for being patient Johnny. As you can imagine, this is a very big deal."

"Yes sir," he said respectfully.

"How old are you?"

"I'm 15."

"You seem like a very mature young man. What grade are you in?"

"10th."

"I want to start by telling you how important it is that you be very honest with me, just like your mom said. You must tell the truth. Do you understand?" he said sternly.

"Yes sir. I will."

"Listen, I think you already know but your sister's friend, Jenny, was killed today."

"Yes," he said looking down at his feet.

"Now tell me what happened after school today." Michaels had his notebook open and was ready to write.

"When I came home, Paige was on the couch crying and her whole body was shaking like she was freezing. I asked what was wrong and she told me Jenny was dead. I didn't believe her. I said, what? And that's when she lifted her head and I saw her eye. I couldn't believe it. I said, what happened? She said she couldn't tell me or he would kill her too. She was crying so hard I figured she was telling the truth."

Michaels was writing and flipping pages in his notebook as fast as he could. "What did you say next?"

"I said who is going to kill you? And she said that big Mexican kid who lives down the street."

"What Mexican boy was she referring to Johnny?"

"I don't know his name. He's a big kid in high school. He lives somewhere in the back of the community near the water."

The pages in his notebook filled quickly. "And then what did you say?"

"I asked if that kid was still in our house and she said no, he would come back and kill her if she told anyone. That's when I called 911 and then I called my mom."

Michaels finished with his final notations, then patted the brave young man on his shoulder. "Thank you, Johnny. You are a brave man and you did the right thing. Your parents are going to be very proud of you. Stay put and I'm going to talk with your sister. Let me know if you need anything."

"Yes sir," he sighed with a big sense of relief.

Michaels walked into the interview room and was pleasantly surprised to hear Bonnie and Paige talking about their favorite thing to do, shop for clothes. Bonnie was a master with interviews and interrogations. She had the innate ability to gain a witness's trust, allowing them to talk more freely. Now, this once questionable witness was ready to tell her story.

Bonnie scooted over allowing him to pull up a chair and sit close to Paige. She was holding a Ziploc bag of ice on her eye. She pulled it from her face and stared at him with a look of desperation. Her eye had completely swollen shut. It angered him so much to think some animal could do such a despicable thing. This innocent child was harmed beyond belief.

"Paige, I just spoke to Johnny and he told me what you said to him. I know the big Mexican boy down the street threatened you but like Ms. Bonnie told you, we are all here and will keep you safe. You don't need to worry anymore Hun," he said while clutching onto her little hand.

Tears poured from her eyes and her hand was cold and shaking.

"But I'm scared. He said he would kill me." Tears streamed faster down her face like a faucet.

"He will never harm you. Never. I promise Paige. That's why I need you to tell me what happened, so we can arrest him and put him in jail forever. We must get him and fast."

She covered her face with both hands and cried. She was petrified. Her emotions weighed heavily on Michaels. Unexpectedly, she uncovered her face and looked at Bonnie with the saddest eyes he had ever seen.

"It's ok Paige. He's here to help you," Bonnie assured her.

"I'll tell you," she softly uttered.

"Take your time Paige. Start from the beginning and I'm going to write down some notes in my book while you are talking."

"O, O, ok". Me and Jenny got off the bus and walked to my house after school. We went in through the back-slider door that we always keep unlocked in case I forget my key. Jenny wanted to wear one of my shirts for school tomorrow." With her trembling hand, she took a sip of her drink, then stared down at the table. She was reliving the horror.

"Take your time. It's fine."

"I went upstairs to my bedroom and when I walked in my room…" Paige's entire body shook, and tears dropped one by one on the table. Michaels continued to hold her hand. "It's ok Paige."

"He grabbed me and put his hand over my mouth. His hand was so big it covered my whole face. It was hard to breathe."

Michaels pen dropped from his hand. He stopped writing.

"He had been hiding behind my door and that's when he swung me around and hit me in the face. It all happened so fast. I think I was knocked out or something, I'm not sure."

Michaels couldn't believe what he was hearing. "Go on Paige."

"I didn't want to do it," she said looking back and forth at Bonnie and Michaels. "I swear I didn't, but he made me. He made me," she cried out.

"What Honey? What did he make you do?" he asked.

"He said he would kill me if I didn't call Jenny upstairs. I didn't want to do it, I didn't want to do it," she cried harder.

"I know you didn't Paige. We understand sweetie, you had to, you had no choice. It's not your fault. Look at me Paige," he said softly. "Do you hear me?" He gently put his hand under her chin and lifted her face. "It's not your fault."

With tears running down her swollen, sad face she said, "he strangled her with my hair dryer cord in front of me while I sat on my bed. I watched Jenny die and then she dropped to the floor like she wasn't even real."

Paige laid her head on the desk and sobbed. The detectives were speechless. They both pictured the nightmare vividly in their minds. Telling the story was a relief to this frightened little child.

"Let's take a little break. Would you like another Coke?"

"No, but can I use the bathroom?"

"Sure Honey lets go to the bathroom and freshen you up a bit. I'll take my purse with me." With that, Bonnie held Paige's hand and walked her down the hall like she was her own child. He watched as they walked away and thought how fortunate Paige was to be alive.

He waited in the room and wrote down everything she had said. Several minutes later, Bonnie returned still holding Paige's hand. She sat back down and took a big sip of her drink. He could tell Bonnie must have brushed her hair and straitened up her shirt and pants.

"Thanks Bon."

"Oh, no problem. We just had a little girl time, didn't we?" Paige nodded her head and smiled. It was apparent she felt much better now that she told some of her story.

"You are doing great. Let's get you settled so you can tell us what happened next?"

She took another taste of her drink and took in a big breath. "He told me to take the sheet off my bed. I didn't know what he wanted it for, so I did, then he made me help him wrap Jenny up." She covered her face and continued to cry once more. "He told me if I told anybody, I would be an accomplice to murder, because I helped him." Petrified, she looked over at Bonnie. "Am I going to jail?"

Michaels looked over at Bonnie. He could see her eyes were filled with tears. It may have been the saddest words they had ever heard. Bonnie got up from her chair and hugged the crying child.

"No, no, no sweetie you're not going to jail. You did nothing wrong Paige. Nothing Honey. I swear to you." The two hugged for a few minutes while Michaels sat looking down at his notebook. After a brief period, Bonnie removed her arms from around Paige, wiped her eyes and returned to her seat.

"What happened next."

"We carried her down the steps, and, and, he yelled at me because I couldn't lift her. She was too heavy. He picked her up and I remember seeing her eyes when the sheet fell off her face. She didn't look real. Then he made me help him drag her outside and down to the beach. He said he didn't want anyone to catch us. We dragged her over to that pipe thing and he stuffed her inside."

She put the bag of melting ice on the table, still crying, she laid her head down in her arms. "That's when he grabbed my neck with his big hand and started choking me, saying if I told anybody I'd end up in there with Jenny. He turned and ran between the buildings toward the road." She slowly raised her head and looked at Bonnie and Michaels. "Am I in trouble?" Michaels' heart nearly stopped beating.

"Absolutely not. You are not in trouble. We are all so proud of you," he said looking deep into her eyes while squeezing her hand.

"Can I go home now? Please?"

"Sure you can. Ms. Bonnie will stay here with you while I go call my boss."

Michaels walked quickly to the front desk where the Booking Officer sat and grabbed the station's portable radio to contact Tommy. "Detective 132 to 130."

Ray's voice came over the radio. "Detective 132, stand by, I'll get him."

After a long pause Tommy answered. "Go ahead Ronnie."

"Call me at Eastern District as soon as possible please." In seconds the Booking Officer answered the phone and it was Tommy.

"How's it going?"

"I know what happened now. What have you guys done at the scene so far?"

Michaels was worried they had disturbed the crime scene in Paige's bedroom not knowing what had taken place or where.

"Not a whole lot Ronnie, just photographs. We're waiting for you."

Michaels could tell from his voice that Tommy was bothered by something because he was calling him Ronnie, not Shithead. Something was up.

"My God Tommy, I don't know why this poor little girl is still alive. Her story is so sad. She told me the girl in the pipe was killed in her room upstairs. This guy, who she called Mexican, strangled Jenny with her hair dryer cord right in front of her and then he made her wrap the body in her bedsheet and drag it down the beach to the pipe. He scared the shit out of her. He said she'd end up in the pipe too if she told anyone. Bonnie and I both believe her."

There was a long silence on the phone. "How much longer will you be?"

"I'm done. I just need to run these two kids home."

"We'll see you when you get here."

Michaels walked toward the interview room and could hear laughter coming from inside. When he got to the room, there sat Bonnie, Johnny and Paige laughing. *Bonnie was a class-act* he thought to himself.

"Ok guys, you two ready to go?"

Both children shouted *yes* at the same time.

Michaels heard the Booking Officer call his name over the loudspeaker. There was a call holding. He took a seat at one of the lieutenant's desk. "Detective Michaels."

"What's going on young man." It was Dredge.

"I'm getting ready to leave. What the hell is going on over there?"

"Captain Gibbons wanted to come into the scene and Tommy wouldn't let him."

"What do you mean Tommy wouldn't let him? Tommy's only a sergeant."

"Oh yeah it's a real shit storm. Tommy said he would lock him up for tampering with evidence if he came in. Tommy asked for Captain Donoho to respond to the scene."

"Wow. Well I got statements from both kids and I'm taking them home now. I'll be there as soon as I can."

He slammed down the phone in frustration knowing he was walking into a scene busting with male egos and power trips.

Michaels called the telephone number Mr. Dodd had given him. Mr. Dodd said he, his wife and their third child were at his sister's townhouse a few streets over from where the incident occurred. He was glad to hear how good his children did and that they would be home soon.

Bonnie and Michaels walked down the corridor behind Paige and her brother. It was touching to see Johnny lay his arm around her shoulders while they walked side by side. It was nice to see, knowing children that age don't typically care enough about their sibling to do such a thing.

In the parking lot Michaels thanked Bonnie sincerely for all her help and they said their goodbyes while the children anxiously climbed in the back of Michaels' car.

"How would you guys like an ice cream from McDonald's?" Michaels asked in a cheery tone.

Johnny immediately yelled out. "I would."

"Paige, how about you Hun?"

"Ok."

Paige was sitting very close to her brother in the back seat. He couldn't bear to think of the nightmares and psychological issues she would endure for years to come.

At the local McDonald's Michaels got Johnny a caramel sundae and two vanilla ice creams for Paige and himself. He parked in the lot to enjoy their treat. Paige put her fresh ice bag on the floor, removed the ice cream lid and dug in. Johnny already had his open and was eating so fast he complained of having brain freeze after three bites. Paige and Michaels both laughed.

"Do you guys play any kind of sports?" Michaels asked trying to keep the conversation light.

Surprisingly Paige spoke first. "I'm on the Riviera Beach soccer team," she blurted out in excitement.

"I'm going to play baseball again this year. I'm a pitcher and a catcher," Johnny said with a mouth full of ice cream.

"Wow that's great guys. You know Paige, I used to play soccer."

She looked up at him with her swollen face. "Yeah one time someone kicked a ball real high in the air and I tilted my head back to hit it off my forehead, but I misjudged the ball and it hit me square in the nose and I fell right on my back," Michaels said.

Both children laughed as they watched the animated detective act out the memory from the front seat. "I was so embarrassed, my nose was bleeding, I was dizzy and couldn't even walk for a bit."

The three talked more and eventually drove from the lot to reunite them with their parents. It was odd, Michaels thought, how he was in no rush to get to the crime scene. It seemed more important to stay with his witnesses and make sure they were ok, especially Paige.

The address where Mr. and Mrs. Dodd waited was four streets away from the crime scene. When Michaels pulled up, Paige quickly opened the door and ran to her parents, standing outside. Johnny was preparing to follow behind when Michaels spoke to him. "Johnny, I'm real proud of you. You were a brave young man. Make sure you take care of your sister."

"Yes sir. I will. Thank you," and with that he bolted from the car to join his family hugging on the front porch. Michaels sat briefly in his car and watched them embrace.

Mr. Dodd walked over to Michaels' car. "How'd she do?"

"They both did very good. You have great kids Mr. Dodd. Paige went through a lot and I mean a lot. Her best friend was killed right in front of her and he made her, and I mean made her help him hide the body. She is beyond petrified. He threatened to come back and kill her. I'm telling you this because she is very scared, and you and your wife are going to need to stick close to her and get her professional help. As for your home, it's a crime scene. This bastard killed Jenny in Paige's bedroom, so we need to process the entire house for evidence."

The children went inside the home with their aunt and Mrs. Dodd joined Michaels and her husband at the car. "Can you tell me what happened?"

"I just told your husband; your daughter is lucky to be alive. In fact, I really don't know why she is." Mrs. Dodd began crying.

"Dear God, please tell us what happened."

He replayed every detail to them. They were speechless. They both cried and held one another. It was as if he were telling them of a horror movie starring their daughter. They listened, trembled and cried as he spoke.

"Do you know who this kid is she's calling Mexican?" They both looked down. They were thinking.

"No, I really can't think right now. There are so many kids in this community," Mr. Dodd said.

"Did she say what he looked like? Or how old he was?" Mrs. Dodd asked.

"She said he was a big kid and was in high school."

"Johnny has a yearbook in his room if that will help," Mr. Dodd offered.

"That's a great idea. I'll make sure we take that with us. Thank you. Let me warn you folks, when we do find out who he is, I'll have to come back with a photographic line up and have Paige pick him out."

"Oh my God, will he see her? Will she have to see him?" Mrs. Dodd asked in fear for her daughter.

"No ma'am, it will just be pictures, that's all. I would never do that to her, I can assure you."

"We need to stay somewhere else for a while Babe. We can't let her back in there now," Mrs. Dodd said to her husband.

"I know," he said to her.

"I have to leave and get to your house and see how things are going."

They both thanked Michaels and remained in the parking lot holding one another crying as he drove off.

The crowd had thinned out at the scene and only one uniformed officer stood outside the front door. Michaels walked up and realized it was his police academy buddy, Officer Rick Gavigan. After a quick reunion, Rick allowed Michaels inside.

"Hi Dad," Michaels said to Ray walking down the steps.

"Hey Ronnie," Ray said carrying two large brown evidence bags in each hand.

"Young Shithead," Dredge said somewhat loudly walking behind Ray.

"Dredge, did you find the hair dryer?"

"Yeah, Jeff recovered it, along with a lot of fingerprints."

Michaels walked upstairs to Paige's bedroom. At the top of the steps, he saw Jeff on his knees vacuuming the carpet in the first room on the right, belonging to Paige. Jeff was so thorough. Given the violent nature of this crime, Jeff was hoping for a hair or two from our suspect.

"Just about done Shithead," Jeff said as he made a few more strokes across the carpet and backed out of the doorway. "It's all yours. Let me know if you see anything else. I'll be downstairs." He gathered his supplies from the hallway and joined the others in the living room.

Michaels stood at the doorway of Paige's bedroom. There was something about the room that called for respect, like a sacred burial ground. The movie raced through his mind in fast motion. He could vividly see a big bodied kid, cinching down on the dryer cord wrapped around Jenny's neck cutting off the breath of life to the startled girl. He pictured her struggling to no avail with her tiny hands and weak arms to release the pressure from the tightening cord. He could see her body fall to the floor like a rag doll, while Paige watched her die.

It was a small room, 10' x 12'. The bed where Paige sat after being punched in the face, was three feet from where she witnessed her friend's brutal death. Michaels stood at the foot of the bed and looked out the window. He wanted to kill this person and end his life, showing no mercy while doing so. The bed was now stripped of its sheets and fingerprint powder was everywhere. There was powder on the foot board, headboard, walls, jewelry box and on the bedside light. When processing a crime scene, detectives and technicians have one shot to get what was needed. It didn't matter if you needed to take part of a wall, a ceiling, a piece of floor or carpet. If it was thought to be evidence, you took it.

After a few minutes, Michaels joined everyone in the living room. "Tommy, what the hell happened today with Capt. Gibbons?"

"Ah, nothing. He just wanted to be nosey and come in here where he had no business. Deputy Chief Russell had to tell him to back the fuck off and leave."

"No fucking way, Damn. You're the fucking man."

Tommy blew it off as nothing, but those at the scene knew there weren't many sergeants who would have told a captain he wasn't entering a crime scene. Tommy had balls, big balls.

While the scene was being processed, Donald and Mark canvassed the neighborhood. Their job was to find anyone who knew the identity of the teenager Paige described. Michaels was talking to Dredge in the living room when Donald busted through the front door. "We got it, we got it." Mark strolled in behind him carrying Paige's yearbook in his hand.

"Calm down son, what did you boys find?" Tommy questioned.

"He lives right down the street. He is a big motherfucker and is only 17. One of the kids a few houses down knew him from Northeast High School. He's a loner and he's got a temper. He found him in the yearbook," Donald said struggling to contain himself. "His name is Peter Alonso. Mark ran his name and found he was charged last month with assault, so his prints are on file if you have any for comparison."

Honing in on the news, Jeff immediately turned to Ray. "Do me a favor and gather up everything here. I'm going to Headquarters to call in a Fingerprint Examiner and pull Alonso's fingerprints. "What bag has the prints we lifted from the bedroom?"

Ray reached down and handed Jeff a clear evidence bag. Jeff walked quickly toward the front door.

"Dredge, I'll let you know what I find."

"Thanks Jeff."

"Good job guys," Tommy said to Donald and Mark.

"What do you need now Dredge?" Donald asked.

Dredge paused and Tommy filled the gap. "I need you guys to put together a photographic lineup with Alonso to show our witness.

"You got it boss. Come on Poodle. We're out of here," Donald said in his typical hyper fashion to Mark. Once again it was true teamwork.

Tommy, Dredge and Michaels went outside to smoke while Ray loaded his van with evidence bags and equipment from the scene. It was now cold and dark, and the crowd had diminished to just a few onlookers. "Follow me boys. We need coffee," Tommy said knowing they had a long night ahead of them and it was only 7:00 p.m. "Call the Dodd's now Dredge and tell them we are finishing up. I gotta get out of here."

Dredge placed a phone call to the cell number. "Mr. Dodd, this is Detective Dave Hart, we met briefly earlier."

"Yes Detective."

"We are just about finished here at your house, so whenever you and your wife want to return, it's up to you." Dredge could hear people crying loudly in the background.

"Thank you. I'll talk to my wife, but chances are we won't be going back anytime soon. That would be way too much for Paige."

"I understand. Just so you know, we are not saying anything to the press, but we believe we have an idea who the suspect may be. I'll let you know more later."

"Who is he? Tell me who he is. I want to kill that son-of-a-bitch."

"Mr. Dodd, I can't tell you that yet. We are still working on a lot of things to verify who he is. Don't worry, I'll let you know if we arrest him." Dredge could hear a woman yelling loudly in the background. *Who is it?*

Dredge ended the call, locked up the house and the scene was relinquished. On the way to the office Michaels had a burning desire to hear his daughter's voice. He imagined what the two families were feeling, and he knew nothing in the world could be as bad as this. Nothing. He called Stacey's cell and Nicole answered.

"Hi Daddy."

"Hi Sweetie-Pie. How's my favorite daughter in the whole wide world?"

"I'm good. Guess what?"

"What Honey?"

"Me and Mommy are going to the movies. We're going to see Shrek."

"Cool beans, that looks like a good movie."

"I know. Mommy said I got to hang up now because we are here. Bye Daddy, I love you."

"I love you too. Bye." Hearing her voice made him smile.

When he made it back to the CID, he could hear Donald laughing halfway across the building. In their office area, Donald was standing at his desk, drinking a coffee and once again, wearing everything but his suit pants, acting as if nothing was out of the ordinary. Michaels sat down and kicked his feet up on his desk and lit a cigarette.

"Must you smoke in here Michaels?" Mark questioned in his normal condescending tone.

"Hey, your partner's smoking, why aren't you on his ass? I'm sorry your majesty, please allow me to let some fresh air in for his Highness." Michaels propped open the back door while Donald laughed at the show in front of him.

A couple of minutes passed, when in walked Dredge and Tommy.

"Dredge here's your line-up," Donald said as he handed him a tan manila folder.

"Thanks." He took the folder and sat at his desk.

"Coffee Dredge?" Michaels asked.

"Sure, Young Shithead, thanks." Tommy walked over and stood behind Dredge as they both looked at the photographic lineup Donald had put together. They both busted out laughing.

"You asshole," Dredge said in his deep monotone voice, throwing the folder down in front of him.

"What? What? You don't think it will fly?" Donald questioned with a big smile on his face. Dredge handed Michaels the folder and cracked up laughing. Inside were eight 4" x 4" black and white mugshots, neatly taped and numbered sequentially above each. The problem was, there were seven white males and only one Hispanic male, the suspect, along with three big red arrows pointing to his face. It was typical Donald humor and just at the right time, when it wasn't expected.

Donald strolled over to Dredge's desk in his striped boxer shorts, still laughing, and handed him the real lineup.

"Now that's better," Dredge said as he opened the folder and studied the pictures. "Thanks, but you're still an asshole."

"My pleasure brother."

The five sat and talked about the case until they decided to grab a bite to eat at Kaufmann's Restaurant. Before they left, Dredge contacted Mr. Dodd and arranged to come by and show Paige the photos at 9:00 p.m. Dredge knew that would be late, but it was crucial.

After dinner, the entire unit ventured back to the office. Tommy called Jeff to learn the status of the fingerprint analysis but, disappointingly, he said he was still waiting for one of the examiners to arrive. The fingerprint examiners worked day shift and it took several calls to find one available to come in. Jeff said the only one he could reach lived an hour away.

Tommy sent Mark and Donald home since they worked all morning, especially if he needed fresh detectives in case something came in overnight or the next day. Dredge retrieved the folder from his desk and he and Michaels set out to see Paige.

They got to the residence where the Dodd's were staying just before 9:00 p.m. Dredge and Michaels were worried Paige might be sleeping and not have a clear mind to look at the pictures. Since Dredge had never seen Paige, Michaels warned him of the damage Alonso had inflicted on her face. In his usual way, he just looked at his partner and nodded with a shake of his head.

Parked out front, Dredge handed Michaels the lineup, "You should do this since she knows you." Michaels agreed, knowing once you have built up a rapport with a witness, especially a young one, you shouldn't keep introducing new people to the equation.

Mr. Dodd was standing in the doorway as the two walked up. "Good timing. We just got home from the hospital." Mrs. Dodd and Paige were sitting side by side on the couch holding one another.

"Hi Paige," Michaels said in a chipper tone.

"Hi," she answered in a very low voice with her eye wrapped in a white gauze, holding a pack of dried ice over the wound.

"What did they say at the hospital?" Michaels asked.

"The x-rays showed three hairline fractures around her eye."

"Paige, this is my partner, Detective Hart."

"Hi Paige."

"Hi," she said barely lifting her head

Michaels knelt next to Paige and her mom on the couch. It was the critical time to show her the photo lineup.

"Paige, remember when you and I were talking earlier at the police station?"

"Yes."

"Remember I said I might have to show you some pictures to see if you could pick out the mean boy who hit you?"

"Yes."

"I need you to take your time and look at these and tell me if he is in here, Ok?"

It got very quiet in the room. Mrs. Dodd and Michaels looked at one another. He opened the folder and handed it to Paige. Her eyes scanned all eight pictures, then stopped. The folder shuttered back and forth in her hands. Her eyes filled with tears, as she was reliving the nightmare. She extended her tiny finger and pointed at picture #5, Peter Alonso.

"That's him."

She dropped the folder from her grip and buried her head into her mother's chest, crying hysterically. Mrs. Dodd wrapped her arms around her and pulled her close. "It's alright. You did great. These men are going to put him in jail. You never have to worry about him. Never."

Once she calmed down Paige initialed the back of the photograph and put the date and time on it as well. It was all over for Alonso now.

Mr. Dodd followed the detectives outside for an update. He looked as if he had aged 10 years since they last saw him a few hours ago. "I want to kill this bastard. Do you hear me? Where does he live?" he said trying to temper the anger in his voice.

"I know," Dredge said. "I have a daughter about the same age. Just let us do our job please."

"So what now?"

"We are waiting to see if we get a match on one of the prints lifted from Paige's bedroom," Dredge told him.

"And if you don't?"

"Then we will get an arrest warrant based on her identification. We just like to stack the deck when building a murder case," Michaels assured him.

"We'll keep you posted Mr. Dodd. Is there any certain time you would prefer not to be called when we make an arrest?" Dredge asked.

"No, no call me any time. I don't care what time it is. I want to know this asshole has been locked up."

"Ok, we'll be in touch," Michaels said.

Back in Dredge's car, his cell phone rang. "Get that Shithead."

"Detective Hart's secretary. Can I help you?"

It was Tommy. "Jeff got a positive match on Alonso's fingerprints from the hair dryer and the dresser. He's fucked now."

"Good, that's good."

"How'd it go over there?"

"Real good. She picked him out."

"See you in a few."

Back in the office, Dredge and Michaels began working on two arrest warrants and a search & seizure warrant for Peter Alonso. Both warrants charged the 17 year old as an adult. One charged him with the heinous first degree murder of 11 year old Jenny Chambers and the second for the brutal first degree assault of 13 year old Paige Dodd. Dredge was also seeking a Search & Seizure Warrant for Alonso's DNA, confident they would find his hair in Paige's room thanks to Jeff's thoroughness.

With the unit's trusty typewriter in front of Dredge and Michaels working on his desktop computer, they both sat briskly hunting and pecking on their keyboards each detailing probable cause on the affidavits. They couldn't wait to come face to face and lock up this ruthless piece of shit. Michaels was done with the search & seizure warrant before Dredge had finished both arrest warrants. To save time Michaels threw a late night phone call to Judge Williams, like he had done so many times in the past. Dredge and Tommy would eventually take the warrant affidavits to the Commissioner's office in Annapolis, while Michaels waited patiently for Judge Williams' signature. Alonso's life was about to change.

As always, Judge Williams was glad to see Michaels. It was 11:00 p.m. and he was in his living room dressed in his robe, pajamas and slippers. When he knocked on the door, the Judge waved him in.

"Good evening Your Honor, thanks for this."

"No problem at all. How's the new job in Homicide?"

"It's going good Judge. But I'll tell ya, it's a lot different than buying drugs for a living."

"Oh, I'm sure it is. What brings you out tonight?"

"I have an affidavit for blood, hair and saliva. This is a bad one Your Honor and so sad."

Michaels sat and watched Judge Williams' face while he flipped through the three pages of probable cause. Several times he shook his head in disgust and grunted in disbelief.

"This is like a mini horror story." He lowered the papers to his lap and looked at the detective.

"I know Judge. That little girl is lucky to be alive."

"She sure is." He picked up his pen and without a second thought, began signing the pages.

"Good luck and be careful."

"Thank you Judge, and sorry to bother you so late."

"That's no problem. It's good to see you again," he said walking him to the front door.

Michaels immediately called Tommy's cell phone when he got into his car. "I'm all signed. What about you guys?"

"Meet us at the entrance of Chase Landing. Let's go get this motherfucker," Tommy angrily said.

"On my way." Michaels stomped on the gas pedal.

By the time he arrived it was midnight. Tommy and Dredge were standing next to Tommy's car.

"Ronnie, the house is dark and there's a silver Cadillac parked in front registered to the suspect's father. If he's home, I want you to transport him to the CID and we'll follow. See what he says to you in the car. Got it?"

"Yes sir."

"Then let's go" Tommy ordered.

Michaels jumped in his car and grabbed his handcuffs. They were finally on their way to arrest this poor excuse of a human being. When they pulled up to the Alonso address, Dredge led the way. He pounded on the door repeatedly until a Hispanic man in his 40's answered.

"Mr. Alonso?" Dredged asked the man standing with a look of surprise across his face.

"Yes, what's wrong?" he asked noticing the uniformed officer and the others standing behind Dredge.

"Is your son here?"

"Of course he is, he's upstairs."

Without asking, Dredge pushed himself past the man and into the foyer.

"Hey, hey, what are you doing?"

"I have a warrant. Where is your son?" Dredge was different. He was visibly angry.

By now everyone had followed Dredge into the home and the five stood in the living room, when they heard movement on the stairs. A large male walked down slowly. It was the bastard they came for, Peter Alonso. Dredge immediately moved toward the stairway, which surprised Michaels, since he had never seen Dredge move with such aggression.

"Peter Alonso, you are under arrest," Dredge announced.

Funny thing was, Peter didn't say anything when Dredge spoke. He didn't ask what or why he was being arrested. He said absolutely nothing. His father, James, responded like most parents and asked what his son had done wrong. He wanted to know what he was being charged with and where he was being taken, but Dredge wasn't answering his questions. His son was a cruel, heartless killer who was being charged as an adult and he was going to be treated like one.

Michaels grabbed Peter's arms and instructed him to put his hands behind his back. With this, Peter's father lunged toward them in a fit of rage. In a flash, the towering uniformed officer wrapped his long powerful arm around Mr. Alonso's neck, stopping him instantly with a choke hold.

"Let my son go," he shouted.

"Sir, if you don't want to go to jail tonight too, I suggest you calm down," the officer warned him.

"Alright, I just want to know why my son is being arrested." The officer loosened his grip.

"I'll call a lawyer son. Don't worry. I'll get you out of this."

With Peter's hands behind his back, Michaels latched the cuffs tightly on the killer's large wrists and escorted him from the home to the front passenger seat of his car. From the house, you could hear Mr. Alonso shouting something inaudible to his son. In a matter of three minutes the arrest was made, and Michaels was alone transporting this killer to the CID.

The trip to Crownsville was eerily quiet. Michaels was alone in a car with a vile, brutal murderer, someone who killed just for the sake of killing. *What was he thinking?* Michaels wondered. *Did he have any remorse? Did he want to escape and kill me?* He looked in his rearview mirror and could see Tommy and Dredge following behind. Dredge was on the phone.

"Mr. Chambers, this is Detective Hart. I'm sorry to call you so late."

"That's ok. We're all still up. Did you get him?" he asked while crying.

"Yes sir, we did. We just arrested a young man who lives just a few streets away from the Dodd's. We are taking him now to the Criminal Investigation Division to interrogate him. I just wanted to give you an update."

"Thank God. Honey, they just arrested a person in the community. What's his name detective? I'm going to put you on speaker phone so my wife and the others can hear."

"Peter Patrick Alonso. He's 17 years old and goes to Northeast High School. He's been charged with 1st Degree Murder and 1st Degree Assault. The press doesn't know yet, so we need to keep this quiet until we finish our interview. I'm just telling you and the Dodd family. How about I give you a call in the morning and fill you in."

"Thanks for the call. My family thanks you. Good luck."

"Goodbye Mr. Chambers."

Michaels watched Tommy's car through his mirror. Neither seemed to be paying attention to Michaels. He looked over at Alonso. He wanted to kill him. Approaching a barren intersection with a red traffic signal, he looked at Alonso with his head slumped down. He showed no emotions. Michaels could do whatever he wanted, including putting a single bullet, justifiably, through his head in self-defense. They stopped at the red light and he looked back at Tommy and Dredge. Just as quickly as the car came to a stop, his hand was gripped tightly on his gun with the cold, steel barrel pressed firmly against Alonso's left temple. He squeezed the trigger and watched as chunks of skull, hair and brains spattered against the window. His head drooped with a massive gaping hole. There sat Alonso, dead. His graphic daydream was interrupted when his phone rang. It was Dredge.

Dredge was talking very quietly. "Is he saying anything?"

"No sir."

"Ok."

They arrived at the CID at 1:00 a.m. Michaels parked close to the building taking the captain's reserved space. He unbuckled Alonso's seatbelt and before he could get out, Tommy and Dredge were already opening his passenger door.

"Let's get him inside and get this show on the road," Tommy instructed.

"Get out," Dredge said while pulling Alonso by the arm from the car.

The four walked quietly to the back of the office. As expected, the building was vacant. Dredge led the way holding tightly to Alonso's left arm. He stopped and opened the door to the interview room. He left the handcuffs on and instructed him to sit down on the chair, furthest from the door near the wall. The small 7' x 8' room was equipped with a 6 foot table, two padded chairs and one metal framed chair with a hard wooden seat for the suspect. Like the rest of the building, it was an old red brick room with no windows located adjacent to Tommy's office, directly across from the coffee room. Dredge threw his car keys on his desk, hung his jacket on the coat rack and pulled out his notebook.

"I'll start the Press Release," Tommy said as he peeled off into his office.

"I'll make us some coffee," Michaels said while Dredge jotted down some notes.

Within minutes Dredge, who was now standing next to his desk with a Miranda Rights form in his hand ready to start the interview with Alonso.

"Ready?" Dredge asked.

"He's all yours partner," Michaels said. They each poured a cup of coffee and made their way into the interview room.

"Stand up," Dredge said firmly to Alonso when they entered. For the first time, Michaels got a real sense of how big this kid truly was. He weighed at least 240 pounds and was a least 6'3". His body seemed massive. His enormous size alone had to be intimidating to Paige.

Dredge removed the handcuffs and he and Michaels sat on each side of the table facing him, He avoided eye contact at all cost.

There are two big hurdles to get past in an interrogation of this magnitude. First was the acknowledgement of the Miranda Rights and the agreement to talk without an attorney present. The second was getting a full or partial confession. Both detectives have always found the best way to get past either was by one of two ways or a combination of both. One way was to establish a trusting rapport with the scum from the get-go. Let him know you are there for him and no matter what he did, you really couldn't blame him. The other technique was to be a straight up asshole and constantly berate the person, calling him a liar every time he opened his mouth, while your partner would sit idle in the room and watch his body language for telltale signs when he is lying. It's the science of good cop, bad cop, which most people do not understand the true complexity of. Regardless of the style used, Michaels preferred the trusting approach to get the suspect to talk without a lawyer.

Dredge laid the handcuffs on the table as a visual reminder to Alonso. "Peter, I'm Detective Hart and this is Detective Michaels. We are going to talk to you but before we do so, I have to read you your rights." Alonso did not speak or bother to raise his head.

Dredge read the first right. "You have the right to remain silent." The two looked at Alonso. "Did you hear me?" Alonso said nothing. "Peter, I can't get your side of the story until we get through these. So, do you understand your first right?" Dredge said irritated.

Alonso lifted his head and looked at Dredge. "Yeah."

"Good, now initial next to each one of these as we go along so we can talk." Dredge handed him his pen which seemed to dwarf in his large hand when he took hold. Dredge ran quickly through the remainder of the rights, which Alonso acknowledged. Finally, at the end he agreed to talk without an attorney present and signed the form.

The first hurdle had been crossed. This was good, but what wasn't, was the feeling Michaels was getting from Dredge. He knew if he could feel it, so could the suspect. You could practically see the steam coming from Dredge's ears and it wasn't fake. You could tell how much he disliked Alonso and Michaels wasn't feeling very confident about a confession at this point. This was no interview tactic, no good cop bad cop, just a pissed off detective who couldn't stop thinking of the victim stuffed in the drain pipe and his own 15 year old daughter.

"Tell us what you did yesterday Peter," Dredge asked firmly.

In interviews or interrogations, Dredge and Michaels always had the lead detective do the talking while the other took notes. Tonight, taking notes was Michaels' job. Alonso sat still without answering and Dredge began shifting in his chair.

"Peter, tell me what you did yesterday after school." This time Dredge said it louder and leaned toward him.

With his head still down, Peter spoke. "I went to school and then walked home to my house and stayed in my bedroom."

"And what did you do in your bedroom?"

He paused, "I laid in bed."

"You laid in bed. And who was home when you got there?"

"My dad came home," he said revealing a cocky smirk.

"I suggest you wipe that fucking grin off your face. I asked you who was home when you got there?" Dredge was hot.

"No one."

Michaels could see they were getting nowhere so he chimed in. "Did you watch any TV before your dad came home?" Michaels was trying to pin down a time based on whatever show he was watching.

"Nope."

Dredge stood up and leaned over in Alonso's face. "You're a fucking liar. We know exactly where you were and what you did. Now let's start all over again and tell us what the fuck you did after school."

Peter did not respond. This interrogation had no chance with Dredge in there and Michaels knew it. Dredge remained standing over Peter as Michaels watched them both. Dredge's face was noticeably red. He was furious. Dredge grabbed the door knob and opened the door. "I need to see you out here," he said to Michaels and he stormed from the room. Michaels followed him down the small hallway to their desks and Tommy joined them. Dredge lit up a cigarette. He was so angry he could barely speak.

"What's going on in there?" Tommy sensed there was a problem.

Michaels lit a cigarette and looked at Dredge. It was Dredge's case and it wasn't his place to intervene. Neither said a word.

"Well? Would someone fucking say something?" Tommy said now getting upset.

"I can't do this Tommy," Dredge said as he looked square into Tommy's eyes. "I don't know what it is, but I just can't do this."

"Ronnie. It's all yours. Get in there," Tommy said like a baseball coach talking to his reliever in the 9th inning.

Michaels walked in the room and Peter was exactly how they left him. He was sitting up in the chair with both arms crossed on his chest looking to his right. It was your classic body language signs of someone protecting themselves. He was lying and Michaels' job was to get the truth.

"Do you go by Peter or Pete?"

"All my friends call me Pete, only my dad and mom call me Peter."

"Well, I'm definitely not one of them so would it be alright if I call you Pete?"

"I guess."

"Sorry, my partner is a little tired and cranky Pete, are you thirsty? Do you need to use the bathroom?" he asked in a friendly voice.

Alonso raised his head. "Do you have a soda and I need to use the bathroom?"

"Sure, we can do both." Michaels was laying the foundation for a rapport between the two of them and this was a good start.

He opened the door and yelled for Tommy when Dredge called to him. "Ronnie come here for a second."

"Stay put Pete. I'll get you a drink and then we will get you to the bathroom."

"Thank you."

Michaels walked to Dredge's desk where smoked filled the room. "What do you need Tommy for?" he asked.

"I'm taking him to the bathroom, and I want him with me."

"You can't go up to the bathroom right now. Tommy is at the front of the building with an attorney and Peter's father. I could hear them talking. They want us to stop talking to Peter and he's telling them to pound sand."

"Oh shit, he can wait. Give me .50 cents so I can get him a soda." Michaels retrieved the beverage, gave Alonso the drink and closed the door.

Ten minutes passed and Tommy rejoined Dredge and Michaels. "They're gone."

"Gone?" Dredge asked.

"Yep, I told them he was charged as an adult and they were not speaking with him. Period. Then I kicked them out of the building."

"You are the fucking man, now come with me so he can use the bathroom."

Michaels opened the interview room door. "C'mon Pete. Let's go take a piss."

"Thanks. I really got to go bad."

Michaels could tell Alonso was starting to feel relaxed by his posture and the way he was talking. He stood up and followed Michaels down the hall toward the front of the building where the bathrooms were located. Tommy walked behind. Michaels had his gun in his desk but felt safe walking with his back to the killer so long as Tommy was following. After Alonso used the urinal, he and Michaels returned to their seats in the interview room.

Michaels was now alone in the room with the cruelest person he had ever met, and it was time to put his interrogation skills to work. First things first. Let the killer know there was no way out of the situation, none. Next, convince him it was in his best interest to tell what happened and how sorry he was for his actions in order to get the best outcome in court. Third, get him to confess. Michaels knew someone like Peter had to tell his story or it would eat him alive. He scooted his chair closer to Alonso until one of Michaels legs was between his. He was in Alonso's personal space by design. He would be unable to cross his legs, which was just another telltale sign of a liar when they unconsciously attempt to cover their genitals. With his arms crossed, Michaels moved in closer.

"Pete, Pete," he said until Alonso looked at him. "It's ok. You hear me? It's ok." He just stared at Michaels.

"Pete, I'm going to stay with you the entire time. I will walk you through the entire process, but you have to tell the truth about what happened and then it's especially important for you to say how sorry you are." Michaels could see he was thinking. He could tell what he was saying was influencing him and he had to keep talking, since he had his attention. Michaels kept using his name in every sentence, speaking softly to him in a reassuring tone.

"Pete, I know everything. We have the girl's body from the pipe. Your fingerprints were on her. The girl you hit in the face told us everything. Your fingerprints are on the hair dryer. Christ, we even have your hair on the sheet you wrapped her in." Some of what he was saying was a bold face lie, but it didn't matter. It was all legal and he wanted a confession.

As he listened, he began to squirm in his chair, and did exactly what Michaels was waiting for. It was a sign. A sign he wanted to tell the truth. He slid his ass forward toward the end of the chair. He slumped his entire torso forward and held his head down and looked at the floor. He took a deep breath. Michaels knew he was almost there and moved his leg closer. His left knee barely touched Alonso's crotch. He reached down with his right hand and held Alonso's large hand like a caring friend. His palms were sweating. He was ready.

"Pete, I don't think you planned for all this to happen. I know you are not that type of person. You're a good kid. I can tell. Is this something you planned, or did things just get out of hand?" He squeezed Michaels' hand tightly. The experienced detective knew his question was a double-edged sword, where an answer on either side would cut him. He began nodding his head in agreement but said nothing. Michaels said the words once more. "Things just got out of hand, didn't they Pete?" Michaels could see his lips begin to move. "Yes. I didn't mean to do it. I didn't want to hurt nobody."

With one hand holding his, Michaels rubbed the top of his Alonso's head with his other hand like a baby. There were no tears or any signs of remorse. He was a stone cold killer. Alonso put the soda can to his dry mouth and gulped down the remainder of the drink.

"I know you didn't buddy. I know you didn't. Can I get you another drink?" He couldn't wait to leave the room and tell Dredge.

"Yes, can I have another one?" Michaels could distinctly hear an obvious sense of relief in his voice.

"Sure, I'll be right back."

He closed the door calmly then raced back to the office where Tommy and Dredge stood smoking by the opened back door. They both had blank looks on their faces. They had no idea what he was about to say.

"Still not talking?" Dredge asked.

"He didn't lawyer up, did he?" Tommy asked.

"He confessed."

"What?" Dredge said.

"You're full of shit" Tommy said.

"No really, he admitted to killing her." By this time, Michaels had the biggest smile on his face.

"Young Shithead way to go," Dredge said.

"Now, while he's willing, I need to take the typewriter in and get a formal statement from him.

"Good job Ronnie." Tommy said.

"Thanks. Now let me cut, wrap and freeze this cold motherfucker."

After retrieving the necessary forms, Michaels unplugged the typewriter sitting on the cart and carried it into the interview room.

"You want another drink, right?"

"Yes."

Michaels called out to Dredge for another soda, while he searched to find an outlet for the typewriter. Dredge leaned into the room and handed Alonso his drink then shut the door.

Michaels inserted the first blank page into the typewriter to begin documenting Alonso's story.

"Am I going to jail?"

He avoided the question, then told him the same lines he had told many other suspects. He leaned forward once more and got close to his face to speak. "Pete, what we are going to do now is get a formal statement to show the courts how sorry you are. Unless you are a stone cold serial killer, which I know you're not, it's important you get on paper that you didn't mean to do this. It's called remorse. Do you understand what remorse is?"

"Yes sir," he said respectfully.

"Pete don't worry, I will walk you through the entire thing," he assured him once more.

The first question was designed to put him right in the Dodd's house and guilty of his first felony. "Tell me how and why you broke into 5566 Blue Herring Court today."

He looked at the detective like he had second thoughts and was about to clam up. Michaels could see it in his eyes.

"Pete, this is the only time we can get your side of the story. This is the only time you can tell me, so I can tell a judge that you are sorry. But if you want me to tell them you didn't cooperate, then fuck it, I'll leave you on your own. I don't give a fuck."

Michaels purposefully paused for a long period and stared at him. Then he took a big gamble and tore the page violently from the typewriter and said loudly to him. "Yup, let's just say fuck it and let everyone think of you as a cold blooded killer. I'll just drop you off at the jail. Is that how it's going to be Pete?" he shouted, and it worked.

"No, no please I'll tell you. I'm just scared that's all."

He sounded as if he didn't want to disappoint Michaels, which is just what the detective wanted. The interview lasted 45 minutes, questioning him about every detail of the crime. He said the reason he entered the Dodd's home was to find money. Michaels didn't buy that, but it didn't matter. He said the rear slider door was unlocked and that was how he entered. He now had admitted to his first felony, 1st Degree Burglary.

"I was upstairs when I heard the girls come in the house. One of them stayed downstairs while the other came in the room where I was hiding."

"Then what did you do?"

"When she came in, I didn't know what to do, so I hit her, so she wouldn't scream." Michaels couldn't believe how calm Alonso was. He had now admitted to his second felony, 1st Degree Assault of Paige Dodd.

"What did you do next?"

Michaels could sense the relief in his voice. "I told her to call her friend up and she did."

"That's logical, then what?"

"She came in the room and I choked her, so she wouldn't scream. I didn't mean to hurt her. I didn't mean it," he said with a blank look on his face.

"You choked her, so she wouldn't scream?"

"Yes sir."

"Pete, that makes sense, things just got out of hand huh?" Michaels said being a smartass without Alonso knowing.

"Yes sir."

Now he had admitted to his next felony, the 1st Degree Murder of Jenny Chambers.

During the entire confession, Alonso showed no emotions, and in fact, he was as cold as ice. Michaels now had a full admission of guilt and a signed Miranda Rights form. It didn't matter what was said or done from this point on, he was finished. Michaels carefully crafted his next question to bring attention to his coldness.

"Once you realized the girl was dead, what did you do?"

"The other girl said to wrap her in a sheet. That wasn't my idea."

"Well, she sure will have to answer for that," Michaels said to give him the feeling that he didn't stand alone in this crime.

Michaels could plainly see, in his own sick way, making Paige sound like she had done something terribly wrong, empowered Alonso. Michaels rolled on through his questions.

"What did you do with the dead body?" he said in order to establish Alonso knew the girl he had just wrapped in a sheet was deceased.

"She helped me wrap the body up and we dragged it down the steps and outside. We took it down the beach to the drain pipe and I left," he said so matter-of-factly.

Michaels could tell he felt more comfortable using the word *we* in his story, to portray Paige as an accomplice. This made him feel good. *This was one twisted fuck,* he thought.

The detective finished up with a few more questions, then placed the typed statement in front of Alonso to sign. This was the final step. "Good job Pete," Michaels said as he handed him his pen.

"Do I need a lawyer?" Michaels couldn't believe his question. Thank God it wasn't earlier in their conversations but first he needed his signature.

"Let's get this signed first and we can talk," he said nudging his pen closer to him while he stared down at the paper. He didn't speak. Total silence filled the room. Michaels was afraid to sound desperate and after a few minutes, he took a shot.

"I told you this was the only way to let a judge know that you were sorry. I said I would walk you through the entire thing." He moved his chair up close to Alonso once more, placing his left leg back between his and put his hand on his shoulder, like a father would. "So, when a judge asks me if I thought you regretted killing this little girl or if you are a cold calculated killer, what do you want me to say?"

"That I'm sorry," he mumbled.

"Then make your statement count and sign this fucking thing," he yelled slamming his pen in front of him.

"I'll sign it," he said holding the pen in his hand and signing each page.

Michaels snatched the papers from the desk. His job was complete. "I'll be back." And he stormed from the room.

Dredge was sitting in the big leather chair in Tommy's office. Michaels tossed the signed confession on his lap.

"What's going on Young Shithead?" Tommy said with his feet propped up on his desk.

Tommy looked like he just won a contest, sporting a Cheshire grin from ear to ear. "Did he give a statement?"

"Sure did, signed, sealed and delivered. He is fucked" Michaels said happily.

Tommy swung his feet off his desk and jumped from his chair. He gave the tired detective a big high five.

"Way to go Ronnie. Good job."

"Yeah, good job Young Shithead," Dredge said lifting his head up briefly from reading the statement.

"Why don't you guys drop him at Western District and go home?" Tommy ordered.

"Can you check on him Tommy? I need to call the Chambers' and the Dodd's. I just can't drop him off at the station, I'll need an Evidence Tech to meet me there to get his hair and saliva. We can get his blood at the Detention Center," Dredge said.

"No problem," Tommy said walking toward the interview room.

"Dredge did you want to call the families with the update or do you want me to?" Michaels asked.

"Would you mind?"

"Sure, let me do that now and then we can leave."

It was now 3:00 a.m. and Michaels telephoned Mr. Chambers' cell, unsure if he would answer. Many times, when emotions run high, the body shuts down and takes over, putting one in a much needed deep sleep. That wasn't the case here. Mr. Chambers answered on the second ring.

"Mr. Chambers, this is Detective Michaels."

"Did he confess? Did he say why he killed my little girl?"

"Yes, he did confess. He gave some lame excuse, saying he was scared. He said he didn't mean to do what he did."

"What does he mean, he didn't mean it? Jesus fucking Christ," Mr. Chambers paused for a few seconds. "What will happen to him now?"

"He will go before a Commissioner and be held without bail in the Detention Center until trial. I can't see them letting him out."

"Well thank you so much. Will we talk again?"

"Yes sir. Detective Hart or I will give you a call in a few days."

"Thanks detective."

"I'm really sorry Mr. Chambers," and he hung up the phone.

Michaels took a deep breath and made the next call while Dredge watched. "Hi Mr. Dodd, this is Detective Michaels. Sorry to call so late but I thought you'd like to know he confessed to everything."

"I'm glad to hear that. Did he say why he killed Jenny and why he broke into our home?"

"Yes sir. He said he was scared and was looking for money."

"But why our house? And how did he get in?"

"Mr. Dodd, I don't know why he picked your house, but I can only assume it was because your slider was unlocked."

"Oh my God. I always tell those kids to lock that door. I should have checked it. Oh my God. Will he get out like the rest of them?"

"We are going to ask that he be held with no bond. The only thing we can do is ask. I suspect the Commissioner will hold him tonight at the Detention Center, but it will be up to a judge tomorrow in a video bond hearing. How is Paige?"

Mr. Dodd took a deep breath and sighed. "She won't leave her mother's side. She has outbreaks when she cries and shakes from time to time without warning. She keeps reliving everything. She is sleeping on my wife's chest now, but she jumps, shouts out and twitches constantly. My wife can't even go to the bathroom without Paige clinging to her. We don't want her to see us upset, so I had to lock myself in the bathroom just to cry. My poor wife can't even do that. Hell, I don't even know why I'm crying. I don't know if it's because Jenny is dead, because my daughter's life was spared, or because I know what this will do to her. I can't see how she will survive this. I don't have the right to cry."

"I don't know what to say sir. You are so right. I'm just glad your daughter lived to help us catch him." Michaels' heart sank.

"Thanks for the call detective. I must say, we are impressed with how fast you guys worked."

"You are very welcome. We will be in touch. Goodnight." With that he hung up the phone.

"Thanks Shithead. Are you ready to get out of here?" Dredge said to Michaels.

"Yeah brother I'm done," Michaels stated while putting his overcoat on.

It was time to take Alonso to the Western District Station to be processed and execute the Search & Seizure Warrant on him. From there he would be taken to the Court Commissioner for a bail review.

"Let's do this." Dredge opened the door to the interview room to see Alonso's head laying on the table sleeping. Neither could believe their eyes. Here was a kid who had committed a brutal murder less than 24 hours ago, charged with 1st Degree Murder which he confessed to and he had the peace of mind to sleep in an interrogation room.

"Get the fuck up," Dredge ordered.

He slowly stood, rubbed his eyes and looked over at Michaels standing in the doorway. Dredge put the handcuffs on Alonso who kept looking at Michaels to help him. "Can I use the bathroom before I leave, can I get another drink?" he asked of Michaels like they were trusted friends.

Michaels looked at him and with a blank look. "You can piss at the station in your cell." His response shocked him.

"But I need to use the bathroom."

Dredge grabbed his left elbow and pushed him out of the doorway. "You'll just have to hold it, now won't you?" It was priceless. Dredge walked him out to his car and put him in the front passenger seat and slammed the door.

Dredge turned to Michaels. "I got this young man. Good job tonight. Go home son."

"Are you sure?"

"Yup."

"Be careful. I'll see you in a few hours."

When Michaels got into his car, he hung his handcuffs on the steering column and looked at his watch. He couldn't believe it was 3:45 in the morning. He pulled from the lot behind Dredge's car and could see smoke coming from Dredge's half open window. Michaels had to smile. He could only imagine what Dredge was saying to Alonso.

He began the long drive home, tired and drained physically and emotionally. He lowered his window while he smoked, allowing the brisk February air to keep him awake. As usual on the way home he passed the Earleigh Heights Tavern, where he nearly killed a man. He replayed those events in his head every time he drove by. Just past the tavern he stopped at a red light on Ritchie Highway, a heavily travelled road, regardless of the time of day. He was first in line at the red light, with only a few cars behind him. The light seemed to take longer than normal to change. Then, unexpectedly, he heard the loud sounds of car horns blasting and tires skidding. Sound asleep, he opened his eyes and noticed his car had drifted into the middle of the road where several cars nearly broadsided him. With his vehicle still drifting toward a large green traffic pole, he slammed on his brakes. In a split second, he had fallen asleep and his car had crept into the middle of the oncoming traffic.

"**FUCK**," he screamed, trying to focus his tired brain. He reached down and turned on his emergency lights and siren. He was stranded in the middle of the intersection and had to somehow get through safely. When he managed to cross the busy roadway, he pulled to the shoulder, threw his car in park and dropped his head on the steering wheel. By now his entire body was shuddering. *Thank God people were paying attention, or I would have been seriously injured or killed,* he thought. He got himself together, lit a cigarette and continued the drive home. He put all four windows down and turned the heat off, with his head hanging out like a dog. Feeling like it was only a dream, his mind could not fathom what had just happened.

By 4:30 a.m. Michaels finally made it home alive and he couldn't get into his bed fast enough. He put his gun on the nightstand and stripped his clothes off, leaving them in a scattered pile in the middle of the room. He closed his eyes but couldn't sleep. His mind was sprinting in fast motion through the potpourri of events which had occurred over the past 13 hours. He had seen a dead child stuffed in a drainpipe, ripped the hearts out of two parents when he told them of their child's murder, heard the horrific story from a brutalized little girl, and he just cuddled up to a heartless killer, stroked his head and held his hand like he cared about him, just to get a confession. As the day ended, he fell asleep at the wheel at one of the busiest roadways and was nearly killed. *What a day it had been. What a job,* he thought as he dozed off.

Mother's Day

It was a beautiful sunny Mother's Day and Michaels and his brother, Steve, made plans to take Beverly to brunch, along with Mel and his mother, Eva. Mother's Day was Beverly's favorite day of the year. She loved being with her boys and Mel who she treated like her own son. This special day was one of the few Beverly had all year with both of her sons. It meant a lot. Growing up, Ray and Beverly took great pride in making sure their boys played baseball, football, went fishing or crabbing or anything that required them to be on a boat. As they grew older, the boys grew apart. They saw little of each other except when it came to Christmas and Mother's Day. This was Beverly's day and she loved being with them.

Michaels picked up Beverly at her house. Her happiness was glaringly evident as she waited for him, smiling on the front steps of her condominium. Steve planned on meeting them at the restaurant.

Everyone met on the parking lot of the Oaks Restaurant, where Michaels and Steve used to frequent when growing up. Mel and Eva were already there, which was no surprise. Mel was always early. "Mom, remember when I was 10 years old and I stole the tip Dad left for the waitress and you guys caught me?"

"Oh, I sure do. You were so sneaky, the way you conned us into letting you go back in, saying you needed to use the bathroom. I was so mad at you." Everyone laughed and they headed inside where their reserved table awaited.

This was one of the best Mother's Day ever. Mel, Steve and Michaels laughed until their stomach's hurt. It was a wonderful time as the men reminisced about the past while Beverly and Eva sat and smiled. They didn't care that they were the loudest in the restaurant. They told stories of adventures that neither Beverly nor Eva knew of. When brunch ended, they exchanged hugs in the parking lot and Michaels dropped Beverly off at her house. She was very happy. It was a good day.

Michaels wasn't on call this weekend. Work had been relatively slow, which gave everyone a chance to catch up on their paper work. Besides the Chambers homicide, there had only been a few non-life-threatening shootings over the last several weeks. No big deal. Michaels' plans for the rest of the day was to take it easy and do some house cleaning that had been ignored far too long. Before going home, he stopped at the liquor store and stocked up on beer, rum and smokes.

Once home, with a full day to himself, he loaded up the refrigerator and cracked opened a cold beer. *Hell, it was 5 o'clock somewhere,* he thought. It was going to be a nice relaxing day. He took one sip of his beer and his cell phone began beeping in the living room.

"What the fuck." He wasn't on-call. Who was trying to reach him on Mother's Day? He retrieved his cell phone from among the empty beer cans next to the recliner, where he had slept the previous evening while watching Saturday Night Live. It was Tommy's number flashing. He couldn't imagine what he wanted, except maybe to say something nice to Beverly, who he knew and loved to joke with.

"What are you doing?" Tommy shouted.

"Um, drinking a beer. I just got home from taking my mom out. What's up?"

"We got a homicide in Glen Burnie. We are meeting on Ordinance Road near a patch of woods. I'm told there's patrol cars there and we can't miss them."

"You know I'm not on-call, right?"

"Yeah Donald is, sorry bud, but I need everybody for now. See you there."

"Son of a bitch. I'll be there in a little bit," he hung up the phone and yelled, "Fuck, who the hell kills someone on Mother's Day?" He started to his bedroom to change clothes cursing to himself.

He sped to the location as fast as his four cylinders would take him with his lights and siren blaring. Having been called out on his day off, he didn't have the patience to dick around with traffic. It took him 12 minutes to arrive on the scene from his home. He could see five marked police cars and fellow Detectives Hauf and Howes' cars parked next to an Evidence Collection van on the shoulder of the road. Donald and the rest of the cops were standing outside talking. When he pulled up, he saw Ray and Mark walk from the woods adjacent to the roadway with looks of disdain on their faces.

He pulled his notebook from the visor and recorded the date, time and location. Ordinance Road extended between a shopping center and a townhouse complex. On one side there was a grocery store, liquor store and a gift shop, along with a few clothing shops and a fast food joint. On the opposite side was a small patch of woods with many paths leading to the townhomes, used frequently by kids and adults as a short cut to the shopping center.

Donald saw Michaels pull up and he immediately scurried over to him to be alone and away from the uniforms. "Hey Shithead, thanks for coming. Doc Johnson and another Evidence Tech are on the way to help Ray."

"What do you have?"

"We got two bodies in the woods leading to the townhomes. They were found by a kid riding his bike. Supposedly, he saw a black guy in his 20's running from the scene. I don't know if he's related or not, but I have all the boy's info, so we can talk to him later."

"What do you want me to do?"

"Let's wait until the others get here before we go in. In the meantime, Mark is showing Ray what to photograph and they are also doing a quick search for evidence before it gets dark.

"Was it a dump job?"

"No, the uniforms said they were definitely killed here."

Donald cut all but one of the police officers loose where he and Michaels were standing to keep people from going into the woods. A second officer was at the other end, at the top of a hill doing the same thing and another was stationed inside of the woods.

Approximately 20 minutes passed, and Doc Johnson arrived, followed later by Tommy, Dredge and Jeff. Donald briefed the newcomers of what little he knew, then together they headed into the woods. They entered on a hard-packed dirt path used over the years by people riding bicycles and walking from the center. Roughly 30 yards in, Ray was seen untangling himself from the 9-foot high canopy of stickers stuck to his pants and shirt's sleeve. Mark was standing off to the side watching him.

Donald led the way to the area where Ray was. As they got closer, Ray stopped briefly to take photographs, while constantly pulling the prickly vines from his clothing. No one, not even Donald, could see what he was taking pictures of. Everyone assumed it was an item of evidence on the ground. They were sadly mistaken. It was a child.

Carefully moving closer, each could see blood droplets sprayed across the leaves, stickers and standing plant life. As for Michaels, this was the most horrific site he had ever laid eyes on. It was a small boy, probably dressed nicely for his mother, in now what was a blood-soaked buttoned-down plaid shirt and what used to be a clean pair of white tennis shoes. The young man's khakis were covered in blood. His hair was short, chestnut brown in color and it too contained dried, clotted blood. The young boy had a thin build. He looked to be about 14 or 15 years old. Oddly enough, his body was deep in the middle of a sticker pile well off the path. The lifeless little fella was draped among the foliage, as if he were hurled from the main path. The picture that burned in Michaels' mind was the site of this poor little guy's head barely attached to his body. His entire neck had been sliced open with an extremely sharp object. His esophagus was severed in two and his entire bloody neck muscles and tendons were exposed. The only body part keeping his head attached was a stretched-out piece of skin with a small piece of muscle attached. Ray photographed the tremendous amount of blood that had sprayed from his neck onto the forest floor, small trees and thorny stickers where he lay. It looked as if his blood spewed from a garden hose.

Doc put on his rubber gloves, while Ray continued photographing the scene. Doc stepped into the tangled mess. Squatting down to inspect the body, he carefully moved leaves from the victim's face. This was the first anyone had seen his eyes. None of those on the scene would ever forget the frozen look of fear that cried out from his dark brown eyes. Ray let his camera hang from the strap around his neck while he stared at him. Tommy, Donald, Mark, Dredge and Michaels stood motionless. Quietly they all looked on, as if they were paying their last respects. There was not a sound to be heard, no traffic, no kids, not even a bird.

Lying next to the path, near the body, was a small white plastic bag. "Ray when you are done, can you put on some fresh gloves and look in this bag?" Mark asked.

"Sure, I'll be right over."

There was plenty of trash in the woods but given the proximity and clean appearance of the bag, it needed to be checked out. Ray donned a fresh pair of rubber gloves and took several photographs and measurements of the bag at various angles. He lifted the small white plastic bag and inspected the opposite side. It read *Hallmark*. It was from the gift shop in the neighboring shopping center. He opened the bag and for the first time Michaels could remember, he saw an overwhelming look of sadness blanket over his father's face. Ray breathed in slowly and took a big sigh.

"What is it Ray?" Mark said kneeling next to him.

"It's two Mother's Day cards" Ray said in a very low tone. He pulled the receipt out to see the date and time they were purchased. "Jesus Christ. These cards were just bought a couple of hours ago."

Michaels saw a sensitive side of his hero he had never seen before. "What cold, heartless motherfucker could do such a thing," Michaels said as a feeling of anger came over him.

"Mark, I want you to stay here and help Ray with whatever he needs to finish processing this scene and get this young man out of these woods," Tommy said drowning in his emotions.

A man from the Medical Examiner's Office arrived for the removal of the bodies. Ray and Jeff assisted him, carefully supporting his neck and head.

"What a way to go. He's way too young," Dredge said under his breath.

Michaels looked at the boy's eyes once more as Jeff zipped the bag closed. Time moved slowly, but eventually the body made its way inside the black, empty Medical Examiner's van.

"Show us where we're going next," Tommy said to Donald.

The group followed Donald nearly 75 yards through the woods up a slight hill in the direction of the townhomes. Ahead they noticed an officer standing a few yards from what appeared to be a pile of clothing at the base of a large oak tree. They continued until Michaels noticed a sandal just off the path. "Donald, did you see this?"

Donald came over to inspect the find. "We'll get Ray to photograph and collect that, just in case." He stopped and placed a blank piece of paper from his notebook on a tree branch above the footwear.

Though there was plenty of debris in the woods, this item didn't appear to be old, nor did it look like trash. They walked closer and closer to the uniformed officer. As they neared, the pile they had seen was not clothing, it was the partially nude body of a young female, approximately the same age as the boy. A second dead child.

"This had to be a true nightmare for these two children," Michaels said now numb and in disbelief of what he was seeing. *This was a scene only Hollywood could create*, he thought to himself.

This victim was wearing a short sleeve buttoned up cream colored blouse, torn completely open with buttons laying nearby on the ground. Her small white bra was stretched and partially torn, exposing her small breast. Dried oak leaves and dirt were entangled in her knotted blonde hair. There was a small sign of blood on the back-left side of her neck and just a quarter size spot of blood on the same shoulder.

Her designer jean shorts were frayed in half, wrapped only around her left ankle. Her pink underwear had been ripped from her body, lying next to her fully spread open legs. Michaels could clearly envision the rage invoked by her attacker from the looks of her pants and undergarments. Both her eyes were half closed with the familiar look on a dead body that he had seen many times before. The other matching sandal was still partially on her right foot.

"This sick motherfucker tried to rape this little girl in the wide-open woods. What fucking vile animal would do such a thing?" Michaels said now furious.

"This is one sick son of a bitch guys," Donald said while writing feverishly. "She must have been running from this sick fuck."

Michaels looked in the direction where the first body was found. "Yeah, the little boy got it first and then she ran for her life until he ended it."

It was not readily apparent how this victim died. Though they could see small signs of blood on her, the cause of death was not as obvious as the young man now laying in the back of the van. Ray and Mark had already photographed and took various measurements around the second body before the others had arrived.

"Hey Doc, we can't tell how she was killed," Donald said to him.

"If you guys are done, we can turn her over now," Doc suggested.

"Ray?" Donald called out.

"All done," Ray replied.

Doc crouched down. Donald stood over him while he gently rolled her body onto her left side.

"Wow, there it is," Donald said to the group standing a few feet away.

"Yup, there it is," Doc said.

Michaels stood next to Donald to see what had caught their attention. There were two prominent stab wounds at the base of the girl's neck. One was an inch to the right of her spinal column and the second incision pierced her spine directly.

"This was the killing wound here," Doc said pointing at the fragmented spine.

Ray joined them, and he too took photographs.

Donald called for a member of the Medical Examiner's Office to bring the gurney to the second body for removal. Ray and Jeff both assisted the gentlemen as they transferred the young girl into a white body bag. The rest of the team watched and the last thing they saw when the zipper was being closed were her half open glazed eyes.

Since it was children who discovered the bodies, the word spread quickly through the community. Parents were searching frantically for their children and the ones who couldn't find their kids were trying to get past the patrolmen guarding the woods. At this point no one had any idea who these two victims were. Tommy's cell phone went off; he didn't realize he had missed a call from the Dispatch Center. "I have to go to my car and make a call. It's Channel 5."

Those still in the woods watched as the gurney made its way into the back of the van next to the first body. The ME employee slammed the double doors and drove off. On the other side of the van, Tommy appeared on the path looking at his notebook. He summoned for Donald and Michaels to join him. Something was wrong.

"What's up boss?" Donald asked.

"Dispatch got a call from a frantic father, a Mr. Bill Ford, who lives not far from here in the townhouses. He hasn't heard from his son in several hours and from the sounds of the description it may be our victim. Here's the address. You know what to do," he said tearing the paper from his notebook and handing it to Donald.

"We got it. Come on Shithead," Donald said and the two walked briskly to Donald's car.

Donald handed Michaels his map book along with the address. Quickly, he found where they were going and directed Donald a short distance through the neighborhood not far from the woods they had just left. Many of the residents were standing on their sidewalks talking and eyeing up the detectives as they drove by.

In the doorway of the address they parked in front of was a clean-cut white gentleman in his mid 40's. He pushed open the door and allowed the detectives in, as neighbors gathered in the roadway watching and mumbling under their breaths to one another.

"I'm Bill Ford, the one who called. Come in, please have a seat," the man said nervously. Both detectives took a seat on the couch, while Mr. Ford sat next to them on the loveseat.

"Is it true? Are there children dead in the woods? You know how rumors are around here. I'm sorry I called, but my son and his friend left hours ago, and they should have been home by now."

Mr. Ford's voice trembled as he spoke, and his hands were visibly shaking. Michaels looked at a table near the television where there was an assortment of family pictures. From where he was sitting, he was unable to make out any faces.

Since it was Donald's case, he was doing all the talking. He started by asking for his child's name, age, height, weight and clothing description. "Daniel's a small boy, he's 14 years old and can't weigh any more than 100 pounds soaking wet. He's very clean cut, with brown hair parted on the side, and I guess he's 5'4" tall."

Mr. Ford wasn't sure what clothing his son had on, which was normal for a male parent. Donald then asked the next big question, knowing full well this would confirm the victim's identities. "And how about the friend he was with. Can you describe that person?"

"Her name is Meagan Baton. She's about the same age as Daniel. We used to live next to the Batons. Those two have been friends since they were babies. They were like brother and sister growing up. She's a pretty girl with blonde hair and about the same height as Daniel, but I'm sorry I couldn't tell you what either were wearing."

Donald looked at Michaels who was immersed in his notebook. "That's no problem. When did you last see them?"

"Meagan's dad dropped her off at 11:00 a.m. and they left to buy their mothers a card at the shopping center. I gave them money and that's the last I saw of them. When they didn't return right away, I figured they stopped at a friend's house. But it's been several hours. I started calling around and that's when a neighbor came by and told me someone was found dead in the woods. I wasn't sure what to do so I called 911."

"Have you talked with Meagan's parents since the kids left?"

"No. I didn't want to alarm anyone if it wasn't necessary."

"Is there a Mrs. Ford?" Donald asked.

"We're divorced, but I have full custody. Daniel's my only child and he's a great kid. His mother on the other hand, well she is a recovering heroin addict. She has put us through all kinds of shit. She lives in Western Maryland with some loser. She won't be here until later if she even shows at all and I haven't told her what's going on either."

Michaels used this clue to walk to the table where the pictures were. As he got closer, he focused in on a picture of two people standing on the shoreline of a river, with kayaks next to them. He could see the picture had a caption at the top which read *Best Buds*. It was Mr. Ford with his arm around a boy, both sporting life-vests and helmets. The teen had a contagious smile. It was him. It was the same boy he had just seen zipped into the body bag. The vision of him lying in the stickers with his head barely attached and a horrified look in his eyes kept flashing through his mind. It was Daniel Ford.

Donald glanced over at Michaels to get a read on his facial expressions like a poker player. He knew exactly what Michaels was doing. Mr. Ford, on the other hand paid no attention. Michaels gave an affirmative nod to Donald, who was about to change the man's life forever. Michaels rejoined Donald on the couch because he knew what was coming. "Mr. Ford, I'm really sorry to have to say this, but your son was killed today." His eyes opened wide in surprise and he shot up from his seat and screamed Daniel's name and cried hysterically. Not knowing what to do, he stood in the middle of the room crying.

"This can't be true. No, no, no, not my little buddy," Mr. Ford dropped to his knees with both hands over his face. "Dear God, No, No, He's all I have." His body fell to the floor, crying helplessly. He stood and walked to the table with the pictures. "No," he yelled knocking all the pictures from the table with one fell swoop of his arm. "Who did this? God damn it, who the fuck did this? he shouted in Donald's face.

Donald remained calm. "We don't know yet sir, but the entire Homicide Unit is on it."

"Oh my God, what about sweet little Meagan. Is she ok? Where is she? They were together. They've been best friends since they were born."

"She was also killed sir. I'm so sorry," Donald said only adding to the man's sorrow.

"Oh, dear God. What did her parents say? I can't fucking believe this. Those poor innocent children. Who the fuck would do this?"

Feeling Mr. Ford's pain, Michaels spoke up. He couldn't keep quiet. "Mr. Ford look at me. We'll find this bastard. I promise. We will find whoever did this."

Mr. Ford kicked over the table where the family pictures once were. "Fuck, fuck, I can't believe this. God why him? Why my little boy and Meagan?"

"Mr. Ford, can you tell us where Meagan lives?" Donald asked.

"Yes, when I was married, my wife and I lived next door to Jim and Karen for thirteen years. Their address is 5 Luther Road, in Meade Village.

Mr. Ford cried harder, returning to the loveseat with his head resting in his hands. The two detectives sat on the couch. There was nothing more they could do or say. Still crying, Mr. Ford asked the dreaded question. "How were they killed?"

Donald paused. He didn't want to answer, but he knew he had too. "They didn't suffer sir."

"I asked how they were killed?" he screamed out.

Donald was forced to reveal the cause of death. "They were both stabbed."

"Stabbed?" Mr. Ford flew out of his seat and began pacing the floor. "Who in the fuck would stab my Daniel? That doesn't make any sense. He doesn't have any enemies. He's the nicest kid you'd ever meet and so is Meagan. I'll kill em, I swear to God, I don't care if I go to jail, but mark my words…I will KILL whoever did this."

He paused and took several deep breaths. "So now what? Can I see my son? I need to see him now."

"Unfortunately, you cannot. He's been taken to the Medical Examiner's Office in Baltimore. You will need to contact a funeral home and they will know what to do," Donald instructed.

"Oh my fucking God. I can't even see my dead son? What the fuck is going on here?" he shouted.

"We are on this Mr. Ford, trust me," Donald assured him. Michaels and Donald stood from the couch.

"Will you let me know when you catch him?"

"Most definitely I will. I'll keep you informed every step of the way," Donald said as he handed him a business card, along with his cell number.

"I don't know what I'm supposed to do now. Just sit here? What am I going to do?"

"Is there someone I can call for you?" Michaels asked.

"No, no I don't know. I guess I'll call my mother or somebody. You all can leave, you need to catch whoever did this. Thank you, detectives," Mr. Ford said as he shook their hands with tears dripping from his eyes.

"Mr. Ford, we are going to the Baton's address now, if you wouldn't mind, please don't call them or take their call just yet."

"I won't, but I'll pray for them."

The detectives said their goodbyes and left him standing exactly where he was first seen, but now with a much different look on his face. For a few minutes nothing was said when Donald and Michaels got in the car.

"That was a bitch," Donald said.

"I know. I hate doing those."

"That makes two of us. It's the worst part of this job."

Michaels grabbed the map book again and began looking up the Baton's address. Both were familiar with the area. It was another townhouse neighborhood approximately 20 minutes away.

"Start heading toward the Meade Village Community and listen, since you did this one, I'll do Meagan's parents," Michaels said.

"Thanks brother."

When they pulled up to their destination, they saw an adult male and female with a small girl who looked to be about 8 years old sitting on the front steps chatting with their neighbors.

"Dear God. This is going to be horrible Donald."

"It sure is. You ready?"

"No, but we don't have a choice. Let's do this."

They opened their doors simultaneously.

Michaels said a quick prayer as he forced himself from the car. Neither wanted to do another notification, especially on Mother's Day.

The two couples sitting with their children had obviously not been watching the news and had no clue what was happening where they had dropped their daughter off this morning.

"Hi folks, are you Mr. and Mrs. Baton?"

"Yes, I'm Jim Baton and this is my wife, Karen. What can we do for ya?"

"We're with the County Police. I'm Detective Hauf and this is Detective Michaels."

"My God, is there something wrong? Is it my brother? Did he get arrested again?" Mrs. Baton asked.

"No ma'am. Is this your little girl?" he said looking over at the child who was playing.

"Yes, this is Becky."

"Can Becky stay with your neighbors for a little bit, so we can talk in private?"

Michaels knew there was no way he wanted to do a death notification in front of a sibling that young, not again. No way. The neighbors sensed the seriousness of the situation.

"Come on Becky, let's go inside. You and Kimmy can play while your mommy and daddy talk to these nice men."

The detectives watched as the two youngsters and the neighbors scurried inside. Michaels found himself short of breath. This was going to be extremely hard to do. They entered the townhouse and walked through the living room to the kitchen. There were pictures on the wall leading upstairs, next to the steps. Michaels followed slowly behind Donald, scanning the wall for photographs of Meagan. Among the pictures was a family shot of two girls and Mr. and Mrs. Baton standing on a beach. Another was a picture of Mr. Baton and the young girl they had just seen outside sitting on the steps. The last photo was of the entire family in a raft at a water park and there sat Meagan Baton, the deceased.

"Take a seat gentleman," Mr. Baton said.

The four took a seat at the table. Michaels knew what he had to do but he just couldn't speak. There was a brief unnerving silence in the room. Donald looked over at Michaels and could plainly see the trepidation on his face. He was about to rescue him when the words spilled from Michaels.

"Mr. and Mrs. Baton, there's no easy way for me to say this. I am really sorry, but your daughter, Meagan, was killed today."

For a moment they both looked at Michaels in disbelief then Mrs. Baton began crying and shouting. "No, she is not, she can't be. What do you mean she was killed? How are you sure it's her and not someone else? You must be mistaken. Dear Lord. No. She can't be, she's at her friend's house in Glen Burnie. She's not even around here."

Mr. Baton was in shock. Michaels could tell he didn't want to believe what he had just heard, so he calmly asked questions while his eyes filled with tears. "How do you know it's Meagan? And what happened?"

"Right now, all we know is that Daniel and Meagan were killed by someone for no apparent reason." Mr. Baton stood up and clutched onto his wife, now both crying. Mrs. Baton was screaming.

"Oh my God, oh my God, what am I going to do? Jesus no, no, no, I can't do this, I can't do this, I need to see her, where is she? I don't believe this, take me to her."

Without warning Mrs. Baton fell to the floor, striking the side of her head on the kitchen table.

"Babe, Babe, Babe," Mr. Baton yelled leaning over his wife. Blood dripped on the floor from a cut on her ear. She was not responding.

"Let me get a paper towel. She's bleeding," Donald said.

Mr. Baton braced her head with one hand and applied the paper towel to her wound. "It's a small cut. She'll be alright. She has high blood pressure. Can you give me some more wet paper towels?"

Donald was getting more towels as she regained consciousness.

"Babe, can you hear me?" Mr. Baton said cradling her in his arms. She slowly blinked her eyes while she attempted to focus.

"Is Meagan really gone?" she said looking up at her husband.

Mr. Baton nodded his head while the tears gushed from his eyes. The two laid on the floor, holding one another and crying profusely for 10 minutes. Mr. Baton's tears dripped onto his wife's face. Michaels remained kneeling on the floor next to their feet while Donald squatted next to their heads, both with tears in their eyes. Quietly, they remained on the floor with the Batons. There was nothing else they could do. It was their job.

Mr. Baton helped his wife up and she took a seat at the table. He wiped his eyes and inquired more about the murders. "How, why, why were they killed?" he stuttered.

Michaels had done enough damage saying their daughter was murdered, there was no way he would mention the attempted rape. From his limited time in the unit, he found being vague and putting everything on the ME's Office was the way to go. He didn't see the benefit of unloading all those details at once. Some detectives might, but not Michaels.

"All we know right now is they were stabbed and neither of them suffered. They are both at the Medical Examiner's Office in Baltimore where an autopsy will be performed."

"Do you know why? Or who? Why would someone do this?" he said as he slammed his fist on the table. "They're fucking kids."

"No sir. We don't know why or who, but a witness saw a man in his 20's run from the woods. We just don't know if it's our suspect or not. The investigation is still very fresh, and things are still unfolding. We haven't released the information to the press, so you must not talk to them," Donald told him.

Mrs. Baton got up from the table. "We have to tell Becky. Jesus, how are we going to do that? She's going to be devasted. She loves Meagan so much. Oh my God. This is going to destroy her. What are we supposed to do without our Meagan? This can't be true." Mrs. Baton left the room and returned with the picture of Meagan in the raft. "How can you be positive it's her?" Mrs. Baton asked rubbing the tears from her eyes.

In a very calm tone Donald looked at Mr. and Mrs. Baton who were clinging onto the picture and any possible hope, "I'm very sorry, but we were both at the scene, we saw that picture on your wall and we've talked with Daniel's father."

The Batons held one another and cried while the detectives sat speechless once more.

As always, Donald obtained their cell numbers and left a business card on the kitchen table. He assured them, they would be kept updated as the case progressed. While the two sat holding hands crying in the kitchen, Donald and Michaels said their goodbyes and let themselves out.

Thoughts raced through Michaels' head as he stepped into Donald's car. *It was tragic to see these young parents have their hearts ripped out because of some thoughtless fucking asshole.*

They drove back to the scene to join Tommy and whoever else was still there. Once again, not a word was spoken for the first few minutes, until Donald revealed something.

"You know Shithead, no one has told you this, but everyone in the unit likes that you have been doing most of the notifications since you've been here. You just know how to talk to people in these situations, better than any of us."

Michaels turned to Donald, surprised to hear his comment. "Thanks man, but just for the record, I absolutely hate doing them."

They chain smoked the entire way, internally reflecting on what had transpired with both families. By now it was dark and when they arrived the patrol cars and Evidence Collection van were gone, in fact, the only cars still at the scene belonged to Tommy and Dredge.

"How'd it go?" Tommy asked.

"Not good boss. The boy's name is Daniel Ford. He's 14, lives with his dad and from all indications he's a real good kid. The father knew of no one who would hurt him. The girl's name is Meagan Baton. She's 15 and sounds like a great kid also. The two have been best friends since birth, Donald said.

"Where's my dad and Mark?"

"I sent Mark home in case something comes in tonight and Ray was on day work. I had Mark and Dredge canvas the shopping center and most of the nearby townhouses."

"Anybody see anything?" asked Michaels.

Dredge spoke up. "A Hallmark employee remembers a young boy, who fits our victim's description, asking her if the card he had selected for his mom was a good one, but that's it. She didn't notice anyone acting unusual."

From his experience as a homicide detective and polygraph examiner, Tommy was very intuitive and an expert at reading people's body language. "Wait here," Tommy said firmly. Dredge, Donald and Michaels looked at each other while Tommy got into his car and sped away. Everyone was befuddled.

Donald spoke up. "Where the fuck's he going?"

Dredge brushed it off, knowing it was useless to try and figure out Tommy sometimes. "Who knows. He's a fucking wild man. So Donald, what's the plan for tomorrow?"

"We need to find out who this black dude is," he answered.

Tommy returned twenty minutes later, driving like a maniac, stopping on the shoulder and nearly sliding into Dredge's car. When his car screeched to a halt, he picked up a large pizza box and a case of Coors Light from his passenger seat and stepped from his car. Still not uttering a word, he dropped the food and beverages on his hood making a loud bang. "Have something to eat and drink fellas," he ordered nonchalantly.

His guys had seen a lot, but they couldn't believe what they were seeing now. Here were three homicide detectives and their sergeant all parked on the shoulder of a well-traveled road, outside of a double murder scene, drinking beer and eating pizza. Tommy knew what he needed to do, knowing what his troops had just endured. The moment was priceless.

The four remained there for the next two hours until the beer and pizza had vanished. When nature called, they pissed not far from their cars and neither of them cared, after all, they had a double homicide to solve. Tommy had a way of making his unit feel untouchable.

They finished up the long day at 10:00 p.m. and they each hopped in their cars and went their separate ways. By the time Michaels got home he couldn't recall half of the drive with his mind playing back the horrific visions he had seen. When he opened his car door he was greeted by Darlene, who was also just getting home.

"Hey neighbor. I guess you've been out all day on that murder of those children? That is so sad. Did you find who did it?"

"Hi Darlene. No, not yet," he said trying to keep his distance to conceal his slight intoxication.

"Well I hope you do soon. Looks like you're ready for a haircut. When do you want to come over?"

"As soon as I get a break, I'll give you a call."

She stopped before she opened her door. "By the way, have you noticed the black SUV that's been driving really slow up and down our street at night? I've seen it twice. All the windows are blackened out and I can't see who's inside."

"No, I haven't. Did you get a tag number?"

"No, both times I saw it was after work when it was dark."

"I'll keep a look out. Goodnight."

"Goodnight. Don't work too hard. I never see your car here anymore."

"Tell me about it."

He flicked on the light and threw his keys in the direction of the bowl but missed. He reached down and yanked his gun and badge from his belt and dropped them on the living room table. Strangely enough, they both landed next to the beer he had opened 10 hours ago, before his plans got drastically changed. It was hard to believe it was still Mother's Day. He took a cold beer from the fridge and worked his way to the recliner. He kicked off his shoes, sat down and lit up. The beers were going down easily, and he wanted more. He continuously replayed the frightened look in Daniel's eyes and the sight of the partially clad female laying violated in the woods. Beer after beer his mind raced and anger overcame him. Like both sets of parents, Michaels was now enraged and desperately wanted to kill whoever did this despicable act.

Michaels knew his new assignment had changed him. He didn't think he could ever cry again over death. He knew he had seen the worst of the worst and there were no emotions left to allow him to cry. The job had robbed him of that ability. Inebriated, he raised his beer and made a toast.

"Don't worry little guys. We'll find the scumbag who did this and if I have the chance, I will kill him for you. I promise. Rest in peace children." He lowered his can and took a big gulp. The distraught, trashed detective continued to drink beer after beer and smoke one cigarette after the next. The ashtray was full and when he tried pouring the ashes into an empty beer can, they spilled onto the table and floor. "Shit," he yelled as he blew at the ashes. Michaels struggled to climb from the recliner and head toward the bedroom. He knew he didn't have to be at work until 3:00 p.m., but he needed to sleep. "I need my fucking sleeping pills. That's what I need," he said out loud, stumbling to the bathroom.

Barely standing, he looked in the mirror before opening the medicine chest. He could see dried pizza sauce on his chin and bloodshot eyes. He searched the medicine chest for the pills Doc Johnson had prescribed him months ago. His new assignment often kept him awake, while he struggled with the death and despair he had seen. He opened the bottle and swallowed four of the pills. It was sleep he needed, not flashbacks.

He staggered to the kitchen to give the medicine time to set in. *"I'm having a fucking rum and Coke in honor of Daniel and Meagan. That's what I'm fucking doing."* He poured a strong drink and plopped back down in the recliner. He lit up a cigarette and stared aimlessly at the wall until his body gave in to the medicine.

"Shit, Fuck, Damn it, he yelled awakened by the heat and smoke from his burning chair. Startled, he jumped up, causing the drink in his hand to spill in his lap. In his drunken stupor, he beat the smoldering furniture with his bare hand oblivious to the burns he was receiving. In a state of panic, he ran to the kitchen for water, only to trip and fall head first into the leg of the dining room table. He managed to get up and fill a glass, which he used to douse the seat cushion and chair arm. Confident the fire had been extinguished and still wasted, he flopped onto the couch, in his wet pants, with burns on his hand and blood running down his forehead.

Two hours later, he awoke once more to the odor of burnt cloth and smoke. The room was a disaster. It looked like the day after a frat party in a college dorm. There were beer cans on the table and floor. The cushion and arm of the recliner were charred. The ashtray was full. Cigarette butts were on the table and rug and a frosted tumbler glass lay on the floor near the television. With a pounding headache, he cleaned the room like he had so many times before, this time spraying the chair with Febreze, then covering it with a clean bed sheet. He peeled off his wet clothes and passed out once more on the couch.

At 7:00 a.m. Michaels heard a strange ringing noise. He slowly lifted his aching head and determined it was his cell phone somewhere under the recliner. He pushed himself up from the couch and retrieved his phone. His left hand was burnt, with two large blisters on his palm and fingers. He attempted to read the number, but he was unable to focus. Quickly, he tried to clear the cobwebs from his hungover state of mind.

"Hello."

"Detective Michaels?"

"Speaking."

"This is Rosemary from the Communication's Center. Your father is being rushed to the North Arundel Hospital. They think he had a heart attack."

"What?" he yelled. "Oh, oh, ok, um, um, ok. Is he alive?"

"All I know sir is he's in an ambo on his way to the hospital."

"Ok," he said, and he pulled the phone from his ear and looked at it. He could still hear the dispatcher talking, but instead he ended the call.

Extremely hungover, Michaels could not figure what to do first. He ran to his bedroom to get dressed, nearly falling from his head spinning. He threw on a pair of jeans, slipped on a t-shirt and a pair of tennis shoes. He scooped up his car keys from the dining room floor, took a Coke from the fridge and with the worst headache in the world, bolted from the front door to his car. Like most retired cops, Ray had high blood pressure, but Michaels never saw this coming.

Driving to the hospital at a high rate of speed with his lights and siren activated, *Simple Man* by Lynyrd Skynyrd played on the radio. He cranked up the volume and lit a cigarette. The hospital was at least twenty minutes from his house. With a cigarette in one hand, he drove 100 plus miles an hour, darting in and out of traffic, sometimes using the shoulder to pass cars and singing every word to the song. The music was turned up so loud it nearly drowned out the shrill noise of the blaring siren. He didn't give a fuck. He was calm yet still managed to smoke one cigarette after the next as he got closer to the hospital.

Strangely, he had no emotions, practically numb but that was just the person he was now. Nothing phased him.

He skidded into a *Police Only* parking spot by the Emergency Room entrance. He threw open his door and stopped to take one last draw from his Marlboro and looked up. The automatic emergency room doors slid open and out walked three longtime friends in uniform. He could plainly see the serious looks on their faces as they walked toward him. He froze in his tracks. Suddenly something came over him, which caught him by surprise. Tears poured down his cheeks, while he fought to keep from giving in to his weakening knees. He couldn't believe it, he was human after all.

His three buddies all hugged him. He thought for sure his dad had been taken from him, never having the chance to say *goodbye* or *I love you* for the last time. Dazed, Michaels could not stop crying.

"Come on in Ronnie. Come talk to him."

"What? He's still alive?" he muttered in amazement.

"Yeah, the paramedic said they shocked him with the paddles 14 times on the way here. They never stopped until his heart started beating on its own, which wasn't until they pulled onto the lot.

"Fuck. I thought he was dead. Thanks guys."

Michaels walked to the small cubical where Beverly was standing next to his dad, holding his hand, crying and trying to talk. She turned when she heard her son and the officers approaching. He joined his mother, while the officers pulled the curtains closed.

He couldn't believe how horrible Ray looked laying on the stretcher. He had a tube protruding from his mouth where a breathing apparatus was attached, still taped to his cheeks and chin. There were wires attached all over his chest hooked to the machine next to his bed. He could see the heart monitor go up and down, numbers flashing on the screen and he could hear occasional alarms sounding. Ray's shirt had been cut open by the paramedics. His breathing was erratic with no apparent rhythm, going from deep to shallow. His skin was pasty white. He looked dead.

Beverly clutched onto her son's hand. "Talk to him Ronnie. He can hear you."

He struggled to speak and held onto Ray's cold hand. "Hey Pop. It's me." He tried to suppress his crying but could not. Ray meant so much to him. Now the man who he was always trying to impress, lay fighting for his life in front of him.

"Dad. I love you. You hang in there. Don't you die on me Pop. Don't you do that to us."

The more Michaels talked the harder he and Beverly cried. He kept his arm around his mother while they both held Ray's hand. With her other hand, Beverly stroked the hair on his forehead.

A few minutes later, Steve arrived. They could tell from his eyes he had already been sobbing but when he took his first look at Ray, he lost it. Big time. Beverly and Ronnie moved to the side so Steve could be close to his father. Balling, he leaned over, kissed him on the forehead and whispered something in his ear. Neither Beverly nor Ronnie could make out what was said. He kept talking in his ear, almost as if they had a secret between the two of them. Oddly, while this was happening, something strange occurred. Ray's breathing changed.

"Excuse me," the doctor said as he drew open the curtain. "Hi, I'm Dr. Benjamin Marshal. I'm the cardiologist on call today. You must be Mrs. Michaels? And these two good-looking men must be your sons?"

"Yes doctor. I'm Beverly and these are my boys, Steve and Ronnie. Is he going to make it?"

"He has suffered a massive heart attack and he has severe blockage in the valves leading to his heart. He has over a 90% blockage in one valve and frankly, he's lucky to be alive.

"Shit, what now Doc?" Michaels asked.

The doctor grimaced when he looked at the dried blood on the detective's forehead and burned hand.

"You should really get that hand looked at while you're here."

The doctor turned to the nurse standing beside him. "While I'm looking at our patient, can you clean up those wounds, and treat his hand please?"

"Yes sir."

Beverly immediately looked at her son's hand. "What did you do? That's terrible. What happened?"

Michaels watched Ray, while the nurse tended to his injuries. "I'm fine Mom. It was stupid. I burned myself on the grill." Michaels looked over and saw the look of disbelief on the doctor's face.

"What's next Doctor?" Beverly asked dabbing her eyes with a tissue.

"Within the hour, he'll be transferred by helicopter to the Shock Trauma Center. There he will undergo bypass surgery depending on his diagnosis. After that he should be as good as new."

"How dangerous is that operation?" Steve asked.

"There was a time when bypass surgery was dangerous but over the years there have been so many advances made, today, it's a very common procedure. Don't get me wrong, it still has its risks because you're dealing with the heart, but he should be fine."

"Should we go to Baltimore now?" Beverly asked hearing the blades of the helicopter nearing the hospital.

"I don't think that's necessary. It will just be a whole lot of waiting and there's really nothing you can do. This surgery takes several hours, not to mention the pre-op before surgery. You'll just end up sitting in an uncomfortable room watching TV and drinking the worse coffee on the east coast." Everyone chuckled.

"What do you recommend?" Steve asked.

"Give the nurse the best numbers to reach all of you and someone will give you a heads up when he gets to the recovery room. I really wouldn't worry that much. He's in good hands."

"Thank you doctor." Beverly turned and kissed her husband on the cheek. "I love you Raymond."

She moved to the side so her boys could say their goodbyes. Ronnie moved closer to the stretcher. "Dad, did you hear that? They are going to clean out the old pipes and your ticker is going to be good as new. I love you Pop. See you in a few hours. Hang in there." Next, Steve put his hand on Ray's shoulder and stared at him while tears rushed down his face and dropped onto his bed sheet. He leaned over one last time and said something in his father's ear. To this day, still no one knows what he said.

Beverly and her sons left the cubicle and walked into the waiting room. Plans were made for Beverly to contact both boys once she heard from the hospital. Michaels would drive Beverly to the hospital and Steve would meet them there, since he lived in Baltimore. Soon the three went home to await the call.

Michaels sat in his car and lit a cigarette. He looked at his hands and his entire body began shaking, he burst into tears. He laid his head on the steering wheel and let himself go, crying like a baby for ten minutes straight. With his emotions releasing, he was unsure if his outpouring was from his father's condition, or that which had been pent up within him.

He pulled himself together and drove home. On the way, he called Tommy to tell him what had happened to Ray.

"Homicide, Sergeant Suit."

"Hey Tommy, it's Ronnie."

"Shithead, what's going on?"

"My dad had a heart attack today."

"What? How is he?"

"They said he's going to be alright. They're flying him to Shock Trauma for bypass surgery now."

"Damn. I'll tell everyone. Does Jeff know?"

"No, shit. I have to call him."

"Don't worry about it. I'll call. How are you holding up?"

There was silence on the phone. His emotions turned to tears once more.

"Ronnie. He's going to be fine son. He'll be home before you know it. What else do you need me to do?"

"I'm good. We are just going to wait on the call from the hospital when he gets into recovery. What are you guys doing today?"

"Donald and the Police Academy Recruits are going to do a grid search at the crime scene to see what they can find."

"That's a good idea."

"Yeah, but hey, don't you worry about this place, you just take care of Ray and your mom. You hear me?"

"I will. Thanks. But if it goes as good as they think, I'll be in later."

They hung up and Michaels made it home. He desperately needed to clean his living room and take a shower. Once again, his body felt beaten and void of any energy.

Opening his door, the inside reeked of burnt cloth and smoke. After he cleaned the entire room, he laid on his bed for a much needed nap while he waited for Beverly's call.

He woke around noon and called Tommy immediately. He was curious about the results of the search by the police recruits.

"How's old Ray doing?"

"They haven't called yet, but it shouldn't be much longer. How did Donald do?"

"We got the fucking knife. One of the Recruits found it," he said with excitement.

"Alright, that is great. Any prints or blood on it?"

"There's blood all over it and Jeff's checking for fingerprints now. Tell your Dad I said we need his ass back to work."

Michaels chuckled. "Ok brother will do. I'll call you guys when we know something."

No sooner did he hang up, his phone rang. It was Beverly. She was crying and couldn't speak.

"Mom, Mom, Is dad ok? Mom answer me."

"Ronnie," she paused again. "The doctor just called. They did a four-way bypass surgery on his heart and put a defibrillator in him."

"Christ, you scared the hell out of me Mom. God. Well that's great news. What else did they say?"

"The doctor said everything went good and the device they put in will act like shock paddles if his heart stops."

"That's good to hear, when should I pick you up?"

"He's been in recovery for a while, so maybe by the time we get there he'll be awake."

Steve was waiting in the lobby when they arrived. A nurse in the cardiac area escorted them to his room. Ray was awake, but still groggy from the anesthesia. The color had returned to his face and arms and he didn't look like he belonged in a body bag anymore. His pupils weren't dilated, and his breathing seemed normal.

"Hi Love," Beverly said as she gave him a gentle hug and a big kiss on his lips.

"Hi there," he said with a little smirk on his face.

"Hi Pop," Michaels said.

"Hey Dad. How ya feeling?" Steve asked.

He made a little groan and grabbed the front of his chest. "It hurts when I breathe but they said that's from cutting me open. What happened? Did I get in an accident?"

"No Ray. You had a heart attack and you just came out of surgery," Beverly said giving him the entire low down from start to finish.

Ray couldn't remember anything. She told him how lucky he was to be alive. The three stayed with him for a few hours until the nurse said he needed some rest. They each gave Ray a hug and left him alone to sleep. They were glad to see him alive.

By 3:00 p.m., Michaels had dropped Beverly off at her home and was already dressed and on his way to the office.

He dialed Tommy's number. "Homicide. Sergeant Suit."

"I'm on my way in."

"What's going on? How's your dad Ronnie?"

"He looks good. They put some device in his chest in case his heart stops and did bypass surgery. They said it all went good and he should be out in a few days."

"A few days?" he yelled.

"Yeah, can you believe that? Bypass surgery is like changing oil in a car these days."

"Fuck Ronnie, that's good to hear. Are you available? Where are you?"

"Fuck, whoever did this needs to die Tommy," Michaels shouted.

"Woah. Woah. Are you ok Shithead?"

"Yeah, I'm fine. I was just up late last night and then all this with dad. I haven't had much sleep."

"I need you to pick up the young boy who discovered the bodies yesterday and bring him to the CID. Donald has already talked to his parents and they are ok with him sitting down with Barb to draw up a composite sketch of the man he saw running from the woods."

Detective Barbara King was a seasoned detective assigned to the Sex Crimes Unit and an extremely talented artist. Outside of her own personal drawings, she frequently did composite sketches for sex crimes, robbery and other cases. Without question, her gifted craft led to many apprehensions.

Michaels went straight to the neighborhood adjacent to the crime scene. He picked up the witness who discovered Daniel and Meagan and saw a black male run from the woods. He drove him back to the CID where he was introduced to Detective Barbara King. He left them alone in her office, along with an 18" sketch pad and a variety of special pencils.

Tommy spent the rest of the afternoon on the phone with the press about the double murder. After a 2-hour interview, Barbara produced a drawing of a light skinned black male, in his early 20's, wearing a do-rag on his head and an evil look on his face. The sketch was so lifelike even the witness was scared to look at it for any length of time. Tommy worked his magic and soon the drawing would find its way to the local newspapers and television stations.

Surprisingly, when Barbara's drawing hit the news few if any, credible leads came in. People in the surrounding communities were ringing the Police Chief's phone off the hook, but he had no new information. The community was on edge and Tommy was feeling the heat to get this one solved.

Since the release of the drawing, Mr. Ford and Mrs. Baton called the office several times to speak with Donald about updates. Most of the time, Donald and Mark were out running leads so Michaels took the calls. On their own, both families had over 5000 copies made of the drawing, which they distributed throughout the community, nearby apartments and single family homes. Every business in the shopping center had one posted in their window and it wasn't unusual for every car to have one under their windshield wiper during all hours of the day.

Two days following the murders, Michaels received a call one morning when he was about to leave for work. "Get ahold of Dredge. I need you guys to go to the Warwick Apartments and interview a lady. Dredge has the address."

"Well good morning to you too sergeant. What kind of wild goose chase is this?"

"I'm not sure. It's probably nothing. She sounds a little crazy and I don't want Dredge going alone. I could hear a male voice in the background when she called."

"Ok, see you in a little bit."

Michaels called Dredge and they arranged to meet at the entrance of the Warwick Apartments. These low rent apartments, located a short distance from the crime scene, was a place where the police were frequently called for fights, gunshots, domestics and much more. As usual Michaels arrived first and waited on Dredge. Several minutes passed when he pulled up next to Michaels driver's window. Smoke blew from his mouth as he came to a stop.

"Shithead, how's Ray?"

"Really good brother. Thanks for asking."

"That's good," the man of few words uttered.

"So, who are we interviewing?" Michaels asked.

"What happened to your hand and your forehead?"

"Oh nothing, I burned it on my grill. So, what do we have?" Michaels said quickly, changing the topic.

"It came through Dispatch to Tommy. It sounds like some goof wants to talk to a homicide detective. It doesn't sound like anything, but Tommy wants us to check it out. I think Mark is canvassing stores that sell knives in the area and Donald is with Jeff at Headquarters with the knife the recruit found."

"I'll follow you to the apartment."

The building was located next to a busy exit ramp off the beltway that led to the heavily travelled Ritchie Highway. There was a 5-foot-high fence that served as a barrier between the apartments and the highway. Kids would frequently climb the wall to get to the predominantly black, middle class community known as Norris Hills.

Both detectives got out of their cars and put their suit coats on. The two young men sitting on the front steps of the building darted inside when they got a glimpse of the two well-dressed gentlemen. He had to smile. It reminded him of his old narc days when they were about to hit a house.

Dredge barely knocked on the door when it opened. There stood a street hardened white female in her twenties with bleach blonde hair and dark roots. She had on faded blue jeans, a teal colored shirt and a blue Walmart vest with the name Jill on the name plate. It appeared as though she had just come home from work.

"Hey, yous guys with the Police Department? Come on in."

Dredge introduced them both. Neither had their notebooks out because they were convinced they were wasting their time.

"Have a seat. My name is Jill and that's my husband, Rocky, at the kitchen table. His real name is Robert, but we call him Rocky."

Robert was a black male in his thirties. You could tell who worked in the family and it sure wasn't him. He had on grey sweatpants, a raggedy t-shirt with no shoes or socks on. The kitchen had dirty dishes spread across the counter and in the sink. It was obvious Robert wasn't the one who called the police, nor did he want the detectives there.

"Rocky didn't want me to call but I said too bad. See, when I got home from work a little while ago, he told me about how this guy, Booker, who I never liked, came over to our apartment Sunday afternoon when I was at work. He said he was acting all fidgety and nervous and kept looking out the window. I heard about those kids being killed and I didn't want Rocky to be caught up in no murder. Hell, he just got out of jail."

The more she talked the more nervous Robert was getting. He wouldn't make eye contact with anyone. Dredge liked what he was hearing but they needed more. "Why did you wait until today to call us?" Dredge asked.

"Because that asshole didn't tell me until I got home today. I told him we ain't getting caught up in no conspiracy."

Michaels went over and sat next to Rocky so he could see his face and make him feel uncomfortable. "Rocky, are you still on parole?" Michaels said already knowing the answer. He wanted him to start processing the thought of having his parole violated if he didn't cooperate.

"Yeah."

"Tell us why you called."

Dredge pulled out his notebook and pen.

"I didn't call you, she did."

Michaels immediately slammed his hand down onto the table causing his ashtray to bounce in the air. Rocky jumped back in his chair.

"We're not here to play fucking games. We got two dead kids at the morgue and I'm putting fucking handcuffs on somebody today and I might as well start with you. So, let's try this again. Raise your fucking head and look at me." Rocky looked at Michaels. "For the last time, why the fuck are me and my partner here?"

"Man, he just knocked on the door and came rushing in like he was all whacked out on rock. He kept saying *I got into some bad shit. I got into some really bad shit*. I didn't know what he was talking about."

"Tell me what happened"

"Look I ain't no snitch."

Michaels stood from his chair and pulled his handcuffs from his waistband. "Stand up motherfucker. You're going to jail."

"No, no, no man wait, I'm going to tell ya. Chill man. His name is Booker."

The cuffs made a loud clanking sound when he dropped them on the table and returned to his seat. "Go on," Michaels pushed.

"Tell him about…"

"*Shut the fuck up,*" Rocky shouted to his wife. "He kept saying *he fucked up* over and over and kept looking out the window. He was getting me nervous, you know. I ain't going back for something I ain't do."

"Go ahead," Michaels asserted noticing Dredge writing from the corner of his eye.

"I said, what kind of shit and he wouldn't answer. He be acting all crazy like he was real paranoid or something, like he was on greens or some shit." Rocky lit up a cigarette.

"Then what?"

"He asked if he could have one of my shirts and if he could take a shower. So, I gave him one and he went into the bathroom."

"What did the shirt look like?"

"I think it was black. It might have had some writing on it. I'm not sure"

"Could you see if there was any blood on the shirt?"

No, I really don't remember. But it was black."

"What did he do with the shirt?"

"He had it rolled up in his hand. He took it with him when he left."

"Where is the towel he used to dry off with?"

"He left it on the floor, but I put it in the hamper."

"Show me what towel in the hamper."

"Shit baby, see, why didn't you tell me that shit, hell, I did laundry yesterday," Jill blurted out. "See if you would have told me...I'm sorry detectives. I didn't know."

"That's ok. What kind of pants did he have on?"

"I think they were black too."

"Shoes?"

"He had red and white Airs on."

"Airs?"

"Air Jordans."

"Did you see anything on the shoes?"

"Anything on the shoes?"

"Blood. Did you see any fucking blood on his shoes?"

"No man."

"Did he say where he was going when he left?"

"He just said *Are we cool*? And left out."

"What did he mean by that?"

"It means don't say he was here." Relieved, Rocky sat up in his chair. "It ain't cool if he killed them kids. They're just kids. Me and her got babies and that shit just ain't right, you know, if he did it."

"Of course. You are doing the right thing. You don't want to be an accomplice and be charged with murder."

Dredge looked up from his notes. "Is Booker his real name?"

"Yup, it's Booker T. Johnson."

Michaels smirked and looked at Rocky. "Are you serious?"

"Yup, that's what he called himself all the time. He bragged like he was someone important or some shit."

"Where does he live?"

"He be staying in Norris Hills with his moms and sometime with some girl he knocked up in the townhouses."

"Do you know what street in Norris Hills?"

"Cherry Lane, at the top of the hill."

"What townhouses are you talking about?" Michaels inquired.

"The ones right next to where those kids were."

"The kids that were killed?"

"Yeah."

"Do you know what street this girl lives on?"

"Nope. I only be knowing she was his Probation Officer in the Cut. That's where they hooked up."

"The Cut as in the Jessup Penitentiary?"

"Yeah."

"So, the girl he got pregnant was his Probation Officer in jail?"

Rocky took another long drag from his cigarette. "Yeah, he got that bitch pregnant and I heard that's why she got fired."

"Did she have his baby?"

"Not yet."

"What's her name?"

"It be like Chello or Mello or some shit."

"Describe her."

"She a chunky light skinned girl. The last I be seeing her she had long braids. She always wears tight clothes that don't fit her, you know, being all pregnant and shit. She around his age, 20 or something like that."

Michaels looked over at Dredge who was burning his pen up, flipping page after page. This was exactly the kind of break Donald needed. They couldn't wait to tell him the news and see his face. Dredge got all their personal information and left them with Donald's name and cell number.

"If he shows up again or you hear where he is, give Detective Hauf a call. His name and number are on the back of my card," Dredge instructed.

Dredge and Michaels walked to the parking lot next to their cars and lit up.

"Dredge, the crime scene is only a few hundred yards straight through these apartments, next to the townhouses. Are you calling Donald, or am I?"

"I think he and Mark are still out canvassing. We'll see him at the office. Do you want to stop and get a coffee?" Dredge asked.

"Absolutely brother. I'll follow you."

When Dredge and Michaels made it to the office, Donald and Mark's cars were in the lot. Exercising much discipline, Michaels forced himself to walk at a snail's pace next to Dredge through the building.

"Dredge, Young Shithead."

"Hey," Dredge mumbled.

"What's going on Ronnie? How's Ray doing?"

"I'll tell you what, he's lucky. His arteries were completely blocked but they did bypass surgery and he's good to go. Thanks for asking brother."

"Hell yeah. We've all been worried about him. So, was that a big waste of time? Some fucking goof?"

"Dredge would you like to tell fuck nuts what we got?"

"No. I think we should just go get a warrant and lock the son of a bitch up ourselves."

"Come on, bullshit, no fucking way," Donald yelled out.

"Don't listen to them Donald. If you assholes would excuse us, we got work to do," Mark said sarcastically from his desk.

"Put it this way. You might want to get on the computer and do a work up on a Booker T. Johnson, who recently got released from Jessup. He's supposed to be a black male in his twenties," Dredge said leaning back in his chair like a captain on a ship.

"Like Booker T. Washington?" Mark said.

"Yup, and that is supposed to be his real name," Michaels said.

"Are you guys bullshitting me?" Donald said now hovering over Dredge and Michaels' desks.

Tommy came walking back to the office. "What's going on?"

"That interview you sent them on wasn't bullshit. They said the guy who killed the two kids' name is Booker T. Johnson," Donald said typing on his computer. Shit, there is a Booker T. Johnson and he's got an address in Norris Hills on the other side of Ritchie Highway."

"Yup, that's him. That's where he stays with his mother sometimes," Dredge said looking over his notes.

Donald continued reading from the screen. "He's a black male, 25 years old, with a shit ton of arrests. Let's see, there's possession of cocaine, a bunch of assaults, passing bad checks, possession of marijuana and aggravated assault. It looks like he did 18 months for the aggravated assault. He got sentenced to 3 years in prison and all but 18 months suspended."

"Donald, listen to this." Dredge began recapping what Rocky had told them and to no surprise, his notes were spot on. After hearing the news, Donald had the biggest smile on his face. He was so happy, he slapped Michaels a stiff high five and planted a big kiss on Dredge's cheek.

"Get the fuck away from me you crazy ass," Dredge said jokingly to Donald.

Michaels chimed in. "Yeah the people we talked to were husband and wife and the husband said he and Booker spent time in the Cut together. Supposedly, Booker knocked up some Probation Officer in prison and she got fired because of it. But the good news is, she lives in the townhouses next to your crime scene and he stays with her sometimes."

"Fucking A! Woo hoo!" Donald yelled.

"Any fingerprints on the knife Donald?" Dredge asked.

"No, everything was smudged."

"Did they say where he's laying his head?"

"He wasn't sure, but it sounds like both Norris Hills or with the pregnant girl, Chello or Mello, something like that."

"Do we know her last name?" Tommy asked.

"No," Dredge said.

"And your saying she worked as a probation officer?"

"Yeah, that's what he said."

"I'm calling up there now," Donald asserted.

"I want to find that shirt and whatever else he threw away. There's got to be blood on it. Got to be," Tommy said exhaling a big puff of smoke.

It was after 4:00 p.m. and the Parole & Probation Department at the prison was closed for the day. Donald spoke with several guards and supervisors, none of which were familiar with Booker or a probation officer named Chello or anything close to that. Donald was getting frustrated with whomever he was speaking to. He felt sure he was getting the run around.

"Fucking bullshit. Like they've never heard of Booker T. Johnson in their jail? Are you fucking kidding me? And a Parole and Probation Officer named Chello or whatever the fuck, really? Like who wouldn't remember those names? Dirty motherfuckers. It sounded like they were covering for him."

"I just tried the rental office for the townhouse Donald, but they're closed too," Mark said.

"Thanks. Come on Mark, let's take a ride to Norris Hills. I'm taking a couple of big trash bags because I'm telling you, if their trash is out, we're taking it. I don't give a fuck if his mother likes it or not."

"Dredge and Shithead go home. Donald, you and Mark go home after you ride by Booker's house, and I'll see you two at 3 p.m."

Tommy looked at Dredge and Michaels who were still sitting at their desk. "Go, get the fuck out of here," he said.

When Michaels made it home, there was an envelope taped to his door. On the outside was a handwritten sticky note which read, *Ronnie, would you please look this over. I have to read this in court next week at Golas' sentencing. Tell me how it sounds please. Thanks, Darlene.* Inside was a copy of Darlene's Victim Impact Statement.

He changed into sweatpants and fixed a straight rum on the rocks. He pulled a frozen pizza from the freezer, threw it in the oven and took a seat on his recliner. He knew all too well what he was about to delve into would be a touching read, jammed full of heart wrenching stories of cherished times spent together, the indescribable emptiness and the enormous loss the family was experiencing all because of the careless addiction of one person. This one would be no different.

The emotionally packed statement was well written and this one especially hit home, since he knew all the players. What took him by surprise was the unexpected jaw-dropping words written at the end.

I remember the words Ronnie said when he told me Mom had passed. I keep having dreams of him in my living room. I wished I would have never let him in. Those were the most devastating words ever spoken to me. It felt like a dream and I feel that if I had not opened the door, it never would have happened. Every time I see Ronnie I want to cry. I can't stop thinking of that night. It haunts me.

Michaels dropped the papers in his lap. He couldn't believe what he had just read. He folded the papers back into the envelope and laid it on the dining room table. He couldn't read anymore. He gulped down his cocktail, helped himself to another and walked outside to his tiny backyard.

He was puzzled as to why Darlene put that part in her statement, but more importantly how she felt about him. It all made sense, thinking that was the reason he hasn't seen much of Darlene since that night. He took a seat on the back steps, smoked, drank and stared at his 12'x 12' grassy plot. *Does every person I've told feel the same way about me?* Depression draped over him like a heavy blanket. *How did I get this way? These things aren't supposed to eat at me.*

His thoughts were interrupted from the obnoxious sound of a smoke alarm. He rushed inside to a smoke-filled kitchen and dining room, with the smell of burning pizza emanating from the oven. Forgetting to set the timer, his dinner was badly charred. He shut off the stove and propped open the back door. He carefully put his extra crispy, charred Italian dinner on the stove top to cool.

With the door open, he took a seat once more on the steps and drank until the air cleared. While waiting for things to subside, he realized he hadn't checked on Ray in several hours. He called Beverly.

"Hi Mom."

"Hi Son. How are you?"

"Well besides burning my pizza, I'm alright I guess."

"You don't sound right. Are you ok? Have you been drinking? You know, you better watch your drinking."

It's funny how mothers have a sixth sense about their kids, he thought. "I know Mom. I'm not drinking much. I can't, I have been working too much."

"Why don't you come over later Hun? I have left over spaghetti and meatballs."

"Thanks, but I need to get to bed early tonight."

"Well you be careful. I worry about you."

"I'm ok Mom. Can I talk to Dad?"

"Here Ray, it's Ronnie."

"Hello"

"Hey Pop. How ya feeling?"

"Pretty good. How's the case going?"

"We got a good call today. Hopefully we'll be making an arrest soon."

"Good. Good."

Talking to Ray was like talking to Dredge, only the bare minimum was said and no more.

"I hope I get to shoot this guy Dad. I want to put a bullet in his head so bad. It would be sadder to kill a deer. And I mean that. I can't stop thinking of those little kids in the woods. That motherfucker needs to die."

"Be careful. Your mother wants to know if you are coming over?"

"No. I can't."

"Alright." Michaels could tell he was ready to hang up.

"Glad you're feeling better Pop."

"Thanks"

"I love you Dad." There was an odd silence on the phone. "Dad?" The phone went dead.

The smoke was all but gone and he closed the back door. The only odor left was the blackened pizza and cigarettes. By now he had 8 stiff drinks and he took a seat in the living room when something frightening happened, making the hair on the back of his neck and arms stand up. Abruptly, he vividly began seeing and hearing the voices of past homicide victims. None of this made sense. These were people he had never seen alive or had spoken to, except Darlene's mother. Some were standing in his living room, some were where their bodies were discovered, and others were at the homes where he told their loved ones of their deaths. One by one each victim scolded him for the way he delivered their death notification. They kept repeating how his method was wrong and how disappointed they were with him.

He couldn't decipher what was happening. This out of body experience made him question his skills but he didn't know what to do. Throughout this surreal experience he kept saying how sorry he was to each victim. The next thing he knew he found himself kneeling in the hallway leading to his bedroom, with his head on the ground crying like a baby. His hair was drenched with sweat, the lights were out, and no TV was on. Confused, he sat against the wall and wiped the tears from his face. He crawled into his bed not understanding what had just happened. Perhaps Darlene's letter had taken hold of him.

No sooner had he laid down when there was a knock at the door. He climbed into his sweat pants and opened the door. It was Darlene. "Can I come in and talk to you?" Michaels could see she had a folder in her hand.

Drunk, he tried not to slur his words, "Sure, come in. I just got home from work."

"What's that smell? Did you burn something?"

"Yeah, I burned my pizza. It's been a crazy couple of days. I've been working that murder, then in the middle of all that, my dad had a heart attack."

"Oh no. How is he?"

"He's good now. He had bypass surgery, which is almost routine these days. What's up?"

She looked down at the bandage on his hand. "What happened to your hand?"

"I burned it on the grill. No biggie."

"Did you find who killed those poor kids?"

"Not yet. We might have a lead but that needs to be kept secret for now."

"Will do. Umm, are you sure you're alright?"

"Yeah, I'm good. I'm just tired is all. What's going on with you?"

"Well I had a meeting at the State's Attorney's Office today and can you believe the guy's lawyer doesn't think he should get any jail time? He killed my mother for Christ sake."

"What did the prosecutor say?"

"They've agreed not to ask for more than five years and that's a joke. This whole thing has been a real eye opener. Did you get a chance to look at my statement?"

"Yeah, I was going to leave it on your door, but here I'll give it to you now. It sounds good." Michaels wouldn't dare tell her how she crucified him in the statement.

"Alright, well I'll leave you be. I hope your dad is ok and I hope you find who killed those children."

"Thanks Darlene."

"Good night," she said giving Michaels a quick hug before she departed.

"Good night."

The next morning Tommy had been pulling his hair out trying to get the Department of Corrections and the Parole & Probation Department to tell him the full name and address of the former employee, once assigned to the Jessup prison, referred to as Chello. After a frustrating hour on the phone, he was able to identify her as Chello March. Though they wouldn't say the reason for her termination, they did provide her last known address after Tommy threatened to have the lieutenant on the phone arrested for Obstruction of Justice.

Michaels had put a nice suit and tie on when his cell phone rang. It was Tommy. "What are you doing?"

"Drinking coffee, about to come in."

"No, write this down. Call Dredge and go to this address on Kent Circle. It's the last address Parole & Probation had for Chello March, who worked at Jessup."

"Is she the chick Booker got pregnant?"

"Sure is."

"Let me give Dredge a call. See ya." Michaels jotted down the address and called Dredge. "Good morning, you big dick motherfucker."

Dredge laughed. "What's going on young man?"

"Tommy gave me an address he wants us to check for that Chello girl."

"Where is it?"

"It's in the same townhouses where Daniel lived, but on Kent Circle. I'll meet you there"

"Ok."

The address was about a 30 second walk to the crime scene. Michaels arrived first and avoided parking in front of the home since he had no idea how long Dredge would be. After a brief wait, Dredge pulled next to him.

"What's going on you bag of shit?"

"Good morning Dredge."

"What house is hers?"

"241. The one with the trash can laying on its side and all the shit in the front yard."

Before they went in, they decided Dredge would be the point man and Michaels would be on notes. The plan was set, and they made their way to the townhouse. When they walked up the steps, through the glass storm door, they could see two black females in the living room talking and one was noticeably pregnant. Dredge knocked hard on the door, startling both women.

"Who is it?" One of the women said with an attitude.

"Police," Dredge said loudly.

The door opened. "I didn't call no police." Dredge opened the door with his badge in his hand and he and Michaels stepped into the foyer. "We are homicide detectives. Are you Chello March?"

"Wait, wait, you all just can't waltz in here like that."

It was obvious Dredge wasn't in the mood to play with witnesses. "I said are you Chello March?" he asked again this time raising his voice.

"Yeah. Why?"

Dredge then turned to the other female on the couch. "Do you live here?"

"No, but I'm her Aunt."

"Good. You can leave."

"What?"

Dredge extended his arm and opened the front door. "You heard me. Leave."

The other female walked toward the front door. "Chello, get his badge number, I'm gonna complain about him. He's rude."

Michaels was enjoying this show because he rarely got to see his partner that cranked up. "Have a seat, we need to talk," he told Chello.

Michaels opened his notebook and Dredge jumped right in. "When was the last time you saw Booker?"

"Booker? A couple of days ago, why?"

"When was a couple days ago?"

"Um, I think it was Sunday. Yeah Sunday, Mother's Day."

"What time did he come over?"

"Oh, I know exactly what time it was. It was 10 in the morning because he done woke me up. He was banging on the door and calling out my name. I already got a letter from the Rental Office. They said any more police at my house and I'm going to get kicked out. I told Booker, I can't be getting kicked out of my house when I'm about to have his baby. That's why I took his key"

"What did he do when he was here?"

"Shit, I just went back to bed. All his little black ass came over for was pussy. He kept trying to pull my gown up and kissing me, but I wasn't having any of that. I told him I don't care what he does I ain't having no sex. I mean look at me." She stood from the couch and stuck out her tremendous belly. "Do I look like I want to have sex? Hell to the no."

Michaels smiled, but Dredge was stone faced. "Then what happened?"

"He got all pissed off like he always do, calling me a bunch of names and shit, then went downstairs."

"What did he do downstairs?"

"I heard him in the kitchen. I thought he was fixing something to eat but he just slammed the door and left. I swear he's gonna get me kicked out."

"Do you have any knives Chello?"

"Shit, what do you mean? Yeah, I got knives. Why?"

"Let me look at your knives."

"Why?"

"Look lady, unless you want to spend the rest of your life in jail being an accomplice to a double murder, I suggest you show me your God damn knives."

Chello jolted her head back and frowned at Dredge. "Murder, what you mean murder? Are you talking about those two little kids? I didn't kill those kids. You think I killed those kids? You all need to be out there catching them instead of talking to me. My knives are in the kitchen."

Michaels followed Chello and Dredge into the kitchen. He hadn't seen Dredge that pissed off since Alonso. At the end of the counter top was a wooden butcher block knife holder with two empty slots.

"Where are the missing knives?"

She walked over to the sink and picked up a long knife. "Here's one. I had Italian bread last night with my pasta."

Dredge walked over to the holder and removed a random knife. It was the same brand as the one found at the scene. Chello opened the dishwasher and looked through the dirty dishes but there was no other knife.

"Now where in the hell is my big carving knife? That little motherfucker. That was a Christmas gift from my aunt too." With a shocked look on her face, her mouth dropped opened and she looked at Dredge. "Oh my Lord, do, do you think Booker killed those kids?"

"Are you sure the knife couldn't be somewhere else?" Dredge asked.

"No, that knife is only used for Thanksgiving and shit. You know for like turkeys and hams." She put her left hand over her mouth. "Booker killed those kids? Oh my God. He couldn't. He couldn't. He just got out of jail. He doesn't want to go back. He said he would die before he ever went back."

"Listen to me Chello. I'm going to leave you my business card, along with another detective's name and cell number. If you hear from Booker or if he comes over, call Detective Hauf right away. If you can't get him, call me. Do not tell him we were here or who knows what will happen to you. Do you hear me? Don't say a word to anyone." Chello was visibly stunned from the news. Even she knew there were too many coincidences for this not to be true.

Dredge and Michaels walked to their cars. "Bingo, we got his ass," Michaels said. "Yup. fucking asshole couldn't get laid, so he takes her biggest knife and for what? Because he's pissed off, he can't get any pussy? Are you fucking kidding me? Jesus fucking Christ Dave. This motherfucker doesn't deserve to live. He needs to die."

"I know."

"I'm serious. This rat bastard doesn't deserve to be on this earth after what he did. I don't want to see Donald lock him up and I don't want to see his punk ass in court. I only want to see him dead with a bullet hole in his forehead. It's that easy," Michaels was fuming.

"Ok, Shithead. Who pissed in your Corn Flakes?"

"Nobody. I just can't stand fucking people like him."

"I know. Let's go tell Donald. I'll see you back at the office."

On the way back, Michaels called Tommy. "We got 'em now."

"Talk to me Shithead. What did you boys get?"

"I didn't do anything. It was all Dredge. He was on fire. He had Chello eating out of his hand and come to find out, she's missing a 10" carving knife too. There's no doubt Booker did this."

"We all agree here too. Donald and Mark had a long conversation with Booker's mother. She last saw him Sunday afternoon around 2 p.m. and he wasn't acting like himself, and since then he's called her a few times for no reason. She asked where he was, and he said at a girl's house."

"If that's true, I don't think he was with Chello. He wants to do the nasty and she's big time pregnant and wants nothing to do with that, which is the reason I think he attacked those kids, so he could rape the girl."

"God damn it. Ok, get in here and give Donald what you have so he can get the warrant for Booker. I want all of us to go find this guy."

"Tommy, I want to kill him. I hope he resists arrest."

"Calm down Shithead, I'll see you when you get here."

After a long day of paperwork, Michaels went home and for the first night in many, he ate dinner and went to bed without indulging in any beverages. He was exhausted.

In the morning, he had an urge to get out and do something to clear his head. He desperately needed to do something other than police work, so he decided to pull out his golf clubs and relieve some frustrations at the local driving range. He packed his golf bag in the trunk. When he pulled into the lot, the range had not yet opened. It was only 8 a.m. and they didn't open for another hour. Accidently, he left his phone at home so now he could only sit and think. Lately, whenever he had a spare moment, his mind drifted to the woods where Daniel and Meagan were slain.

With time to spare, Michaels opened his notebook and began to jot down his feelings in the form of poetry, a long-lost past time. The words came easy. He was writing so fast he could barely read his own scribble. At times, he could feel himself welling up. This so called therapy at the driving range would forever be called, *The Sadness I Feel.*

The sadness I feel seems to come almost daily

The bodies of two young children lie motionless in the woods

Leaning against a tree, I imagine the horror and fear that must have taken place and I keep asking myself why?

Why take the precious gift of life from an innocent child?

Why leave their families without their loved ones, never having the chance to say I love you for the last time?

This feeling of helplessness comes when a man who calls himself a policeman, a man who is responsible for solving crimes and being impartial, must now tell a mother, father, sister or brother that they have lost a family member.

That someone without any regard for their feelings, their love, or their lives has taken the future away from someone dear to them.

This is when that hardened man must remove the emotionless barrier and become personal, be a friend, lend a shoulder, hold a hand and preserve their life when they feel like giving up.

This is a time when a policeman no longer wants his job.

He asks the Lord if this is his punishment.

He asks the Lord to help him.

He finds he feels sorry for himself for having to perform such a task, but soon realizes where his sorrow should lie, with the families.

As they cry, scream, faint, break things and then hug you. You, a man whom they have never met until now. They clutch onto you for help, for the return of their son or daughter.

You stand there, returning their hug fighting back the tears and feeling helpless. Like being sent to a job without your equipment, there is nothing you can do.

Finally, you leave their home and they thank you, thank you for being so kind, so nice, so helpful, while all along you felt useless.

You drive off, quiet and drained of all your energy.

No one will ever know the pain you have seen, the sorrow you feel responsible for.

Needless to say, he never hit a single ball, but he did get to dump some of his feelings on paper. Not realizing how much time had passed, he closed his notebook and drove home to prepare for the evening's man hunt. His life had become consumed with work and he sorely missed Nicole. He hadn't seen her in several days.

It was still too early to go to work, so he did things around his house to keep his mind occupied. He finished the laundry, emptied the trash and cleaned up his burnt Italian cuisine, still on top of the stove. He pulled out his gun cleaning supplies and wiped down the five shot .38 caliber revolver Ray had given him years ago. He dryfired it several times, going through the motions of a smooth trigger squeeze in case he had the chance to kill Booker. Never had he felt such a compelling desire to kill someone like he did now. Booker, he thought, needed to pay for what he had done and being catered to by the judicial system would not suffice. *I don't even think God himself could forgive an animal like Booker.* Michaels was certain of that.

When he got to work by 2 p.m., everyone from the unit was sitting at their desk, anxious to find Booker T. Johnson. "Young Shithead," Tommy yelled out as he saw him walking toward their office.

"How's everyone?" All of them acknowledged, except Mark. He had a smartass comment of course.

"Nice you could make it in Michaels."

"Fuck you, you poodle headed looking bitch."

"Did you get the warrant Donald?" Michaels asked with excitement.

"I'm almost done, then I'm going to drop it at the Commissioner's Office."

"Cool. Do you need me to do anything brother?"

"Nope." Donald pulled the sheet of paper from the typewriter and announced, "Done. Now, we just need to find him." Donald and Mark left the office. Tommy had already called the on-duty commissioner and told him they were on their way and to make it a priority. He agreed.

By 5:00 p.m. Donald and Mark returned with a 1st Degree Murder Warrant for Booker T. Johnson. Now the hunt would begin. Tommy devised a plan for the unit to split up. It was ingenious. Dredge and Michaels were to ride together and saturate the townhouses where Chello lives, along with the Warwick Apartments where Rocky and Jill lives. As for Mark and Tommy, they would stay in the Norris Hills community where Booker's mother resides. Tommy hoped he would show up at one of the two locations or be seen walking in the area. The most important and classic assignment was for Donald. Tommy ordered him to stay at the office and partially disrobe, like always, for good luck and communicate regularly with Jill, Booker's mother and Chello. The direct order was explicit and firm causing Donald to immediately begin removing his pants.

"No, no, not yet asshole. Wait until we hit the streets."

"Yes sir," Donald said as they all laughed.

Another task assigned to Donald was to have Dispatch broadcast a lookout for Booker. In no time, every police department in the Baltimore Metropolitan region simulcasted the name and description of Booker and the 1st Degree Murder warrant that was on file. On top of that, Donald was coordinating with the department's Public Information Officer to have all local television stations plaster Booker's face on every news channel and his description on every radio station, in hopes of receiving tips of his whereabouts.

Donald handed everyone in the unit the most recent mug shot of Booker. Michaels studied it and put it in his rear pocket. Booker's face was already burned in his brain and the picture only enhanced his rage. The entire unit, minus Donald, left the building at the same time to begin the search. Michaels grabbed his handcuffs from his car and tucked them in his waistband. Dredge would be driving and the young one would be the eyes. Once settled in Dredge's car, Michaels placed the mug shot on the console, so Dredge could see his face.

The sun was starting to set, and their search began in the townhouses. They drove up and down every street, saying little to one another, eyeing up everyone. This was a hunt like no other for the unit. Periodically, Donald would get on the radio and tell them that none of his sources had heard or seen the suspect. Donald and Dredge laughed picturing Donald standing at his desk, transmitting on his radio, wearing a heavily starched white shirt, blue tie, purple boxers and shiny black shoes.

In two separate cars, the unit combed the areas for the next several hours without a sighting of Booker. By now every cop working in Anne Arundel, Baltimore County and Baltimore City knew of the lookout. At 9:00 p.m. Dredge and Michaels met Tommy and Mark in the shopping center where the kids shopped just before their senseless death. Parked side by side smoking and chatting,

Tommy's cell phone rang. It was Donald. Tommy had a concerned look on his face while he wrote in his notebook. Whatever he was being told, they could see it was important.

"That was Donald. He just spoke to Rocky. Booker called and said he saw his picture on television and he knows he's wanted. He's supposedly chilling at some girl's townhouse and is going back to Norris Hills soon to score some crack. Jill said he doesn't have a car and when he goes from the townhouses to Norris Hills, he normally crosses the wall at the Warwick Apartments."

"Ronnie, come here," Tommy said stepping from his car and leaning against the trunk. This was odd, Michaels thought.

Tommy lit up a fresh cigarette and spoke in a very low voice to Michaels. "Do you know where this crossing is?"

"Yup. I sure do."

"Have Dredge drop you off somewhere near there and if you see him, well you know what to do."

"Got it."

"You good?"

"You fuckin A, I'm good," Michaels said looking Tommy directly in the eyes.

Tommy and Mark sped away to surveil the Norris Hills' community. Michaels directed Dredge to the exit ramp between the apartments. A grassy area next to the roadway leading to Ritchie Highway had an old tree and a row of bushes growing.

"Stop here Dredge. Let me out."

"What?"

"Just drop me off here and drive around in the area and keep your radio on. I'll be behind that tree," he said pointing to a large maple.

Dredge was a Vietnam Vet. He understood and knew the value of killing the enemy. The aging timber would give Michaels enough cover and concealment and allow him a prime view of the location where Booker would most likely cross.

"Be careful son."

Michaels snatched the mug shot from the console. At the tree, he cleared brush from the ground to silence his movements, then crouched down. He turned his radio volume to low, then removed the clean Smith & Wesson from his holster and clutched it firmly. He was hunting, but this time it was for a man.

From time to time traffic would pass by Michaels, causing him to hunker down. He laid Booker's picture on the ground in between him and the tree. From his vantage point, he could see the worn out path less than 20 feet away, leading to the short barrier where people crossed. Michaels visualized his every action if Booker were to appear, down to the final shot.

An hour passed when Donald's voice came over the radio. "Listen up guys, our suspect was just seen leaving the apartments. Stand by. Keep your eyes open."

Everyone knew what apartments he was referring to and Michaels repositioned his body behind the tree. He was ready and determined to kill this motherfucker. Listening closely, he could hear a noise coming from the direction of the apartments. It was the faint sound of someone walking.

The detective remained still, like he was hunting a trophy buck. His eyes shifted from side to side trying to pick up movement. His senses were heightened. Suddenly he saw someone approaching. From the slight glimmer of the nearby streetlight, he could make out a short black male, with the same build as Booker. The person was still too far to identify his face, but he was walking fast as if he was in a hurry. Michaels lifted his right hand and leaned his forearm against the tree for support. He put pressure on the trigger while he leveled the sights from his handgun on his torso. After a few more steps, he stopped. Michaels looked down at the mugshot then back to the person in his sights. He believed it was Booker but needed confirmation. Increasing the force on his trigger, he was ready to send a .38 caliber hollow point into the man's body. Life was about to end with a few more pounds of pressure on the trigger. In the distance Michaels heard the voice of another male. Raising his head, he could see a second black male walking in the same direction.

"Jimmy, wait up," yelled a younger looking male to the first subject.

"Fuck," Michaels whispered lowering his head and exhaling. He lowered his weapon and loosened his grip. He watched while the two young men scaled the fence and made their way to the Norris Hills' community.

"Ronnie, did you see those two just come through?" Dredge asked.

Disappointed, he answered. "Yeah, it wasn't him."

An hour or more had passed with no sightings or incoming information from any of the sources. Only two sets of females crossed the wall, still no Booker.

Tommy came on the radio with unexpected news. "Is everyone on the air?" Donald, Dredge and Michaels all acknowledged him.

"I just got word, our suspect is DOA in the city. He was shot a few minutes ago in a suicide by cop attack." There was a brief pause over the radio. "Everyone meet back at the office."

"Ronnie, I'll pick you up in 30 seconds," Dredge advised.

Michaels yelled out, furious from the news. He wanted to be the one to end Booker's existence. He looked down at the mug shot laying on top of the leaves. He pointed the barrel of his weapon directly at the face on the picture. He swiftly unloaded five rounds into the photograph, obliterating it into pieces. He shoved the gun back into the holster, when he noticed Dredge's car pulling up to the nearby shoulder. The picture, now speckled with bullet holes, remained at the base of the tree. Michaels sternly planted his foot on it, mashing it into the ground before he walked to Dredge's car.

"Did you just hear gun shots?" Dredge asked Michaels when he climbed in his car.

"No, that was a car back firing."

"Oh, it sounded just like a gun."

They drove back to the office. The entire unit couldn't wait to hear what had happened in the city. Part of Michaels was happy and another part angry. The first person everyone could see when they approached the office was Donald, dancing in his boxers, singing his own version of Ding Dong the Witch is Dead. He was extremely happy. No one, except Tommy, cared to embrace Donald in his boxers but Dredge had no choice when he threw his arms around him and laid a big wet kiss on his cheek. Dredge stood there with his arms to his side and a big smile on his face. "Get the fuck off of me, would ya?"

All the members of the unit took a seat at their desks, while Tommy placed a call to his friend and comrade, the Commander of the Baltimore City Homicide Division. After a short conversation, he came out to brief the anxiously awaiting detectives.

"Listen up. It's still early but what they know so far is patrol responded to a disorderly subject, who appeared to be all fucked up, yelling crazy shit and carrying a knife. He was told to drop the knife, which he refused to do and then started screaming like a wild man, charging at 3 police officers. Some or all of them shot and killed Booker. They said it was an obvious case of suicide by cop. So, there you have it. Case solved. Donald, call Doc Johnson. We're all going to Kaufman's to celebrate. It's on me tonight."

"Boss, I'll be running a little behind. I want to call both families and let them know what happened before they hear it on the news," Donald explained.

"We'll see you there. Budweiser bottle, right?"

"Fuck yeah."

"I'll have a cold one waiting for ya Donald," Tommy assured him.

The night was a celebration for the closure of a terrible double murder, hosted by the illustrious Sergeant Tommy Suit, a leader like few others. It was hard to describe, but Tommy had the look of a proud dad on his face when he ordered drinks for his men. He knew he had developed an unstoppable, genuinely talented group of professionals. While the evening progressed, not only did he have his four detectives together, but surprisingly, Doc Johnson even showed. During the evening's festivities, Michaels had Doc retrieve his antique camera and take a picture of the unit. Everyone was delighted.

The night consisted of laughter, high fives and plenty of alcohol. Donald and Michaels purposefully omitted discussing the two depressing death notifications for obvious reasons. Michaels quickly learned since being in the unit that no one ever talked about death notifications. Ever. It was as if a wall was put up to forget they ever occurred. They enjoyed plenty of food, smoked an inordinate number of cigarettes and drank alcohol like prohibition was starting the next day. Everyone got shitfaced, including Doc.

"Who, who is on call tonight?" Tommy slurred.

"What's tonight?" Dredge said as he took a big drag from his Merritt.

"I don't know. Shit, I don't know what today is," Tommy said in disbelief.

"It's Friday you dumb asses," Doc said.

"Today's Friday?" Donald asked in amazement.

"Young Shithead is on call," Tommy yelled out.

"What? Aww fuck, that's bullshit, I'm done," Michaels yelled out.

"What? You ain't done Shithead. Have a victory shot with all of us first," Donald insisted.

Three toasts later with the cheapest house Tequila, Michaels made his way to his car and began his drive home. It was a bitter sweet night for Michaels, one full of mixed emotions. Once home, he parked and hurried to open the car door, spewing vomit across the floorboard and onto the pavement.

"It should have been me, me. It should have been me who shot him. I wanted to kill that worthless asshole," he yelled tripping toward his front door.

Hearing the commotion outside, Darlene opened her door. "Ronnie are you ok?"

Michaels tried his best to straighten up. "Hi Darlene."

"What are you doing?"

"Oh, I'm just coming, coming home from work. I'm a little tired."

"Goodnight and if I didn't say so, thanks for reading my statement."

"You're welcome. Good, goodnight Darlene." After several attempts he managed to get the key in his door and push it open. He staggered to the kitchen and poured himself a rum on the rocks. Haphazardly he threw his gun, badge and wallet on the table, using a dining room chair to brace himself. He peeled his suit coat off and attempted to hang it on the chair to no avail. He took one sip of his cocktail and dropped the glass on the table. Mentally worn out from the past few days, he was on the verge of passing out.

Inebriated, he laid down on his bed once again seeing the faces of young Daniel and Meagan lying in the woods. He struggled to open the bottle of sleeping pills on his nightstand and swallowed the last three. He knew he needed to sleep. Finally, he felt the pills, along with the alcohol taking effect and his eyes grew heavy.

Almost an hour passed when Michaels was startled. He squirmed in bed, shuttering his eyes open and closed, while he tried to identify the wakening noise he was hearing. Realizing he wasn't dreaming, he sorted his thoughts and determined it was his phone. He turned the nightstand light on and reached around with half squinting eye lids for his phone. Even with blurred vision, he could make out the familiar numbers of the Dispatch Center. He looked at the clock and could see it was almost 1 in the morning and he was still fucked up.

"Damn it, give me a break," he yelled. He fell back onto his pillow and let out a big sigh. He knew he had to answer the call, but he needed a moment to gather himself. "Fuck," he said while the phone kept sounding. The Dispatch Center was desperately trying to reach him. "Jesus fucking Christ ok, I'm coming," he shouted ripping the blanket from his body and stomping into the kitchen where his notepad was. "Fuck." He pressed the call button on his phone. "Hello," he said in a grumpy voice.

"Hi Detective Michaels, this is Leo from Channel 5. How are you?"

Now what kind of question is that he thought at 1 a.m.? "I'm fucking sleeping. How do you think I am?" He took a seat at the dining room table.

Shocked by his comment, Leo relayed the call to Michaels. "Sergeant Suit told me to call you. We have a messy triple murder in Brooklyn, and he wants you to respond as soon as possible. Do you want the address now or do you want to call me when you get into your car?"

"*Motherfucker,*" he yelled in disgust. "A triple homicide? Really? I can't catch a fucking break. God damn it. Fuck it Leo, I'll call you," and he threw the phone as hard as he could onto the kitchen cabinets. The phone shattered with pieces of plastic and electronics flying across the floor. "I can't fucking do this, I can't fucking do this anymore, dear God."

He took four big gulps from the warm rum still on the table. He slammed down the empty glass and looked at his wallet. He reached down and pulled out his favorite picture of him and Nicole sitting on a park bench at Herrington Lake in Western Maryland. His eyes filled with tears. She was the precious age of four at the time of their only father/daughter weekend. He laid the picture in front of him. The tears flowed from his eyes. "We had such a fun weekend together. I wish we had more time Honey. I'm sorry." The undeniable feelings of guilt overtook him. "Daddy loves you Honey."

His entire body quivered as he was losing all control over what was happening to him. A peculiar cold rushed through his veins. He was painfully saddened, and his body and mind had been badly beaten. He didn't want to do this anymore. He couldn't do this anymore. He no longer could be the bearer of the worst news anyone could ever imagine. He pulled the .38 caliber Smith & Wesson revolver from the holster and struggled to say these words. *I'm sorry Dad. I hope I've made you proud.* The distraught detective put the cold steel barrel in his mouth while staring at Nicole's smiling face in the photograph. She looked so beautiful. He was so proud of her. He squeezed the grip tightly with his trembling right hand then placed his thumb across the grooved trigger. He could feel his heart beating rapidly. Tears dropped onto the cylinder, his clenching hand and the table. His eyes were open. He waited as he watched the hammer of the gun rock slowly backwards. In an instant he felt warm again and his body stopped shaking. He was at peace.

Michaels came to as Paramedics hovered over him while the blood pressure cuff was strapped to his upper arm, pumping tightly to his bicep. Startled and confused, he focused on Tommy looking down at him on the living room floor.

"Ronnie, Young Shithead are you ok buddy?"

Michaels lifted himself to a sitting position. "What the fuck happened to me?" he said rubbing his pounding head. His sight cleared, and he quickly scanned the room in confusion when he noticed pieces of his shattered phone on the kitchen floor and his gun laying on the table next to a picture of his daughter. The dining room chair he normally used was lying on its side at his feet.

"I think you were just run down from being up so much the last few days and then on top of that you had a few cocktails brother. You'll be alright."

"His pulse is 120/80 sir. He's fine. Would you like us to take him to the ER for a head X-ray in case he injured himself from the fall?" one of the paramedics asked.

"No, no, I'm good. My head is fine. Let me get off this floor. Jesus fucking Christ." With help from Tommy, he took a seat in the chair the paramedic had set upright.

"Thanks guys. I appreciate your help. You can go and let's not talk about this. We don't want to make more of this than what it is. Ok fellas?" Tommy asserted to the seasoned paramedics.

"Yes sir. No problem," the older paramedic assured him while he tore the Velcro strip from Michael's arm. They packed their gear into their trauma bag and were soon gone.

"What the fuck happened Tommy? The last thing I remember was getting home."

"We were all still out when the Dispatch Center called me and said they notified you of a triple murder. The dispatcher said you cussed at him, then he heard a loud crashing noise over the phone, and it went silent. They couldn't get you on the radio or phone, so they called me. I remembered where you kept the extra key, so I had the paramedics meet me here." Tommy retrieved a water bottle from the refrigerator. "Here, get some water in you boy."

"Thanks." He pointed to a small shelf above the kitchen sink. "Grab me four of those Ibuprofens please. My head is killing me."

Tommy looked concerned. "How are you feeling?"

"I'm good Tommy. Really. I'm fine."

"Get a shower and get some sleep. I'll see you in a few hours at the office."

"Sounds good. I'm sorry you had to do all this. I'll be alright. So who's working the triple homicide?"

"It ended up being a double murder/suicide. Mark said it was a horrible crime scene, but an easy case. It was the double murder of two young kids and the suicide of their mother who stuck a 9mm handgun in her mouth and blew the top of her head off.

"God damn it. I'm sorry. Fuck. I don't know what happened to me Tommy."

"The boys got it Ronnie. Don't worry. Get some rest son. I'll see you later."

After Tommy's departure, Michaels poured the contents from the half filled, watered down rum and Coke in the sink. In seconds, the frosted cocktail glass was refreshed with rum and a splash of Coke. The time was 2:00 a.m.

The next morning at the office, Tommy was first in and Michaels drifted in shortly behind him just before 8:00 a.m. Michaels raised his semi-filled coffee cup to Tommy who was kicked back in his chair talking on the phone. Michaels sat at his desk, took a deep sigh, and thought about what he had almost done the previous evening.

"Shithead, come here," Tommy yelled out. Michaels sprung from his chair with his coffee. "Shut the door," Tommy instructed him as he stepped into his office.

Michaels closed the door with a puzzled look on his face. "What up's man?"

"Relax, have a seat." He lit up a Marlboro and offered Ronnie one.

Michaels reached over and grabbed the lit cigarette from Tommy's hand. Tommy had a peculiar look across his face. "Here take this," Tommy said handing him a piece of paper containing a handwritten name and number.

"Who's this?"

"It's an acquaintance of mine, Dr. Esterling. Don't fucking freak out, but this doctor specializes in cops. I want you to call the number. No, correct that, I'm telling you to call."

"What? Is this a psychiatrist?" he questioned.

"Yes. But no one in the unit needs to know. I want you to promise me you will go at least twice."

"I'm fine Tommy, why do I need to do this?"

"Look son, I've been around this job too long. Just do me this favor. Trust me Ronnie, it'll be good for you."

Michaels knew Tommy had seen what he had experienced over the last months. He wondered if Tommy had seen the shrink himself.

For the next several days Michaels and Dredge handled a few near fatal drug related stabbings and one case involving the murder of a four year old boy. As it turned out, the little fella was struck in the chest by a stray bullet while playing ball with his father in their front yard. Neither detective could give a shit about the stabbings, but the .40 caliber projectile seated deep in the toddler's sternum left an indelible vision in their minds. Their investigation led to one dead end after the next. From the trajectory of the bullet, there were no witnesses, no suspects and no clues.

The morning following the latest murder, Michaels woke up on his living room floor with his disheveled clothes still on. He couldn't remember how he got there, but the empty bottle of sleeping pills on the floor reminded him of the horrible dream he had prior to taking them. He could only recall a small part of his dream. The part where he cradled the child in his arms, staring down at the bloody hole in his soft white skin. He took the paper Tommy had given him from his dresser and dialed the number. A woman answered the call. "Dr. Esterling's Office. Can I help you?"

Michaels paused. He thought of hanging up. "Hello. Is anyone there?" The woman on the phone asked.

"Umm, yes my name is Ronnie Michaels. I guess I need to make an appointment?"

"Hi Mr. Michaels. Yes. When would you like to come in? Dr. Esterling is free the remainder of the week and we have a few spots available next week. Do you know where we are located?"

"No ma'am."

"We are in a discrete location behind the Severna Park Business Center. Are you familiar with that?"

"Yes, I am. I'm on nightwork this week so I guess sometime in the morning?"

"How is 9:00 a.m. tomorrow sir?"

"As good as ever, I guess."

"Then we will see you then."

"Thanks. Goodbye."

"Bye bye now."

Michaels hung up and took a deep breath. He couldn't believe he had just made the call.

The next evening Dredge and Michaels canvassed the homes within ¼ mile from where the toddler was killed. They were both skeptical anyone would talk given the violent nature of the community, but they were hopeful the age of the victim would encourage someone to come forward. They were wrong.

At no time during the night did Michaels mention his appointment the next morning. He didn't want to reveal such weakness to the man who always said, *it's their grief, not ours,* when it came to death notifications. By the end of their tour, Michaels went home and after one stiff drink, he forced himself to sleep in his own bed before passing out in a drunken stupor.

The following morning, he woke up semi-refreshed and reluctantly drove to the doctor's office. "I can't believe I'm fucking doing this. Why am I going to see a shrink? I ain't crazy. Hell, I must be, I'm talking out loud in my car and no one else is here. Oh boy."

A tall, attractive woman in her early 30's greeted Michaels in the waiting area just inside the office entrance. "Hi, you must be Ronnie?"

"Yes, hi. I'm here to see Dr. Esterling."

The woman smiled and shook Michaels' hand. "Nice to meet you. I'm Dr. Katie Esterling."

"Oh, oh, I'm sorry Tommy never told me. I just had a last name," Michaels said fumbling to speak.

"You must be with the Police Department," she inquired.

"Yes ma'am. My sergeant, Tommy Suit, said I should give you a call."

"How's my buddy Tommy these days? Is he still running the Homicide Unit?"

"Yes ma'am he his. He's crazy as ever, well you know what I mean. I didn't mean crazy as in crazy."

She laughed. "It's ok, I know what you mean. He's a good guy. Follow me please. Do you work together?" She had one of those voices that was pleasant to listen to he thought.

"Yes ma'am. I'm in the Homicide Unit."

Dr. Esterling was jaw dropping gorgeous, he thought. She was 5'9". Her long wavy brunette hair extended to the middle of her back. Her smooth olive skin and puffy lips were eye catching. Dressed in a black conservative skirt, heels, and an expensive white silk buttoned down shirt, he followed behind her into the office in awe. She looked like a model from a Fortune 500 magazine. Breathtaking, he thought.

"Come in and have a seat." She pointed to the expensive light brown leather couch. Her office reflected her fine taste. It was decorated with comfortable leather furniture, mahogany end tables, well-crafted black iron-based lamps, and fresh flowers. It was elegant and professional.

He took a seat on the couch and Dr. Esterling sat across from him in a straight back padded leather chair. She started the interview with a notebook in her lap, where she documented Michaels' personal information. After jotting down his age, marital status and number of children, she turned the conversation to his job and placed the notebook on a nearby table. He filled her in about his brief time in patrol and then his lengthy exciting tenure working undercover as a narcotics detective. She was intrigued. From there he transitioned to his assignment in the Homicide Unit.

Dr. Esterling immediately noticed a change in Michaels' demeanor. She could tell something was amiss. "How do you like being a homicide detective Mr. Michaels?"

Her open-ended question released the flood gates, something Michaels had been holding in for nearly six months. He was no longer enamored by the beauty of the person sitting across from him with her legs crossed. It was now all business. "Dr. Esterling, solving a murder is one of the most gratifying things I have ever experienced as a cop.

It's like getting a record seizure of drugs and cash every time. It's exhilarating, but so different at the same time."

"How's it different?" She looked directly at Michaels with an attentive look on her face. He knew she was an excellent listener.

"All of the death and sadness just wears on you. It's one thing if the victim is a piece of shit. You know, like a rapist or a gang banger who doesn't give a fuck who he shoots. That doesn't bother me, hell half the time I'm glad the person is gone from this earth. It's the good ones that rip my heart out. If the victim is a child, or genuinely a good person, that just fucks me up. Oh, I'm sorry Doctor, excuse my language, this stuff really gets to me."

"No worries Ronnie, your language doesn't bother me. I've been in this business way too long. I want you to be yourself. This is interesting, tell me more."

"It's such a change from being a narc. This line of work is so depressing, especially when Tommy sends me to do a death notification. I fucking hate those."

"Tell me why you dislike doing them so much."

"It's hard to explain. It's just hard being the bearer of bad news so often. And to make things worse, Tommy has been giving me the majority of them since I've been in the unit."

"Why do you think that is?"

"I figured it was because I was the new guy. I'm sure the rest had their fill. I don't know."

"Maybe he thought you were the best person to deliver such news."

"I don't know, but whatever the reason, it still sucks. I know this will sound weird, but when I tell someone their loved one is dead, I almost feel responsible for the person's death. I feel like every time they see me after that point, they must think back when I delivered the news to them. To see me must be a horrible reminder of what was probably the worst day of their life. This will sound strange, but to add to all these emotions, I feel like if I don't solve a murder, the family will hold me to blame, the bearer of the news."

"When you are giving a death notification, how do you act?"

"Well." He turned his head to the side and thought for a few seconds. "I do it the same way I would want my mother to be told of my death. Exactly. I do it with compassion and true feelings of caring. The way I see it, you have one chance to say the right words, one time. And whatever you say and how you say it, will be remembered forever by the person you are telling."

"Do you think everyone you work with shares that same philosophy about doing death notifications?"

"I don't know. I've never thought about that. I'm not sure."

"Has Tommy ever been with you when you did one?"

He paused and thought for a moment. "No, as a matter of fact he has not."

"Well just from the passion I am seeing from you today, I think he's made the right choice. Sorry, I know that's not what you wanted to hear, but I think Tommy recognizes the real importance behind a death notification, and that's the delivery. The other members of your unit have probably told him about how you do such a great job at them."

"Fuck."

"How have you dealt with all of your emotions since being exposed to so much death?"

"I've been drinking, smoking and working a lot lately. I have needed sleeping pills to help me sleep sometimes. I guess it's my escape. I get so drunk it's embarrassing to even say. I do all this to avoid the nightmares I've had, but I still have them. I guess it's my personality, just like when I was in the Narcotics Section. I go all in with my job. Investigating murders is my whole life. It's all I do."

"How often do you see or talk to your daughter?"

"Yeah that's a joke. I just work so damn much. That's pretty much the reason my marriage didn't last in the first place. It wasn't that I had a bad wife, I was just having an affair with my job. I was never home."

"You are a very caring man Ronnie and I must say, more so than many others I have run across over the years in your field. The department, hell the citizens of this county, are truly lucky to have someone caring like yourself. That is nothing to be ashamed of. I think that was a good first session." He looked at the clock on the wall, shocked an hour had passed so quickly. "Let's meet again in two days and I want you to walk me through some of your dreams and if we have time, an actual notification."

"Sounds good. Thanks for meeting me so soon. I appreciate that. It felt good getting some of these things off my chest today," he said sounding relieved.

"It was my pleasure. Be careful out there and I want you to try taking better care of yourself, with a little less drinking and pills."

"Thank you." He stood up and shook hands with Dr. Esterling. This was the first time he had ever shared his feelings with anyone since being in the unit. Any feelings of infatuation toward Dr. Esterling were swiftly replaced with respect.

Their next meeting was scheduled for 1:00 p.m., two days later. Working the evening shift at 3:00 p.m. would allow him to have his hour-long session and then drive straight to work. But on this day, things would turn out differently. Michaels' cell phone rang at 11:45 a.m. on a hot July morning. "Detective Michaels?" the female asked on the other end of the phone.

"Speaking."

"This is Diane from Channel 5. Sergeant Suit needs you to respond to the Friendship Trail at the Park Observation Area. They have a body discovered in the woods. The other members of your unit are also on their way."

"Shit, ok, I'll be there in a few." he hung up and quickly slipped on a pair of light brown suit pants and a white polo shirt. This wasn't the day to be dressed in a suit and tie, given the intense heat expected. Michaels picked up his cell, searched through his recent calls and pressed a number.

"This is Dr. Esterling. May I help you?"

"Oh, hi Doc, this is Ronnie Michaels. I didn't expect you to answer. I need to cancel my appointment. I just got called out for a body that was discovered."

"Hi Detective Michaels. I understand. Call me when you're able and we will reschedule. Talk to you soon and be safe," she said with her soothing voice.

"Yes ma'am. Thanks." Michaels hung up, snatched his badge and gun from the dining room table and rushed out to his car.

The observation area was a large piece of land with a parking lot, benches and playground equipment for children. The mini park was designed for people to observe planes up close as they took off and landed at the Friendship Airport located just a few hundred yards away. Adjacent to the gathering area was a bike trail, which stretched for miles and miles throughout portions of the county. It was used daily by people of all ages for exercise, whether for biking, jogging or walking. On this day the tranquil family gathering space would be the staging area for the Homicide Unit and crime scene technicians.

"Detective 132 radio," Michaels said with his portable radio close to his mouth.

"Go ahead Detective 132," answered the dispatcher.

"Put me out at the scene please."

"10-4."

"Ronnie, wait for Dave, then come down the path and you'll see us," Tommy blurted over the radio.

"Yes sir."

"I'll be there in 2 minutes," Dredge sounded over the radio in his deep voice.

"Standing by," Michaels advised.

The parking lot had been cleared of the plane watchers and was now full of marked police cars, two Evidence Collection vans and the unmarked cars belonging to Captain Donoho, Lieutenant Tank, Sergeant Suit and Detectives Howes and Hauf. From the looks of the brass present, Michaels knew something was up.

"Hey Dredge. How the fuck are ya?" Michaels asked as Dredge climbed from his car.

"Damn Shithead, all the bigwigs are here. What's going on?"

"You know as much as I do. We're supposed to meet Tommy down the path."

Michaels and Dredge walked across the parking lot and onto the trail where they were greeted by longtime friend, Officer Paul Stammer, who was maintaining the Crime Scene Log, capturing who was entering the scene.

"Hey Paul, how'd you get stuck with this detail?" Michaels jokingly asked.

"I don't know. My sergeant is an asshole and he's got a hard on for me, I guess. I don't care. It's shady here. How have you been? You and Mel been fishing lately?"

"Shit, I wish. I'll let you know when we're going. Put me and Detective Hart on your log at 12:18 p.m. brother."

"You got it. Good luck. This is one sick motherfucker."

Michaels and Dredge looked at one another in bewilderment and walked a few hundred yards down the 8' wide, black asphalt path. Though the sun was brightly shining, the path where the group of cops and techs stood was dark from the heavily shaded forest. Getting closer, they could see the immediate scene had additional crime scene tape stretched across the path to keep those in command close enough to see, yet far enough to keep from fucking anything up. Tommy was heard talking to Jeff and Ray. Both were carefully stepping through the woods, taking photographs at various angles of a body lying on the ground.

"Hi Dad," Michaels said to his father, who had his camera placed firmly to his face snapping off pictures. "Good to see you back at work."

"Hi Ron. Yeah it's good to be out of the house." Like always, Ray was a man of few words, especially while working.

Both Detectives greeted Captain Donoho and Lieutenant Tank who stood behind the secondary crime scene tape tied to the trees. Captain Donoho was heard briefing Chief of Police Bill Lindsey of the murder on his cell phone. Dredge and Michaels stood next to Tommy and Donald who remained staring. They could not believe their eyes. Approximately 15 feet from the paved trail, under a large oak tree was a deceased elderly female lying on her back. From the looks of her white colored hair and face, she appeared to be in her early 70's. Her eyes were fixed open with that familiar blank stare. There were obvious signs of a scuffle from the disturbance of the leaves next to the path, which turned to drag marks on the ground. A thin distinct ligature mark was visible around the front of the victim's neck. The device used left cutting abrasions on the skin. This murder was planned and brutally violent. The dense foliage made it perfect for an attacker to hide and remain unseen until it was too late. It was clear that whoever did this made a concerted effort to move the woman far enough from the trail that the attack could not be readily seen by anyone approaching.

Michaels moved closer to examine the injuries. This was like no scene he had ever witnessed or studied in any death investigation school. The victim's body looked fake, like a mannequin he thought to himself. Lying on her backside, arms were deliberately placed perpendicular to her body by her killer like she was mounted to a cross. Her black pants and underwear were sliced open with a sharp instrument from the waistband, down to her crotch, exposing her vagina. The cutting implement left a clean incision on her skin, from the top of her waist down to parts of her clitoris, which was also perforated. There was no doubt the swipe of this blade was done with precise force.

Her shirt was sliced open like an autopsy cut from the top of the neck to the bottom, and clean through her white bra, uncovering her breasts. Michaels was dumbfounded that another human could do such a thing. It was unfathomable, foul and vicious. One of the victim's nipples had been completely torn from her breast and was nowhere to be found. Most likely the killer did so to remind the sick fuck of his kill. From the remaining flesh attached to the nipple, the object used for this gruesome removal was not the same sharp device used to pierce through her clothing. The visible teeth marks clearly showed the cannibalistic act was done by another human mouth.

If this unbelievable scene was not horrific enough, the killer left yet another unique signature, which most likely would be a telling sign. Whoever ended this poor woman's life, took the time to evenly douse accelerant around the torso and limbs, tracing the entire body and set it ablaze. The body itself received no burns, but the surrounding sticks and old leaves were charred. These were the marks of a sick minded killer.

"This is one sick motherfucker," Tommy said lighting up a cigarette.

"Do we know who she is? Any ID on her?" Dredge asked.

"The cyclist who found her said he's seen her before. He said she was a regular walker. The grey Mercury Marquis in the parking lot belongs to her. That's being towed to headquarters," Donald said.

"Where's Mark?" Michaels asked.

"He just left before you got here. He's going to take a statement from the guy who found her," Tommy replied.

"Are we considering him as a suspect?" Michaels fired back.

"Not sure. Just acting a little weird. Wanted to leave in a hurry and didn't want to get involved," Tommy said.

"Well shit after seeing that, who could blame him?" Michaels said still disgusted from what he had seen.

"Yeah that's what Donald said, but fuck it. I figured let's do it now before the man starts talking to people and clams up completely," Tommy said.

Tommy walked over close to where Michaels and Dredge stood, still looking in disbelief. "Dredge, the victim's car is double listed to a male in his early 50's. Can you go see what you can learn about her? See if she ever had any problems on the trail and do the notification for me?"

Dredge nodded his head blowing smoke from his cigarette. "Yeah Tommy."

"Donald, give Dredge the information about the victim's car."

"Sure Boss." Donald opened his notebook, flipped through a few pages and tore one out. "Here you go brother."

"Thanks," Dredge said folding the piece of paper and placing it in his shirt pocket.

"Do you want me to go with him?" Michaels asked.

Tommy paused and looked at him. "Are you alright?"

"Fuck yeah," Michaels assured him.

"Ok, but Dave, I want you to do this one," he said in a serious tone.

Michaels turned and began walking away in his typical hurried fashion. "Come on Dredge, let's do this."

"Hold on Shithead. How much longer are you guys going to be here Tommy?" Dredge asked.

"Probably a while. Jeff wants to take samples of the soil where the accelerant was poured, and he wants to gather the leaves under and around the victim to search for DNA evidence."

"I'll give you a call," Dredge said before he turned and walked away.

"Thanks, and Dredge remember I want you to do this one," Tommy repeated emphatically. Dredge nodded his head and started down the path where Michaels was already several yards ahead of him.

When the two reached the lot, Dredge pulled the paper from his pocket and handed it to Michaels. "I'll drive. You check the map book and tell me where I'm going. See if you can get a photo emailed to you of the registered owners so we can positively identify our victim."

"I know where 2nd Avenue is Dredge. It's only a few miles down the road, close to my old elementary school."

"How about the pictures of the owners?" Dave asked impatiently.

"Yes sir. They just came through." Michaels looked briefly at the photographs of the two registered owners on his phone. "Yup it's her alright. No doubt about that. This other guy looks pissed off. He must have had a bad day when this photo was taken."

In a few minutes the detectives arrived at the address where the victim's car was registered. The home was a two story single family house built in the 50's. The yard was well groomed, and the window frames and shutters recently painted. Having grown up a short distance away, Michaels knew most people who resided in these homes did so for a lifetime. It was a true family oriented community, where you could yell at someone else's kids and not hear shit about it. Everyone looked out for each other. That's just the way it was.

Parked out front was a newer black pickup truck. The two got out of the car and by habit Michaels put his hand on the hood to check its temperature.

"Someone's here," he said to Dredge.

"I know. He's looking out the bedroom window," Dredge said surprising Michaels with his keen observation.

The screen door opened swiftly and there stood a stout, well sculpted, bald, shirtless white male, approximately 50 years old. He was wearing a black pair of gym shorts and black tennis shoes. He was a hard-looking man. "Whatever it is your selling gentlemen, take it somewhere else. I suggest you turn around and leave." The man said in a deep, intimidating tone. His voice, along with the scowl on his face, was daunting.

"Semper Fi Brother," Dredge said to the man.

Hearing those words, immediately the seemingly angry man relaxed his posture. Michaels was amazed. He thought to himself, *it was like two opposing warriors who shared a common bond but were meeting each other on the opposite ends of a battlefield.*

"Sir, I'm Detective Hart and this is my partner, Detective Michaels. We're with the County Police." Dredge's wallet was open with his badge displayed.

"What's your first name Marine?" the man demanded.

"Dave."

"When did you serve brother?"

"Long ago. Two tours in Nam in the 60's."

"Hoo ra. I'm honored. You're welcome into my home anytime sir. Come in."

Detectives Hart and Michaels walked into the living room where the towering man insisted they would be more comfortable on the couch.

"Please excuse me, let me get a shirt so I can talk to you gentlemen." The man left briefly and returned wearing a camo green t-shirt. Both detectives quickly scanned the photographs hanging on the wall and situated on the tables throughout the room. They saw several pictures of the victim standing with the giant of a man they had just met. Among the pictures were some with the same man posing with several bearded men, wearing tactical clothing, armed with AK-47's and other automatic weapons. He took a seat in the old vinyl chair.

"What can I help you with?"

Mesmerized by the man's appearance, Michaels finally noticed the Marine tattoo on his massive forearm. Dredge knew exactly the type of soldier he was dealing with, a true badass, who didn't want to be jerked off about a death notification. He knew he had to get to the point and fast.

"Are you Mr. Abrams?" Dredge politely asked.

The man extended his oversized hand to Dredge. "My apologies brother. Yes, Ken. Freshly retired Captain Kenneth Abrams. I served proudly for 32 years in the Corps sir."

"SF?" Dave asked in code to answer his suspicions that Ken was a member of the Special Forces Unit.

"I served with some great men," he answered affirmatively without answering the question.

Dave got right to the point. "How are you related to Mildred Abrams, Captain?"

"She would be my mother." Suddenly, the man's forehead clenched tightly, and a grave look appeared across his face. "What happened to her. Did she get into another accident? I told her she needs to stop driving."

"No sir," Dredge said.

Ken stood quickly from his chair, high above both detectives. He was ready to fight. He looked at Michaels then back at Dave with an eagle like stare. "What happened to my mother gentleman?" he said once more.

"I'm very sorry, but your mother was killed today sir." Dave looked the fellow Marine in the eyes, then bowed his head out of respect.

"What? What do you mean my mother was killed today? How? By who?" the retired Captain shouted. Michaels remained silent.

"If you would have a seat sir, I can tell you what limited information we know so far," Dredge asked respectfully. The man eased himself slowly in the chair. His eyes had changed from a look of concern to one of an intense focus like he was about to go into battle.

"Sir, your mother was killed today while on the county hiking trail. Michaels looked at the Marine when Dredge broke the news waiting for his reaction, but there was none. The chiseled man's face stayed rigid, void of any emotions. Dredge continued. "Please understand, it's early in our investigation, but as of now, we are trying to find someone else who may have been on the trail who could have seen something. At this point there are no witnesses. We are very sorry sir."

"What weapon was used to kill her?"

"At this point it appeared she was strangled," Dredge answered.

"With what?"

"A thin object."

"A wire?" the Marine questioned Dredge, referring to a special strangling device issued to Special Forces members for silent kills.

Dredge knew exactly the weapon he was referring to. "Perhaps sir."

For the first time, the detectives saw the tiniest hint of emotion from the Marine. "Excuse me gentlemen." He stood from the chair and walked into the kitchen. A loud banging noise was heard which startled both detectives.

Ken joined them a few minutes later and returned to his chair. The knuckles on his right hand were bleeding.

"Sir, do you live here also?" Michaels asked the man.

"Yes, I've lived here for the past six months since my retirement. I spent my last two years commanding special operations in Afghanistan. I moved in with my mom because she's getting up there in age and she needed help maintaining this house and yard."

"Is your dad still around?" Michaels asked.

"Fuck no. That worthless slug left us when I enlisted in the Corps. We haven't seen him since."

"Did your mom walk the trail often?" Michaels continued.

"Everyday. Every single day. Ken stopped talking and lowered his head, looking at the ground. Quickly he cleared his throat, composed himself and raised his head. "She would leave like clockwork at 11 a.m., right after she read the newspaper, had her breakfast and drank her coffee."

"Did she ever mention seeing someone who she had a bad feeling about?" Dredge asked.

"No. She said a lot of the same seniors would show up and walk. She didn't like to walk with the others. She preferred to be alone." Ken stood again and walked to the end table nearest Michaels. He picked up the picture of him and his mother and smiled. "This was just two weeks ago. She said she wanted to go back to Ocean City before she got too old. She said she loved taking me there when I was a kid. We had so much fun walking on the beach. She watched me body surf for an hour straight. I felt like a child again. I'm glad we had the chance to do that." He sat the picture carefully on the table and walked to the door, where he stood looking out. "Was she assaulted?" he asked with his back turned to the detectives.

Dredge didn't want to lie to his fellow Marine. "Yes, but we don't know to what extent at this point. There is some testing that needs to be done."

"What can I do?"

"Nothing at this time sir. We have her car at our headquarters. Once we look at it, I'll give you a call and we can make the arrangements to have it picked up," Michaels informed him.

Still standing in the doorway, Ken turned and faced them. "I don't give a fuck about her car. What can I do to help find this asshole?"

"I understand sir," Michaels spoke up.

"No, you don't understand young man, was your mother killed?" Michaels did not respond. "Answer me, was your mother killed?" he shouted.

"No."

"Well then don't sit there and tell me you understand." Ken turned again and peered out the glass door. "I'm sorry detective. I was out of line. That was uncalled for."

"It's ok sir, and I'll tell you this. You have the best team of investigators you would ever want on this case." Michaels said to him.

"Captain, it's the kind of team you are used to," Dredge added.

Ken walked over to where the two were seated and extended his hand. "Thank you, gentlemen."

Dredge and Michaels stood and shook the man's large hand. "Though we are all working this case, Detective Donald Hauf is the primary detective, so you will be hearing from him mostly about updates. I put the number to his desk on the back of my card," Dredge told him.

"Thank you. Semper Fi."

"Semper Fi," Dredge said and before long he and Michaels were on their way back to the scene.

"Boy, everyone is different, aren't they?" Michaels said.

"What do you mean?"

"Every death notification is different. That guy barely showed any reaction to his own mother being killed. I'm sure there's a big hole in the kitchen somewhere. That sounded like an explosion."

"He's the real deal. There is no question about it. I'm sure he's seen many of his brother Marines killed, which has made him a hardened man," Dredge explained.

By the time they returned to the scene it was crawling with every news station and heartless reporter around.

"Call Tommy and see what he needs from us."

Michaels called Tommy on his cell phone while he scoured the parking lot looking for a spot away from the mayhem of media. "Hey man, we are back in the parking lot, what do you need from us? There's a shit ton of press here."

"Can you guys help the officers out? Those vultures keep slipping by trying to film our crime scene, I don't know if it's a fucking reporter or if it's a suspect." Michaels could hear Tommy's agitation.

"Sure, me and Dredge will gladly remove the little fuckballs for you. Are you guys almost done?"

"We'll be a little longer. Jeff called the rest of his Evidence Collection Unit, and I have ten cops all searching the woods now. Doc is here. We are just waiting for the Medical Examiner's van. If you see it, have them drive all the way down to where we are Ronnie."

"Ok, will do."

"What does he want us to do?" Dredge asked.

"Tommy wants us to keep the bottom feeders away. Come on let's go."

Dredge parked away from any of the media vehicles and the two walked around most of them. Before long one of the maggots approached the detectives. "Excuse me sir, are you with the Police Department?" asked a man sweating profusely.

"Nope. We're with Parks & Recreation," Michaels quickly answered then turned his back to him.

They walked up to Officer Paul Stammer, who was still standing on the trail holding a clipboard. He had a look of disgust on his face. "What's going on brother?" Michaels asked.

"That one little pimple faced reporter with the Annapolis Times is getting on my fucking nerves. He needs to get locked up. Do you know who I'm talking about? The liberal asshole that always writes bad shit about the Department."

Michaels laughed. "Oh yeah, you got to be talking about that pussy, Rick Davis."

"Yeah that's him. I told him once he wasn't allowed past this point and then he tried again a little while ago."

"Ok Paul. We are going to nose around in the woods for a little bit to make sure no one gets back to the scene."

"I'll be here. Jesus Christ, what the fuck is this?" Officer Stammer looked in surprise down the path. "Somebody's going to get locked up. I'm telling ya."

The detectives both laughed, and Michaels spoke up. "It's ok brother, it's the Medical Examiner's van. They're here for the body."

"Oh, sorry. Those little bastards are getting on my nerves. I can't tell you how many have tried to get past me."

"You better call Tommy and tell him we are going in, so we don't get shot," Dredge wisely advised his partner.

"Good idea," Michaels said pulling his phone from his pocket.

"Tommy it's me. What part of the woods is being searched now?"

"The opposite side of the woods, which would be south of the victim," Tommy responded.

"Got it. Dredge and I are going hunting."

"What?"

"Tell the search team we are going in the woods closest to the parking lot to clear this end."

"Ok."

Dredge and Michaels entered the woods next to Officer Stammer. The woods were comprised mostly of tall pines, scattered oaks and small saplings. The property was owned by the airport and was kept relatively cleared of brush and debris, making it easy to see a long way through the forest. They both had their weapons drawn, pointing forward as they eased through the woods. Their weapons were out not for the pesky reporters wandering through, but for the killer who could still be lurking nearby. Many times, sick bastards stay close to their crime scene to get their rocks off from the massive response they caused.

Without speaking, the two walked slowly through the narrow section of trees, which widened as they extended further toward the body. Michaels caught a glimpse of what appeared to be a man hiding between a large rotted stump and a thick patch of honeysuckle vines. Using hand signals, Michaels alerted his partner. Dredge honed in. The subject was completely unaware of the detectives bearing down on him. Michaels knew they were nearing the crime scene. Between the overhead planes, Tommy's voice could be heard.

"Don't move motherfucker or your dead," Michaels shouted. The person was noticeably startled but continued to look forward. "You heard me. Let me see your hands now." Michaels was unable to recognize the subject. He knew Davis was a white male in his twenties, who sported an oversized pair of glasses. Dredge crept forward using the large trees for cover, while Michaels continued with his commands. "I'm not going to tell you again asshole, put both of your fucking hands where I can see them or I'm going to stick a bullet in you, now." With that, the man's trembling hands raised slowly above his head. Dredge was now ten feet away with his sights fixed on the subject's torso. Michaels advanced forward. The person was a white male with a few leaves stuck in his hair. From the looks of the plant life and dirt on his clothing, it was obvious he had been hiding in the woods for some time. With both guns aimed at the subject, they approached the man.

"Is that you Davis?" Michaels asked the visibly shaking man. With his gun held tightly in both hands pointed closely at the person's head, he walked around to get a better view. "You motherfucker. Do you know how close you were to being shot? Stand up. You're under arrest for Obstruction of Justice, Interfering with a Police Investigation and anything else I can fucking find. Stand the fuck up."

The 140 pound reporter, with his leaf ridden bowl style haircut, stood up and began sobbing like a little bitch. "I'm sorry. Please don't arrest me. I was just doing my job."

"Yeah, well guess what you little asshole? So am I. These are called consequences. That's what happens when you don't respect the police. You were told not to go past the officer on the trail, weren't you?" Michaels asked.

"Um, I guess."

"Look, he pissed himself," Dredge pointed out.

Michaels holstered his weapon and pulled his handcuffs from his waistband. "Put your hands behind your back. I'm going to love this. And make sure you get that quote right and don't forget to report how you balled your eyes out and pissed your pants because the big bad cops almost shot your ass." Michaels slapped the cuffs on and the two escorted him to the trail where Officer Stammer awaited.

"Oh, look who you guys found." Stammer laughed and shook his head. "I warned you not to go past me, now look. Did he piss his pants?"

"Yup, I don't think this is going to read well in the newspaper," Michaels said sarcastically. The three laughed and the detectives escorted their arrestee down the trail toward the reporters, eagerly awaiting the arrival of the Department's Public Information Officer. Many of the reporters took notice of the handcuffed man coming from the direction of the murder scene. Davis kept his head down, but this time Michaels and his partner took their time parading the wannabe journalist in front of the media to Michaels' car. Many shoved their microphones and cameras in their faces, shouting questions about the arrest. Both detectives maintained a stone face, while the whimpering Davis was placed in the front passenger's seat of the unmarked cruiser. Given the timing and circumstances it could have easily been construed their arrest was related to the murder. Having been wronged so many times in the past from this local trashy paper, this was a slice of poetic justice for both men.

"I'll see you at the office when you're done," Dredge said. They looked at one another with big grins across their faces.

"See ya in a few partner," Michaels said before he drove through the parting sea of media types, scattering like ants to avoid being struck by Michaels' car.

Several hours later at the office, things were moving rapidly. You could sense the urgency of the investigation in the air. Donald sat next to Dredge's desk as he was briefed on the information gleaned from the victim's son. Mark was drafting a Nationwide all-points bulletin about the homicide. Lieutenant Tank and Captain Donoho were in Tommy's office on a conference call with Chief Lindsey arranging beefed up patrols on the trail, in case the killer decided to strike again. Tommy's cell phone laid vibrating on his desk as one call after the next came in from a plethora of news reporters. Michaels sat at his desk and worked on the report from his earlier arrest.

Once the media learned of the victim's sex and age, they were relentless. Every television network, newspaper, podcast or social media buff covered the story. Every blood sucking journalist with a heartbeat stood at the scene and filmed the location where the victim lay. The area was recognizable from the soil and leaves Jeff and Ray had removed for testing. Everyone in the unit knew coverage like this would only fuel a sick killer like this one. Tommy had a great rapport with most of the media, but despite his repeated requests to avoid sensationalizing this crime, they continued to do so.

By 10:00 p.m. everything that could have been done had been. The back door of the office was propped open. The smoke-filled air swirled about the homicide unit's space. Tommy appeared from his office with coffee and cigarette in hand. He wasn't smiling like normal.

"I don't like it," he said. He took a long drag from his cigarette and blew the smoke out forcefully. "This ain't good."

Everyone had the same thoughts, but just hadn't vocalized them. The four detectives sat at their desks watching Tommy when Donald came to life slamming his fist on his desk making a loud bang. "Shit, Tommy this motherfucker doesn't have any clue who he's up against. We'll get this bastard, mark my words. He doesn't want to fuck with this unit." Donald leaned back in his chair, kicked his feet up on his desk and lit up.

"Let's get the fuck out of here. Donald and Mark, I'll see you guys in the morning. Dredge and Shithead stay close to your phones in case something breaks, otherwise I'll see you all at 3."

Finally home, Michaels poured himself a strong rum and Coke and made his way to his recliner. His mind switched back and forth from the horrifying site of the murder scene, to the victim's son. He wondered what emotions, if any, a warrior of his caliber would have, once alone. Would he cry? Or did his job strip him like it had so many others of their ability to experience sadness? Michaels sipped from his glass and placed a late night call to Dr. Esterling's office.

"Hi Doctor, this is Ronnie Michaels." He unsuccessfully tried masking his slurred speech. "It's late on Thursday evening. I just got home. Give me a call so I can make another appointment. I'm not scheduled to work tomorrow until 3 p.m. Thank you. Goodbye."

Michaels fixed several more drinks and could not stop thinking of Captain Abrams. Like many times before, he wanted to spend time with the surviving family member, the one whose life he had changed. He thought, even a tough Marine had to vent sooner or later. Drunk, Michaels decided to go visit Abrams. He looked at the clock and it was shortly after 1 a.m., but he didn't care.

He grabbed his keys and opened the front door. He was finally going to satisfy this urge he had felt so many times before. When he opened the door, he noticed a man lying halfway underneath Michaels aging truck. The man jumped to his feet and sprinted across the street through the opening of the townhouses. In a flash he was out of sight.

Michaels yelled out. "Hey what the fuck?" The wasted detective was in no shape to give pursuit but decided to inspect the undercarriage of his truck. Nearly falling, he looked underneath, but nothing appeared to be tampered with. He returned to his feet and held onto his side mirror for balance, then puked profusely on the street. After a few bouts of barfing, he stumbled to his front door, aborting the idea of visiting Mr. Abrams. He made his way back to his bedroom, quickly downed five sleeping pills from the bottle on his nightstand and in seconds he was out.

By the next morning, panic had blanketed the area around the airport. Senior citizens were afraid to walk the trail and parents wouldn't allow their children to ride their bikes there. Only a handful of male joggers and bikers could be seen on the path most of which were probably oblivious to the news. The county was in fear and rightfully so. This case would be a true test of the unit.

At 9 a.m. Michaels was awakened by his phone. Not bothering to open his eyes to see the caller ID, he answered. "Yeah."

"Good morning Detective. This is Dr. Esterling. Did I get you at a bad time?"

"No, no you didn't" he said sitting upright in his bed and trying his best to sound awake.

"I got your message this morning. I must say you sounded a bit intoxicated. I was calling to see when you wanted to schedule our next visit."

"I can come in this morning, say by 10:30 if you're available. Sorry about the late night call."

"Oh, no apologies. Believe me, you're not my first drunk call. I'll see you then. Goodbye detective."

"Goodbye."

By 8 a.m. Donald had been on the phone with Ken Abrams for the first time. He had not had the opportunity to meet the man and was a little taken back when he received his call. "Detective Hauf, this is Kenneth Abrams, son of Mildred Abrams. Detective Hart said you were the contact person for my mother's case. I'm calling to inquire as to the status of your investigation. Have you determined the killer's identity?"

"Hi, Mr. Abrams. Umm, no sir, but it is very early. Sometimes in cases like this it may take a while." Before Donald could continue to speak, he heard a dial tone. Mr. Abrams had hung up. Perplexed, Donald looked at the receiver in his hand.

Without warning Tommy yelled from his office, "Donald."

"Yes sir."

"Get the fuck in here." Donald jumped from his seat, grabbed his coffee cup and walked briskly to his office.

"Yeah Boss?"

"I just hung the motherfucking phone up with a homicide supervisor at the Bureau of Criminal Investigations in North Carolina. He just read Mark's bulletin and your crime scene matches a murder his office investigated in April of this year. According to the sergeant, their crime scene was on a similar path that stretched through a lengthy wooded area between two parks, frequently used by people for recreation and exercise."

The modus operandi was nearly exact, including lighting accelerant around the body. In their case, the victim's nipple wasn't bitten off, but it looked as if most of her pubic hair had been cut. This came as no surprise because any seasoned investigator knows a deranged killer will increase his level of violence with each murder to either satisfy their sexual needs or personal gratification.

Within hours of the news, Donald and Mark were touching down in North Carolina where they were met at the airport by Sergeant Rick Tabor. Inside of an hour, they found themselves at the Bureau of Criminal Investigation's headquarters in the heart of Raleigh.

In Maryland, Michaels arrived for his second appointment with Dr. Esterling, feeling much more comfortable than he had on his initial visit. "Hi Detective Michaels, come in please. Have a seat," Dr. Esterling said with a cheerful smile. Both occupied the same seats they had before in her office. Without her notebook in her hand,

Dr. Esterling recapped everything Michaels had told her in the previous session without once referring to notes. He was thoroughly impressed.

"So, you said you got called out to a homicide? I guess that's the one I've been watching on the news. That was horrible. I know the investigation is still on-going, so I won't ask you any questions about that."

"Oh, that's ok. It's a real, *who done it,* as we say in my line of work when you have a case with no clues, no witnesses and no suspects."

"What do you do? How does it get solved?"

"Physical evidence, DNA, witnesses. Normally in cases involving the elderly, it's either money related or the killer is a true whack job. Sorry Doc."

"No, I totally agree. Continue, this really interests me."

"When there's no clear motive like robbery, a big insurance policy or a Will, then the person killed for the pure enjoyment or whatever demented reason they've conjured up in their head. There is no question about that in this case. The way I see it, a piece of garbage like that doesn't belong on this fucking earth breathing my air." Michaels could feel his face getting red with anger. "You wouldn't believe what this sick fuck did to this poor old lady who just wanted to take a nice walk like she does every day."

"No please don't tell me. I've read enough books that say certain details of the crime are kept secret, so only the killer and the police know."

"Damn, Doc, listen to you."

"Did you carry out the death notification for this murder?"

Michaels leaned forward and scooted to the edge of the couch. Dr. Esterling didn't know what to expect. "I accompanied my partner, who told the victim's son."

"Was that a relief for you to see someone else carry out that task?"

"Maybe, but part of me felt like that was my job. It's weird. I hate doing them, but there I was thinking I should be doing this. In this case Dredge, I mean Dave, my partner, was perfect for this notification. He and the victim's son were Marines and there was some sort of bond because they both had served in combat I believe."

"Yes. I totally agree. I would think in every circumstance, the person delivering the news should have some connection with the surviving family member, whether it be through their job, age, race, or even parental or marital status."

"That's a good point. I've never looked at it that way."

"Hey, you have your talents. I have mine." The two laughed. This technique was Dr. Esterling's subtle way to relax her patient, get him to trust her advice and ultimately appreciate her knowledge. "I heard on the news the victim was in her 70's?"

"Yes ma'am."

"So, I take it her son was older. How did he react?"

"Like a fucking ice cube. He was some Special Forces Commander, pissed off at the world. You could tell he had been through a lot."

"He showed no emotions what so ever?"

"Nope. He did walk away briefly, and then returned, but there was not a single tear in his eyes."

"That's not healthy. Bottling up grief and stress makes for a ticking time bomb. It must be released but in a healthy way, not through drugs, alcohol or violence, like I've seen some do. What else have you gotten yourself into?"

In Raleigh, Donald, Mark and Sergeant Tabor stood around a large conference table reviewing autopsy and investigative reports, crime scene sketches, photographs and one witness statement. Jokingly, Sergeant Tabor said he was pleasantly relieved when he read the crime bulletin sent by Detective Howes. For the past two months since their murder, the entire county had been on edge. Tabor said the County Executive fired the Chief of Police and transferred the homicide supervisor when the case wasn't solved after the first month. Tabor said that he and his crew have worked overtime nearly every day trying to solve their case, to no avail. Mark asked Sergeant Tabor if his investigators had ever reached out to the FBI Behavioral Analysis Unit in Quantico, VA for an in depth look at their case. Tabor was unaware if any such contact had been made.

Learning of the news back in Maryland, Tommy was quick to notify his colleagues at the Annapolis FBI Office of the link between the murders in both states. The agents assigned to that office primarily assisted local law enforcement in bank robbery and counterfeiting cases, but this one became an immediate priority. Thanks to Tommy's relations with the Bureau, in just a few hours there were two FBI Agents assigned indefinitely to the Anne Arundel County Police Homicide Unit. With one phone call, a much needed mini task force had been formed. Sergeant Suit was amazing. He made things happen. With a second call, Special Agent Brooks Hollman, supervisor of the Behavioral Analysis Unit, agreed for his group to accept and review all pertinent documents from both the North Carolina and Maryland murders.

"Ronnie, today if you feel comfortable, I want you to walk me through one of your actual death notifications. Start from the beginning and tell me how the events unfolded. Do you think you can do that?"

Michaels dropped his head back on the couch while he shuffled through the multitude of cases in his mind. "Yeah I have one. This was so strange. You can't make this shit up."

Dr. Esterling sat forward in her chair like she was about to watch a movie, but without the popcorn. Michaels began.

"It was a July weekend, a little over a year ago when I was sitting at the office on a Saturday, studying for the upcoming Sergeant Promotional Exam. I was using the office computer when my cell phone went off. It was Donald. He told me to meet him at the fast food joint across from the Sport Center, near the Chesapeake Bay Bridge. I wasn't on call that weekend, but that never mattered. I packed up my shit and drove out to see what he needed. Doc, I remember every dead body I have ever seen. Each one of them are filed permanently in my mind and play back like movies. This one was a 35 year old white female named Sharon Fowler, with a single gunshot wound in her left temple, the size of a .32 caliber. She was slumped over in the front passenger seat of a utility van fully dressed, along with her purse that contained money, credit cards and her driver's license. It was obvious whoever did this wasn't trying to rob her or conceal her identity. Plain and simple, it was a flat out dump job on our side of the Bay Bridge. Anyway, the address on her driver's license was #11 Maple Street, in Easton, Maryland, not too far on the Eastern Shore in a neighboring jurisdiction. The only thing Tommy said to me and Donald was, *go see what you guys can find.* That's it. That's all he said, and we left."

"Once we entered the small town of Easton, we easily found Maple Street. Like idiots, Donald and I drove up and down the same road, unable to find #11. We found numbers 12, 13 and 15, but we couldn't locate number #11. I saw this black guy, about 30 years old, standing on a corner smoking a cigar, watching us ride back and forth. Finally, I told Donald to stop so I could ask him where the stupid fucking address was. Well, wouldn't you know it, he knew exactly where it was. He pointed down a long, gravel driveway right in front of us. We thanked him and as we were about to pull off, he said, *who are you looking for?* Donald abruptly stopped the car and I said Sharon Fowler. To our surprise he said, *that's my girlfriend.* Now what are the odds of that? Now Donald and I were looking at each other and we didn't know what the fuck to do. We didn't plan for this to happen, so Donald told him to get in. He said his name was Tavon and he proceeded to tell us he and Sharon were on and off boyfriend and girlfriend. He said she lived alone at her address. I asked Tavon if he knew where she was. He said he hadn't seen her in a few days and was getting worried. I said, I hate to tell you this bud, but your girlfriend has been killed. This guy got really quiet and started crying. Donald and I couldn't believe what was happening, so we proceed to question him about when he last saw Sharon and where he was the previous evening and his story was solid. Understand Doc, this didn't count as a true death notification in my mind because they weren't married, nor was he family. He told us her only other relative in the state was her mother, who resided 45 minutes away in a remote place known as Taylor's Island. He didn't know the street address, but he knew how to get there, so he volunteered to take us."

"The three of us were on our way to the sparsely populated island. During the long drive Tavon told us about Sharon's enemies, to include the name of her former husband and a few of her recent boyfriends, none of which were happy she was dating a black man. We eventually found her mother's address, which was in a trailer park, with one of those long wheel chair ramps leading to the front door. Donald, Tavon and I walked up together. Her mother opened the door and recognized Tavon and allowed us in. The place was cluttered with magazines, newspapers and junk everywhere. It smelled like cat piss and mildew. Her mom was at least 65 years old. Her hair was kept nicely, and her shirt looked clean. Cats were everywhere. Bound to a wheel chair with only one leg, she was quick to explain how diabetes had taken its toll on her body. Hazel was her name. She gave us a warm greeting, demanding hugs from everyone. There was something special about her, like she was a person you were meant to meet. Forget about what she didn't have, there was something very sweet about this woman. You couldn't help but to like her. She was one of those people who had a unique glow. Donald stood by the front door, while Tavon and I stood on each side of the wheelchair. I remember she was holding mine and Tavon's hands. I'll never forget her words. *Tavon, where's my baby Sunshine?* That's what she called Sharon. She was a wise old woman. She could immediately sense something was wrong. She pulled us closer to her and then she looked up at me with the prettiest blue eyes I have ever seen. She asked *What is your name young man?* and before I could answer, tears streamed down her face and she squeezed my hand. *My baby sunshine has been taken away from me, hasn't she?* It was everything I could do to keep my composure. She pulled me and Tavon down to her chest and hugged us as she cried harder. Her tears were all over my face and shirt. I remember watching Tavon and her cry. She kept saying how Sharon was the only one that took care of her and how there was no one else. No one to take her to the doctor, get her food or her medicine. It was beyond sad. After an hour or so we left this crying, crippled lady all alone. There was nothing else we could do."

Michaels took a deep breath, let it out slowly and looked at his shoes. He looked up and watched as Dr. Esterling reached over to the end table and pulled a tissue from the box. "Wow," she said dabbing her eyes. "Boy, now I can see how something like this can have an effect on you. Excuse me. That was a first."

Michaels looked up at the clock and he had already exceeded his appointment by 30 minutes. "Sorry Doc. You wanted to hear one."

"Yes, I did. I must say, I was not ready for that. So, who killed her?"

The smirk on Michaels face was clear. "Tavon. In fact, while he was in custody, he worked over two correctional officers using his martial arts skills and escaped for a few days before he was apprehended. Oddly enough, he would only confess to me."

"And to think he accompanied you to do the notification to Hazel and even cried. Ok detective call me when you can. I'll see you soon." Surprised and embarrassed by her actions, Dr. Esterling rushed to get Michaels from her office.

For the next few days every member of the unit, along with veteran FBI Agents Jim Wilson and Christina Smith assigned to the Annapolis office, worked vigorously on the Abrams murder. Realizing the magnitude of these cases, the FBI pulled two agents from their Raleigh Office, Agents Jeff Kelly and Kevin Moore, to assist Sergeant Tabor. The cops from both local agencies were deputized as Federal Marshalls courtesy of the FBI. First, the two teams would jointly focus on attempting to find the needle in the haystack. Their job was simple or so it sounded. Who had moved from Raleigh to sleepy ole Anne Arundel County in the last two months?

In both states, agents and detectives painstakingly looked through countless boxes of documents from their respective Motor Vehicle Administrations. The boxes contained hundreds of new drivers' licenses issued in Anne Arundel County or cancelled drivers licenses in North Carolina. Nothing was found. They reviewed, researched and studied photographs of every prisoner with a violent record released from the Department of Correction facilities in both states, who took residence near Raleigh or Anne Arundel County around the time of the murders. Their efforts were fruitless. Reward posters seeking information about their cases were hung throughout the community in both jurisdictions, repeated news articles and special bits appeared on TV, including a special TIP hotline. Still, no credible leads.

The reports and photographs from both investigations were forwarded to the FBI National Academy in Quantico, Virginia. Agent Hollman began his timely and thorough analysis of each case. Based upon extensive research on human behavior, traits and characteristics he would craft a detailed criminal profile of the suspect or suspects. Often this would serve as a helpful tool for investigators, especially in serial rape or murder cases.

The following week, Michaels found himself seated once again before Dr. Esterling. He felt very relaxed, and he needed to talk. "Doc, I keep having these dreams about something my neighbor said to me last year."

"What was that Ronnie?"

"You see, my neighbor is a friend who cuts my hair. Long story short, her mom was killed in a car accident and I did the notification. For trial she wrote an impact statement and in it she said how every time she sees me, she thinks of that horrible night. Doc, I can't stop thinking how everyone I've ever told must feel the same way. Lately, I keep dreaming of all these notifications and no one wants to be around me because of what I've said or what more bad news I may bring. It's tearing me up." Tears poured from his eyes. "I'm sorry Doc."

"You're human Ronnie. It's ok."

The room was quiet and soon Michaels abruptly said goodbye and excused himself from her office. He rushed to his car and drove to work with tears dripping from his eyes.

One month had passed since the Abrams murder with still no suspects. Members of the task force were slowly running out of leads and the team's confidence was diminishing.

Laboratory tests showed no semen present in, on or around Edith Abrams. Several Caucasian male pubic and head hairs were discovered in the leaves beneath and surrounding her. Evidence of the pubic hair revealed that at some point during or after the murder, the killer exposed his genitals. From the hair, DNA proved to be an exact match to those retrieved in North Carolina. Unfortunately, there were no matches in the FBI data base. One thing they knew for sure is they had a transient, white male serial killer on their hands.

It was a Monday morning in late August when Tommy walked from his office holding the FBI Behavioral Analysis Profile. Half of the task force was present along with Dredge and Michaels. "Here it is. Let's see what they have to say about our suspect."

Tommy's eyes darted back and forth, reading silently through much of the narrative. Both Dredge and Michaels leaned back in their chairs drinking their coffee and enjoying a morning smoke. FBI Agents Wilson and Smith sat at their newly acquired desks, now crammed against one another near the back door.

"Well? Say something. Don't just read it to yourself," Dredge anxiously said to Tommy.

"Oh, sorry. So, this says we are looking for a middle aged or older white male, who most likely has a college education, possibly divorced and is currently, or once served in the military. He most likely has a history of assault charges, arson and sexual offenses. Let's see, it says he had a troubled upbringing, most likely raised by a strict grandparent or guardian. He was most likely a Christian and believes in God. It is surmised from the way in which he positioned his victims before he set fire around their bodies that he was cleansing them of their sins. It says he believes the fire was the devil and once it has burned out, the victim had been forgiven for their wrongful sins." Tommy looked up at Michaels and Dredge.

"If that's true, that's one sick bitch," Dredge said with smoke trickling from his mouth.

Tommy flipped to the next page. "Fuck check this out. *A killer of this type will readily admit his actions once apprehended. It is key for the interrogator to show respect and understanding for his actions.* That's something Donald could do." Tommy scanned the remaining pages and sat the packet on Donald's desk. "There you have it. That's who the FBI says we are looking for."

Michaels' cell phone sounded. "Hello."

"Hi Daddy."

Michaels' face lit up. "Hey Honey. How was your vacation at Grandma and Grandpa's?"

"It was really fun. We went to the beach and rode waves and Grandpa took me fishing at Mount Trashmore and I caught a sunshine fish. But I didn't touch it, Grandpa did all that cuz that was yukky."

"That's great Honey. Are you home now?"

"Yes. Mommy wants to know when you're coming to get me."

"Tell her I'll be over after work today."

"Can we color those placemats?"

"Of course we can. I'll see you in a few hours. Love you, can't wait to see you."

"I love you too Daddy. Bye."

"Ronnie what's going on?" Stacey said before he could hang up.

"Hi to you too. It sounded like she had fun."

"Yeah she had a blast. She really needs to see you. It's been way too long."

"I know. I'll be over after work to take her out to dinner."

"If you say so."

"Stacy, I'll be there. Give me a break."

"I have Ronnie. A lot of them. I got to go. Bye."

Soon after the call, Michaels gathered his things to head home for an evening with his daughter. Tommy and Michaels walked out of the CID together.

"So Shithead, how are things?"

"Good, I'm going to see my daughter tonight. I haven't seen her in weeks. First, she was on vacation with her mother, then with her grandparents but that's alright she's having fun."

"Have you seen my doctor friend?"

Michaels laughed. "The one you failed to tell me was some hot, classy babe?"

Tommy chuckled. "Sorry, I just didn't think you would talk to a woman that's all."

"We've talked a couple of times now. I really like her. She's got her shit together."

"Do you think she is helping you?"

"Yeah, I think so. A little. Thanks for asking Tommy. I'm ok."

The evening went just as planned. Michaels and Nicole had pizza, laughed and colored the restaurant's placemats like always. He was his typical care free self, placing slices of pepperoni over his eyes, causing Nicole to spit Coke from her mouth and nose in laughter. The night was perfect and much needed. They said their normal goodbyes with butterfly kisses and Michaels ended the evening feeling happy.

An Angel

It has been three months since the Abrams murder. Michaels had a few more visits with Dr. Esterling, making slow progress in managing his stress. The residents of Anne Arundel County slowly began living life again as normal. The police presence was sporadic on the trail and seemed to lessen each week.

Zack and Samantha Bates were brother and sister who enjoyed riding on the trail most Sunday mornings. The 17 year old twins unloaded their bikes from the car rack and started toward the trail located just a few yards away from the small Park & Ride commonly used on Heights Road. Oddly enough, the Park & Ride was located next to the bar Kathy Jarvis was last seen and where Michaels was seconds away from killing an armed man. It was a windy morning and the two were enjoying their ride. There were few people occupying the trail, which made for a relaxing excursion. Not long into their ride, Samantha noticed her front tire had gone flat.

"Uh oh Zack, it looks like I got a flat. I hope you have your repair kit with you."

"Oh crap. I do, but it's back at the car. Have a seat on that bench up ahead and I'll go back and get it."

"Ok."

Zack turned his bike around and began peddling to the car. Samantha moved her bike off the asphalt, leaned it against a tree and took a seat on the bench.

Several minutes passed without seeing a single passerby. The wind howled and drowned out any of the cars in the distance. She looked across the trail and something caught her eye. She walked to the tree line but still could not confirm what she was seeing. She took a few steps when she saw something brown. Still unsure of the object, she worked her way deeper past the trees and brush. Unexpectedly, what she was focusing on jumped to its feet. Frightened, she grabbed her chest while the brown and white speckled fawn struggled to walk away. Only days old, the injured deer hobbled through the trees dragging it's broken front leg. Saddened, she walked quickly toward the animal in hopes of rescuing it. Weak and broken, it continued to labor through the forest, occasionally making a high-pitched crying sound. Samantha snaked faster and deeper through the woods until she was stunned by another sight partially visible behind a fallen tree. It appeared to be a white sock on a foot. She called out to the person but got no answer. Now scared of what she may have found, she moved past the fallen timber and stopped quickly in her tracks. Caught by surprise and astonished, she screamed. It was an older woman lying on her back, with her private parts exposed. There was a large blood spot above her forehead among her wavy frosted colored hair. Her skin was pale. One eye closed and the other half open. She could tell the woman was dead. Fear rushed through her body like she had never felt. She turned and ran toward the trail, scurrying to get her backpack off and retrieve her cell phone. The strong winds caused a large branch to crash next to her.

Barely able to unzipper her backpack, the petrified teen fumbled for her phone and nervously pulled it from an upper pocket, dropping it in the thick, dried leaves. She could hear noises around her, and some sounded very close. She started to cry as she searched for her phone. Once located, she scrambled to call her brother. There was no answer. She could hear a sound approaching her from the trail and fear jolted through her body like a transfusion. Running toward the bike trail, she tripped over an old log and fell into prickly stickers, dropping her phone once more. Somewhat entwined, she pushed herself up and swiped her phone from the ground. The sharp stickers scratched deep into her legs and forearms causing blood to trickle from her wounds. She continued running but was unable to see the asphalt path.

"Sam," Zack called out as he came riding up.

"Zack, Zack, over here. Help, oh my God, oh my God, come here, over here, help," she cried.

Zack jumped from his bike and it crashed to the pavement. He could hear the panic in his sister's voice as he raced between the trees to get to her.

"We gotta call 911. Oh my God, call 911," she said as her voice cracked.

"What happened? Jesus, calm down. Damn, why are you shaking?"

She grabbed him by the arm and squeezed his bicep. "There, there, over there's a dead lady right behind those trees," she frantically said pointing to the shaded area.

"No way, what are you talking about Sam? Are you sure?" Zack stepped into the woods when he made another discovery. "Hey, there's a tennis shoe over there," Zack said pointing a few feet away.

"Jesus Christ Zack, really? No, I didn't see that," Samantha said blowing the dirt from her phone. "I'm calling 911."

"Show me what you're talking about. I don't see anybody. Are you sure?"

"Zack, where are we? What are we near?" Samantha asked while talking to the 911 operator.

"Tell them we're a good way down from the Park & Ride on Heights Road."

Samantha hung up the phone. "They want us to wait here. The police are on their way."

"Show me where this person is," Zack demanded.

"I'm not going back there again. No way. See that big fallen down tree?" Samantha pointed into the woods. "She's right next to that."

Zack weaved around piles of brush and made his way to the fallen tree. Peering through the limbs, he could see part of a leg dressed in a pair of light green polyester sports pants. He made his way closer until he was able to see the woman who was sprawled in a cross-like position. He could not comprehend what he was seeing. One tennis shoe remained on her right foot and only a sock soiled with dirt and leaves on the other. Her long sleeve shirt and white sports bra had been cut open. Her slacks and underwear were cut from the waist band and torn to one side, revealing her vagina. Smoldering burnt leaves outlined the deceased corpse like in a horror movie, he thought to himself staring in amazement. In the center of her forehead, evidence of dried blood could be seen which had streamed down to the bridge of her nose. He noticed a distinct horizontal line spanning across her neck where she had clearly been strangled. The curious young man was shocked when he saw a 3" x 4" section of her scalp missing. The sight of the lady's skull repulsed him causing him to vomit. He turned and walked toward the trail. He could hear sirens getting closer. Walking faster, he noticed his sister speaking to a white male sitting on a black colored mountain bike, wearing a dark baseball cap and sunglasses.

"Sam," Zack yelled out.

"Over here," she shouted. The man she was speaking with swiftly ended his conversation and sped off in the opposite direction he had been traveling. Samantha paid the man no attention and joined her brother. Finally getting to his sister, they both could hear police radios around a nearby curve in the trail.

"We're down here," Zack yelled. A male voice acknowledged his call from a distance.

Michaels just returned home from purchasing shotgun shells for the goose hunt he had planned with Mel for next weekend, when his phone rang. "Ronnie, you're on call this weekend, right?"

"Yep. Why?"

"We got another one on the trail."

"Fuck, where?"

"In Severna Park. Meet me at the Park & Ride on Heights Road."

"On my way." Michaels put on a pair of khakis, freshly polished cordovan colored shoes, a light blue buttoned down shirt and his blue blazer. In mere minutes he was out the door.

The Park & Ride was jam packed with police cars and evidence vans just like the airport observation lot a few months earlier. The media was quick to respond to this scene and were staging in mass in the Tavern parking lot a hundred yards away. The uniformed cop allowed Michaels into the taped off parking lot. He took his notebook from his visor and shoved it inside his jacket pocket and shot out of his car.

This had to be the fastest response ever from the entire unit, including FBI Agents Wilson and Smith. Everyone had a vested interest and they wanted it solved at all costs. From the looks of it, no one had plans on this particular sunny Sunday morning, no one, except for the killer. Jeff was already standing by at the staging location waiting for Tommy and company.

"Which way down the trail is the body? North or south?" Tommy asked Jeff.

"South. They said it's a little over a quarter mile from here."

"Agents Wilson and Smith, I want you guys along with Dredge to start interviewing people on the trail. Mark and Donald start canvassing the homes close to the trail." Everyone agreed and set off to their assignments.

A uniformed officer approached Tommy and his team while they stood talking. "Excuse me, but do you guys want me to cut the kids loose who found the body? I have their statements and personal information. They are standing over by my car. My sergeant said to ask you first."

"Ronnie talk to them. We'll meet you at the scene," Tommy said.

Michaels turned and walked toward the teens. "Hi guys. I'm Detective Michaels from the Homicide Unit. I understand you found a body in the woods?"

"I didn't. She did," Zack said pointing to Samantha.

"I know the officer got a statement from you both, but when you guys were riding today, did you notice anyone or anything out of the ordinary?" Michaels inquired.

"No. There really weren't a lot of people on the trail today" Samantha said.

"Here's my card. Call me if you can remember anything else. You guys are free to leave. Thank you," Michaels said.

The detective walked down the trail and had his name entered onto the Crime Scene Log by the rookie standing eagerly on the path. "Hi Dad. Hi Jeffrey," Michaels said to the two men working in tandem with a tape measurer.

"This is one deranged individual Ronnie. Do you see what he did to her head?" Jeff asked pointing to the victim's skull. Michaels and Dredge stepped in for a closer inspection.

"These scenes are all identical. This is a true serial killer and he has no plans on stopping," Dredge said while he put a cigarette in his mouth.

"My God, he scalped her like a fucking Indian. What the fuck?" Michaels blurted out in astonishment.

"The mark around her neck looks the same also," Dredge pointed out.

"Whatever kind of blade he is using, is awful fucking sharp. Damn, look how it sliced through both layers of her clothing and the material never even frayed," Michaels stated examining the body from head to toe.

"Where is her other shoe?" Dredge asked Jeff.

"It's about six feet off the trail. If you noticed, there are only a few drag marks. It looks like he may have walked her most of the way back here," Jeff concluded from the lack of disturbance on the ground.

"Oh yeah, I see that. Maybe he coaxed her back deeper with the ligature around her neck like a leash," Michaels added.

"Most likely," Dredge said in agreement.

"Damn it," Tommy shouted. "Let me guess. No witnesses. No one heard shit?"

"That's what I'm told. She was found by a teenager who was biking with her brother. They didn't notice anyone strange. The victim doesn't have any ID, so we are going to run the tags on the cars in the parking lot until we find something close," Michaels said.

"I'll have the patrol lieutenant start on that. Where was the bike patrol when this happened?" Tommy asked.

"Who fucking knows, but I can tell you they weren't here," Michaels muttered.

Tommy was pissed. "I hate to say it, but I don't want him to leave."

"What do you mean? You don't want who to leave?" Michaels asked in shock.

"I don't want our killer to leave. A bike trail is one of his signatures and though they stretch for miles through the county, it still limits his striking areas. Hell, if he took this killing spree to the streets, we'd be fucked," Tommy exclaimed.

"And if he leaves our state and starts fresh somewhere else, he can keep killing and killing and killing," Dredge said in a very low voice while he puffed on his cigarette.

Michaels perked up with an epiphany. "What about Christina?"

"Who the fuck is Christina?" Tommy asked with a puzzled look on his face.

"The FBI Agent, Christina Smith."

Still not grasping Michaels' thoughts. "Yeah, what about her?"

"She's 50 something. How about she dyes her hair grey and we use her as a decoy."

Tommy's eyebrows lifted, and his eyes opened wide. "That's a great idea Shithead. Listen Ronnie, I'll stay here with Jeff and Ray. The entire academy class is on their way to search the woods, or at least several hundred yards worth. Dredge, do me a favor and find out where the fuck the bike patrol guys were and what, if anything, they have. Ronnie, I want you to pull the security tape from the convenience store up the street and see what you can find from this morning. Search for anyone who looked like they may have been going on the trail, you know buying drinks, wearing exercise clothing, anything. After you do that, get with the patrol lieutenant and see if we can ID this poor lady's car so we can tell her family."

Dredge and Michaels left the scene to complete their assignments. Everyone knew they needed to develop a lead before this deranged fuck took another life.

Michaels drove to the nearest convenience store located a short distance from the Park & Ride. As he walked into the store, he was greeted by a Pakistani man working behind the counter. With his badge and credentials prominently displayed, he greeted the employee. "Good afternoon. I'm Detective Michaels from the County Police. Are you the Manager?"

"No. No. Not Manager. Habib is Manager. He's in office," the man said in broken English, pointing to a closed door next to the ATM machine.

Michaels proceeded to the door with his credentials still in hand. He reached down and opened the door. Frightened from the sudden unannounced entry, the man arched back in his chair and reached down to zipper his shorts. On the computer screen in front of him was a video of an older middle-eastern man getting a blow job from a teenaged boy. The man fumbled on the keyboard pressing buttons until the video ceased playing.

"Who, who are you?" the man stuttered to Michaels.

"See this." he stuck his badge and ID in his face. "I'm the police. I'm from the Homicide Unit. You comprehend, homicide?"

"Yes police. Police. I do nothing wrong. Nothing. I'm just day Manager."

"Listen Habib. I'm investigating a murder while you're sitting here jerking off. I need today's security tape from 8 a.m. until 1p.m. I'll need your DVD, CD, VHS or whatever the fuck you got. Understand?"

"Security tape. Oh no. I must get permission from owner first. He is not in country."

Agitated, he hovered over the man with his handcuffs visibly displayed in his free hand. "Listen pal. How do you think the owner is going to feel when I tell him you were getting your nut off watching some little boy suck off some old dude's cock while you were working? I don't give a fuck where your owner is. I'm leaving with your security footage from today if I have to rip the machine off the fucking wall. And then I'm going to arrest you for being fucking stupid, you copy me?" Michaels said sternly.

With his entire body leaning back in his chair in fear he responded, "Yes sir. Yes sir. I get DVD. You take DVD. I put in new one." Michaels stood back as the man recovered the hardware from the security system and turned it over. "Here sir. Can I get you a Coke? Cigarettes? Take whatever you want. My treat."

"No thanks Habib," Michaels said, and he turned and walked from the store.

Back at the Park & Ride, Michaels met up with the patrol lieutenant whose men were running the tags from the 10 plus cars that were parked in close proximity to the trail. At the onset, none of the registered owners' descriptions seemed to match the victim but there were still more vehicles to be checked.

"Detective, the only thing I can tell you is to be patient. The MVA system is extra slow today, so my guys are going as fast as they can," the silver haired seasoned lieutenant told Michaels.

"Yes sir. Can I give you my cell number in case something comes in that looks promising?"

"Sure. Give it to my sergeant standing at the top of the parking lot," the hard ass commander said before he walked away.

Michaels started toward the uniformed sergeant when his cell phone rang. It was Tommy. "Yes sir."

"Where are you?"

"At the Park & Ride talking to General Patton."

"Who? Oh, never mind. Get over here. One of the recruits found the victim's fanny pack with her ID." Tommy hung up the phone.

Michaels rapidly walked to Tommy's location where he saw a light brown leather fanny pack laying on the path. "Where was this found?"

"It wasn't too far from the body. How far Ray?" Tommy asked.

"12'4" from her right shoulder," Ray said while snapping close up pictures repeatedly of the woman's head injury.

"The strap was cut in the front and it looks like it may have just been thrown off. It was probably in the killer's way. The leaves leading up to where it was recovered were not disturbed." Jeff remarked.

Tommy handed Michaels a driver's license, keys and a cell phone from the fanny pack. "Here Shithead, Go do this notification. Take one of the guys with you when you do it."

"You got it." Michaels looked at the cheerfully smiling lady pictured on the license. Her wavy light grey hair was neatly styled. The wrinkles surrounding her eyes were a visual reminder of her age, but not enough to hide her beauty. From the picture, he got the feeling she was someone who took care of herself and was particular about her appearance.

"Allison Withers. What a fucking shame and only 63 years old," Michaels said shaking his head in disbelief and looking back at the body. "1401 Ives Drive. That's no more than a mile from here. Hell, she may have walked."

Michaels tucked the victim's phone and driver's license in his coat pocket while walking to his car.

He pressed a speed dial button on his phone. "Dredge."

"Yeah."

"We found the victim's fanny pack along with her ID. I'm headed over there now to see what I can find out."

"You need me to go with you?"

"No. I got this. I'll call you when I get back." The call ended, and Michaels took a quick glance at his map book. Familiar with the neighborhood and only a short distance away, he arrived in under three minutes. The address was a new Colonial style home and one of the nicer houses in the community. Parked in the driveway was a shiny black Mercedes Benz SL500.

"Well it looks like someone's home," he said aloud taking one last hit from his Marlboro. "Fuck I hate these. Fuck," he said banging his fist on the steering wheel. He kicked his door open and flicked his hot-boxed cigarette to the ground. He walked up the sidewalk toward the front door and was startled when the door swung opened and out walked a teenaged girl.

"Oh, you scared me," the child said.

"I'm sorry, I'm looking for anyone related to Ms. Allison Withers."

"That's my grandmother. My mom is in the back yard if you want to talk to her." With that, the girl called out to her friend and ran up the street.

He took a deep breath and walked to the rear of the residence. It appeared the azaleas bordering the front of the home had been freshly trimmed and landscaped. When he made his way to the backside of the house, he saw a lady spreading mulch carefully around a set of mature rose bushes. She was wearing a pair of old jean shorts, a yellow top, tennis shoes and gardening gloves. Her hair was loosely tied in a bun on top of her head. Oblivious to Michaels' presence, her back was turned while she continued her landscaping. He made a slight coughing sound trying not to startle her, "excuse me ma'am."

Caught by surprise, the lady uttered a short scream and placed both hands over her heart. "Oh my gosh you startled me," she said turning toward Michaels. A distinct look of surprise edged over her face. "What are you doing here?"

He couldn't believe his eyes. Dumbfounded, he could not speak. It was Dr. Katie Esterling.

"Detective Michaels. Clients don't come to my residence and that includes police officers. I'll need you to leave right away, please. Call me Monday morning at the office," she said sternly. He stood frozen looking at the agitated woman.

"Did you hear what I said? You need to leave now."

"I'm sorry Doctor. Believe me, I wish I could," he said in a somber tone.

"Well then if it's that urgent, I'll meet you at my office in an hour," she said frustrated.

"I'm sorry, but your mother was killed today," he said softly with his eyes locked on Dr. Esterling's.

Standing with a stunned look on her face, her arms fell to her side and both hands went limp, dropping the moist brown mulch from her grip. Collapsing to her knees, she burst into tears and cried out. "What? No. No. Where? How? My God, she was on the trail, wasn't she? Wasn't she?" she bellowed.

"Yes ma'am she was," he sadly answered joining her among the shrubs.

She cried harder and harder. "But you said you had extra patrols watching the path. You said that, you said that. I told her it was ok. Where were they? Answer me. Where were they?" she yelled.

Michaels stood speechless as the sadness he had just caused overtook him. "I'm sorry Doctor." His head dropped down.

"How? How? How was she killed? Oh my God I can't believe this is happening? Are you sure it's her? Positive? It can't be. You have to be mistaken." She reached in her rear pocket and pulled out her phone. "I'll call her." She pressed a few numbers on the keypad and within seconds she could hear the phone ringing. With the phone to her ear she raised her head and looked toward the sun. "Come on mom, pick up." Michaels lifted the victim's ringing phone from within his jacket pocket. Recognizing her mother's phone, she saw what was happening. He terminated the call and Dr. Esterling's head fell into her dirty hands crying.

He knelt next to his sobbing counselor. He could not believe he was delivering this news to the woman who he had sought help from. The same type of news which caused him to land on the couch at this very person's psychiatric office. He put his hand on the weeping doctor's shoulder. "I'm really sorry Doc. I really am. Is there someone I can call for you, like your husband?"

Still crying, she lifted her face now covered with mulch from her hands. "No, there is no one, only my daughter and my sister, who lives in Texas. I'll have to call her. My God, my daughter." She cocked her head back and faced the sky letting out a loud shrieking scream at the top of her lungs.

"Doctor, I believe I met your daughter when I arrived. What about her?" he asked.

She jumped up from the ground. The front of her body was soiled with the mulch she had just put down. "Oh God, Kathryn. She is going to be so upset. I have to tell her." Frantically, she looked up at a nearby window and shouted her daughter's name. Tears poured down through her dirt covered face.

"Kathryn, Kathryn."

Michaels stood up. "Doctor."

"Kathryn," she continued to yell.

"Doctor. Doc, She's not here."

She turned to him plagued with sorrow. "What do you mean?"

"She ran up to her friend's house when I arrived."

"That's right. God, I'm such a mess. I'm so sorry." She walked out of the area where she had been working and began pacing back and forth on the freshly cut lawn. "I can't believe somebody would do something like this to her." She stopped pacing and walked over to Michaels standing in the landscaped area. "Did she suffer? Tell me she didn't suffer. Please tell me she didn't suffer."

"No ma'am. I don't think she did."

"How was she killed? No, don't tell me. No, I need to know. Can you even tell me? No. I don't want to know. You said she didn't suffer. That's all I want to know."

"Let's get you inside and clean you up a bit so you can find your daughter," he suggested.

"I'm so sorry you had to do this. Christ, this is why you came to see me and now look at me. My God, I'm so embarrassed."

"No, no don't be. Doc, you just lost your mother. How else are you supposed to react? Don't apologize. Come on, let's get you inside."

The two walked into the home through a rear entrance. Once inside, she excused herself and walked up the steps to her bedroom. He heard the door close and immediately she could be heard crying. He walked into the living room from the kitchen. The house was immaculate, decorated like a model home, everything in its place, just as her office was except for two birthday balloons suspended from a kitchen chair.

The front door opened, and Kathryn walked into the foyer. She slipped off her shoes and with a big smile on her face she greeted Detective Michaels once more.

"Hi there. I'm Kathryn."

"Hi." he paused reluctant to say his title. "I'm a friend of your mom. My name is Ronnie Michaels." He extended his hand to shake.

"Nice to meet you Mr. Michaels." She grabbed his hand and gave him a firm hand shake. "Do you know where my mom is?"

Unsure what to say, he tried to delay the inevitable until Dr. Esterling had time to gather herself. "Um yeah, she's upstairs cleaning up from doing yard work, so you may want to wait down here with me."

"Oh, that's ok. I have to ask her something." The young girl disappeared up the steps.

Kathryn knocked on her mother's locked bedroom door calling for her. He could hear the door open and close and then it happened; she began screaming wildly. He heard Dr. Esterling talking then they cried simultaneously. He thought how in just a few short minutes, the lives of these two people were changed forever. One minute they were happy and normal and now they were devastated, overtaken by grief.

Twenty minutes later Dr. Esterling walked down the steps with her arm around her daughter. Kathryn's head leaned on her mother's chest, continuing to weep. "Sorry detective. Thanks for being so patient. So, what do we do now?"

"Contact a funeral home, they know what the process is. I can assure you we have an entire team of detectives and FBI agents working on this case. He walked over to them standing at the bottom of the steps and placed his hands on both their shoulders. I promise we will do everything we can to find who did this. You have my word."

Dr. Esterling reached forward and hugged Michaels. "I know you will and thank you."

"I'll be in touch." Michaels walked to his car and called Tommy on his cell. "I just made the notification to the victim's daughter and you're not going to believe who it was."

"Who?"

"Dr. Katie Esterling."

"No fucking way," Tommy said in disbelief.

"Yeah, I couldn't believe it."

"Was it a bad one?"

"Horrible. Along with her young daughter, too."

"Jesus fucking Christ. Ok Ronnie, Jeff and Ray are wrapping up here. The others are just about done. Everyone is going to meet at the office. Ronnie are you ok?"

"Stop. I'll see you at the office." Michaels hung up the phone.

An hour later the office was full of detectives and agents. The canvassing of the nearby homes and folks remaining on the trail yielded nothing. No one had seen or heard anything unusual. This case came to a halt quickly.

On Donald's desk was a message from Mr. Abrams. Donald was sure he had caught the latest news and was calling for an update.

"Mr. Abrams. This is Detective Hauf. I just got back to the office and saw your message."

"I saw the news detective. Same guy?"

"Yes sir. We think so. Both scenes have the same M.O."

"You don't have any leads, do you detective?"

"We have some physical evidence, but…"

Mr. Abrams interrupted Donald. "You got nothing at this point, correct?"

Knowing he couldn't bullshit the man, Donald answered him. "No sir. But we are not giving up." The phone went dead once more.

Sitting at his desk Michaels slipped the DVD from the convenience store into his computer. For the next two hours he fast forwarded through the frames searching for anyone who was dressed like they might be headed to the trail. Surprisingly, there were many people who fit the profile. There were couples who arrived by bike, wearing their matching outfits, while others were dressed in exercise apparel, captured buying drinks or snacks. An athletic looking white male was seen arriving at 8 a.m., riding a black mountain bike, wearing a black baseball cap, a black sweat suit and sunglasses. He purchased a Power Aid, which he secured in the holder beneath his seat. After scanning through hours of footage, Michaels made it to the end. Disappointingly, no one appeared suspicious.

"Listen up everybody. It's 6:30 p.m. I want everyone to go home and get some rest and we'll meet here in the morning. Agent Smith," Tommy said loudly pointing at Christina.

"Yes sir."

"I need you to wear some type of exercise clothes to work every day until I say otherwise. Clothing like a Senior would wear. Go to the store tonight and buy yourself some grey hair dye. Congratulations, you're going to be our decoy."

Surprised, the witty 53 year old FBI Agent responded. "Thanks, Sarge. What are you trying to do? Get me killed before my retirement? I'll bet this request came from my husband," she said sarcastically.

"No Christina, it was actually Michaels' idea." Everyone laughed.

Smiling, Michaels looked at Christina. "Hey sorry, I don't have tits, or I'd do it."

The laughter continued, and she returned fire. "Fuck, neither do I, so what's that got to do with anything?"

"That's enough. I'll see everybody in the morning," Tommy ordered.

Almost home, Michaels approached the top of his court when a black Tahoe, parked next to a fire hydrant, caught his eye. Suspicious by nature, he slowed to take a closer look. There was no registration plate on the front and the windows were blackened out. From the light of the illuminous full moon, he could make out the silhouette of a person behind the steering wheel. He continued down his street when he caught a glimpse of movement in his rearview mirror. The vehicle was leaving in a hurry. Closer to his home, he saw the figure of a tall man walking away from the front of his residence. With his curiosity peeked, he sped down and whipped into his reserved parking space. He jumped from his car and walked hurriedly toward the break between the townhomes. Standing close to the building for concealment, he placed his hand on his gun. Something in his gut didn't feel right. His eyes dashed side to side looking for movement. He listened carefully for dogs barking or any noises, but there was nothing. He retreated to his home, on edge from his observations. Something wasn't right.

He stripped himself of his jacket, gun and badge and kicked off his shoes before he fixed a strong cocktail. He made himself comfortable in the recliner, took a deep breath and lit up a much needed cigarette. As he reflected on the day, his mind started racing, cluttered with the traumatic events. His thoughts centered on the latest victim. The thought of a serial killer lurking in his county did not sit well. His emotions shifted to Dr. Esterling. How strange was it he thought, that he had just completed a death notification to his own psychiatrist?

He detected a slight noise outside his front door. He jumped up and unholstered his Smith & Wesson lying on the dining room table. He crept over to the picture window and slowly pushed the drapes to the side. From the moon's light, he could see the shadow of at least one person on his doorstep. He readied his gun and quietly moved toward the door. With his opposite hand, he carefully turned the dead bolt to the unlocked position. He placed his hand on the doorknob and tightened his grip on his weapon. He swung the door open and leveled his barrel on the figure standing on his steps. The person stepped toward him with an object in one hand and both arms extended in his direction. Stunned, he lowered his weapon. It was Dr. Esterling.

Falling into his arms holding a wine bottle, the intoxicated, distraught woman cried out of control on his chest. He helped the unsteady doctor into his foyer. He gently took the near empty wine bottle from her hand and sat it on the table, along with his revolver. Crying loudly, she clung onto him as he walked her to the living room couch. Still in his arms, the two sat side by side. He noticed she had no shoes on her feet. She lifted her head. Her shirt was wet from tears and fluids were dripping from her nose.

"I'm so sorry. I'm sorry, I shouldn't be here, but I didn't know what to do," she cried.

"It's ok, wait here. Let me get some napkins for you." He grabbed a wad of napkins from the dining room table and rejoined his unexpected guest on the couch.

Her head was buried in her hands. "I can't stop crying. I don't know what to do. Tell me what to do Detective Michaels," she said raising her head and looking at him.

"Doc, call me Ronnie please."

"I'm supposed to be a professional at handling crisis and look at me," she said in the midst of blowing her nose and wiping the relentless tears from her eyes.

"Doc, it's ok. You're still a person. You just lost someone you loved. Someone who you were close to."

"Don't call me Doc. I'm Katie. I'm anything but a doctor right now. I can't even explain my emotions. I can't begin to pull myself together any longer than five minutes. I'm hurt, sad, ashamed, angry. Fuck, how could someone do this to my poor mother? She never hurt anyone. I've never wanted to hurt another human being so bad in my life, but now I do. I'm not supposed to think that way. Jesus Christ, some psychiatrist I am." She slumped her upper body onto the couch.

"Can I get you some water or coffee?"

"No, but I'll take some more wine. God, listen to me. I'm so pathetic. I had my ex take my daughter for the night. I drove drunk to my office and got your address. Now I'm balling like a baby at a client's house. I should lose my license." Katie struggled to push herself up to a sitting position. She put the napkin once more to her eyes and soaked up the tears. Drunk, Michaels saw her eyes roll upwards while she mumbled. "I should leave now."

"No Katie. That's not going to happen. You're in no condition to drive. I can't let you do that. You are staying here tonight. I have an extra room upstairs or you can sleep here on the couch, whichever you prefer."

"The room is spinning." She sniveled a few more times and closed her eyes. The room went silent. She was sound asleep. He lifted her legs onto the couch, grabbed a blanket from the hallway closet and draped it over her. He took a sip of his drink and was completely bewildered. He freshened his beverage, turned off all but one light and returned to his chair. He chained smoked one cigarette after the next and downed two more drinks while he watched his psychiatrist lay curled up on his couch, body twitching, passed out cold. Murder was so cruel, he thought to himself. It had no boundaries, no preferences, no age or sex limitations and definitely, no rules or restraints. He clicked off the light next to his recliner and called it a night.

Early the next morning, he awoke to the sound of the shower running on the first floor. He slipped on some sweatpants and started a pot of coffee to begin the day. Knowing he had a long day ahead, he took advantage of the upstairs bathroom to get ready for work. By the time he walked downstairs he noticed a handwritten note propped up on the table, between his gun and the bottle of red wine.

Dear Detective Michaels,

Please accept my sincerest apology for coming to your residence last evening. My condition, my actions and my behavior were inexcusable, and I would not blame you for making a formal complaint to the State Board. I am beyond embarrassed and mortified. I would understand if you never spoke to me again. I hope you catch whatever monster killed my darling mother.

Katie

He laid the note down and put his badge and gun on his waist and started out for work.

Michaels stopped in the doorway of Tommy's office. "Shithead, I need you to coordinate the decoy operation with Agent Smith. Captain Donoho has six bike patrol cops on their way here, and if you need more, just say the word. You know how to do these things. Just make sure she doesn't get hurt. We don't need that right now."

"Tommy, you will never guess who visited me last night."

"Later Ronnie, I can't talk right now. I got too much shit going on."

Michaels entered the office with a big smile stretched across his face. "Wow Smith, how you've aged overnight. Man, this job must really be getting to you."

"Fuck you Michaels," she snapped back.

At this time, six bike patrol officers walked into the office where Michaels and the entire task force were. Half were dressed in jeans, the others in athletic clothing. Some wore hats, some did not. It was a good mix Michaels figured, and just enough to provide Agent Smith with adequate cover, besides her own .40 caliber Glock concealed in her custom fanny pack. With 24 ½ years on the job, Agent Christina Smith had her share of undercover assignments. Regardless if she was posing as an arms dealer, a counterfeiter or a bank teller, she had walked the walk many times, and she surely knew how to handle herself.

"Listen up everyone. I want Christina to start at the Park & Ride on Route 460 in Annapolis every day. For the next several days we want to start her on a routine, arriving each day at 9 a.m. and walking for one hour north on the trail and one hour back to her car. I'm sure our killer is watching his victims closely and honing in on those he can pattern. No one is to talk with her on the trail or where she parks. We will be on encrypted channel 4C. Christina will be equipped with the covert wire microphone which only I'll be able to hear. She will not have a police radio with her, only her cell. The radio and cell reception in this area sucks. Christina you know how this works, if you come upon someone be sure to talk so I know what's going on and I can communicate with the team. Don't take any chances. If something doesn't feel right, say the word *help* and we'll move in. Everyone stay alert. No fucking around. Pay attention. This could turn bad, really quick. Christina, when you leave, be sure to do counter-surveillance maneuvers before you make your way back to the office in case you're being followed," Michaels instructed.

"Got it," she acknowledged.

Now wired up with a hidden radio device, the operation was set, with the aid of the bike officers and Detective Michaels. Arriving at the parking lot shortly after 9:15 a.m., Christina stepped from her rent-a-car sporting her new grey hair and older style apparel. She began her stroll down the county rode that lead to the trail. Dressed appropriately, Michaels wore his concealed police radio earbud in one ear and from another earpiece he could hear Christina over the wire. Posing as a walker, Michaels also set out for the trail. Bike units were scattered in three pairs. One pair was to travel back and forth on the trail slowly near Christina, while the second pair remained stationary a short distance from the Park & Ride. The third team was to jog the trail north and south, never traveling too far from the undercover agent.

Back at the office, Tommy hung up the phone and joined the remaining detectives sitting at their desks. "Donald, I need you and Mark to go to the Eastern District. Last night the midnight shift locked up a peeping Tom outside the Arnold Senior Living Center. I want you guys to go interview him and see if he's our guy."

"You got it boss. Come on Poodle," Donald said to Mark.

At the station, Donald and Mark met up with the arresting officer in the squad room. The officer proceeded to tell them how he arrested a subject after the department received calls from two different women at the home. Both women live on the ground level of their building and both observed a man standing outside their window while they undressed and prepared for bed. One of the women is 83 years old and the other 76. The officer said the man claimed he was just walking his dog, but the circumstances and their statements proved otherwise. The case was strong.

The two detectives interviewed the pervert for hours. When asked if he ever frequented the trail, he said he had periodically, but soon clammed up. This got their attention and they intensely questioned him about the two separate homicides. He claimed to be unsure of his whereabout on either of the dates. They keenly noticed that his answers and demeanor changed when the questioning was geared toward the trail murders. The suspect became fidgety in his chair, constantly rubbed his hands together and avoided eye contact at all cost with the detectives. Then Donald sprang the tell-all question to the suspect. He asked if he would give up a DNA sample voluntarily. The subject gained control of his anxiousness, raised his head and looked Donald square in the eyes and asked for a lawyer.

For three hours, Christina and her back up officers slowly traversed the two miles of trail, walking at a slow, vulnerable pace. Knowing the location of the trail was merely a shot in the dark, the team kept at it. Christina noticed that various points along the trail became unusually dark based on the time of day and cloud cover. Another observation she made was most of the people occupying the trail were men. At noon the operation ceased.

Riding back to the CID, Michaels called Dr. Esterling's office. "Dr. Esterling's office, may I help you?" the young girl answered.

"Is Dr. Esterling in, this is Detective Michaels?"

"No, she's not. I think she's taking care of funeral arrangements today. She told me you were investigating her mother's case, so I guess I'm allowed to give you her cell number."

He called Katie on her cell. "Hello," Katie said softly.

"Katie, this is Ronnie. Ronnie Michaels. Did I get you at a bad time?"

"Ronnie I am so sorry. I can't tell you how ashamed I am of my actions."

"Stop Katie. Stop," Michaels insisted.

"I'm so embarrassed. Please accept my apology," she begged.

"Katie. No more apologies. Deal?"

She paused, "Deal. Do you have anything yet Ronnie?"

"Nothing now, but as I told you, we have an unbelievable team of investigators on this."

"My mother is getting buried tomorrow. It's going to be a rough day for Kathryn and me."

"Listen, when you finish up tomorrow and if you want to talk, give me a call. I can give you an update. If not, just call me when you feel up to it."

"Ronnie. Thank you so much. You are very good at what you do."

"I have to catch this piece of shit first. Then you can say that."

"Thanks. I'll give you a call. Bye now."

"Bye."

For the next two days, Christina and the team repeated the operation arriving at 9 a.m. and leaving promptly at noon. Still, nothing appeared out of the ordinary and Michaels had not heard from Katie.

At home one evening Michaels opened a bottle of Merlot and was about to fix himself some pasta when he heard his cell phone ringing in the living room. Fearing it was yet another dead body, he reluctantly went over to the end table and picked up his phone.

Taken aback by the number on the phone, he answered. "Hi Katie." The only thing he could hear were sounds of crying in the background. "Katie. Katie," he repeated.

"I can't stay here. I can't be in this house anymore. I keep hearing my mother's voice. I think I'm losing it," she said barely understandable.

"Are you home?"

"Yes."

"I'm on my way. Don't move."

He quickly grabbed his keys, poured his wine into a plastic cup and bolted from his house. He raced to Katie's home, where he saw her sitting on the steps outside her front door. She noticed Michaels' speeding car halt to a stop in front of her home as she stood up and with both hands, she half-heartedly attempted to wipe her eyes. Weakened from insomnia, alcohol and emotions, she fell to her knees on the sidewalk crying hysterically.

He opened his door and ran to her. "Katie, Katie," he yelled bending down hugging her with both arms. The two remained in the front yard for several minutes. She wreaked of wine. "Come on, let's get you to my house," he said slowly lifting her to her feet. "Where is your daughter?"

"She's staying with her father," she struggled to say.

They drove to his house and Katie continued to weep. Inside his house, he helped her onto the same couch where she had slept a few nights before. By now Katie had suppressed her tears enough to speak.

"I'm sorry to do this to you again. Look, here I am once more on my client's couch, when you're supposed to be on mine," she said attempting to interject some humor into the moment.

"It's ok Katie. It's really ok."

"Burying my mother the other day was so difficult. So final. I can't believe I'll never see her again, that we'll never talk or go shopping or work out in the yard together. She was my best friend. My only friend. Of all people, I should know how to handle this, but I don't know what to do. I can't stop crying and I want to hurt whoever did this. I know that's terrible, but it's just not fair."

He reached over and held her hand. "Katie, I'm here for you, believe me, I understand."

She squeezed his hand tightly and looked at him. "Thank you. I really appreciate it." The two embraced with their arms wrapped tightly around their bodies. Both could feel emotions toward the other growing.

"How about you jump in the shower. You'll feel better. I'll get you a clean pair of my sweatpants, a shirt and some socks. I was about to make some pasta when you called. We can eat and talk. How's that sound?"

"You are such a good man Ronnie. I can't thank you enough." She leaned forward and kissed him gently on the lips and walked into the bathroom. Shocked, he stayed seated for a moment. This was the first he had felt this way in quite some time.

Standing in the kitchen preparing their food, he turned to put the plates on the table when he saw Katie standing by the refrigerator wearing his oversized clothing. "Damn, you scared me," he said. "How long have you been standing there?"

"Just a few seconds. I like watching people when they don't know they're being watched. Do you mind if I hug you again? I'm sorry." The two clung onto each other. A special closeness ran through their bodies.

"You never have to say you are sorry to me," he said pressing his lips against hers. The two kissed passionately while they held each other closely. After their kiss, they separated and looked deeply in each other's eyes.

"I must say detective, I never saw this coming."

He released his hold on her and stepped back, eyeing her from head to toe with a smile on his face. "Well Doc, I have to say my sweat pants and t-shirt have never looked better." The two managed to laugh, took a seat at the table and began eating.

They ate their meal and finished off the bottle of Merlot he had opened just before her call. Now on their second bottle, the two moved to the living room where they talked for hours about Katie's life and how her mother was such an inspiration for her obtaining her doctorate's degree in psychiatry. He could tell she was happy to open up and talk about the good times she had with her mother. The two laughed, cried and laughed some more. Unmindful of the time, they talked for hours about the on-going investigation and finished off the Merlot. This was an evening of therapy she desperately needed, and he was still perplexed how he went from client to counselor overnight, but was glad, nonetheless.

"Shit, do you see what time it is?" Michaels said.

"I have no idea."

"It's 1:30 in the morning. I have to get up early. Why don't you sleep in the spare room tonight instead of this hard couch?"

"If it's alright with you, I'd rather just sleep here. I don't want to intrude any more than I already have."

"Now you stop that. Come on, let me show you where it is. You'll have your own bathroom and everything. As a matter of fact, there is a pack of new toothbrushes and toothpaste in the cabinet under the sink. Help yourself."

"Thank you so much. You don't know how much this means to me. I had such a great time tonight. Thanks for dinner and thanks for listening to me." She kissed him softly on his lips and they hugged once more. The two said goodnight and retreated to their separate bedrooms. Each laid in their beds thinking about the other until their eyes closed for the evening.

The next morning, he woke to the smell of bacon in the air. He put on his gym shorts and found Katie fixing breakfast. "Good morning, breakfast? In the last few years, the only person who has ever fixed me breakfast was my buddy Mel when we went hunting."

She laughed. "Well tell Mel to step aside because scrambled eggs and bacon are being served. I was going to fix you pancakes, but the box in the cabinet expired two years ago." Michaels laughed and pulled a chair up to the table.

"Thanks again for last night. Will you be able to drop me off at my house this morning or should I call a cab?"

"Of course, I will. Will you be alright at your house? Do you want me to go in with you?"

"No Ronnie. You've done enough. I have to learn to handle this."

He reached over and held her hand. "Katie, I wish it wasn't under these circumstances, but I felt something between us. I laid in bed thinking of you all night, like I was in high school again. It actually felt special."

She smiled. "That's funny. I did too."

"I haven't felt this way in a long time."

"Likewise," she said.

"I'd like to see you again," he confessed.

"That would be nice. I'd like that, but you can't be my client anymore," she giggled, now you're much more. You're a friend.

He smiled. "I know."

A short time later, he dropped her off at her home. The two shared hugs once more and kissed again before he pulled off to reconvene the decoy operation.

On day three at 9:45 a.m. Christina came upon a man in his late 40's dressed in blue jeans and a light weight, dark green jacket. He was crouched down just off the asphalt looking at his bike. She alerted Michaels over the wire about the man she was about to engage. Immediately, she noticed the subject's appearance didn't fit the profile of the other riders she had observed.

The man noticed Christina and nervously looked up and down the path like he was looking for someone. Michaels gave the word and quickly the team converged closer to her location yet remained out of sight. The section of trail was heavily sheltered from the large towering oak trees, making it unusually dark.

"Good morning. Problem with your bike so early?" Christina said in a friendly tone.

The man's eyes scanned Christina from head to toe before he spoke. "Yeah my chain broke. I'm glad you're here. I could use your help. It normally takes two people to put one of these on," he told her.

"Sure, I can help you." She knelt next to the man who was removing the chain from the bike's sprockets. "I must say, I've never seen a chain off a bike," she said so Michaels could hear what was transpiring.

"Does anyone have eyes on her?" Michaels transmitted over the radio. There was no response. "Does anyone have eyes on our undercover?" he said louder.

"I'm working my way through the woods trying to find her. What is she near?" Officer Penn from the Bike Unit whispered.

"She is just before the Woods Road crossing," Michaels said getting frustrated.

Christina had a bad feeling about the man. He constantly looked up and down the trail. Something didn't seem right with him. Next to his side was a camouflage backpack that was partially unzipped. Without a kickstand, the man held the seat with one hand and pulled the long chain and placed it over his arm. Christina was quick to notice the chain contained no grease. She wondered if this could have been the object used to strangle the victims. Her heart began to race.

"Can you hold the bike up for me? I'm going to need both hands to do this," the man asked.

Michaels hurried down the path to close the gap. "Officer Penn, do you have her yet?" Michaels anxiously repeated.

"Not yet, but I think I'm getting close. I see something up ahead," he said attempting to sneak through the woods undetected.

"10-4."

Now with the man behind her holding the chain, she kept the bike upright with her right hand on the seat and her left on the rear tire. Christina felt extremely vulnerable. She looked down at her fanny pack where her gun was. She knew there would be no way she could get to it fast enough if she was being strangled. Her only hope would be her backup. She kept turning her head to watch the man who was now holding the broken chain with both hands behind her. He carefully studied the chain for no apparent reason.

"What um, are you going to do with that chain?" Christina asked.

Michaels detected the fear in her voice.

"I got eyes," Penn finally said. "This doesn't look good. The subject is standing behind her holding a bike chain with both hands with our undercover on her knees."

"I have to put a new one on. I should have one in my backpack." With the chain stretched out in both hands the man leaned toward Christina and draped the chain over the frame near her head. "Do you come here much?" the man weirdly asked.

No stranger to undercover work, Christina responded. "No, I just retired and moved in the area and thought I'd start exercising. I'm not getting any younger. What about you?"

"Yeah I just moved here also. I like trails like these."

"I need everyone to stay close and be ready to move on my command." Michaels moved up enough to where he could make out Christina and the subject 50 yards away.

Now with his gun drawn, Officer Penn was about to key up the microphone and give the go sign. Everyone was on edge. Michaels felt a horrible knot in his stomach. Oddly, no other people had come down the trail since Christina came upon the man. By now, the sun had disappeared behind the clouds and the woods became gloomy. *This had all the ingredients of a perfect storm*, Michaels thought to himself.

"You mean, you have a new chain with you?" Christina asked.

"Yeah, I should have just what I need. I'll just need to put my gloves on first," the man said reaching into his backpack.

"He's putting gloves on Ronnie. I don't like this," Officer Penn said quietly inching his way closer, trying not to make any noise.

"Why do you need gloves?"

"Because the new one will have grease on it." The man pulled out a box and squatted down behind Christina making it impossible to see him in her peripheral vision. He laid the small box on the ground between him and the agent, then reached over her right shoulder and took grasp of the broken chain.

"What are you going to do with that?" she nervously said over the wire.

The man did not respond. Christina tried to move her head to see what he was doing but was unable to get a good look. She removed her hand from the seat and grabbed the zipper on the fanny pack and started to open it slowly.

Worried, Michaels keyed up his radio. "What's happening Penn?"

"He just put the old chain in the backpack."

"Oh, you do have a new chain," Christina said to keep Michaels abreast of the situation. Her once fast beating heart began to return to normal.

The man fed the new chain onto both the front and rear sprockets then with a pair of pliers, he snapped together the adjoining links.

"There, that should do it," the man said taking control of the bike.

The agent stood while the man closed his backpack and slung it over his shoulder.

"Thank you," he said before he rode off.

"Have a nice day," Christina said watching the man pedal down the path.

"All clear everyone. All clear," Penn said over the radio.

Michaels could feel his cell phone vibrating in his jacket pocket. It was Christina. "Jesus fucking Christ Ronnie. I thought I was done. He could have easily killed me."

"I agree. That was a little touch and go. You couldn't see, but he was standing behind you with the bicycle chain extended in his hands. I almost gave the signal to move in. We had your back though. We still have another hour so keep walking."

"That's easy for you to say, but it'll take me a while to stop shaking first."

Michaels hung up the phone and got back on the radio. "Listen up everyone. We still have an hour left, so let's stay on our toes. What just happened was a good test."

"Heck yeah it was." Penn added.

The final hour was uneventful, and the team returned to the CID with no arrest.

The next morning was overcast and a chilly 49 degrees. At 9 a.m. Christina arrived at the Park & Ride and began her daily walk while the others took up their positions. Today, there were even fewer people using the trail, especially females. At 10 a.m. Christina saw an adult male stopped on the side of the trail sitting on a black mountain bike looking into the woods. Christina told Michaels of her observation while she continued toward him. Once he noticed her, he turned his bicycle around and rode off in the opposite direction. This seemed very suspicious and she informed Michaels of the man's actions. Michaels was seated on a bench next to the path just 100 yards away from the subject and in seconds, the man she had just seen, rode past her and Michaels. This further heightened their suspicions. He wore black sunglasses, a black ballcap, a black sweat suit and black and white tennis shoes. His appearance sparked Michaels' curiosity as well. He had seen him somewhere before.

"If anyone sees a white male riding a black bike, wearing all black and a baseball cap, attempt to follow him. I'm interested if he drove a vehicle here or not. If so, get a tag number please," Michaels announced over the radio.

"He just blew passed me. I'll see if I can catch up," Penn said.

Michaels dialed up Agent Smith on her cell phone. "Christina."

"Yeah."

"Do me a favor and stand where the subject you saw on the bike was standing. Once I mark your location, keep walking. I want to peek in the woods where he was looking."

"Will do," Christina said.

Michaels saw Christina standing up ahead as he walked in her direction. Not seeing anyone, she rubbed her foot in the dirt to mark the spot for Michaels. He nodded, and she continued on. After a brief search of a small section of woods, Michaels returned to the trail. Still puzzled, he continued to rack his brain about where he had seen the man before, suddenly it hit him. He was on the store security camera the day of the second murder.

"Anyone got an eye on that subject riding the bike dressed in all black?" Michaels asked the team.

The units responded, but no one had him in sight.

"If anyone sees him, stay on him. He may be of interest. I'll explain later."

Christina chimed in, "I'm walking up on a subject near the one-mile marker, sitting on the bench with a grey colored bike."

"All units, our undercover is coming up on a rider with a grey bike, sitting on the bench near the one-mile marker. Stand by," Michaels informed everyone.

"Hi, oh no don't tell me your chain broke again," Christina said to the man she assisted the previous day.

The man chuckled. "No, I just thought I'd take a breather and drink some water."

"Yeah, at least it's cool out."

"How many miles do you put in?"

"I do four miles a day. Two miles up and two back to the Park & Ride."

"That's good. I have an extra water if you need one," the man offered.

"Thanks, but I have one in my fanny pack."

"By the way, I'm Jack. Thanks again for your help yesterday," the man said reaching out and shaking Christina's hand.

"Nice to meet you. I'm Tina. And it was no problem, my pleasure."

"Well I guess I should get going. Enjoy the rest of your day."

"You too. Goodbye," Christina said.

"All units stand down, it's the gentleman she helped the other day with the broken chain. She's clear from him and on foot again," Michaels stated over the radio.

Following another unsuccessful day on the trail, Michaels returned to the office to review the store security tape. He pulled the DVD from his thickening case file and placed it in the computer. Impatiently he waited for the device to load.

"C'mon motherfucker. This piece of shit," Michael exclaimed.

Tommy emerged from his office. "You have something Shithead?"

"Maybe, if this dinosaur ever loads my DVD."

Tommy laughed and stood behind his chair when the footage finally appeared. Michaels hit the fast forward button and skipped through several frames until he found what he was searching for. The bicyclist in all black with the ballcap and sunglasses.

"Yup. That's him. That's him right there. It's a shame there's no real good frontal shot of him. These are so grainy. But, no doubt, we saw this dude today. He was stopped on the grass next to the trail sitting on his bike."

"What was he doing?" Tommy asked.

"Looking in the woods. At what? I have no idea. He drove off like a bat out of hell, I searched where he was looking, but there was nothing."

"Maybe he was looking for a place to drag his next victim," Tommy suggested.

"Now that you say that, it was a dark section where he stood."

"Why don't you print out that frame and make a bunch of copies for everyone. I would just try to ID him, but not in a way to scare him off."

"I agree. I'll take care of that. It just seems weird to me that the same guy is so far away from the store on Heights Road. What's that 10 miles?"

"At least. Good job Shithead."

"Thanks."

During the drive home, Michaels telephoned Katie. Her phone went straight to voicemail. He then tried her office, surprisingly she answered.

"Hi there. It's me. So, you are back to work?" he said glowing from ear to ear when he heard her voice.

"Yes. I'm actually trying to practice what I counsel people to do. Keep the world turning. Stay busy. Keep my mind occupied with something other than my emotional trauma. So, any luck today?" she said switching topics.

"I did see someone on the trail today who sparked my interest."

"I'd like to hear about it if you're able to share. How about you and your daughter join Kathryn and I for dinner at our house tonight?"

"That sounds great. I'll check with Stacey."

"Ronnie, I have someone waiting for me. See you at 6?"

"Looking forward to it. I'll bring the wine."

"Bring two. Goodbye."

"Goodbye."

They spent another pleasurable evening together indulging in tender filets on the grill, chilled white wine, more laughs and fewer tears. Kathryn enjoyed Nicole's company and the two spent most of the night playing hopscotch on the sidewalk. The feelings between Katie and Michaels were growing exponentially beyond either's imagination. The evening turned out to be extremely pleasant for everyone.

The fifth day of Operation Decoy kicked off at the normal time. With the weather unusually warm, there were more than the normal number of people occupying the trail. By 11:30 a.m. Christina finished her walk when she encountered a small group of people gathered around a 10 year old girl laying on the ground crying loudly. Christina alerted Michaels who instructed the team to converge inconspicuously to her location. Once closer, she learned the young cyclist had accidently fallen from her bike after riding over a branch. Jack, whom she had seen twice early in the week, was busy providing the injured child's mother with sterile wipes and bandages for the scrapes on the youngster's knees and hands. Once in place, the mother helped her daughter to her feet and the two thanked Jack for his able assistance. Still whimpering, the brave girl climbed back onto her pretty pink bike once Jack had repositioned her crooked handlebars. By now, most of the team had made it to Christina's location, posing as regular users of the trail.

"You're the man Jack," Christina remarked.

"What can I say? Grandma taught me to be prepared," Jack said while zippering his backpack. "I gotta run."

Back at the CID, Michaels filled Tommy in on the uneventful day. In the meantime, Donald and Mark were busy trying to locate the pervert obsessed with naked seniors. Because the incompetent State's Attorney for the county was unsuccessful in getting the sick bastard held, the man was released with nothing more than his signature. Scrambling to write a search warrant for the man's DNA, Mark and Donald found themselves in a District Court judge's chambers. Now armed with a Search & Seizure Warrant, the rest of the team was in the field, attempting to locate the son of a bitch.

Finishing up a hectic week, Tommy instructed everyone in the task force to take the weekend off to get refreshed. On the way home, Michaels and Katie made plans to have dinner, since it was Kathryn's weekend to spend with her father. Again, the two spent a wonderful night eating and drinking. They dined at Michaels' favorite restaurant, the Riverdale Tavern, located off a quiet cove on the Magothy River. Following dinner and drinks, they decided she would spend the night for the first time. The two had grown so close, they found themselves feeling alone if they weren't at least talking on the phone. Their happiness and joy for one another was obvious and long overdue for both.

Following dinner, their irresistible passion was unleashed as the two entered his townhome. Clothes dropped to the floor while their lips explored every inch of each other's bodies. Both slightly inebriated, they moaned as they found themselves entangled in one another's arms and legs like two wild snakes on the living room floor. Their desire for each other took control like a feverish frenzy for several minutes. Fully aroused, Katie took hold of Michaels full erection and inserted him into her. While she lay on her back, he propped himself above her bare body, locked his elbows straight and with one thrust, he pushed himself deeply into Katie. He looked into her beautiful brown eyes. Katie placed both her hands on her lover's hips experiencing his deep penetration for the first time. As their desire grew, he could feel her hips move forward, and her eyelids squeezed shut while the two exploded in simultaneous orgasms. Michaels groaned with pleasure, as Katie shouted in ecstasy.

The next afternoon the couple was closer than ever. Sitting at the dining room table drinking iced tea, Katie couldn't resist. It was a question looming in her mind for days. "Ronnie, how are you handling the issue you were dealing with? You know, the one that caused us to meet."

Jokingly, he answered, "Ladies and gentlemen meet Dr. Katie Esterling."

"You're so funny. I'm just curious. I care."

"Honestly, I'm glad it was me who told you. I don't mean because, you know, you and I now, but because you deserve to be treated special. And it's kind of different for me to be the person someone reaches out to and not just as a cop. I don't know. It's hard to put into words."

"That so sweet. You're a good person Mr. Ronald Michaels." Katie clutched onto his hand and gently kissed his cheek.

"Can I be honest with you?"

"Of course. What is it?" Katie replied.

He paused and looked away. "I've always had this thing; once I told someone about the death of their loved one, I found myself wanting to see them again. I'm not sure why, but now I get to do that, because I'm with you. But it's in a way I never dreamed of. Life is just so funny. But I always think once I leave, they blame me. Do you?"

"Look at me." she pulled his hand to her chest. The two looked at one another. "I don't blame you. I'll even go a step further and say, I'm sure none of the people you've told blame you. It's honorable you care so much. That makes you different, unique, special. What people like me want, are these animals, these horrible people caught." Her tears dropped onto their hands.

"Thanks Katie, or should I say Doctor?" they both smiled. "So now you tell me, how are you handling all this?"

Her eyes immediately welled up. "I miss my mother so much. I keep hearing her voice in my head. The other part of me is full of anger. I haven't asked you what the killer did to her, because part of me doesn't want to put you in that position and the other part of me doesn't want to know. I catch myself gritting my teeth and clenching my fists, then crying uncontrollably. I want to hurt whoever did this so bad and I'm not like that. I've never been in a fight in my life. Heck, I graduated from college by the age of 17 and had my Doctorate at 19. I'm a book worm and I owe it all to my mother, who some sick asshole took from me. I guess I shouldn't tell a homicide detective, but I want him dead."

"Believe me, I understand. I hear that often from family members. It's just a natural reaction, practically everyone says it. So, on a happy note, how would you like for me to fix something on the grill tonight? I'll get us some burgers and fries at the grocery store, then shoot over to Harbour Liquors and grab some stuff to make margaritas and we'll have us a party? How's that?"

"I'd love that Mr. Michaels. I'll jump in the shower while you're gone." The two kissed and he headed to the stores, neither of which were far from his home.

She walked toward the bathroom, when out of the corner of her eye she noticed a large red accordion folder leaning against his recliner. She walked closer to get a better look and saw the words *Friendship Trail Case* written on the outside cover. She stopped and contemplated looking inside, wondering if there were any pictures of her mother in the folder. She was cautiously eager to see exactly what had happened. She looked at the file, then looked at the door. She knew where he was going was just a short distance away. Pondering over what to do, her morals took hold and off to the bathroom she went.

Finished with her shower, she stood in the living room wearing Michaels' robe and brushed her long dark hair. She kept looking down at the folder. She dashed to the front window and glanced out to the street. She hurried back to the floor where she sat next to the case file, frantically flipping through the folders until she found one marked *crime scene*. She hesitantly opened it only to see her nude mother, head partially scalped, with one eye half open and sprawled out like a mannequin with her clothes sliced opened. She yelled out, then placed her hand over her mouth as she began to cry. Immediately a sickening feeling came over her. She slammed the folder shut, stunned by what she had just seen. A sea of emotions channeled through her mind, the last being pure rage. Unaware of how much time had passed, she saw a notebook with the words *Abrams Case* at the top. It was a reporter's style notebook, with every page containing Michaels' handwriting. She wildly flipped through the pages, expecting Michaels' home any minute. She sprinted to the front window and could see his truck coming down the street. Madly, she grabbed her phone when she heard a door close outside. She ran to the door and turned the dead bolt to the lock position. Using her cell phone camera, she snapped several photographs of pages from the notebook then shoved it back in the file. Michaels began knocking on the door. She propped the file against the recliner and rushed back to the door as it opened.

Pulling his key from the deadbolt, he looked confused. "What's going on? Did I just hear you lock the door?" he asked.

"Yeah. I'm sorry. I saw it unlocked. I'm sorry. I'm still scared. I didn't know it was you."

"No, that's my fault. I'm so dumb. I should have locked it when I left. I'm sorry babe."

The two hugged when he noticed Katie's eyes. "Have you been crying?" Katie dropped her head on his shoulder and tears streamed down her cheeks. Do you think you'll ever find this person Ronnie?" she uttered while sniveling.

"I hope so Katie. I hope so. We just can't seem to catch a break and if we did, who knows what our liberal courts would do. He would probably walk."

"I'm going to take a quick shower," he said.

"I'll make the hamburgers and cut the tomato while you're doing that," she told him.

She stood at the kitchen counter slicing the tomato. She could hear the shower running and Michaels singing his rendition of Lynyrd Skynyrd's *Simple Man,* when his phone lying on the dining room table sounded. On the screen the caller ID said *Dispatch.* Afraid it may be important, she answered the call.

"This is Detective Michaels' line. Can I help you?" she said in her professional voice.

"The is Leo from Communications. We just received information from an anonymous caller and my supervisor said to give it to Detective Michaels since he's on-call. Is he there?"

Katie looked, the bathroom door was closed, and the shower was still running. She took a notepad and pen from her purse. He's busy right now, but I'll take the information for him."

"We received a call today from what sounded to be an elderly male. He said there's a white man living in a one-bedroom apartment in his basement at 710 View Avenue in Linthicum next to the trail. The caller said the man moved in with nothing but a bike and a small suitcase about the time the first murder on the trail occurred. He's supposed to be driving a faded blue Saturn with North Carolina tags 91270E, with a bicycle rack on the trunk. That's all he said then he hung up."

"Got it, thank you. I'll make sure he gets the message. Goodbye."

"Goodbye."

She stared at the information, looked back to the bathroom and thought about what Michaels had just said. She closed her pad and placed it in her purse, then picked up his cell phone and erased the number listed as Dispatch. The bathroom door opened, and she slid the phone across the table.

Following his shower, he slipped on some comfortable clothes and joined Katie in the kitchen. "Lynyrd Skynyrd huh? Not bad. Not bad," she said as the two laughed.

"Did I hear my phone ring?"

"No that was mine, it was my sister."

They spent the afternoon learning more and more about each other's lives. Their evening mirrored the others, packed with smiles, laughter and on this evening, war stories from his days as an undercover narcotics detective. She was fascinated about the role he had played and the cases he had made. The night ended wrapped naked in one another's arms making love once again. Never once did she tell him about the call she had intercepted.

The weekend passed, and Michaels was focused once again on Operation Decoy. Tommy made the decision this would be the last week of the detail. Donald and Mark still had not picked up their peeping Tom. With a new batch of Metro Crime Stopper flyers posted at most of the businesses, a barrage of endless leads lit up the phone on Donald's desk. Half the task force was now committed to the decoy detail, while the others were combing the county looking for Donald's suspect.

It was a cloudy overcast morning at the start of day nine of Operation Decoy. With the threat of rain and being a weekday, the volume of people on the trail was minimal. The detail kicked off as usual, except the first half of the morning only included Michaels and Penn as foot surveillance on Agent Smith. The others had morning criminal court and weren't expected until 11:00 a.m. In an attempt to switch up their tactics, Michaels instructed Penn to remain stationary at Christina's normal turn around location, while Michaels monitored her actions from his car at a second parking lot a short distance from the Park & Ride.

"Ronnie I'm starting my walk now. I'm…the trail," she said barely audible with some of her words fading out when she spoke.

Christina walked the trail at her normal pace, taking notice how dark certain portions were due to the cloud cover. She commented over the wire about the shadowy conditions, but Michaels was unable to hear her transmissions. The batteries in her wire device had weakened over the past eight days and the extra distance where Michaels had moved made communications impossible. Christina was on her own.

For the first half mile, Christina only saw three people. The first was a young black male jogging at a rapid pace and a middle-aged white couple riding bikes. Strolling along, she noticed the laces on her right shoe had come untied. For safety, she stepped off the pavement after first checking her surroundings.

"I'm stopping close to the half way mark to tie my shoe. Boy, those clouds don't look good. It looks like a storm is coming." Unbeknownst to either, her words could not be heard. Pulling tightly on the laces, one unexpectedly snapped in her hand. "Fuck, my shoelace broke. Damn it. I'm going to have to go back to the car and go buy a pair." Still Michaels heard nothing. With part of a shoelace in hand she hobbled 40 yards down the trail where she took a seat on a bench to temporarily rig her laces for the long walk back to her vehicle.

Suddenly, the skies opened up and the rain poured from the clouds mixed with hail. She took cover under a tall pine tree with a massive canopy of branches above her. A loud clap of thunder rung out and shocked the lone agent. The mixed precipitation pelted her and even the dense branches couldn't keep the deluge of rain from drenching her hair. She hunched her shoulders and crouched down to keep the cold rain from chilling her neck. Loud clashes of thunder bellowed through the woods. The shrill sound of lighting cracked sharply in the sky, startling the agent. Christina felt uneasy seeking cover under the towering tree during such an intense lightning storm. Then without warning, it happened. Caught by surprise from behind, she felt the overpowering force of wire piercing through the skin of her neck and crushing down on her esophagus. By instinct the trained agent reached back to disable her assailant, but the attacker intensified the compression of the strangulation. She attempted to call out for Michaels but was deprived of her voice. She was hastily fading from consciousness while she felt herself being pulled into the woods. Her body went limp. Neither Michaels nor Penn had any idea of the nightmare unfolding a short distance from them. FBI Agent Christina Smith was about to die.

Waiting less than a mile up the trail, Penn radioed Michaels. "This doesn't look good. What's the plan?" he asked briskly walking to his car.

"Just hang in your car until this passes. I'm going over to the Park & Ride. I haven't heard from Christina for a while. If she's not there, I'll start walking the trail. I'm going to try her cell."

"10-4. I'm already wet, so I'll start down the trail from this end."

"Roger that."

Unalarmed, Michaels placed a call to Christina's cell phone. After ringing several times, it rolled to voicemail.

"Christina, its Michaels. Call me."

The storm continued while the jarring reverberations of thunder echoed through the trees. The brutal accoster panted heavily while he struggled to drag Christina's limp body over the fallen timber.

Abruptly, her near lifeless body fell to the ground. The vicious killer's grip gave way and the ligature swathed around her neck dropped beside her. The 10" diamond sharp stainless steel blade pierced in and out of the attacker's carotid artery from a second assailant behind him. Without hesitation, the first attacker's head quickly jerked to the right, snapping his vertebrae like a fresh piece of wood. Bright red blood erupted from the piercing hole, spewing high in the air. The darkened pine needles were now saturated with bubbling red fluid. The rain droplets bounced in the puddles of blood. The flaccid corpse collapsed to the forest floor simultaneous with luminous flashes of lightening. The unseen person vanished quietly from the area.

"Penn, any sign of Christina yet? I'm at the lot and she's not here."

"Not yet, but she can't be much further. That storm came out of nowhere."

"I know. I'm drenched. I'm almost on the trail now, coming your way."

With her severely damaged airway now partially open, Christina coughed in pain while she gasped for the slightest breath. She attempted to open her eyes, but her vision was blurred from the hemorrhaging caused by the strangulation. She slowly lifted her aching body to a sitting position when she caught a glimpse of someone behind her. Barely conscious, she manipulated her fanny pack and pulled out the .40 caliber Glock. Unable to focus, she painstakingly turned toward the figure with her weapon resting loosely in her hand. She was too weak to pull the trigger, so she twisted her body to confront her adversary, only to be astounded when she saw the body of a man lying on his stomach in a gushing river of blood. With one of his arms blocking his face, she could see his left eyelid open. His cold dead stare sent chills through her body. A backpack draped down his left arm. Confused, she wondered how her life was spared and by whom. Now several yards into the woods she knew she had to make her way out to get help. She held onto a small tree and lifted herself to her feet. Her neck was tender and throbbing in pain. With her gun still in her hand she stumbled through the woods moving from tree to tree for support. The reality of her near death weighed heavily on her when she realized she was following the marks on the ground where she had been drug. Looking ahead, she could faintly make out a person walking on the trail. It was Penn. She tried to call out, but her wind pipe was too damaged. The abundance of trees between them made it impossible for him to see her. She tucked her handgun in the pack and pulled out her cell phone while she watched Penn walk out of sight. She called Michaels.

Soaked from the torrential downpour, Michaels continued on the trail looking for Agent Smith. He was relieved when he heard his cell phone ring and saw her name displayed.

"Hey Christina, damn girl I was starting to get worried. You must be soaked too." He laughed, but there was no response. "Hello, Christina."

Christina attempted to speak but could only make soft moaning noises. Michaels could barely make out the sounds but knew something was wrong.

"Christina," he yelled. "Where are you? Are you ok?" Michaels stopped and listened intently. The moaning noises continued as she struggled to speak.

"Help," she painfully uttered.

Michaels keyed up his police radio. Penn, I got Christina on the cell. She's in trouble. She needs help. Where are you?"

"I'm on the trail. I can't find her," Penn responded.

Scared, Michaels scrambled to pin point her location. "Christina, guide me to you. Are you on the north side or south side of the path?" Michaels cupped his hand over his earpiece. Barely audible, he could hear her mumble the word *north*.

"Penn call a Signal 13. We need cars here now," Michaels screamed over the radio. "She's on the northside of the trail." Michaels could feel his heart racing. He pulled out his gun and began walking faster through the woods shouting for Christina. Penn, too, entered the woods with his weapon drawn coming from the opposite direction. They both could hear the approaching sirens blaring in the distance. Christina continued to creep through the woods. She could hear Michaels and Penn shouting her name. Michaels finally saw her wilted body leaning against a tree.

Penn also saw her and the two ran to where she had fallen to the ground. Her hair, shirt and pants were covered in wet dirt, dried leaves and pine needles. She clutched onto her neck while her eyes rolled beneath her lids.

"Call for a paramedic," Michaels shouted. Kneeling next to her, he could not believe his eyes. He was looking at the exact same reddish colored markings on Christina's neck, just as he had seen on the two previous victims, except this one was on a cop who was still alive.

"Hang in there girl. We gotcha," Michaels told her.

Christina's eyes were beet red with blood hemorrhaging spots speckled throughout. She unsuccessfully tried focusing. She lifted her arm and struggled to point behind her. Michaels and Penn could see she was trying to alert them to something. She tried desperately to speak but was unable.

"She's telling us something is back there." Michaels got closer to Christina and put his ear close to her mouth. He could hear the word *dead, dead.*

"She's saying dead. Is someone dead back there?" Christina painfully nodded.

Michaels, Penn and Christina saw six uniformed officers charging down the trail in their direction. Penn waved them over. The rain had stopped as fast as it started, and the dark clouds were replaced with hints of sun.

"Thanks for coming guys we just found her. This is Agent Christina Smith with the FBI. One of you stay with her, and two of you come with me and Officer Penn. She keeps motioning behind us and saying dead."

The officers along with Michaels stood side by side and began stealthily making their way through the timber with their weapons drawn. Michaels could hear the sound of an ambulance arriving at the Park & Ride lot. The four cops scanned the woods. Michaels' hair stood on his neck when he saw Christina's drag marks on the forest floor. Ahead Penn saw a figure on the opposite side of some thick brush. He signaled to the group making them aware of his observation, then cautiously moved forward until he realized it was the deceased body of a white male.

"Shit. He's got one hell of a hole in his neck. Jesus Christ," Penn said in amazement. "Man, those FBI agents are some bad ass dudes."

"Detective 132 to radio."

"Go ahead," the dispatcher answered.

"Can you advise Sergeant Suit that I need him ASAP and get ahold of Evidence Technician Cover and tell him I'll need him and another tech here also? We have a deceased male in the woods at our location."

Michaels bent down and looked closer at the dead man's face. "It's Jack."

"Who?" Penn asked.

"Jack. The guy who Christina helped with his bike. The guy who helped that little girl."

"Oh shit, that is him," Penn replied.

"Detective 132, Sergeant Suit is already en route, and I'll advise Technician Cover."

"I'm almost there Ronnie," Tommy said with his siren wailing in the background.

Michaels was amazed at the amount of blood which had gushed from the subject's neck, covering his brown long sleeve shirt and the ground surrounding his torso. Without moving the corpse, Michaels looked the body over. Beside the gaping incision to the middle right portion of his neck, he could tell the neck had been snapped by the unorthodox way his head lay. Just a few feet away, it was obvious the dried leaves and dirt were disturbed. Among them was a two-foot-long piece of thin flat wire with 1" rings attached at each end. It was the weapon used by the sick bastard to wrap around Christina's neck and at least three others who weren't as fortunate to survive. Michaels noticed both victim's eyelids were stuck wide open with a cold, unique look of surprise on them. He knew all too well this was common in attacks such as these where the fatal wound is instantaneous.

"Penn stay here. I'll need one of you guys to remain at the trail and start a Crime Scene Log," Michaels told the cops with him. Michaels and the two uniformed cops walked out to the trail where Christina was now on a stretcher being attended to by paramedics. "Don't take her yet," Michaels yelled walking faster toward them. He pulled his notebook from his rear pocket and stood next to Christina. She looked up at him, winching her face in pain. "Unstrap her. I need her to write something. Christina, tell me how the guy in the woods got stabbed." He handed her his pad and pen.

She gingerly took the pen from his hand and wrote. *Don't know. One sec I'm being strangled then I come to on the ground.* She turned the notebook around, so he could read her message. Michaels read her words and was even more confused. "So, if you didn't kill him who did?"

Christina turned the pad back around to write, when tears began rolling down her cheeks. She jotted down two simple words and handed Michaels the pad. *An Angel.*

"Guys get her out of here and take extra good care of her. Not long after Christina was put in the ambulance, Tommy, Jeff and Ray arrived. The two immediately began processing the scene.

"What happened Ronnie?" Tommy asked.

"I don't know. There weren't many people out today because of the weather and either Christina didn't see anyone, or the wire died. I'm not sure. The storm came through and she called but couldn't talk. Our killer got her Tommy," he said with an astonished look on his face.

"What do you mean, he got her?"

"He fucking strangled her and none of us knew. She didn't say a word. There was no warning. Nothing. He dragged her into the woods. She is so lucky to be alive. I can't believe it," Michaels said shaking his head in disbelief.

"The dispatcher said you had a dead body. Did she shoot him?"

"No, someone stabbed the guy in the neck. It's the weirdest fucking thing. And Christina never saw whoever it was that saved her."

"What? You're fucking with me," he yelled.

"No man. Our killer is right back there in the woods, deader than shit with a big ass hole in his neck. Check it out," Michaels urged.

"How bad is Christina?"

"She's real fucked up. It's so strange seeing the same marks on her neck that were on the other bodies, except she's still breathing."

"I wonder who the Lone Ranger was? This is unbelievable." Tommy said out loud while walking through the woods toward Jeff and Ray.

Standing on the trail talking with a uniformed officer, Michaels' phone sounded. It was Katie. "Hi there," Michaels said.

"How's my favorite homicide detective? Did you get caught in that storm?"

"Katie, you're not going to believe what happened," Michaels said excitedly.

"Ronnie, are you ok?"

"Babe, the person who killed your mom is dead." There was silence on the phone. "Katie, you there?"

"He's dead? The one who killed my mother?"

"Yeah, fuck yeah," he said with excitement. "He'll never be able to kill again Babe. He's dead. It's a real cr....."

"I gotta go Ronnie, I have a call coming in," she interrupted sounding oddly troubled by the call. She immediately hung up the phone without another word.

"Shithead." Donald shouted hurrying down the trail with Dredge and Doc walking much slower behind him. Donald was beaming with an oversized grin.

"I can't believe this," Michaels yelled out.

The two detectives were amazed when they heard the story of the mystery killer who Christina dubbed as the *Angel*. Michaels escorted the men into the woods, following the markers Ray had placed along the ground where Christina had been drug.

Back at the scene, Jeff and Ray were busy taking photographs and measurements. Doc slipped on a pair of blue rubber gloves and squatted next to the body to inspect the injuries. "This was a direct hit to the carotid artery. No chance of surviving this. Damn, looks as if his neck may be broken also. Wow," Doc said pulling out one photograph after the next from his camera. "Jeff, is it ok to take his wallet from his pocket?"

"Sure Doc. I was waiting for you before I did anything with the body."

Doc pulled out a thin black leather wallet. Inside was a North Carolina driver's license, a credit card and other miscellaneous forms of identification.

"What's his name Doc?" Michaels inquired.

"Let's see." Doc removed the license from the wallet. "Jack Andrew Stewart." Oh, you'll like this. "He's got an address of 2819 Michigan Court in Raleigh, North Carolina."

"There you go. Sergeant Tabor is going to love hearing that, especially when he has to do the death notification. But where the fuck is he laying his head here? We need that address, or we'll never find the missing body parts and who knows what else," Donald interjected.

"I don't see any other addresses in here, but here's the accelerant he was using," Doc said lifting a 24-ounce container of lighter fluid from the backpack. Doc rummaged through the bag when he pulled out something strange; it was an antique rosary. "Man. He's got all kinds of shit in here." He began carefully looking through its contents. "There's a first aid kit, gloves, a lighter, one of those big ass Rambo knives, and a bicycle repair kit for tires. Let's see what's in this pouch." Everyone watched as Doc pulled out two pieces of paper. "These look as if they were torn from a Bible. Holy shit, this dude was out there. Listen to this from the book of Corinthians. He's got this highlighted."

> *But what I am doing, I will continue to do, that I may cut off opportunity to be regarded just as we are in matter about which they are boasting, for such men are false apostles, deceitful workers, disguising themselves as apostles of Christ.*

He flipped to the second piece of paper. "This one has a section underlined. It's from the book of Peter."

> *And especially those who indulge in the flesh in its corrupt desires and despise authority. Daring, self-willed, they do not tremble when they revile angelic majesties, whereas angels who are greater in might and power do not bring a reviling judgement against them before the Lord.*

By the time the van arrived from the morgue, Jeff and Ray were finished with the crime scene. Each item from the backpack was catalogued, photographed and packaged separately. The wire used to strangle Christina and the others was photographed and secured for DNA testing. The bloody leaves and soil were collected and placed in larger bags. The two gentlemen from the Medical Examiner's Office pulled the gurney through the trees, stopping at the prominent crime scene tape.

"You can tear through that, we're done here," Tommy said to the men.

The tape was severed, and the gurney was lowered to the ground. The white body bag was unzipped, and the limp body was rolled inside. His head bobbed sideways, unattached from the spine. The familiar noise of the zipper could be heard through the still woods. For once, they all thought, this was a good sound, not a sad one.

"Good riddance motherfucker," Donald exclaimed.

Michaels laughed. "Yeah, have fun at the morgue bitch. Don't cut yourself."

"Ok guys, everybody grab something and let's get out of here. Let's go find out who the Angel was."

"Ronnie, you and Dredge go over to the hospital and take a statement from Christina. When you're done, go tell the Marine that we found his mother's killer, and Ms. Withers' family too."

"Yes sir. We sure will," Michaels answered.

At the Emergency Room, Christina laid in a small cubicle with a tube extending from her forearm into an IV bottle hanging from a shiny pole. The beeping noise of the blood pressure and heart monitor kept Christina's eyes open. The cuff around her neck was placed to immobilize her prior to surgery. Her crushed windpipe was in dire need of medical attention. She squinted in pain when Michaels and Dredge filled her doorway.

"Laying down on the job again Agent? Damn Feds," Michaels said sarcastically.

Christina picked up the sticky pad and pencil from her lap and scratched down a message. She ripped the paper from the pad and handed it to Michaels. *Don't make me laugh.*

"Oh shit. I'm sorry." Michaels reached into his front pants pocket and handed Christina the driver's license of her attacker.

Christina's eyes opened in shock. She feverishly began writing on the pad. *That's Jack. The guy with the broken chain.*

"Christina, he's the guy who tried to kill you."

Fuck, she wrote.

An older female nurse entered the room. "Agent Smith. I take it these two good looking men are friends, family or co-workers?"

Christina scribbled on her pad. *All of the above. Has anyone gotten ahold of my husband?*

"Yes. Tommy spoke to him. He's on his way," Michaels assured her.

"Well, I'm sorry gentlemen, but it's time to take this lucky lady to the O.R. The doctors have a little work to do so she can sing again."

"Sing? I don't know if we need all that," Michaels said with a big smile.

Christina smiled once more in pain.

"Hang in there girl. We'll see you in a few hours," Dredge said while she was being wheeled from the room.

"Come on Dredge, let's go to Glen Burnie first and notify Mr. Abrams. I'll let you do all the talking. I'm sure he's going to love this."

When they pulled up to the Abrams' residence, the Marine's spotless Chevrolet pickup truck was parked in the driveway with a black mountain bike in the bed.

"At least he's home and we can be the ones to tell him and not the press," Michaels pointed out.

"Yeah," Dredge mumbled stepping on his cigarette he had dropped.

Michaels followed Dredge to the front door. They saw the main wooden door open which allowed Dredge to see inside to the living room. Michaels remembered the last time they were there and how he watched Mr. Abrams standing at the same door holding back his emotions. Before he knocked, Dredge peered inside through the glass. Quickly, he turned to Michaels. "Fuck."

"What?" Michaels asked hearing the surprise in Dredge's voice.

He quickly opened the door and barged in with Michaels following close behind. Slumped on the couch was the deceased body of Retired Captain Kenneth Abrams. On the right side of his head, at his temple, was a hole the size of a medium caliber bullet with blood still oozing from it.

"What the fuck?" Michaels yelled.

"He just did this," Dredge said looking down at the .45 caliber handgun on the floor. "It's got the Corps emblem engraved on the side. It must have been his retirement gift." Dredge turned and walked toward the dining room and lit a cigarette. He did not like what he was seeing.

Michaels walked to the table next to the body where he saw a cell phone. He picked it up and observed a small piece of paper lying beneath it. His jaw dropped, and his head fell forward when he unfolded it and recognized the name and number, It said *Katie Esterling 443-555-1779.* Unnerved, he grabbed the paper and crammed it in his side pocket before Dredge could notice. Unaware of his find, Dredge's attention was drawn to something on the dining room table.

Holding another piece of paper in his hand, Dredge called out, "Ronnie, you need to see this. This was inside of this black ballcap along with those sunglasses."

Still stunned from seeing Katie's number, he took the paper from Dredge's hand.

Mission complete. Semper Fi.

The End

Made in the USA
Las Vegas, NV
15 January 2022